Publisher's Note. This is a work of fiction. Names, characters, places and
incidents are a product of the author's imagination. Any resemblance to
a
person or persons, living, dead, or undead, business establishments,
events or locales is
purely coincidental.

First Publishing; Crystal-Rain Love: May 2020

VAMPIRE'S HALO

A BLOOD REVELATION NOVEL
CRYSTAL-RAIN LOVE

ACKNOWLEDGEMENTS

S pecial thanks to Christle Gray, always my first reader, and Greg Bennett, editor extraordinaire.

PROLOGUE

Inky black fingers of night crept over the moon, stealing what precious little light shone into the darkened alley. A breeze skimmed over the young girl, adding more cold to the chill already raising the hair on her arms.

"Quit folding your arms, girl. You can't see your goods like that!" Harvey jerked her thin arms down, his pudgy fingers sending yet another chill through her small body. She'd always thought of the devil as a red creature with horns and a pointed tail. She'd had no idea he was a fat slob of a man with bad breath and a balding head. "Look alive. Here comes a paycheck."

She watched the headlights of the approaching car with nausea filling her belly. Why had she run? Her stepfather was a monster, but life at home had been better than what Harvey was about to put her through. She'd just traded one nightmare for another.

The black car rolled to a smooth stop and a tall, dark figure emerged from the driver's side. Harvey instantly stiffened, preparing himself for a fight in case the man was a cop. The other girls spaced themselves apart, ready to scatter if there were trouble.

"What's up, man?" he asked, scrutinizing the stranger as he approached. "I ain't seen you before."

"I'm new in town," the man responded, his gaze roving over each of the girls. "I heard you had young girls."

Harvey nodded, stepping forward. "If you heard about me, you know the drill. Turn around and put your hands on your head.

The man did as ordered and Harvey frisked him, checking for weapons, or a wire. The girl held her breath, hoping he'd find a badge. Maybe the man could save her from the hell she'd been caught in. Her hope shattered when the man was allowed to turn around and lower his arms.

1

Harvey grinned, relaxing his stance. "Take your pick, man. You pay upfront."

The shadows released the moon from their dark cover, allowing it to illuminate the stranger. There was a brief flash of hostility in his eyes before he answered. "Yes, of course."

Harvey grabbed a blonde by the elbow and ushered her forward. "This is Bambi. Twenty-five years old and very limber. She—"

"I heard you had younger selection on the menu." With a frown, the man turned his head to stare straight down at her as she trembled at Harvey's side. His frown deepened; his eyes filled with sadness. "How old is this one?"

Her trembling increased as Harvey caressed her bare arm with his fingers. "Jewel here is my pride and joy. Twelve years old and still intact. You get the honor of breaking her in, you have to pay the damage fee."

She gulped, finding it hard to swallow with her throat so tight and dry. Tears started to form and she fought to hold them back. Harvey didn't like tears, much like her stepfather. She had the bruises to prove it.

"Of course." The man placed a long finger under her chin and tilted her head so she was forced to look him in the face. Something in his eyes whispered an apology before they quickly turned dark and hard once more. Turning toward Harvey, he released her. "Put her in the car while we handle payment."

Harvey grabbed her arm tight enough to hurt, making sure she didn't bolt at the last moment. "You understand the damage fee is pretty hefty."

The stranger looked at Harvey's hand on her arm and tightened his own hand into a fist. "I assure you I have the funds, which you should remember from checking my wallet."

"I'll be taking all of it." Harvey's grin reeked of evil.

"Put the girl in the car or you'll get none of it."

Harvey stiffened at the man's authoritive tone, but prodded the girl along. She tried to dig her heels in but Harvey shoved her into the car effortlessly. "Run and die," he warned, his rank breath blowing over her face before he slammed the door closed to get payment for the theft of her virtue.

"Oh God, help me," she whimpered, letting a tear escape.

She jerked as something crashed against the hood of the car. Looking up, she saw Harvey's round face shoved against the windshield, blood leaking from his nose and mouth. There were screams, followed by the rapid clicking of heels as the other girls scattered. Harvey's body was lifted from the car but the two men moved in a blur of speed she couldn't keep up with. Two more bangs and three grunts later, the driver's side door opened and the mystery man, her first john, slid into the seat.

She grabbed for the handle of her door, but he locked the doors from his side and burned rubber out of the dark, narrow alley. "You are safe now," he said calmly as he maneuvered the car onto a main street and navigated it through the seedy little neighborhood she'd made the mistake of entering after running away from home.

"Is Harvey dead?" She regretted the question the moment it slipped out. If the man was dead, she was a witness to the murder.

"I do not kill," the man replied matter-of-factly. "He is severely hurt, enough that he won't be a bother to anyone anymore."

She'd gathered that much from the blood leaking out Harvey's face. The man who'd bought her, or pretended he was going to buy her, had moved like the wind, pummeling the heftier thug to a pulp in no time at all. She studied him as he drove. Short, dark hair, tall with a lean build. Very cute for an older guy. He looked around twenty or so, with dark blue eyes and a baby face that belied his ferocity. He was dressed in black pants and a black long-sleeve T-shirt, clothes a robber might wear. Or a john planning to beat up the pimp he got his girl from. She cringed, knowing she wasn't out of danger yet, regardless what the man might have said.

"What is your real name?" The man looked steadily ahead as he asked the question.

"How do you know Jewel's not my real name?"

"Harvey wouldn't want your real name known in case the authorities are looking for you." He glanced back at her. "When did you run away, and why?"

She shrugged, unsure how to answer. Would he kill her if he thought the police were looking for her? Maybe thinking so would save her life. Or make him kill her faster.

"I won't hurt you, little one."

He sounded nice. He looked nice. But Harvey hadn't exactly had PIMP tattooed on his forehead either when he'd offered her food and a place to sleep. "What you're going to do to me will hurt no matter how slow you go," she whispered, pushing the words out with effort. She'd taken sex education class last year and knew what was going to happen. Fresh tears fell at the thought. *Please, God. Please, please...*

The man pressed down harder on the gas pedal, snagging her attention. His mouth was set in a grim line, his jaw clenched tight. He took a hard left and slammed on the brake before putting the car in Park.

She looked up at the building before her and her jaw dropped in surprise. A moment later, the door next to her opened and the man stood there, looking down at her. "Come on out. It's all right."

She stepped out of the car, her legs shaking, and glanced around. "We're not going in there, are we?"

The man studied the large building before them. It was a small white brick building with a big wooden cross towering over the center. "Yes. I own the church. You will be safe here."

Numb, she obeyed as he gently prodded her toward the big doors. She was going to be violated inside a church. By the time they made it inside to where red carpet rolled out before them, lined on both sides by pews, she was sobbing.

"My name is Christian," the man said, ushering her down a hallway and into a small room. It was white, furnished with a small cot, dresser, and lamp. He flipped the light on and gestured for her to sit on the bed.

All her limbs trembling now, she did as instructed, instinctively tucking her knees beneath her chin and wrapping her arms tight around her shins to guard herself the best she could.

Christian looked at her and his eyes softened, the blue pools swirling with sorrow. "I will not touch you. No one will touch you in my care." He squatted before her, putting him at eye level. "Are you hungry?"

Her stomach rumbled at the offer but she shook her head.

He rose to a stand and lay his hand on her head, patting her hair. "I will bring you food and something to drink."

He stepped out of the room, closing the door behind him, and she looked up at the poster hanging on the wall in front of her. It was a picture of Jesus sitting with a group of children and animals. "Did you hear me, God?"

She whispered, afraid her voice would carry. "Please let him not be crazy, or worse."

Christian returned and set a plate—a slice of pumpkin pie, a ham sandwich, and an apple—and a bottle of water on the dresser and turned to look in distaste at what she wore. He left the room, but returned shortly with clothing. He handed the clothing to her, placing it next to her on the bed when she refused to unwrap her arms from around her legs. He'd given her a pair of gray sweatpants and a long-sleeved white T-shirt close to her size, along with thick, white socks.

"These clothes are more appropriate for your age. I will find you better shoes in the morning."

She took the clothes, glad to rid herself of the spaghetti-strapped mini dress, fishnets, and heels, and held them close to her chest. Would he want to watch her change? Was that his sick pleasure?

"Rest well, little one, and we will talk more in the morning. When you trust me enough to confide in me, I will help you find home again." He smiled at her, the gesture sad and apologetic, and left the room.

She stared at the closed door for long into the night, waiting for it to open. Chewing on the food he left, she kept waiting for him to intrude and push her down on the bed, ripping the sweatpants from her thin body. What felt like an eternity later, she fell asleep.

Still, he did not come.

CHAPTER ONE

"Rent's due on the first of the month, Jadyn!"

Jadyn cringed as the landlord yelled the reminder she was late again, and continued running up the stairs, praying she made it to her apartment before he realized what she carried in her arms. "I know, Mr. Guerra. I'll get it to you this week, I promise!"

The stocky man cursed a blue streak in Spanish and slammed his door. Jadyn wished she'd picked out one of the apartments in the back of the building so she didn't have to pass his on the way to hers every day. She'd been late with the rent for months, and was scared she might actually skip this month. Thank goodness Mr. Guerra's bark was worse than his bite or she might face the possibility of being homeless. As if she didn't have enough to deal with.

She entered her small apartment and kicked the door closed behind her before quickly stepping over to the small kitchen area. She set the bag of small breed dog kibble on the counter, dropped her keys next to it, and moved toward her bedroom to check on her babies.

"They're not my babies," she reminded herself as she shed her hoodie and tossed it on the bed. In the corner of her room, four black and white balls of fur teetered around inside a rabbit cage. "You guys are getting better at walking. You'll be ready to go out into the world before I know it." She took a deep breath to keep her tears at bay, and laughed a little as she bent down to open the cage. "I know I shouldn't be this emotional, and I'll be able to work more gigs once you're released, so that's an upside. Still, all this stress of worrying about Mr. Guerra finding out I'm harboring you and scraping all my pennies to keep a roof over all of our heads while I take care of you is worth it when I see these cute faces."

She carefully wrapped the baby skunks in blankets, tucking their tails down to avoid an accidental spraying and moved them into a small dog carrier she kept for emergencies. "You guys hang tight," she told them as she quickly set to work cleaning out the cage. "I think I liked it better when I had to stimulate you to use the bathroom, but this is good that you go on your own now. Yep, you'll be on your own in no time." Her voice hitched, and she shook her head, feeling silly. She knew she couldn't keep wild animals forever, and it wouldn't be good for them if she did, but she'd worry about the little guys once they were on their own in the big world with all its predators and other dangers. Once the cage was clean and restocked with fresh blankets, she grabbed the water and food bowls. "I'll be back with yum yums," she told the little cuties as she took the dishes to the kitchen and washed them out in the sink.

Noticing the time on the microwave, she walked over to the living area off the side of the small open kitchen space, and turned the TV on to check the news, letting it play as she returned to finish preparing the babies' dinner. She filled one of the dishes with fresh water and opened the bag of dog food as the news anchor recapped a story about a drug dealer being arrested. She scooped dog food into a bowl and started adding in water a little at a time, making sure to get it soft enough for the kits, but not completely mushy.

"... local minister helped the police in the capture of..."

Jadyn glanced up from her task to focus on the television. She'd always had a weak spot for do-good ministers since having her own life saved by one several years ago in her birthplace of New Jersey. The image of the man who went by the name of Christian flashed through her mind and she gasped as that same image popped onto the television screen.

"No way." She abandoned the food and rushed toward the television, staring at the image which faded away too quickly. Grabbing the remote from where she'd left it on the coffee table, she thanked goodness for DVR and rewound the newscast to the point where his picture was shown. The picture was just a still from a security camera and it appeared he was purposely averting his face the best he could, so the image wasn't as clear as it could have been, but it was enough. She would recognize that man anywhere... especially since he hadn't appeared to have aged a day. And how was that possible? It had been eleven years. He should have been showing some sign of age. Heck, he didn't appear to be a day over twenty years old, and she was twenty-three herself. She'd only been twelve when he'd saved her from the clutches of a very bad man in a dark alley. He had to be at least thirty years old by now, and that was at the *very* least.

Jadyn focused on the story, learning that Christian had personally delivered a wanted child molester to the authorities and left the police headquarters before they could get much information from him, such as his name or occupation, but they had his image from their security cameras and another officer had recognized him as a minister at the Blood of Life Non-Denominational Church, a church located in Baltimore.

Jadyn raced over to the old desk she'd found in a rummage sale and booted up her computer, immediately plugging the name of the church into a Google search. Not much information came up for the church, but she did find what she needed most. She now had the location of where to find the man who'd saved her life so long ago... and a place to go to in order to find answers to the burning questions that had haunted her for the past decade.

Christian was no ordinary man. There was something about him, some strange aura, like a cloak of power that surrounded him and separated him from the rest of mankind. His lack of aging over the past eleven years proved this even more. Jadyn would find the man and thank him for what he did for her... and she would learn just what exactly made the man so special, and maybe, find out what was wrong with her in the process.

"I DON'T KNOW HOW YOU drink that garbage," Seta said, her delicate nose—and not much else about the fiery woman could be considered delicate—scrunched in distaste.

"Nothing that preserves life could ever be considered garbage," Christian stated as he turned the glass of blood freshly warmed in the microwave up and swallowed its contents. He'd gotten used to drinking it cold straight out of the bags, but since he'd drunk from a living donor five years earlier, Christian had again developed the taste for warm blood. He'd also started picking up on the sound of heartbeats without even trying, a part of being a vampire that he'd never enjoyed. It came in handy when in danger, but otherwise it just made him feel like a predator.

"I suppose." Seta turned away from the statue of Mary one of Christian's artistic parishioners had recently made for the church, a thank you for the room he'd given the young woman after she'd fled from her abusive boyfriend, and shrugged her shoulders as she paced the floor at the front of the chapel. "Interesting artwork."

Christian grinned as he admired the large stone statue that now sat to the side of the doorway leading to a row of rooms left of the chapel. Most statues of the Virgin Mary showed her with a serene expression on her face, or cradling the infant Jesus in her arms. In this statue, she smiled brilliantly, and the artist had somehow managed to create a sparkle in her eyes. How that was possible to create from stone, Christian did not know, but he admired the talent and skill it took. "Carly is an amazing artist," he said. "This is one of my favorite pieces."

He'd received a lot of art in the several centuries he'd been a vampire. He'd always been some sort of holy man. Regardless of the denomination, regardless the role, he'd always been an important, highly esteemed member of a Christian church, or a traveling minister. As far back as he could remember, that was all he could remember. That, and the artwork. He helped people whenever he could, felt it like a call from God himself, as if he were put into the world to spread God's love. Often, those he helped would thank him with gifts, many of those gifts of an artistic nature. He glanced around his church, noting the various framed paintings and sketches lining the walls, the statues, large and small, which rested wherever he could find space. None of these works of art were painted by famous artists, just normal everyday people he'd helped in some way. Some he had helped by rescuing them from a living nightmare of some sort, some he helped with just a simple shoulder to cry on or an extra voice when reciting a prayer, but he'd made a difference and they'd thought enough of him to gift him with beauty. Not one piece of art in his church would sell for millions at auction, but each piece was priceless to him. As were the humans he helped in whatever way he could, each one of them helping him redeem himself and live with the fact of what he was, and what he was not.

He was not a monster, or a demon. He lived on the blood of others, but he had never taken it by killing. He had never abused the power flowing through his veins, though to do so would have been too easy. At his age, he was among the strongest vampires walking, whatever age that was. He could not remember when he began, just that he awoke bloody and battered, left for dead. Unlike the other vampires he knew, he did not recall much of being human. He'd been turned into a vampire not long after the beating that took his memory. There were times he questioned if he had ever really been human at all.

"Are you even listening to me?"

Seta's sharp bark snagged Christian's attention, and he realized he'd allowed his mind to wander. He offered an apologetic smile to the rosy-cheeked woman, knowing the flush of color was from irritation. It didn't take much to ruffle the vampire-witch's feathers. "I'm sorry. Could you repeat what you said?"

"I said it is time." Her voice was stern, eyes grave. There would be no budging on the subject.

Christian sighed. He'd had this conversation far too many times, and it never got easier. He could never stay in one place for long. A decade here, a decade there. No more. Often less, depending on the circumstances. He didn't age, and people noticed that. They wondered about it, investigated it. And they found out far too much if they were successful. Even if they were not successful themselves, their musings often reached the awareness of others who were dangerous. Slayers. Exterminators of his kind. A vampire could never hang around, watch the neighborhood change with time.

"I've done good here," Christian said. "There are still people here I need to help. I'm making so much progress. I had wanted another few years, at least."

"Then you shouldn't have taken that monster to the police station." Seta's already dark brown eyes deepened to chocolate. "There was another way to take care of him."

"That way is not always the right way," he answered, starting yet another conversation that had been repeated far too many times.

"It's the permanent way, and far more satisfying to the victims," Seta countered, a small grin turning up the corners of her full lips, "and extremely satisfying for the executioner."

Seta had been horribly abused the night she was changed over into a vampire, beaten and thrown over a cliff to be exact. Losing her human life in such a way left a permanent mark on her, a desperate need to exact vengeance. It didn't matter if her prey harmed her personally, or someone else. She still reveled in the thrill of taking what she deemed to be worthless, wasted life. Although Christian didn't condone murder, he knew in his heart the woman's soul was good. If ever an innocent was in trouble, he would find no greater protector than the vampire-witch, and any who fell at her hand were already marked for hell.

"I'm no executioner." Christian drained the last of the blood from his glass and walked the length of the hallway to the right of the chapel before entering the small kitchen to rinse the glass in the sink. Seta followed on his heels. "The man was not an imminent threat to anyone at the time I captured him. The human system of law sufficed. I did what was right."

"And when he is released because human law hasn't figured out that child molesters are vile monsters who need to be locked away or *shut down* for good?"

Christian frowned. "Fortunately, they now have sex offender registries."

"Yes, like those stop them." Seta huffed out a breath. "Enough stalling. It is time for you to go."

Christian leaned back against the counter and crossed his arms. "No one has come yet."

"They will, and you know it." Seta waved an elegant, long-fingered hand in the air, and an image appeared. "I have already had the vision."

Christian watched in dread as the scene played out before him. His beautiful church burned to the ground as slayers who had caught wind of him came to take his life... or try to. "Do I die in the vision?"

"No." Seta snapped her fingers and the image dissipated into mist. "Because you will not be in the church when they come. Whether it takes the easy way or the hard way, you will be long gone and far away."

The easy way being he would pack his belongings and leave as soon as possible, the hard way being Seta would grow tired of his refusal and use her magic to teleport him somewhere far away without his consent, and without his beloved treasures. "It still hurts my heart every time I think of those beautiful pieces of art I lost in Denmark."

Seta grinned, the expression full of righteousness. "Then don't make me send you away without your possessions again."

Reluctantly, he nodded his head, and straightened. "I will need a moving van."

"There is one parked outside, waiting to be filled."

"Seta..." He projected a warning tone into his voice.

"I paid for it," Seta snapped with a roll of her eyes before her expression softened. She placed a hand on his shoulder. "I hate that you have to do this. I know you enjoy being accessible to the humans and providing them a safe haven, and I know you have enjoyed Baltimore. I pray for the day you stop getting so attached. It only makes these times harder on you."

That day would never come, but Christian nodded his head and offered a small smile despite his unhappiness. This was his calling, this was *him*. "I need to get my affairs in order, and then I give my word I will leave. You don't have to stay and watch over me."

"Good, because I will be leaving Baltimore as well, as soon as I leave you, in fact. Njeri cast her first spell today."

Christian's jaw dropped, his mouth left hanging open in surprise for a moment before he could form a thought coherent enough to verbalize. "She is only four years old!"

"Yes, she is." Seta grinned, pride glistening in her eyes. "My grandchild is no ordinary vampire-witch."

"Are any of you?" Christian smiled, knowing Seta was well aware she may in fact have been the first of her kind. To their knowledge, no other witch had been turned into a vampire, and both had lived long enough to have heard stories if such an event had happened.

"No, but Njeri is even more extraordinary," she answered, "and her power is going to be stronger than anything any of us has ever seen." A dark cloud passed over her eyes. "Power like that draws attention. Slayers will come in droves, as will demons, and all those working as Satan's hand."

Christian nodded his understanding. Njeri was one of two special children born four years ago as part of the Blood Revelation, a prophecy older than Seta and Christian put together. Under normal conditions, a vampire could not reproduce, but Njeri had been born to Seta's son, Rialto, who Seta had given birth to a year before she'd been turned, and who she herself had turned as he lay dying on the same cliff her body had been thrown over twenty-eight years earlier.

His mate was Aria, a woman who, as the daughter of a born witch, carried the gene. Turned by Rialto in order to save her life, she was also now a vampire. Together, they had created one of three prophesied children, warriors like none other. One of them would save mankind from Satan's wrath.

"Has Slade shifted?" Christian asked, wondering if the other prophesied child, a child born right next to Njeri in this very church had started showing his own power. Born of a slayer and a pantherian-vampire hybrid, he would also show amazing strength.

"Not to my knowledge," Seta answered, "and believe me, I have questioned Jacob and Nyla often. That one will be a danger as he grows into his abilities."

"As will Njeri."

"Yes." Seta nodded. "That is why I am leaving with her. She must be trained, and I am the only one powerful enough to be put in charge of that duty."

"Where will you take her? As her power grows, she will be tracked by those who sense it."

"We will not stay in any place long." Seta's eyes slightly widened, showing the briefest hint of fear before she raised her chin defiantly. "I will cloak her the best I can, limiting my own power to stay undetectable, and I will teach her how to defend herself. When I am through, I pity the unfortunate fool who dares to lay a finger or touch of dark magic on her."

Christian pitied any fool unfortunate to touch anyone Seta cared about. "You know how to reach me if you need to."

"Yes." She looked away, sadness evident in her frown. "You are actually the strongest vampire I know next to Eron, and until he decides to rise..."

Christian's heart went out to the tough-as-nails vampire-witch. For all her power and strength, her heart was a fragile thing, her love not something passed around freely. She had given it to Eron a long time ago, but the two were both stubborn and had yet to figure out how to coexist without constantly trying to seek dominance in their relationship.

Eron had nearly died five years before, chained to a wall by a demon and constantly bled out for months. Once rescued, he'd buried himself deep in the earth in order to replenish all that had been taken from him. Every day that passed without him rising, Seta worried he never would, though Christian was the only person she'd confided in about that. Christian hadn't dared tell her what he thought: that Eron knew he was in for a serious tongue-lashing, and maybe even a good beat-down once he finally faced the petite but deadly woman. Christian thought that despite Eron's immense power, the vampire was plumb scared to rise.

"I will gladly give my aid to you until Eron rises, and long afterward." He stepped forward, but stopped himself before he lifted his arms to pull her into a hug. The vampire-witch would see the gesture as a sign she was weak, and Seta never showed weakness. Then again, maybe she had, but knowing her as he did, Christian was confident if she had shown weakness before a witness, that unfortunate soul hadn't been able to speak of it afterward. He prayed her need to prove herself powerful didn't backfire. "I know there aren't many vampires of our age or power that can be trusted, but what of the vampire you've been associating with in Kentucky? Rider Knight? You go back far with him, and of all I've heard, he is very powerful and good. He's rescued many vampires from abusive sires, breaking up evil nests before they could become plagues on mankind. Can you not ask for his help guarding the children?"

Seta stared back at him for a moment, thinking. "He owes me favors, and has quite a network of vampires, shifters, and witches at his disposal, all who are dedicated to him, but you know as well as I these children are hunted. The more who know about them, the graver danger they are in. His direct help with the children would only be if absolutely necessary, but I will take his help in other matters." She pursed her mouth in thought. "He can help you if I have to go deep underground with Njeri. Once I get her somewhere secure, I will set up an introduction in case something happens and I am unreachable."

Christian nodded. "I appreciate that, but try not to be unreachable. I know you well enough to know it will be because you are trying to keep me from danger. You are my family, as are Rialto, Aria, Nyla, Jake... and these very special children. I would lay down my life for any and all of you."

"As would we for each other." Seta's lips curved into the slightest of a smile, her eyes glistened with unshed tears which were quickly blinked away before she raised her chin, shoulders back, taking the stance of a regal queen. "That's settled. Be gone from here soon, Christian. You will find that you will regret having to receive my aid if you fail to do as I have told you and get yourself captured or dead."

"How will you harm me if I get killed, Seta?" He grinned, anticipating the answer.

"Because, my dearest friend, I will find a way to raise you from the dead only to flog you with fire whips every day for the rest of eternity."

Christian chuckled. "I don't doubt your word. That is what I believe they call tough love."

"That is love," she spoke softly, her eyes warm with the emotion before she cleared her throat and stepped back a bit, regaining the space she liked to keep between herself and others. "I'm feeling very charitable today. Picture in your mind all of the things you want to take with you and hold that image there."

Knowing why she'd made the request, Christian did as instructed while Seta closed her eyes and raised her hands, holding them out by her sides, mid-torso high. Christian pictured every beautiful piece of art he had been gifted, his clothes, the cash he kept on hand in his home that had been built under the church and protected by Seta's wards, and a few other items he didn't want to part with.

"It is done. All of your belongings are in the moving van." Seta opened her eyes and Christian could see the strain in them.

"I could have packed my things the old-fashioned way." Guilt assaulted him as he realized how overexerted the vampire-witch was. "You need your strength to take care of Njeri."

"I will be good as new as soon as I feed, and I will have Rialto and Aria with me," she quickly replied, waving off his concern. "Trust me, this was nothing in comparison to the favors I've been doing for Rider. That man truly does owe me a great deal. Besides, if you pack for yourself, you will waste precious time reminiscing over every piece of art you own."

Christian grinned, knowing she was right. He held on to memories as best he could. He imagined it was the result of not knowing anything about his life before he had been changed into a vampire. Memories were precious, but those fortunate to know where they came from didn't fully appreciate just how precious they were. "Go feed and take care of Njeri. Call me any time you need my help."

"After you." Seta gestured toward the door.

"I promise I will leave soon. I just need a few moments to look around, and seal this image in my mind."

Seta shook her head in exasperation. "If you get in trouble and I have to save you because you dawdled, you will be one very miserable vampire," she muttered. "Call me when you find a new residence and I will ward it."

She disappeared, teleporting herself elsewhere.

KIARA DIPPED HER FINGER into the cold, crystal blue water, stroking her finger along Christian's jawline, or at least the image of it. Sorrow weighed down her heart, and fear was a hardened lump she could barely swallow past. A throat cleared behind her, and she sighed.

"In all of Heaven, you have to be here right now?" she asked, knowing who stood behind her.

Zaccharus settled next to her and peered into the vision pool, one of many small pools of water which allowed the angels to see Earth or whichever planet or realm they needed to view. This particular pool was Kiara's favorite, for it was placed in the Garden of Tranquility. It had been Christian's favorite place.

"I worry for you, Kiara."

She raised her head, managing not to take her gaze off of Christian as she did so. "Why?"

"You are in danger of falling."

Startled, she took her gaze away from the vision pool to look at Zaccharus. With long, wavy hair, almost as deep a shade of gold as hers, and light brown eyes, he was stunningly attractive. The sharp angles of his face made him even more alluring, but his beauty, while appreciated, had no

16

effect on Kiara. Others might swoon in his presence, but not her. He was a brother to her. Narrowing her eyes, she raked her gaze, now burning like hot coals, over him, allowing him to feel her ire before she spoke. "What did you dare say to me?"

Zaccharus swallowed hard, recognizing Kiara's authority. "It was not my intent to offend you. I just spoke honestly of my concern. To lie to you would be a great disservice."

"As would speaking so poorly of me." She tilted her head to an angle that allowed her to look down her nose at the lesser-ranked angel. "Whatever gave you such a ridiculous idea?"

Unspeaking, Zaccharus nodded toward the vision pool, where Christian's image swam.

"What of it?" Kiara asked, hackles raised. Zaccharus was not the first to notice the time she spent watching over the vampire.

"You are enamored of him. You spend hours watching him, both here and ... there."

So her personal visits to Earth had been noticed. Kiara frowned, wondering what gossip was being spread among the others. "He was a dear friend. Of course I watch over him."

"With longing in your eyes." Zaccharus quickly looked away as her glare burned hotter, letting his gaze fall upon the image in the pool. "He fell because he longed for something of that world, just as you long for something in him. I hold you dear, Kiara. Please do not allow yourself to fall. Aurorian is damaged. Unclean."

"He goes by the name Christian now," Kiara managed to get out, although each word was a growl, "and he is the most spiritually clean man walking the surface of Earth."

"But he is just a man," Zaccharus countered, his jaw set stubbornly. "Man is beneath us."

"Mankind is our Father's creation," she reminded him. "Are you saying what our Father made is unclean?"

Zaccharus's eyes widened and pure fear shone through as he realized what he had insinuated. "No! Never! I... I wouldn't dare... You know that's not what I meant."

Kiara arched a golden eyebrow, knowing she had stopped his meddling for the moment. To doubt their Father in any way, shape, or form was a grave offense. "I think you should leave now, Zaccharus, and not bother me with any more foolishness."

"My apologies, Kiara. I am only concerned because I care." He swiftly rose to his feet and walked away, no doubt quaking with worry over whether she would report what he had said, as if their Father didn't already know.

Kiara watched the white-clad angel until he disappeared, traveling by thought to his destination, and turned back to the vision pool. She sighed as she recalled their conversation and wondered again how many of the others had noticed her preoccupation with Christian's welfare. A few had mentioned her lengthy presence at the vision pools, more had frowned as they caught glimpses of who her most viewed subject was. None had dared say a word, but now she knew they were thinking a horrible thought.

She would not fall. She'd known angels who had, and what became of them. To be created as such a blessed creature, only to throw that gift away was the ultimate slap in their Father's face. Angels lost more than their wings when they hit the ground. They lost their purity, the part of them that made them pristine. They felt the same urges as humans, and because those urges were so new to them, they gave in easily, quickly succumbing to a sinful life.

Khiderian, one of her dearest friends and brothers, had not even made it an hour on Earth before he sinned. He'd chosen to fall because he wanted to feel things like humans. His human emotions new to him, he confused love with lust, and he allowed an adulterous woman to seduce him within the blink of an eye, immediately starting him on a long life of sin. However, he did eventually see the error of his ways, and he had done great good, helping to aid the Blood Revelation prophecy and eradicating a *drac chemare*'s power, saving mankind from what could have been a horrible curse. He had redeemed himself and sacrificed his life out of honest, pure love.

Then there was Aurorian, whose reason for falling was not clear. Kiara could remember him talking of mankind's beauty, amazed by the way they put their hearts and souls into everything they did. He loved to watch women mothering their children, to see men building things with their hands. He felt the sadness when small children wept over the loss of their beloved animals, hurt for them when they scraped their little knees. He

18

adored the humans, but he never spoke of any urges to be like them. He only wanted to help them, as was his job. They all helped the humans, their Father's children. There was no need for him to fall.

Yet he did. With all Kiara had seen in her time, nothing shocked her, but she had been stunned to learn of Aurorian's falling. She'd nearly accused the others of lying to her even though she herself had felt his loss as he descended. She'd wanted to go to him immediately but was not allowed to. When an angel fell, no other angel was allowed to go to them until after they dealt with their first great temptation on Earth.

Khiderian's first temptation had been a woman. Kiara had waited until after he'd given into his temptation and fornicated with the woman to admonish him for what he'd done and warn him he'd doomed himself to hell. It had been she who had been sent to kill the *drac chemare* he had fallen in love with centuries later... She who had run a sword through him at his request in order to save the *drac chemare*. She who had wept a single tear as his sacrifice gave both he and the *drac chemare* new life, and saved his soul from eternal damnation.

She who had watched helplessly from the vision pool as Aurorian woke in his human form on Earth. He'd barely walked a mile before he'd been jumped by three men. They'd beaten him severely in an attempt to get gold that he did not have, and left him for dead in the road. She could not go to him, for he had not yet been tempted or put into a position to make a major choice. She'd watched helplessly as he lay bleeding on the ground, but he survived that cruelty at the hands of men only to face a far greater cruelty not long after.

Aurorian hadn't even lived a month as a human before being changed into a vampire. He'd gone from a being of light to a being of darkness in a blink of time, and she'd done nothing to prevent it. Couldn't have done anything. So she did the only thing she could do. She'd warped space and time to position Eron, a good vampire she knew of, near enough to Aurorian to sense the presence of the newly changed vampire and help him.

The beating Aurorian had received before being changed into a vampire had damaged his memory. It was a blank slate. He'd had no recollection of ever being an angel. Kiara had watched from the vision pool as Eron asked his name. She'd watched as Aurorian looked Eron straight in the eyes and said, "I am Christian, for I serve the Lord."

In that instant he had rejected every new vampire's temptation of fully embracing their dark side. He had dealt with his first great temptation, allowing Kiara to go to him, but before she could, an order was put out that no angel was to aid him in regaining his memory. Aurorian, now Christian, had to make it through his new life on his own, and if he made the right choices, he would be the first fallen angel with a shot at actually coming back home, wings and all.

Kiara didn't dare go to him, afraid she would not be able to hold back the truth of what he was, so she only watched him from above, constantly amazed by his ability to resist darkness even as a vampire. As time passed, her admiration for him grew, and now that admiration had her brothers and sisters talking, wondering if she was next to fall. She would not, not even for Christian, but she would watch over him and protect him as best she could.

She tensed as she stared into the vision pool, watching as a woman walked through the doors of Christian's church. "Oh, Christian, you should have left immediately as Seta had instructed," she whispered as she instinctively felt the trouble the woman walking down the aisle of his church brought with her.

CHAPTER TWO

J adyn pushed open the front door, relieved to find it unlocked, and entered the Blood of Life Non-Denominational Church. A long, red carpet swept out before her, sectioning off two rows of long pews as it continued on several feet to the pulpit. The walls were bare, plain white, totally different from the church she remembered in Jersey. That church had been decorated with paintings, drawings, and sculptures of all shapes and sizes.

Christian had loved art, and during her time with him she'd made him a drawing as a gift for saving her. She'd never forget the beautiful smile he gave her in return. It was the first time in her life she'd felt worth something, and the moment she'd fallen in love with her hero. She'd cried so hard when she'd had to leave him.

"Can I help you?"

Jadyn jerked, so lost in thought she hadn't noticed anyone enter the chapel. Turning her head to the right, her breath caught in her throat as she set eyes on the man who'd rescued her eleven years earlier. The same man. The same exact man right down to the age. How was that possible?

Her mouth went dry as she raked in the sight of him, from his short, dark hair, and piercing blue eyes, to the slim but strong build of him wrapped in a cream sweater that looked soft to the touch, and black slacks. He cocked his head to the side as his brow furrowed, and stepped closer. "Are you all right?"

Realizing she was probably gawking and hadn't answered his first question, Jadyn quickly nodded, biting back the disappointment that he didn't recognize her right away and call her by name. How could she expect him to? Unlike him, she had changed very much in the past eleven years, and besides that, she knew he'd probably helped hundreds of people since she'd last seen him. He was just that kind of a soul.

"Christian?"

"Yes." He frowned. "Have we met?"

"A long time ago."

His eyes widened in alarm before his gaze swept the room. His body quickly became rigid, the sight reminding her of a dog preparing to attack, just waiting to see if the threat was worth it, before his gaze returned to her. "How long ago?"

Sensing she'd said something wrong, Jadyn swallowed, her heart pounding furiously. She'd never been scared of this man, well, with exception to that first night, but now she was as frightened as a doe in headlights. The power she'd sensed from him before seemed to thicken, any more so it would surely be visible.

"Oh, just a while ago," she said, doing her best imitation of casual, praying her voice didn't crack under the nerves she felt. She waved her hand in the air as if to say the time wasn't important, and added a nonchalant shrug. "I imagine you've listened to so many people's problems we all start to run together after a while."

His eyes lost their predatory gleam as his face softened, his jaw no longer so tightly clenched. "All of my parishioners are important to me."

"Oh, without a doubt," Jadyn quickly said, realizing he'd taken her comment to mean she thought he didn't bother with the task of remembering those who came to him for help. She smiled. "I admire what you do."

"I am only a messenger." He shifted his feet uncomfortably before gesturing toward a pew with his hand. "I'm actually due to leave soon, but if you need to talk to someone, I can spare a moment."

"That would be kind of you. Very nice," she almost stammered, nerves getting the best of her. She hadn't intended to come into an empty church and face him so soon. She'd hoped there would be someone else inside the chapel. She recalled parishioners dropping in at all hours in the church he'd ran in New Jersey. With someone else there, she wouldn't have drawn so much attention to herself, and could have observed him awhile. She also hadn't realized how seeing him again in the flesh would affect her.

She wiped her damp hands on her jean-clad thighs as she situated herself in the pew, a thousand questions running through her mind. What would she ask him? How would she ask? Now that she was face to face with him there was no doubt he was the very same man who had rescued her eleven years ago, but he hadn't changed a bit. Nobody went an entire decade without aging the littlest bit, and no plastic surgeon was this good. Christian's skin was flawless, totally unharmed by the elements, and what she could see of his body was beyond fit. His eyes sparkled with youth and his hair was so thick and lustrous his picture belonged on shampoo bottles. He was beautiful, like a piece of art come to life.

"What weighs on your mind?" he asked as he perched atop the back of the pew before her, his hands folded together in his lap, but the rest of his body was as taut as a bow string. His gaze kept shifting around the chapel as if expecting someone to jump out of the shadows at any moment.

What are you? Jadyn bit her lip to keep the strange question that had just entered her mind from pouring out through her mouth. The man already looked as if he expected trouble. She didn't want to be that trouble... but she did want answers. There was something very different, almost mystical, about him, and she felt if anyone was capable of helping her, or at least understanding her, it would be him.

"You have absolutely flawless skin," she heard herself saying, and heat suffused her face. Once the compliment slipped out, she went with it. Maybe the best approach with him was a roundabout one. "You seem so young to be a minister. How old are you... if you don't mind my asking?"

His face hardened into a mask of caution as his eyes narrowed. "Age doesn't matter as much as wisdom, and despite popular belief, one doesn't always increase the other."

Jadyn once again got the feeling she had said the wrong thing. Instead of frightening her this time, excitement bubbled up inside her. He obviously didn't like being questioned about his age. That, and the fact he kept looking around as if expecting an ambush, confirmed her suspicions something was off about him. There was something about his lack of aging that equaled more than just good genes.

"I will need to be leaving soon." He glanced toward the window to his left. "I have a lot of miles to cover before morning."

Jadyn recalled the U-Haul sitting in the parking lot and suddenly the bare inside of the church made sense. When Christian had said he was leaving, he didn't mean he was making a run to the store for snacks. He was *leaving*, church and all. No way could that happen before she discovered the secret she knew was somewhere hiding inside him.

"Please wait." She clamped her hand on his forearm without thinking, then quickly pulled it back, feeling as if she'd touched something she wasn't worthy of, an odd feeling seeing as how she'd known him from before, and despite that air about him that he was more than just a man, she'd never felt like that before. Then again, she'd been a child and he'd been her hero. She wouldn't have felt strange about being in awe of him then. Now it was a little... weird. "I'm sorry. I just... I have so many questions I need answers to."

"And you came to church to find them." His expression softened again, though his eyes still held a trace of wariness. "Those must be some heavy questions. I will help you as much as I can, but first you must ask them."

Jadyn laughed self-consciously, realizing she must seem pretty scatterbrained. "I'm sorry. I'm just a bit nervous and unsure how to start."

"Start at the beginning," Christian suggested.

Jadyn swallowed the hard lump that suddenly formed in her throat. The beginning? Why not? And why not be honest with him? From what she remembered, he was one of the most generous people she'd ever met. Surely he would help her ... unless he thought she was crazy. Taking a deep breath, she steadied herself and hoped for the best. "When we first met, you were saving me from a life of prostitution."

Christian's entire body stilled to the point he looked as if he'd been carved out of marble. After what seemed an eternity, his gaze slowly rolled over her, studying her every feature, and Jadyn knew he was trying to place her.

"I was twelve years old and my hair was longer." She tucked a shoulder-length, dark-hued curl behind her ear, feeling awkward under his intense scrutiny, like a bug under a microscope.

"What's your name?"

"Jadyn Lee."

"New Jersey," he murmured before rising from the pew and stepping into the aisle, giving her his back as he raked a hand through his hair. "You saw the news story and recognized me."

"You were easy to recognize," Jadyn stated as she stood from the pew. "You look exactly the same as you did the last time I saw you, after you put the fear of God into my parents."

He turned around. "Did they ever try to contact you again?"

"No. They did as you told them and signed me over to my aunt and uncle to raise, then forgot I existed." Jadyn shook her head. "I never understood how you got them to agree to that. My stepfather didn't fear anyone, but he sure followed your orders as if his life depended on it."

Christian shifted his feet again, a muscle ticking in his jaw as he shrugged. "I've been dealing with people like that a long time. I guess I've just got a talent for finding the little spark of good inside bad people, and appealing to it."

"Well, you were certainly my guardian angel. I don't think I could ever repay you for what you did for me, but I've dreamed of it. I've always wanted to come back and thank you for what you did, for giving me a chance at a real life not led under a brutal hand." She looked around the chapel. "I went back to your church to thank you, but you were gone. I never knew your last name so searching for you on the internet was pretty impossible, and believe me, I'm good at finding information. It's one of my strengths, I guess."

His eyebrow rose in interest at this. "Are you a detective now?"

Jadyn laughed at the idea of her being something as normal as that. "No, no, no. Nothing near that, I'm afraid. I ... I've been working temp jobs a couple of years now."

"There are worse ways of making a living."

Jadyn nodded solemnly. "Yes, there are. Thank you so much for seeing to it that I didn't have that misfortune."

"Thank God, Jadyn. I only work as His hand when I can."

"You're a very rare and special person, Christian."

"We all are in our own way." He looked toward the door again, the wariness in his eyes sharper than before.

"Are you expecting someone?"

Worry lines creased his brow. "No, I just need to be on my way." He turned his attention back to her. "So your upbringing was good after we parted ways? The rest of your childhood was pleasant?"

Jadyn nodded. "I was never homecoming queen or anything like that, but I had a good childhood once you rescued me from the nightmare it started out as."

"Great. Any problems now? Any burdens on your mind?"

Jadyn bit her lip. *Just tell him,* she mentally coaxed herself. *But what do I say? Tell him the truth. He'll think I'm crazy. He helped you before. That was a totally different issue altogether.*

His eyes narrowed a bit as he angled his head to study her. "Are you all right?"

"Yeah, sorry." She let out a little nervous laugh. "I was just kind of having a conversation with myself."

He grinned. "Do you do that often?"

"No, maybe, I mean I guess we all do a little bit."

He looked toward the door again, angling his body toward it, clearly ready to leave. *Just say it, Jadyn!*

"Sometimes I talk to animals."

He turned his attention back to her, and smiled, his teeth dazzling white against his tanned face. "I remember your love of animals."

"Sometimes they talk to me," she quickly added before she lost her nerve.

Christian stared at her, blinked, and opened his mouth to say something, but his body went rigid before he said anything. His nostrils flared as his head quickly jerked to the right, slightly cocked as though he'd heard something, but she had heard no sound. Before she could blink, she found herself on the floor, Christian covering her as a popping sound rang out, and a hole blew out of the pew next to them.

"Stay down," Christian growled as he roughly shoved her between two pews, and raced off, faster than she could see. He moved in a blur and within seconds she heard a grunt and a shrill cry as a light fixture near the far corner of the chapel burst, another bullet finding a place to destroy.

Jadyn realized she had gasped louder than the sound the broken glass made and forced herself to slow her breathing and calm down as she carefully sat up, ignoring the aches in her body from being shoved down none too gently. Afraid to raise her head above the pews with all the commotion going on around her—grunts, gasps, shrieks, and growls, obvious sounds of fighting—she folded her legs underneath her and crawled to the end of the pew, where she could peek her head around it, and see up the aisle at a level that she prayed the intruders wouldn't think to lower their gaze to.

Blood stained the back wall, a trail of it leading down to the slumped-over form of a bulky man, moaning as he held his head. Blood trickled through his fingers as it seeped from his skull. He was alive, but Christian had definitely immobilized him.

Jadyn swiveled her head, letting her gaze roam from the back of the chapel to the front, but saw nothing except for a pair of feet sticking out beyond one of the pews at the front of the room. How Christian had managed to fight down there and at the back of the room without her ever seeing him was lost on her. He moved like the wind. There was no way to explain how that was possible.

The sounds of fighting now seemed to come from the hallway trailing off of the right side of the chapel. She recognized the layout as similar to the church Christian had run in New Jersey, and she figured it would be safe to bet the hallway contained a small kitchen area and a few small rooms with nothing more than a cot and dresser, rooms he kept for people in need, people like the person she had been eleven years ago.

She started to turn around so she could crawl to the other end of the pew and look around it, see if she could catch a glimpse of anything at the beginning of the hallway, but the fine hairs along the nape of her neck quickly rose as a chill kissed the skin there, forming small bumps along the flesh. Someone was behind her, and had snuck up on her as silent and invisible as the air she breathed.

"Please don't kill me," she beseeched whoever stood behind her, too afraid to turn and see the person who would be making the decision of whether she lived or died.

A strangled cry was her response, followed by the sound of something large hitting the wall behind her, before she was grabbed by the shoulders and yanked up to stand. Her knees wobbled, nearly giving out, before she was turned around, forced to face Christian as he stood between the pews with her.

His eyes still sparked with silent fury; his chest heaved as his fierce glare pinned her in place. "Who are they?"

Jadyn gulped, the low timbre of Christian's slow and controlled speech scarier than a yell, and shook her head. "I could only see the face of that man over there by the back of the room, and I don't know him." Tears filled her eyes as she realized the implication. He thought she was a part of whatever this was. "I came here alone. I don't have any clue what just happened, or why it just happened."

Christian grabbed her shoulders again, and maneuvered her around him so she now had a good view of the person who had been behind her. He'd apparently thrown the man into the wall behind her, managing to take out a good chunk of drywall as he'd done so. Jadyn frowned as she took in the badly beaten man's short, light brown hair and freckled face. The gun he'd brought inside of a church and planned to hurt Christian with, the gun he would have most likely also used to hurt her with, rested on the floor near his open hand.

"Who is he? Why did you bring them here?"

Jadyn blinked, the second part of Christian's question scaring and infuriating her enough to snap her out of the trance of disbelief she'd been in. She met Christian's calculating, narrow-eyed gaze and refused to cower. "I don't know who this man is, and I didn't bring him here with me. I told no one I was coming here today, at this time. I definitely didn't invite armed men to come inside a church and attack a minister, especially not the minister who once saved my life!" She took a deep breath, having expelled her long response without pausing once. "Just what kind of person do you think I am? If you think I would organize such a thing against someone who saved my life then you should have never saved me."

Christian's brow furrowed as he penetrated her with his gaze, seeming to look through her skin, right into her soul, and checking if it had any dirt on it.

"I swear I don't know these men," she told him, hearing the crack in her voice as tears slid down her cheeks, the initial shock of the situation having worn off. She pointed at the man who'd crept up on her. "That one had a gun at my head. He was going to kill me." She started breathing faster, panic rising. "I came here thinking you could help me. I didn't think there would be danger."

"There is always danger with me." He looked over toward the church entrance and growled. "Oh, great."

Jadyn followed his gaze and saw the same streak of blood running down the wall that she'd noticed earlier, only this time it didn't lead down to a person. The man had escaped. "Will he come back here for you?"

"Yes, but I won't be here," Christian answered as he guided her to the aisle and directed her toward the entrance. "Did you tell anyone about me?"

"No." She stopped, forcing Christian to stop. "Why did they come here for you? Why are you asking if I told anyone about you?"

With his hand on her lower back, Christian lightly pushed her forward, determined to get her out the door. "It's better you don't know, better you forget all about me."

"How will I ever forget this?" She looked around the chapel before they reached the front doors, memorizing the scene. "Are you just going to leave them here?"

"I never kill," Christian answered firmly.

"Kill?" Jadyn swallowed hard. "I wasn't asking if you were going to kill them. I just thought maybe we should call the police. They came in here armed, and attacked you, maybe determined to kill you."

"My death was definitely their intention," Christian answered without emotion, as if he were discussing something as mundane as the weather. "Calling the police will only draw attention to this, and I don't wish for that."

"But surely someone heard gunshots and called. They will probably be here any minute, and it won't look right if you just leave two injured men behind."

"It takes more than gunshots and screams to get the police called in this neighborhood," Christian answered as he flung open the front door and ushered her into the cool night air.

Jadyn wrapped her jacket tighter around her as the cool breeze blew over her, and noticed Christian didn't seem the least bit bothered by the cool October evening air despite not wearing a jacket over his sweater, a sweater now streaked with blood.

A loud pop rent the air, and they both looked toward the sound to see a trio of men standing near an SUV parked near the edge of the parking lot. The one in the middle held a strange weapon she'd never seen before. He smiled as smoke wafted from the barrel of the weapon and the church went up in flames behind them. Another man raised a normal looking gun and fired. Time seemed to slow as the air shimmered in front of where she stood with Christian. In that shimmering air, a woman appeared, raising her hand just in time to catch the bullet that had been speeding toward them.

The golden-haired woman in the long, white dress glanced over her slim shoulder and pinned Christian with eyes the same golden hue. "You should have left immediately like you were told to do," she snapped before throwing the bullet at the man who'd fired it, blowing his gun out of his hand with it.

Jadyn screamed.

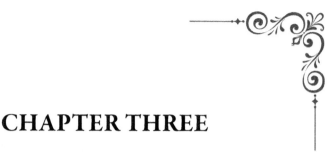

CHAPTER THREE

I know her. The words flowed through Christian's mind on a tidal wave of elation as chaos erupted around him. The shooter's gun fell to the ground as the man dropped to his knees, holding his bloody hand as he screamed in pain, blood pouring onto the pavement below him. The remaining men raised their guns and started to fire upon them as a red pickup truck careened into the parking lot and screeched to a halt. Two burly thugs climbed out of the cab as four men jumped from the bed. All had weapons.

Between Christian and them stood another weapon. She looked like an angel spun from gold. A warrior angel. And he knew her.

"Take the girl and leave," she yelled over her shoulder as she stretched her arms out and formed some sort of wind barrier, protecting Christian from the bullets flying in his direction.

Christian froze, his brain struggling to process the vision before him. Was this actually happening? Then he heard the screaming.

Turning his head, he saw Jadyn holding his arm in a death-grip, begging him to move in-between her panicked screams. Tears rained from her eyes as she pulled on him, urging him to move, to escape the danger.

He couldn't. He knew the golden-haired woman. For the first time in his centuries-long life, he knew someone from his hidden past... but who was she?

"Go, now!" the woman commanded, her eyes glowing like the sun. Such an odd, yet beautiful color. Almost as if she were created from the sun and the moon and stars... everything beautiful and wondrous.

"Christian!" Jadyn's fingernails sank into his arm in her desperation to escape with him. "Let's go! Now! Come on!"

Christian turned toward her just in time to see a group of men coming around the side of the church. Behind her, they weren't held back by the other woman's energy shield. Christian heard a whooshing sound and knew their protector had released her energy, throwing it at the men she'd been holding back.

Behind Jadyn, the approaching men raised guns, aiming for them. He saw fingers push triggers and instantly reacted. Jadyn's panicked cry cut off abruptly as he grabbed her around her waist, dropped to the ground with her, and rolled as bullets flew over them. She gripped his biceps as he rolled them toward the moving van with his hand covering her head protectively. Once close enough to the van, he pried her death grip from him and positioned her so the van provided a barricade between her and the men attacking them.

"You saved my life again," Jadyn gasped.

"I haven't saved it yet," he murmured as he absently brushed tears off her cheeks and checked the perimeter. A brick wall enclosing the area behind them protected her from an attack from that direction. The golden-haired woman had released her energy shield, knocking out the majority of their attackers who were now lying on the ground to his far right. That only left the group who had shot directly at him and Jadyn.

"Stay here," he cautioned the shivering woman as he crouched down and maneuvered around toward the front of the van.

The trio who had shot at Jadyn saw him the moment he emerged and released a storm of bullets to rain upon him. The world stood still as his gaze, drawn like a magnet, locked onto golden eyes. The woman nodded at him once before twisting with one arm flung out. The bullets froze in mid-air as the ground shook, the weight of the woman's power hitting the atmosphere like soundless thunder.

Knowing what needed to be done, Christian ran toward the men, using his vampiric speed to strike them before they could see him arrive in front of them. Their eyes still open wide in astonishment at what the woman had done, they didn't even blink as Christian struck each one in rapid succession, knocking them unconscious before they knew they were being attacked.

Breathing heavy as the last one hit the ground, Christian turned toward the woman, and was once again struck by shocking familiarity. Her name danced around his fingertips, but he couldn't grab on to it. He needed to. He needed to know who he was, and if he recognized her, she had to recognize him. Why else would she appear out of thin air to aid him?

With his heart in his throat and tears in his eyes, he took a step toward her, ready for the answer to the question that had haunted him for millennia. Who was he?

She smiled, a soft, warm upturn of her mouth he felt down to his very soul. Like a mother offering hot chocolate to a child coming in from the cold, she was going to give him exactly what he needed, what he longed for to make everything all right.

The air shimmered around her and her eyes grew wide as panic filled them. Instinct kicking in, Christian picked up the pace and ran toward her, knowing this opportunity to finally know who he was and where he came from was about to slip right through his fingers.

Despite the use of vampiric speed, the two men in white who appeared, stunningly attractive despite the deep scowls on their faces as they clamped strong hands around the woman's arms, snatched her before he could reach them.

The three of them disappeared, simply vanished in an instant, as Christian skid to a stop, the woman's anguished expression swimming in his memory as he growled with rage and fell to his knees, his palms connecting to the pavement the woman had just stood on. She was real and had stood right there, a missing link to his past. She had been right there only a second ago. Water burned behind Christian's eyes as his heart sank back into place. He didn't even know who she was. How would he ever find her again?

A scream snagged his head up, bringing his attention back to the world around him. Turning his head toward the sound, he saw Jadyn fighting off the man who had held a gun to the back of her head. No longer unconscious, the man dragged her toward the open passenger door of the van, ready to steal her and Christian's getaway vehicle, but the woman was not allowing him to take her so easily. She bit into his arm, bringing a cry of pain from the brute as he raised his other arm, fingers closed in a fist.

Christian stood before him before he had the chance to swing it. One-handed, he crushed the man's fist until bone cracked. "Get in the van," he ordered Jadyn as he used his other hand to grab the man's forearm and spun, lifting the man from the ground before flinging him across the parking lot.

Sirens wailed in the distance, indicating they had finally made enough commotion in the crime-infested neighborhood to warrant a call to the police. Deciding not to wait around, Christian slammed the passenger door closed as Jadyn fell into the seat, and raced around the front of the van to climb into the driver's seat.

"Hold on," he warned as he started the engine, put the moving van in Drive, and took off, leaving the mess behind for the police to try and figure out. From the corner of his eye as he navigated the dark streets of Baltimore, he saw the glint of tears roll down Jadyn's cheeks as she struggled to breathe normally. He recognized the action. Fighting panic was something he had seen more times than he wished to recount. Considering the woman was only human, she was doing a good job.

"Why did he grab you?" he asked as he careened around a corner, his goal to get away from the scene of the crime as quickly as possible.

"What?" She looked over at him, eyes cloudy and dazed, as if distracted from some deep thought.

"If it was me he came after, why did he snatch you when he came out of the church? Why didn't he come straight for me?"

Jadyn blinked before redirecting her gaze to the street. "He said I was bait, and you would come to save me and that's when they would make their move."

"That's what I was afraid of," Christian muttered, taking another curve at too high of a speed, but he managed to avoid an accident. The men had to be hunters, maybe even slayers, and those types were known to lay traps for vampires. If they thought the woman meant something to him, then she was in as much danger as he was. "Where do you live?"

Jadyn gave him the address, and sniffed, fighting back tears as her mind undoubtedly tried to come to terms with what she had just witnessed.

Christian took a deep breath and shook his head. This was why Seta warned him against getting close to humans. Once they knew you, they were in danger. There was no way to avoid it. He couldn't let that stop him from saving children though. Saving children was how he redeemed himself for being what he was. It was the light that countered the darkness inside him. He would deal with this problem, lead Jadyn back to safety, and he would go on saving all the innocents he could save. It was the only way to keep the darkness inside him from spreading.

With a few directions from Jadyn, Christian found her apartment building and parked along the curb, lucky to find space for the large U-Haul. He stayed her hand when she reached for the door handle, and shook his head. "Not without me."

He exited the van and walked around to her side, carefully surveying the area for signs of danger. The hair along the back of his neck rose as an uneasy feeling swam in his stomach. Danger still chased him, and from the feel of it, it wasn't far behind. He helped Jadyn out of the U-Haul, his attention never straying from the task at hand: Guarding her life.

"Try not to make any noise," she said in a near-whisper as she unlocked the main door to the building and crept up the stairs, "I don't want to deal with my landlord right now."

Christian frowned at her request, but quickly shrugged off his curiosity as to why she would be avoiding her landlord. He already had enough questions in queue needing to be answered, some of them life or death.

They reached the landing and Jadyn came to an abrupt stop. Christian grabbed her shoulders, narrowly avoiding slamming right into her. Before him, one of the apartment doors stood wide open, hanging on by its last hinge. "I'm guessing that's yours."

She nodded, mouth agape, as he moved past her and cautiously stepped toward the apartment. He shielded his body behind the protection of the wall as he peered inside. The place had been ransacked, a clutter of Jadyn's belongings scattered all over. Dishes were broken in the kitchen area, smashed like the screen of her television. The stuffing from her sparse furniture was in so many places it looked as if the sofa and chairs had exploded, and three men lay bleeding into her carpet. None of that surprised Christian. The man standing in the middle of it all did.

"Christian." The tall, dark-haired man nodded his head in greeting as he unfolded his arms to shove his hands into the pockets of his dark jeans.

"Jonah."

Christian stepped inside the small apartment, pulling Jadyn along into the living area with him. He sensed the terror rising in her and gently covered her mouth with his hand, stifling a scream before she could alert neighbors of the situation. "Surely this wasn't quiet," he commented, noticing the signs of a fight among the bruises Jonah and the men shared, not to mention the smoke wafting up from a hole in the wall. "Your wife's fireballs didn't set off the smoke detectors?"

"They aren't made of smoke, or normal fire for that matter," came a feminine voice behind him.

Christian turned to see Jonah's wife, Malaika, enter the apartment. With light chocolate skin and caramel eyes, she was a vision of beauty, but it was her warm smile as she nodded toward him that was her most striking feature. She was one of the prettiest witches he'd ever met.

"I assume you've bespelled the building's occupants?"

"Of course." She smiled as she walked over to her husband, the human detective, Jonah Porter, and wrapped her arms around his waist. "It kept me busy while waiting for you to show up."

"And just how did you know I would be showing up?" Christian asked, already figuring the answer as he removed his hand from Jadyn's mouth. She'd calmed down enough that he didn't fear a scream, just a few tears over her trashed home, which she shed in silence.

"I saw it." She shrugged. "Of course, in the version I saw, these men were lying in wait and attacked you the moment you stepped through the door. They seemed hell-bent on getting the girl, and in turn, getting you. There will be more."

"There always is," Christian muttered as he raked a hand through his hair. It never ended. Despite his good deeds he would always be hunted for what he was, but this was unexpected... and confusing "I was just ambushed at the church. At least I thought I was ambushed, but if Jadyn's apartment is trashed... which one of us are they after?"

"So, these two are with you?" Jadyn asked him, gesturing toward Jonah and Malaika. "They're not dangerous?"

"Yes, I mean no." He shook his head. "Yes, they're friends. No, they're not a danger to us. This is—"

"My babies!" Jadyn ran down the hall, leaving Christian with his mouth hanging open, completely baffled.

He looked at his friends. "Babies?"

Malaika's nose scrunched, her lip curling back. "Oh hell. I thought those nasty things were left here by the bad guys. They're her pets?"

"Pets?" Christian asked.

"That girl's got *skunks* in her bedroom."

Skunks? Christian stood still a moment, processing that. Skunks. He looked at Jonah and could tell by the way the man's shoulders shook with silent laughter that Malaika wasn't lying. Skunks in her bedroom. Wow. He shook his head and decided to move past that. He had bigger problems. "Is this because of the Blood Revelation?"

"I'd say so," Malaika answered. "I got enough off of these guys to know they were ordered to bring you back to whoever sent them, some vampire whose name I couldn't pull out of them. The girl was just a way of finding you."

Christian took a moment, stunned. "How? Jadyn is a young woman I rescued over a decade ago and haven't seen or heard from since. How did they know she would lead them to me? How did they know I'm even involved with this prophecy? I'm not one of the chosen ones."

"You know the chosen ones," Jonah answered, "and I'm sure they knew about her the same way they knew about Malaika. They have their own psychics and witches. They were watching Malaika long before she ever delivered Rialto and Aria's baby."

"We are all connected," Malaika explained, "because we protect those children and their parents. They think that if they capture us they can capture them, or at least know who the special children are."

"If they can see us, why can't we see them?"

Malaika frowned, shoulders sagging. "I try. I've tried countless spells along with Seta."

"It's not your fault, Malaika. Never think that it is." Christian glanced toward the room Jadyn had disappeared into. "The Blood Revelation is a prophecy, and prophecy works on its own time. Besides, the prophecy says we win, remember?"

"As long as they don't get the children," Jonah reminded him.

Malaika backhanded him in the gut, drawing a grunt.

"Hey, one of those kids is my nephew. I'm not being insensitive. I'm just stating the facts," he explained. "We can't take it for granted that this prophecy is going to come true and just twiddle our thumbs, waiting for things to work out."

"He's right," Christian conceded. "God helps those who help themselves. We have a duty to protect the chosen and their offspring."

"Well, you need to help that girl on out of here so we can take care of this mess," Malaika said, taking in the damage to the room. "We didn't make it in time to keep these dirt bags from destroying this place, and some got away. There's a lot of mess to clean, and I'd rather do it before any more come back."

Christian nodded, and stepped toward Jadyn's room, wondering how things had gotten so crazy so quick. He sent up a thank you to God for blessing him with good friends. The night would have been a lot worse if not for Jonah, Malaika, and... the golden-eyed woman. He swung back around. "Jonah, is Khiderian available?"

"He's out of state on a special job, but Marilee is here in the city. Why?"

He frowned, wondering why he'd thought of Khiderian. The man was a fallen angel, turned human after he sacrificed himself to save Jake's half-sister, Marilee, and in the process stripped her of her ability to call forth demons. Jake had brought the pair to his home while they recuperated from the ordeal, and Christian had been in awe, standing in the presence of a former angel, but Khiderian had shrugged off his many questions, claiming to not remember much of his existence as an angel. He did, however, retain his knowledge of everything that had happened to him since falling centuries ago, and he knew of beings Christian hadn't even heard of before. That must have been why he felt the urge to talk with Khiderian. "We were ambushed at the church and a woman just appeared out of nowhere to help. She was powerful, probably the most powerful woman I've ever encountered, but don't tell Seta I said that."

"Clearly not a human woman." Jonah cocked his head to the side. "What was she?"

"That's what I was hoping Khiderian could tell me. I didn't get the sense she was a witch, definitely not a vampire, but she was able to slow time, or at least it seemed that way. She caught a bullet in her bare hand and threw it back at the shooter with enough force to shatter his hand."

Jonah's mouth fell open as he stood blinking.

Malaika's eyes narrowed. "She didn't introduce herself after helping you?"

"Two men, just as powerful as her, appeared out of thin air too. Before I had time to blink, they latched on to her and disappeared faster than Seta can." Christian's gut twisted as the woman's face appeared in his mind. She'd looked caught. He hoped she didn't get in trouble for helping him, whoever and whatever she was. All he knew was she was on their side, and that was all that mattered. That, and the fact she was somehow linked to the past that he couldn't remember. "They were extremely attractive, almost seemed to radiate beauty, and all three were dressed in pristine white. She had golden eyes. Not brown, not hazel, but gold like a golden coin."

"I'll ask Khiderian if he knows of anyone who can catch bullets bare-handed, has golden eyes and a thing for white," Jonah said with a frown before gesturing down the hall with his head. "I'll ask Jake too the next time he checks in. You need to head on out of here and take the girl someplace safe. Call us and we'll come take over watching her while you move on."

"What?" Christian shook his head. "She's staying with me."

Jonah and Malaika exchanged a look of surprise before he replied. "You want a strange woman with you while you're on the run? What if she finds out what you are?"

"She doesn't already know, does she?" Malaika's eyes grew wary.

"No," Christian answered, though he suspected she was close to it. "With all that's happened she knows I'm not a normal man. She knows none of us are normal. I've got a lot of explaining to do."

"A simple spell would resolve this. I can wipe her memory once we set her up somewhere safe."

"No," Christian nearly growled before restraining his sudden flare of temper. "Like you said, our enemy knows who she is and that she would end up leading them to me. Whether you wipe her memory or not, she's still going to be bait because the men after her won't believe her when she says she doesn't know me. They'll think she's just protecting me." And he wasn't fond of wiping memories unless necessary.

"Well, it's not safe for you to be with her if they're tracking her in order to find you," Malaika argued. "They find her now, they find you. Game over."

"Then I'll just have to keep them from finding her."

CHAPTER FOUR

Jadyn had immediately dropped to her knees before the cage and opened the door, checking over the precious kits inside, oblivious to anything else. Now that she had assured herself they were fine and had one of them wrapped in a blanket, snuggled against her chest, she allowed her brain to catch up.

She'd found her long lost hero, and had walked into an ambush she'd thought was for him, but then she'd almost been abducted, and strange men had been waiting for them in her apartment. Strange men who appeared to be dead. *In her apartment.* She'd thought Christian could help her, that he was some powerful hero, but his friends... What were these people?

"Maybe I'm dreaming," she murmured to herself as she stroked her finger down the kit's back, imagining where the white line of fur would be under the light blanket. "Having a very vivid nightmare."

"You're very much awake."

She jerked, her head instantly swiveling in the direction of the deep voice that had surprised her. Christian stood in the doorway of her bedroom, one shoulder leaning against the frame, the rest of his body anything but relaxed. This was a man not used to truly relaxing, ever letting his guard down, and if he'd had many nights like tonight she certainly understood why.

"Sorry. Didn't mean to frighten you." He surveyed the small room, which wasn't much to brag about. A full-sized bed with a dark blue afghan for cover, a couple of oak nightstands topped with plain white lamps, and a distressed dresser she'd gotten off of a curb several months ago. A large poster of the *Footprints in the Sand* poem hanging on the wall above the headboard was her only décor. His eyes lingered on it for a moment before he turned his attention to the skunks, eying the ones in the cage curiously before focusing on the one she held. "Don't those tend to spray some really foul-smelling stuff?"

"They generally don't until they're about three months old, although they are capable of doing it earlier. I'm careful not to startle them and holding them with their tails tucked between their legs helps to make sure they don't. I normally don't hold them because I'm only caring for them until they're weaned and can be released..." She realized she was starting to ramble on. "I was afraid those men had hurt them."

"If they made it back here before Jonah and Malaika arrived, they probably took one look at those things and ran the opposite way." He grinned, but it only lasted a blink of time before he shoved his hands into his front pockets and expelled a breath. "It's been a rough night, and I wish I could tell you everything is good now, but I don't think that's the case."

Feeling her anxiety level rise and not wanting to transfer the emotion to the kit in her arms, Jadyn put the sweet baby back into the cage and closed the door. "What happened tonight?" she asked as she stood and crossed the room to her small bathroom, carefully washing her hands after handling the kits. Christian followed her, but didn't step through the doorway. "I see you on the news, discover you're actually in the same city I currently live in, haven't aged a day, and I go to your church just in time to get caught up in some sort of ambush. Some woman who looks too beautiful to be real just appears out of nowhere and catches a bullet in her freaking hand..." She dried her hands off on a towel, and turned toward Christian. "I'm nearly snatched, then I come back and there's dead guys in my apartment because apparently they wanted me all along? Or wanted me as bait all along? When I didn't even know I'd be seeing you until earlier today, and never told anyone. How is —" She stopped speaking, noting Christian's sweater no longer had any blood on it. "You had blood on you. There were streaks all over your sweater."

Christian looked down at himself and shifted uncomfortably.

"I've lost my mind." Jadyn gripped her temples as everything seemed to sway around her. Her knees weakened and bent.

"Whoa, whoa, whoa." Christian gripped her by her arms and guided her to the bed, helping her sit at the foot before he lowered himself to his haunches, putting himself at eyelevel. "You're not crazy. Everything you saw actually happened."

"I saw blood on you."

"There was blood on me." He ran a hand down his face and took a breath. "Look, you saw everything so you know I'm telling you the truth when I tell you we're in a dangerous situation. My friends stopped those men who were waiting on us here, but there will be more. I'll explain everything to you, but we need to go now."

"Go? Go where?"

"I don't know yet, but we need to leave here immediately and get ahead of whoever is after us."

She stared at him for a moment, until he became blurry and she felt herself sway.

"Jadyn." He gripped her shoulders, holding her still until the dizziness faded away. "We probably need to get some food in you or you need to sleep or something. You're really pale. We'll figure it all out on the road. Do you think you can pack some clothes or do you want me to do it for you?"

She sat still, blinking, replaying his request. "No," she finally said.

"No, you don't want me to pack for you or no, you don't think you can do it?"

"No, I'm not leaving." She stood, fighting through the dizziness as she swept him aside. "I can't leave."

"Do you want to die?" Christian asked, standing. "You're not safe here."

"If I'm not safe, neither are they!" She pointed to the kits. "I know most people don't care about skunks, but I'm not leaving those babies to die, and they can't be released yet."

Christian looked at the caged animals and ran his hand through his hair before returning his gaze to her. "Do you remember what those men did to my church?"

"Yeah, they set it on..." She gripped her stomach, suddenly feeling even more ill. "Would they do that to my apartment? There are innocent people in this building."

"We're innocent people, Jadyn. They want to kill us anyway, and they won't care at all about those skunks." He looked at them again. "We can't take them with us. We have no idea what we might run into."

"I can't leave them." She started to cry, imagining them abandoned, or worse, on fire. "I can't let those people hurt them, and they'll never make it on their own right now, not until they're weaned."

"Pack some clothes and whatever you absolutely need, write down complete instructions for their care, and I promise you they'll be taken care of." He walked over to the door, stopping to look back at her. "You have five minutes. Pack what you need and write those instructions down. If you're not done in five minutes, we're out of here with only the clothes you have on now." Then he left.

Jadyn stood in the middle of her room for a moment, just processing, or trying to. The more she thought about the events of the night, the crazier it all became. All she knew for sure was she had to take care of her babies, and if there was any chance that someone could hurt them, well, it was a chance she couldn't take. She walked over to the cage and squatted beside it.

"I'm so sorry, babies," she whispered as she gazed lovingly upon the three sleeping, and the bigger one moving around on his tiny legs. She hadn't named them, knowing it was a bad idea when she'd have to release them, but she'd grown attached anyway. Now she didn't even know if she'd be there to see them when they were able to go back to the environment they belonged to.

She only had five minutes. "Dang it. I'm so sorry, babies, but I do know Christian is a good guy. He saved me when I was little and surrounded by predators. He'll do the same for you."

She quickly grabbed the instructions for care she, herself, had researched and printed off her nightstand, and took out a pad of paper and a pen, quickly adding more detail about the kits' current feeding schedule. She boxed up all the supplies she had in the room and put the instructions on top. Only then did she grab a duffel bag from her closet and start packing for herself, tossing in all her necessities from the bathroom before even worrying about clothes.

"Five minutes are up," Christian said, stepping back into her room and frowning as he saw the open, and barely filled, duffel bag resting on her bed.

"It took a while to get the skunks' supplies together and write out detailed instructions. They're not even two months old yet. They need close, and very specific care." Her voice broke and she sucked back a deep breath as she stuffed clothes into the duffel, willing herself not to fall apart.

"I understand you're upset. I wish this hadn't happened, and that you weren't brought into this mess."

"And what exactly is this mess?" She jammed as many socks and undergarments as she could fit into the bag and zipped it up. "People are dead. Some of them in my apartment! Some woman just poofed in and out of reality. What the—" Jadyn quickly zipped her lip before cursing in front of a minister. Despite knowing he fought like no minister had any business fighting, she still regarded him as one and would not disrespect him by cursing at him. At least not until more bullets came zipping at her head. Then all bets were off. "What the heck, Christian? What the *heck*? Just explain to me what is going on."

"I will. I will explain everything once we're on the road."

"And I'm supposed to be okay with that?" A small laugh escaped Jadyn's throat despite the situation being anything but funny. "I came to you in the sanctity of a church and found myself in the middle of a frigging war! Bullets were everywhere. Then I come home to find my apartment torn apart, dead people on my floor, and it's your friends in the middle of it all!"

Christian stepped inside the room, crossing the short distance to stand before her. "It will all be explained, but now is not the time. Unless you want to see more bullets and blood, we need to go now."

"Where?" She stepped back as he reached a hand out to her. She didn't want anyone touching her right now, especially not people who she didn't even know really were people anymore. She frowned at the thought, but she'd certainly seen enough craziness to warrant it. "Where are we running to anyway?"

"I'm not sure yet." He ran a hand over his eyes, his youthful face appearing tired. "I usually take off by myself and I just end up wherever I end up."

"You say that like running away is a normal thing for you. What do you run from? This?" She flung her arm out in the direction of the living room where his friends remained with the three corpses on her carpet. "Do your friends kill a lot of people? And what are they? You said something to the woman about *bespelling* people!"

"They are friends, and if not for them you would probably be dead right now." His eyes grew darker, his jaw set firmly. "I told you I will explain everything to you once we are on the move. I'm sorry, but we don't have time for this now. If you want to keep those skunks safe, let's go."

He picked up her bag and walked out the door with it. Jadyn stared at the empty doorway, mouth agape. He'd just left, taking for granted she would follow him. She fisted her hands in her hair and crouched down, elbows on her knees as she rocked back and forth. What was she going to do?

Only an idiot would take off into the night with a stranger, especially after seeing how dangerous that stranger was, but Christian wasn't a stranger. Oh, she definitely didn't know him as well as she could, but he'd had a major influence over her life. The man was more of a mystery than anyone else walking the earth, but she knew him. He'd saved her life once. Twice, if she counted tonight.

He was a minister, a man of God. He protected children, and his protection apparently didn't stop after they grew older. Despite the danger chasing him, he didn't seem to do anything to warrant it. She certainly hadn't done anything to deserve being hunted, unless they somehow knew her secret... but was it worth killing for?

Blowing out a steadying breath, she rose to a stand and glanced over at the *Footprints in the Sand* poem. "Please walk with me now, Lord. I need you more than ever." Then, to the innocent kits she'd rescued after their mother had been killed, she said a tearful goodbye, sent up a prayer for their protection, and left the room on shaky legs while she had the willpower to do so.

Three sets of eyes turned toward her as she entered the living area, one full of such regret it made the pit of her stomach feel hollow.

"Ready?" he asked, one foot out the front door, and her bag in his hand.

"I don't really have a choice." Jadyn nodded toward the men on the floor. "Dead men are in my living room and I have no way of explaining it. I guess I'm pretty much on the run for my freedom as well as my life."

"Don't worry about the law," the woman named Malaika said. "When we are done cleaning this mess, no one will know what happened. They won't even remember you living here."

Jadyn frowned, wondering how that was even possible. "My landlord will remember me. I owe him enough rent money for him to curse me forever."

The woman smiled, a strange, knowing look in her brown eyes. "It will all be forgotten."

"We should go, Jadyn."

"All right." With a strange feeling in her stomach, an almost warning sensation in her gut, she glanced back toward her room. "What about my babies?"

"You know those things are skunks, right?" Malaika asked, her nose wrinkled in disgust.

The man gave the woman a look and she shrugged. "Don't worry about them," he told Jadyn. "We've made a call to our friend, Marilee. She's more than happy to look after them. Apparently, she's cared for baby squirrels, raccoons, and opossums. With your instructions, she shouldn't have any issues at all. As for Malaika, she might not be thrilled about them, but she wouldn't harm a fly."

Jadyn looked past them at the men lying lifeless on her carpet.

"Oh, I'll harm the hell out of some murderers sent after my people," Malaika told her, "but I don't hurt animals, not even nasty, stinky ones."

"I give you my word they will be well cared for," Christian promised, jerking his head toward the hall, "as long as we get out of here and allow Jonah and Malaika time to get them to safety before more trouble comes this way."

The image of her apartment on fire with the kits inside flashed through Jadyn's mind again, getting her moving. She looked back over her shoulder at his friends, taking in the woman's serene smile and the man's hawk-eyed gaze and stiff posture as they watched them leave.

Christian quickly ushered her down the stairs and onto the street, pausing just long enough to survey the perimeter before he gripped her beneath her elbow and directed her toward a dark gray Taurus parked on the corner.

Jadyn frowned as he unlocked the trunk and deposited her bag there. "We came here in the moving van."

"And we're leaving in a Taurus. This is Malaika's car. She and Jonah will be putting my belongings in storage until I can safely retrieve them, and they'll take the U-Haul back for me. It's not the best escape vehicle."

Jadyn nodded her understanding. Her gaze caught on another bag as Christian closed the trunk. "They have a bag in there. We should put it in the van for them."

"That's my bag," Christian said as he guided her to the passenger side of the car and opened the door for her, closing it after she settled into her seat.

A flare of warning twisted Jadyn's gut as he rounded the car and slid in beside her. She replayed the time spent packing in her room through her mind, sure she hadn't been very long before Christian had joined her. Something wasn't right. "When did you have time to get your bag out of the U-Haul and put it in the trunk of this car?"

His jaw clenched as he turned the key in the ignition and started up the engine. "Malaika moved it for me."

"Oh." That made sense. She figured the woman would have had time to take care of his stuff for him if she'd left right after Jadyn had gone to her room and returned shortly before. Jadyn shook her head. She was getting paranoid, certainly understandable after the night she'd had. It was a wonder she wasn't screaming.

"Maybe I'm not awake after all," she murmured as Christian pulled away from the curb. "No way would I be this calm right now with all that has happened."

"I wish I could tell you this was all a dream, but you're not sleeping." Christian's eyes spoke of apology as they glanced her way briefly before his focus returned to the road.

"Why am I so calm then? So... numb? Dead men are in my apartment. A woman disappeared before my eyes. I should be completely freaking out right now."

"The numbness is a gift. It gets you through what you otherwise couldn't handle."

Like leaving innocent kits behind for a stranger to care for. "This Marilee is a good person?"

"She's a wonderful person who I trust completely to take care of your little ones."

Jadyn stared out into the night, thankful for the numbness that kept her from losing her mind as she came to the realization she'd stepped into a living nightmare, but maybe she should have expected something like this. Why would she have a normal life when she herself was anything but normal?

"JUST WHAT EXACTLY DID you think you were doing?"

Kiara shrugged out of Zaccharus and Amuel's hold, surveying her dark surroundings. She recognized the cave from the times she had come to meet the Dream Teller in the witch's realm. She didn't see the woman around. "Why are we here?"

"Answer my question first." Amuel's deep growl of a voice rolled out like thunder to echo off the stone walls. "Do not forget your rank."

Kiara swallowed hard and turned to face her raven-haired, silver-eyed superior. Her stomach churned with disdain, knowing she'd called rank earlier against Zaccharus and now the lesser angel had the satisfaction of seeing the same done to her. She was a warrior angel, and one of the best at that, but Amuel was far more superior. He was one of the absolute elite, an archangel.

"I know my place, Amuel, and I acknowledge and respect yours. I would never willingly disrespect you."

"Yet, you went against orders and showed yourself to our lost brother."

Kiara glared at Zaccharus, narrowing her eyes on him as he attempted to shrink away.

"Do you really think I needed Zaccharus to tattle on you?"

She turned her attention back to the angered archangel. "Of course not. An archangel would never need the assistance of such a lower level angel to assist him in something so simple as tracking a warrior angel," she said before allowing herself a little smile, happy to have gotten in the subtle dig at Zaccharus.

Amuel frowned his displeasure at the behavior. "Aurorian is off limits. You know this."

"Yes."

"Then why did you go against orders and seek him?"

Kiara sighed. "He was in danger and I protected him. It's my job as a warrior angel to protect—"

"To protect humans!" Amuel roared forcefully enough to blow Kiara's hair back. "He was an angel and is now a vampire, a very powerful one. It is not your job to protect him."

"He was outnumbered!" Kiara shouted back, knowing that doing so was an offense, but her anger outweighed her sense of duty. "What if he'd been fatally wounded?"

"You are not to interfere!"

"But—"

"Silence!"

Again, Kiara's hair blew back as the archangel's voice boomed through the cave. His dark, lethal gaze bore into her as he stood before her, nostrils flaring and chest heaving as anger coursed through his muscular body. Despite the pristine white of his silk button-down shirt and slacks, he was a dark and formidable force to be reckoned with. Regardless, Kiara refused to wither before him. She raised her chin and stared right back into his silver gaze, not outwardly defying him, but letting him know she would not cower. She had stood up for what she believed in, what she knew to be right. For that, there would be no apology.

"I helped Christian because I believed him to be in extreme danger, and helping him felt the right thing to do. As a warrior angel, I fight for the side of good. Tonight was no different." She waited for another angry response, but received none. "I answered your question. Now, why am I here in this cave? Why bring me to the dream realm instead of home?"

"It seems I have a new roommate."

Kiara turned toward the old, withered voice of the woman who had the dream realm all to herself. Most who laid eyes upon Krystaline saw her as an old, hunched over witch, a hag for lack of a better description, with ropes of thick gray and white hair falling from beneath her hooded cloak, endless rivers of wrinkles flowing within her leathery skin, a large hook nose, and platinum eyes blind to the world. They knew her only as the Dream Teller, a powerful witch who had guided them along the course fate had set before them, a blind old hag who could see far more than any of them.

Kiara and the other angels of her rank and above saw the real woman. Krystaline. Her long platinum blonde hair flowed like silk as she approached through the cave entrance, shoulders proudly held straight as her dainty chin rose just a fraction. She never dared think herself superior to the angels. She knew her place, and despite hating the curse placed upon her to make her appear ugly to all others, she did not cry out against it. The angels had not placed the curse upon her, but they would be the ones to lift it when the time was right.

As Krystaline looked at her with narrowed blue eyes, eyes that couldn't actually see, Kiara knew the woman was displeased. "Welcome to my humble abode."

Kiara ignored the sarcasm dripping from Krystaline's greeting, instead focusing on the implication. Her eyes burned with anger as she turned them on Amuel. "What is the meaning of this?"

"You are to stay here with Krystaline," the tall archangel answered. "Your recent behavior has not gone unnoticed, and some of our brothers and sisters are calling for you to be cast out."

"What?!" Kiara's voice ricocheted off the stone walls. "Only one angel has ever been cast out, and I have done nothing nearly as horrific as Lucifer!"

"You also did not perform your last assigned task."

Kiara blinked back tears of rage. "The *drac chemare* is no more. I ran a sword through Khiderian in her place, eliminating the threat without taking a life. I could not have handled the situation better."

"Your order was to slay the *drac chemare.*"

"I killed the part of her that called the demons forth!"

"Why did you have to?" Amuel cocked his head, eyes narrow and inquisitive. "Why did the situation reach the point where there was a decision to be made?"

Kiara frowned. "I do not understand this question."

"Yes, you do." Amuel stepped forward until she had no choice but to crane her neck to look into his smoldering eyes. "You were given a task to perform, a task that could have been performed at any time after the *drac chemare* had been used to save Jacob Porter. Instead of performing the task as instructed, you put the duty onto the slayer to perform."

50

Kiara backed up a step, remembering handing the assignment off to Jacob in this very cave after having Krystaline call him there in a dream. "He is a slayer. It was the most effective way to see the threat removed."

"Since when does a slayer wield more power than an angel?"

"Sometimes it's not about the power."

"Really?" Amuel grinned, the sight reminding Kiara of a snake readying to strike. "You chose the time, place, and person for the attack because you did not want it to happen. You knew Khiderian would intercede and once Jacob knew the *drac chemare* was his sister he would refuse to deliver the death blow."

"I planned for the chance of that happening and was ready to step in and do my duty," Kiara argued as sweat ran the length of her spine.

"Were you really?"

"Yes." Kiara swallowed, the task of getting the lump in her throat down a great effort. "Had Khiderian not offered himself in her place, I would have executed her. It was a hundred times harder to run the sword through Khiderian, but I did. It was my duty. I have never backed out of my duty."

"Yet." Amuel stepped back to allow her some space. "You will stay here, Kiara, while I await word on what to do with you."

"What is my crime? I helped a brother—"

"A former brother," he corrected, "and one who is off limits to our help. You know you were violating the rules when you stepped into that battle to aid him and the woman. Aurorian must seek his own path, fight his own battles. We cannot sway his direction."

The archangel turned toward Krystaline, who had been listening to the exchange in rapt silence, and nodded his head toward her before turning his attention back to Kiara. "Stay here, sister. I have lost enough of my brothers. I do not wish to lose one of my sisters as well."

He disappeared, taking the traitorous Zaccharus with him. Kiara frowned. Zaccharus was hardly a traitor. There was no sense blaming him for her folly, even if she truly did not believe what she had done to be folly. There was nothing wrong in protecting a good person. It was her duty.

"Christian is safe," Krystaline said softly as she turned toward a pathway in the cave and gestured with her hand for Kiara to follow. "Come. Have a look yourself."

51

Kiara followed along, her fingertips trailing along the words of the Blood Revelation prophecy carved into the cavern walls as they traveled down the narrow passage. Kiara gasped as they stepped out of the cave's murky darkness into a bright, sunlit garden full of lush, colorful flowers blossoming among tall, healthy trees and dense green foliage. A pebbled trail led to a large birdbath shaped like a heart standing in the center of the garden.

Krystaline turned to face her as she reached the birdbath, and gestured toward it with her hand, bowing slightly. "This is the only place where I can see with my eyes, not just with my power. I think you need this gift more than I right now."

Kiara stepped forward and looked down into the birdbath, recognizing the water as the same found in the vision pools in Heaven. A myriad of colors swirled within the crystal blue water then took form. She saw Christian driving the dark streets, escaping the danger on his trail as the woman who'd brought it to him slept in the passenger seat.

"Can I ask you a question, Krystaline?"

"Of course," the Dream Teller answered as she gazed into the water with her.

"If I am the only one helping Christian, who is doing that?" She pointed to the glowing white cross marking a building safe for Christian. She had done it in the past when he had to flee with no idea where to go, but the cross she saw glowing in the water now was not of her doing.

"Clearly, you are not the only one aiding him."

"Then who else is helping, and why am I the only one being reprimanded for it?"

CHAPTER FIVE

"What happened?"

Chuck swallowed, the dryness of his throat making it seem as if he were swallowing a prickly ball. Fear twisted his gut as he looked into the murky gray eyes of the man who'd sent him on the failed mission. "What... what had happened wa—"

"Kneel, you pathetic waste!"

Chuck flinched as the man's voice roared over him. He hadn't budged from the throne-like chair he rested in, hadn't tensed a muscle. To the naked eye, Jaffron appeared completely relaxed, unbothered. He didn't just sit in the chair, he lounged in it, his posture the epitome of carefree. His right elbow rested on the right arm to support his body, his left leg draped over the other arm, but Chuck could feel in his bones that the man was coiled to strike, and when he did he would be far more aggressive than his sharp tone.

"I beg your forgiveness." Chuck kneeled, his wobbly knees almost giving out and sending him to the floor faster and rougher than he'd intended. He almost laughed at his sudden lack of balls. He'd been a linebacker in high school, and never backed down from a fight. No one and nothing scared Chuck Lester... except for this scrawny little man with the long red hair sitting in front of him in the prissy black leather pants. The man looked like a pussy through and through, a wimp if ever he'd seen one, but it was what lay beneath the man that made him lose three drops of piss every time he saw him. It was the promise of pain in his voice, the power that seeped from his pores, the soullessness in his cruel, dark eyes. It was the monster inside human skin.

"What happened?"

Chuck licked his cracked lips, tasting the salt. Whether from blood or tears, he didn't know. He thought it possible he may have cried a little once he'd realized he'd screwed up and lost the frigging minister. "He got away."

"Of course he got away, you idiot. Otherwise he would be here now bleeding out. *How* did he get away?"

Chuck swallowed hard, saliva sliding down his throat in a painful lump, before answering. "He took us all out. He was just too quick."

"He's a vampire." Jaffron leaned forward. "You call yourself intelligent yet you expected a vampire to move as if human."

"No, no, of course not." Chuck licked his lips, barely wincing at the sting caused by his tongue touching the open skin. The pain he truly feared was far greater than a little cut. "But we were heavily armed and thought we could get him while he was distracted with that girl, but he seemed to sense us. One of my guys took a shot, missed, and then he went into action. He moved quicker than we thought he would."

"Idiot." Leather rustled as Jaffron settled back into his chair. "How much damage did he do to your men?"

"He hurt them pretty bad. They're in the hospital. I got the least of the damage." Chuck raised his hand the best he could with his arm in a sling. He hadn't gone to the hospital, but had instead taken care of his own injuries the best he could. He'd known that if he'd kept Jaffron waiting for a report he'd suffer far greater injuries than a concussion, busted hand and dislocated shoulder. He hoped getting back before sundown earned him some points and the vampire would have one of his witches heal him, at least the shattered bones in his hand. "I knew you'd want a report so I skipped the hospital myself."

"How noble." Jaffron's tone practically dripped sarcasm. "So, the vampire killed no one?"

"No." Chuck shook his head. "He roughed us up, defended himself pretty good, but he never drew a weapon or used fang. He fought more like a boxer than a vampire. The woman did more damage than he did."

"The one I had you follow?"

"No. There was another." He raised his head, daring to hold Jaffron's gaze. "She appeared out of nowhere. I don't know what she was, but she wasn't human."

Jaffron leaned forward, interest piqued. "Do I have to draw this out of you detail by detail? I asked you what happened and you take this long to mention he had help? Tell me everything, you fool!"

"Yes, yes, Jaffron. My apologies. I'm a bit jumbled. I think it's from my head injury."

"You will have greater injuries if you keep trying my patience."

"Yes, sir. Of course, sir." Chuck licked his lips again and started to speak, but couldn't remember what he was going to say, preoccupied with holding his bladder. Damn if the prissy vampire didn't scare the piss right out of him.

"The woman!"

"Oh yes, the woman!" Chuck nodded his head, his brain waking up. "The church was on fire and Horowitz had a clear shot at the vampire so he took it. I don't know how to really describe what happened, except to say it was like time slowed down and the air shimmered between the vampire and Horowitz. This woman just appeared right there in the shimmer. She grabbed the bullet with her bare hand and threw it back at Horowitz, obliterating his hand. Everyone we had in front shot at her and she just... shielded herself and the targets with, like, air. I swear there was nothing there. It was like magic, but I've seen witches and she wasn't no witch."

Jaffron leaned back in his chair and rubbed his chin. "What did this woman look like?"

"She was gorgeous," Chuck said, allowing himself a moment to savor the image of the woman from his memory. "She was tall, slim. Not skinny, but strong, but not like a body builder. Her hair was long and I'd say blonde, but it was more of a gold, and her eyes looked gold too when she turned to say something to the vampire. They were like whiskey and they had a shine to them that just wasn't natural, not that gold eyes are natural at all. Nice shape." He smiled, remembering.

"What did she wear?" Jaffron asked, not seeming to care about the woman's body.

"A white dress," Chuck answered. "It was shiny and silky, and whiter than anything I've ever seen. It didn't have sleeves. It was like a white version of that dress Amara wore on *Supernatural*."

"*Supernatural?*"

"Yeah, yeah. The TV show."

"Do I look like I have the time or low brain cell count to waste my days watching made up stories on television?"

"No, sir." Chuck lowered his gaze again. "That's for lower life forms like me. Uh, it was a long dress, like a gown, and it dipped down in the front."

"That's enough detail on the dress. Did she have a sword?"

"No, no weapon. She kind of just used her hands."

Jaffron continued rubbing his chin. "You said Christian knocked you out. Was she still with him then?"

"No. Two men appeared and grabbed her, then they disappeared with her. They wore white too. Really bright white." Chuck looked up and noticed the annoyance on Jaffron's face. The long scar running from his eye to the corner of his mouth seemed to stand out sharper. "I've never seen clothes so white."

Jaffron's nostrils flared. "What did they look like?"

"Dudes," Chuck answered, looking back down after catching the glint of irritation in Jaffron's eyes. He didn't have as clear a memory of their images as he did the woman. The woman was hot. The men were just men, and they'd disappeared as quickly as they'd appeared. "One, uh, had dark hair. The other one had blond hair, almost gold, but not like the woman's. Hers was really, really gold. They felt like her though. All three were really powerful and different. That was another reason why we didn't get the vampire. We weren't expecting those three. It really threw us off."

Jaffron stared at him for what felt an eternity before finally speaking. "Take him away."

Chuck raised his head as he was roughly jerked to his feet by two of Jaffron's burly shifter guards. Pain ricocheted down his injured arm, pulling an anguished cry out of him.

The red-headed vampire cast him a bored glance before making a shooing motion with his skinny, long-fingered hand. It was a feminine hand, Chuck noticed, right down to the black lacquered nails that extended the length of his fingertips. But it was a hand that had killed many, he knew in the pit of his stomach. A hand that had promised to kill him if he disappointed.

"Take him to the witch and have him healed," the vampire instructed the guards before narrowing his lethal gaze on him. "You will have one more chance. Come back here empty handed and I will feast on your blood."

THE CROSS GLOWED BRIGHT through the dark night, drawing Christian to it. He'd had no plan once he'd started Malaika's car and pulled onto the street, but had followed his gut, heading south. Jake and Nyla had to focus on their son's protection. Seta was with Rialto and Aria, doing the same for her granddaughter. Christian wouldn't bother them when the lives of those special children were far more important to mankind than his own. Marilee was caring for Jadyn's animals, Khiderian was off on some assignment for Jonah, and the detective had stayed in Baltimore with Malaika, cleaning up his mess there.

He didn't want to bother any of them with his problems. Yes, they were a family, but they had their own troubles. This wasn't the first time he'd had to flee without much notice. There'd been times he'd had no notice at all. Yet, this time was different. The Blood Revelation changed everything. He no longer worried that enemies were after him, but who he knew. Who he loved.

And he'd never had a mysterious warrior woman appear out of nowhere to help save his hide, a woman he knew, but couldn't remember. Who was she? Who was he? Who led his way with the glowing crosses?

He'd seen them before in similar circumstances. He'd thought they were the Lord's way of answering his prayers for protection and guidance, but no one he knew had ever had the same thing happen. Eron told him he must be special, that he seemed to have his very own guardian angel perched on his shoulder, but the thought bothered him. Try as he might to live a most holy life, he was still a vampire. He drank blood. He hurt people, even if he didn't kill them, even if they were villainous. He wasn't so arrogant to believe himself better than anyone else.

Just five years before, he'd been prepared to kill if necessary, to save the life of Rialto's beloved. He had killed that night, but he hadn't used his hands and he hadn't taken human life. He'd obliterated a demon with the power of his prayer. But he still hadn't killed a human in all his centuries... that he could remember. He had no idea what he'd done before he'd opened his eyes that first night as a vampire. Did the golden-eyed woman know?

He pulled the car to a stop outside the small house and cut the engine. He knew he'd be safe to rest there as he looked up at the glowing cross only he could see. Next to him, Jadyn slept, her head resting along the window. She couldn't be comfortable, but comfort didn't matter when you were tired enough. She'd been through a lot. He was used to danger and even he was tired from the events of the night.

Deciding to let her rest until absolutely necessary to wake her, he carefully opened the driver side door and eased out of the vehicle, gently pressing the door shut behind him before pocketing the keys. The house was small, one story, and didn't appear to be occupied. Still, he crept toward it with caution, his footfalls soft along the grass just in case. He peered in a window, his excellent night vision allowing him to see his assumption was correct. The main room was empty except for a battered sofa and what looked like stacks of boxes and a pile of junk that had been shoved into a corner before whomever had once lived on the property abandoned it.

He stepped to the front door, covered the knob with his hand, and swung it open with absolutely no effort. He glanced back at the Taurus, saw Jadyn still slept, and stepped inside the house. Beyond the living room, he found a kitchen, a tiny dining room that still held a wooden table and chairs, a bathroom barely big enough to contain the toilet, sink, and narrow shower, and one bedroom. There was no bed, but a mattress had been left on the floor. He inhaled and nodded, satisfied there was no mold or other dangerous substances in the building. His ears didn't pick up any scurrying, leaks, or other potential problems. There were no other buildings within viewing distance. This would be safe long enough for him to rest.

He moved around, locking the windows and the back door off the kitchen before returning to the living room. His thigh tingled as he approached the front door and he stopped to retrieve his cell phone from his front pocket. He looked at the screen, sighed, and raised the device to his ear.

"I know, Seta. I should have left the moment you told me to."

"It's bad enough you didn't listen, and now you take away my opportunity to say I told you so."

He grinned. "I'm sure you will have plenty of other opportunities."

"Unfortunately." Her disapproval carried through the phone. "Jonah and Malaika told me everything. Does the woman with you know what you are yet?"

"No." He walked to the front door and leaned against the jamb. "And I know what you're thinking, how coincidental it is that I was attacked after she came to my church, but you know as well as I do we can't jump to that conclusion. When the sirens were killing men four years ago it would have been easy to accuse Malaika of being involved. This could be the same type of situation."

"It could be, or she could be involved and you've decided to keep her."

"I'm being careful. The men who came for me didn't seem to care about sparing her life. I can't leave her behind to be hunted, and I don't want to leave her with Jonah and Malaika. They have a child to care for. It's best I draw this whole mess away from everyone."

"If this is related to the Blood Revelation, you can't handle it alone. Don't be stubborn."

"I'm not being stubborn," Christian told her as he studied the sky, the awareness of the soon-to-rise sun prickling his skin. "I'm heading south, toward Kentucky."

A beat of silence met his announcement, and stretched out as the sky started to subtly lighten. "Good idea," Seta finally said. "I'll let Rider know he's come due on the favor he owes me. Leave your phone on so his tech team can track you."

Christian nodded although she couldn't see it. "I will. Take care of your granddaughter," he added in case the vampire-witch got any ideas about helping him personally.

"Don't make me regret not being there," she warned him. "If you get yourself killed, I'll find a way to bring you back just to make you miserable."

"I love you too," he said, and hung up, saving the prickly woman from having to respond in kind.

Ribbons of orange and yellow slashed across the sky above the hills in the distance. Considering his age, Christian had built some immunity to the sun's rays, enough that he wouldn't immediately burn, but it still weakened him and would kill him with enough time.

Not willing to risk it, he ran to the car and opened the passenger side door, waking Jadyn in the process. If not for the seatbelt strapping her in to the car she would have fallen out of her seat. She blinked a few times, rubbed her eyes, and startled as she saw him leaning toward her.

"It all coming back to you?" he asked as he watched the confusion evaporate in her eyes.

She nodded, the movement slow as she came out of sleep, and unfastened her seatbelt. "I guess it wasn't a dream."

"Unfortunately, no. We're resting here for a bit. We'll continue at sunset."

She stepped out of the car, looked around, and frowned, nose scrunching as she saw the abandoned house in the middle of nowhere. "Where are we?"

"Somewhere in West Virginia."

"West Virginia?" Her voice rose three octaves as she turned her head toward him. "Why aren't we still in Maryland?"

"Bad people who want to kill us were in Maryland. We're trying to stay ahead of them until we can regroup and find a way to end this."

She stood still for a moment, green eyes slowly blinking at him, her mouth slightly parted, then shook her head as she appeared to come out of her momentary shock. "And you decided to drag me to West Virginia? What about my job? My family? My life?"

"You're a temp and currently between jobs, your aunt and uncle still live in Jersey and you haven't visited them in several months, and I brought you along with me so you could keep your life."

She stared at him, mouth agape.

"Jonah's a detective. He ran a check on you as soon as we left."

"This can't be happening. This is insane." She raked her fingers through her hair, fisted the dark curls at the top of her head, and took a deep breath. "Where are we going?"

"South," Christian answered as he closed the car door and ushered her toward the house.

"Wait." She planted her feet and twisted around. "You said you would explain everything to me once we were on the road, then you said you'd tell me when we were farther away from the imminent threat. We've been on the road and now we're in a different freaking state, and I still don't know half of what's going on."

"I know," he said, "and I will tell you what's going on, but I'm tired. I need to rest a bit and then we'll be back on the road by sunset. I will explain things after I sleep."

"Well, I'm wide awake now." She looked back toward the car. "Tell me where we're going and I can just drive while you sleep."

"That's too risky." Christian prodded her toward the house again, the sun dangerously close. "I will be doing all the driving. If the people after us catch up while we're on the road there will be split-second decisions to be made. You're not used to this. I am."

"How are you used to this?" She backed away from him. "You're a minister. You shouldn't be used to being on the run. This is crazy!"

Christian stared at her and sighed, at a loss for words, and almost at a loss for time. His exposed skin already tingled in warning. He had to get inside.

"You know I'm more than just a minister," he said, then picked the woman up and slung her over his shoulder.

"Put me down!" She beat at his back as he sprinted into the house, kicking the door shut behind him.

"Enough!" He set her down and turned to lock the door. With the bolt thrown, he turned around and looked down at her. He hadn't immediately recognized her when she'd set foot into his church, a decade of time having passed since he'd last seen her, but once she'd given her name, he recalled the scrawny dark-haired girl with the pale skin and timid green eyes. She'd taken time to warm up to him and tell her story, but once she did, she'd given him her complete trust. He'd practically had to pry her off of him when he'd delivered her to her aunt and uncle. The memory of her tear-stained eyes watching him leave had haunted his sleep for years, but he'd done what was necessary to give her the best chance at a good, safe life. Her soft green eyes glistened with unshed tears now, tearing at his heart. "I saved you once, Jadyn. Please trust me to do it again."

She opened her mouth to say something, then shook her head and turned away, putting distance between them before turning back around to face him. "What choice do I really have?"

"You have a choice. You could wait for me to sleep and try to hurt me. You could try to run away on foot." Christian slid his hands into his pockets and tilted his head, watching her. "But I hope you remember me well enough to know I would never hurt you, and to remember I'm one of the good guys."

"I do," she said softly, holding his gaze, "but I know this is all too out there, and I know you're hiding something major."

Her eyes narrowed as she studied his face and Christian knew he'd have to tell her what he was. She already questioned how he looked exactly the same as he had the night he'd saved her in New Jersey. "I know you have questions, and you have every right to, but we're not completely out of the danger zone. Let me get some rest and I'll answer your questions. Please, just be here when I wake up."

She bit her bottom lip as she thought, and nodded. "I guess I'm going to be the lookout, which is something I never thought I'd say."

"I'm sorry you have reason to say it," he said as he walked to the front window and adjusted the blinds that had been left covering them, allowing enough light in for Jadyn to see her way around, but not enough to disturb his sleep. "I'll sleep on the couch," he advised, deciding it best he sleep close to the exits in case she decided to try her luck on her own. "There's a mattress in the bedroom in case you grow tired after all."

"I doubt that's possible after my long nap in the car. I'm surprised I slept at all after what happened."

"You went through a lot of excitement, stress, and emotional overload. The human body can only take so much of that before you crash."

"You didn't crash."

"Good thing. I was driving."

She rolled her eyes. "You know what I mean."

"Yeah, I know. Tonight wasn't my first time getting shot at or having a church set on fire."

"You really have a lot to explain."

"Yeah, I know that too." His eyes started to close and he forced them open. "But, I think it's my time to crash now."

She looked around the room, walked over to the light switch, and sighed when flipping it up did nothing. "Well, try not to sleep too long or I might die of boredom. I can't even charge my phone and I don't want the battery to die so no Panda Pop for me."

Christian looked over at the boxes piled against the wall and tore one open. He looked through it, finding doilies, magnets, action figures and other odds and ends. He rooted around until his hand closed around a deck of cards. He tossed them to Jadyn and smiled. "I'm not sure what Panda Pop is, but Solitaire should keep you entertained."

She opened the small box, checking the cards inside. "Yay."

"Trust me, it could be worse." Christian walked over to the couch and stretched out across it, not caring that his feet hung over the arm. His eyelids seemed to weigh a ton.

"Are you sure we're safe here?"

"As long as you stay with me, I promise to keep you safe," he said before the day sleep pulled him under.

"CHRISTIAN?" JADYN STEPPED closer to the man as he lay supine on the couch, both hands resting over his stomach. She said his name again, but he didn't respond, knocked out. He hadn't been lying about it being his turn to crash.

She checked the lock on the front door before settling on the floor to play Solitaire, feeling safer the closer she was to him, and silently chastised herself for worrying. She'd seen the glowing cross on the house when she'd stepped out of the car. Whatever Christian had done to make men hunt him, whatever secrets he hid, she was safe with him. She'd seen the same glowing cross on his church the night he'd saved her in New Jersey.

CHAPTER SIX

Jaffron stood directly before the pentagram his witch had painted on the bare floor in virgin blood, his feet positioned so he stood between the lower two points of the five-point star. No natural light reached the cellar, not that he needed it, but a bare bulb hung overhead, lighting the symbol as it cast shadows along the poured concrete walls.

The sun had risen, and it called to him to rest, but he would not lay his head to his pillow until he knew. "Are you sure this will work this time, Minerva?"

The witch, short and wrinkled, looking every bit of her three hundred years, turned her head to look up at him from where she crouched beside the pentagram, painting intricate Enochian symbols between the points. "If the one you seek has been on this earth recently, it will work."

She stood, picked up a pitcher of oil and poured it on the floor, tracing the pentagram's circle. Once finished she dipped her finger in the pitcher then traced his scar with the oil. It burned his flesh, but he gritted his teeth and bore it, unwilling to show any weakness before the group of shifters standing at attention in the small room. They didn't serve him out of loyalty, but out of fear. He was not so stupid to believe they cared for him, nor did he give a single shit as long as they did as they were told.

"Light the flame," Minerva told him, her voice raspy with age, the complete darkness of her magic having stripped all the youthful vigor from her body. Magic always came with a price. The darker the magic, the higher the price. She produced a match. The flame came alive as she passed it to him and stepped away.

Jaffron held the matchstick in his long fingers and took a deep breath. He'd been disappointed so many times, and he'd had enough of it. His prayers unwanted, he made a silent wish and tossed the match, carefully stepping back as he did.

The matchstick touched the oil and fire sprung forth with a *whoosh*. It raced around the line of oil until the entire circle surrounding the five-pointed star blazed. The overhead bulb blew out, but the fire gave off enough light to see the pentagram clearly. The heat of it assaulted his flesh, forcing him to take another step backward. His kind did not fare well in fire.

The witch spoke in Latin, her voice rising with each word as she gestured wildly with her hands, her eyes rolled up until only white showed. Jaffron took his gaze from her and returned it to the pentagram as he waited impatiently.

"You assured me that this time—"

A figure appeared in the center of the pentagram, his blinding white clothes a stark contrast to the darkness of the room. The witch quieted, retreating into a dark corner of the cellar to await further instruction, if needed.

The man inside the circle looked around, eyes wide as he took in his surroundings, realizing he'd been summoned. Jaffron wasn't sure if his kind's eyesight worked as well in darkness as his, but could tell by the narrowing of his eyes and flaring of his nostrils as he looked around that he could see the shifter guards he'd positioned in the room. The man rested his gaze on him and his lip nearly pulled back in a snarl. "You."

"Me." Jaffron grinned. "It's been a long time, partner."

CHRISTIAN CAME AWAKE uneasily, immediately sensing himself under intense observation. He sat up in a flash of movement, causing Jadyn, who had been sitting cross-legged on the floor, watching him, to jump, her green eyes wide. A sharp gasp spilled through her parted lips.

"I'm sorry." He held his hand out, palm down, as if she were an animal he'd startled and now needed to calm. "I could feel you watching me," he explained, "but I didn't know it was you. After what we went through last night, I guess my fight or flight reflex kicked in."

"You sat up quicker than I've ever seen anyone sit up." Her eyes narrowed. "Faster than I'd imagine anyone being possible of moving."

"Good reflexes." He smiled, attempting to look more approachable as he ran his fingers through his short hair and looked at the window. The sun still filtered through the blinds. "How long was I out?"

"Long enough for me to know I never want to play a single game of Solitaire again."

He chuckled as he situated himself so he could pull his cell phone free of his front pocket to check the time. He had a text notification. He pressed it with his thumb, bringing the message up.

SETA SAYS YOU NEED HELP. I'M TRACKING YOUR PHONE AND SENDING AN ESCORT. RESPOND IF YOU FIND YOU NEED IMMEDIATE ASSISTANCE. – RIDER KNIGHT

An escort? Christian shrugged. Additional help could come in handy if whoever had attacked them in Baltimore caught up to them. Better that help be Rider Knight's people than his own family, who were probably being targeted by the same hunters who'd burned his church. He noted the time before slipping the cell phone back into his pocket. He'd slept most of the day, but still had a good stretch before the sun started its descent.

A good stretch of time to spend in the small house with the woman currently studying him with an intensity that made him feel like a bug under a microscope lens. "Have you been watching me for long?"

"Yes."

Direct. He grinned, liking it.

"At one point you stopped breathing. Completely. I thought you were dead."

Crud. Christian nodded. "I do that sometimes. I sleep very, very deeply." The deep sleep mended him, strengthened him, but it also completely immobilized him to the point he appeared dead. He could imagine how odd that would appear to a human. "I'm sorry if it frightened you."

"You never breathed."

"I'm fine." He smiled and held out his hands. "See?"

She shook her head. "You didn't breathe, Christian. I put my hand on your chest and there was nothing there. It was like laying my hand on a rock. No one does that."

He nodded. "I understand how that must have looked—"

"What are you?"

He stilled, looked into eyes staring straight back at his, eyes full of determination that wasn't going to just be swept aside. "I'm a minister, Jadyn. I'm someone who helps people, someone who helps children."

"You're someone who hasn't aged a day in over a decade, who doesn't breathe for a long period of time when he sleeps, who gets covered in blood and it just disappears, who takes out multiple armed men without a weapon, and moves faster than a man should." She barked out a laugh that seemed more panicked than jovial. "Either you're some kind of superhero with superpowers or I'm losing my mind. You said you'd give me answers after you got some rest. You slept. No more delaying, Christian. Explain what happened, explain everything."

He took a slow, deep breath to help him think as he watched her. She'd positioned herself so she'd be directly across from him when he woke and sat up. Her jaw was set, her back straight, hands clasped, eyes unrelenting. She was done being put off. He had to tell her, but how much? He didn't want to lie. He avoided lying by omitting truth or twisting his words so although he didn't lie, he kept his secrets well hidden, but she was looking at him with the fierce eyes of a Rottweiler and the truth was her chew toy. However, there were reasons why his kind didn't tell their secrets. Once he got her to safety she'd be on her own again, and it wasn't good for either of them if she knew too much.

"I trust you, Christian. I've pretty much put my life in your hands. Isn't that enough to get the truth from you?"

Wasn't it? "I'm not a superhero," he said as he struggled for how to tell her the truth without telling too much. In all his centuries he'd never come out and said he was a vampire to anyone who didn't already know they existed. "I do try to help people as much as I possibly can, and I do have ... a condition ... that affects the way I age, and it affects the way I sleep, eat, drink, move, pretty much everything."

She angled her head to the side, considering this. "Like a disease?"

"That's one way to think of it," he murmured, dropping his gaze to the floor.

"Why the big secret? And what does this have to do with the men burning your church down and trying to kill you, and where do I come in?"

He sighed. "This, uh, condition... People generally react in two ways. Either they don't understand, think the worst, and try to kill what they see as a threat, or they want it for themselves, at least the parts they think are positives. I have to keep this condition a secret from both groups for my own protection, and the protection of those I care for."

"You think they burned your church down and attacked you because of your condition?"

"Yes," he answered truthfully. Whether they wanted him for who he was or who he knew, it was all because he and his friends were vampires, or other paranormal beings.

"That doesn't explain me. Maybe it would if they'd just tried to grab me while I was with you, but men came to my apartment to wait for us. They knew where I lived. How would they know that? How would they know I know you? We haven't seen each other since you left me in New Jersey when I was just a kid, but they were there in my apartment. Why would they even think to be there if they wanted you?"

Christian frowned, realizing he'd never questioned Jadyn's presence in Baltimore. "What were you doing there? In Baltimore, I mean. You're not in school and you work temp jobs. What made you decide to move to Baltimore of all places?"

Jadyn stared back at him, her eyes frozen as her lips parted softly, then closed again. "Um..." She grabbed the hem of her hoodie with three fingers and absent-mindedly twisted it a moment before shrugging. "I just did. I wanted to go somewhere new, and I ended up in Baltimore."

"Without a steady job?" He looked at her clothing: a dark blue hoodie with LOVE spelled in all caps and a paw print in place of the O, jeans that were very well worn and washed out, and white canvas sneakers that had seen better days. She didn't scream money, and from what he knew of her family, none of them did either. The house her aunt and uncle had lived in when he'd dropped her off was small, and in a lower middle-class neighborhood. She'd also mentioned owing rent to her landlord. "What brought you to Baltimore?"

"The bus," she answered, narrowing her eyes. "You're supposed to be answering my questions, remember? You still have a lot of explaining to do."

"I'm trying. You popping up in my church the night someone decides to torch it is a pretty big coincidence. Finding men in your apartment takes that coincidence from big to huge. The fact you happened to have moved to Baltimore of all places, while I was there? I don't believe in coincidences of that magnitude."

"What are you saying?" Her voice elevated. "Are you saying I had something to do with this?"

"Yes. That's exactly what I'm saying." He huffed out a frustrated breath, seeing the confusion and anger in her eyes. "Whether you knew it or not. They knew you would be at my church. They knew we'd known each other, that you would come to my church to see me."

"How?" She shook her head. "How could people I don't even know have any clue about that? I just saw you on the news earlier in the day. I would have never known you were at that church if I hadn't seen you on the news. No one could have known any of that."

"They could have if they were using a psychic or someone knowledgeable in dark magic."

"Dark what now?" Her gaze slowly lowered to his sweater, and her breath hitched.

"No, I don't dabble in dark magic," Christian told her, sensing she was remembering the blood on his sweater, and how it had miraculously disappeared. "There are psychics and there are witches. There are bad ones, and good ones."

"Your friend." Her voice came out barely above a whisper. "You asked her if she'd bespelled the tenants... and your sweater..."

"Malaika is one of the good witches."

Jadyn sat perfectly still, other than her eyelids, which blinked slowly as she stared at him. Air left her parted lips in a soft whisper of breath.

"Jadyn? Are you all right?"

She continued to stare at him for a moment before finally nodding her head. "Yeah, yeah, I'm... I'm fine. Witches are real and I'm fine. I'm fine. Everything's fine."

"You're about to flip out, aren't you?"

"Well, who wouldn't?" she almost yelled, snapping out of the near trance-like state she'd been in. "Glenda the Good Witch killed men in my apartment!" She scrambled to her feet and started to pace the floor, her arms folded. "OK, so if your friend is a witch, what were they? What was the woman who caught the bullet in her hand? Was she a witch too?"

Christian caught a flash of the golden-eyed woman, a quick glance that escaped before he could fully latch on to it. She was smiling at him, shaking her head as if he'd said something silly. It wasn't from the attack earlier. It was from another time and place, as if it were a memory.

"Earth to Christian."

He looked up to see Jadyn had stopped, and now stood near the spot she'd been sitting, arms still folded as she stared at him, brows raised in expectation. "I'm sorry. What?"

"Who was she? The woman with the gold hair and eyes."

"I wish I knew." He ran his hand over his chest as he struggled to grab the memory back, but it was gone, leaving behind a strange feeling in his core, like a sliver of light burning from somewhere deep inside him. "She didn't feel like a witch."

"Wait, you can *feel* witches? Like, you can sense them?"

He nodded. "I'm able to pick up on paranormal beings. Witches have a unique feel to them. She didn't feel like a witch."

"What did she feel like?"

Home. Christian shook his head, unsure where that thought had come from, but the thought didn't shake out. The woman had felt like home, like family, like ... somewhere he'd been or had come from. She felt familiar in a way no one ever had before. He rubbed his chest again, the odd sensation flaring, just as it had flared when he'd first seen the woman... and when he'd first seen Jadyn in his church, although the feeling hadn't been as strong with her. He'd still felt something unusual though. That was why he'd stopped to talk to her instead of ushering her out so he could be on his way.

He stood and walked the few steps to place him in front of Jadyn. The feeling expanded a little, not with the force it grew when he remembered the other woman, but he definitely felt something odd around Jadyn. He ignored the curious look in her eyes as he searched them, inhaling deep, and opening all his senses to her. She was human, but there was something deep inside her,

70

some little piece of something that seemed to call out to some little piece of him. He got a flash of Khiderian so strong in his mind it rocked him back a step. *What in the world?*

"Christian? You're kind of freaking me out."

He was kind of freaking himself out. He straightened and studied the young woman again. Definitely human, but definitely special. Had he sensed it all those years before? No, he didn't believe so, although he'd certainly cared for her a great deal. Part of him hadn't wanted to leave her with her aunt and uncle, but the underground lair of a vampire was no place for a young girl. He'd done what was best for her.

Looking at her now, her Asian ancestry was a little easier to see, although she still seemed to have mostly taken her father's Caucasian genes. She was still a little thing, on the short side and very slender, from what he could tell of what he saw not covered by the bulky hoodie. Her features were small, soft, but pretty. Her hair was darker, the big curls bouncier. He wrapped one around his finger, marveling at how silky it felt. Yes, she was very pretty, but that wasn't what called to him. "Jadyn, what led you to Baltimore?"

She held his gaze, biting her lower lip.

"Why?" he asked again, knowing she hadn't simply picked the city at random. "What led you to Baltimore?"

"You wouldn't believe me."

He nearly laughed. "I have witches for friends, remember? I'll believe almost anything. What led you to Baltimore?"

"Crosses," she said softly. "Crosses lit my way."

Christian stumbled backward again, releasing the lock of Jadyn's hair to cover the center of his chest with his hand. Whatever it was he felt inside certainly reacted to Jadyn's revelation, flaring almost painfully. "Crosses? Glowing crosses?"

Her eyes widened as she quickly, very enthusiastically nodded. "You've seen them too?"

"Yes."

"You saw the one on this house? That's why you came here?"

He nodded as he backed far enough away that he could lean back against the wall, needing the support. All his life, all the centuries of it, no one else had ever seen the glowing crosses. "How long have you seen them?"

She pursed her lips in thought. "The first time was the night you rescued me. I saw one on your church. After that, I didn't see them again until about two years ago. I followed them to Baltimore."

"Where I was." He ran his hand down his face, taking it all in. It hadn't been a coincidence. Something or someone had led her to the same city as him, to where she would eventually find him. But why two years ago? Why hadn't she always seen the crosses like he had?

"Is that when you started seeing them?"

"I've seen them as long as I can remember," he told her. "They guided my way every time I had to flee. No one else ever saw them. Not one person."

She shifted her feet. "So, is it a good thing or a bad thing that we see them?"

He frowned. "They've always led me where I needed to be. They're crosses. A sign of the Lord. Why would that ever be a bad thing?"

Her brow furrowed as she opened her mouth to answer, then she winced, touching her temple. A small strangled sound escaped her as her eyes squeezed shut.

"Jadyn?" Alarm slammed into Christian's gut. He rushed toward her. "What's wrong?"

She jerked her head up as he reached her, her eyes wide and glossy. "Something bad is coming. We have to go."

"What?" He looked toward the window, noting the sun still shining through the blinds. He had no sunscreen, not that it did that much good while in direct sunlight for extended periods. Leaving wasn't an option. "The cross was on this house. We're safe here."

"Is it on the house now?" She whimpered a little, again holding her temples as if in pain. "I'm going to bet it's not. Something is coming."

Christian looked at the window and sucked in a breath. It wouldn't take long to go outside and look to see if the cross was still on the house, but sun was a major energy zapper, and if by chance something bad was headed their way, he needed all the power he had. He didn't even have blood with him, and he was *not* going to feed from Jadyn. Telling her about Malaika was one thing. He'd rather not have the vampire discussion unless it became absolutely necessary.

She became very still, another small whimper escaping her as she lowered her hands from her temples. "Uh oh."

That didn't sound good. "What do you mean, uh oh?"

She moved to the window and opened the blinds all the way, revealing what looked like an Alfred Hitchcock film resting outside. Christian stared out the window, jaw dropped, as he took in the sheer number of birds of every size and color that had landed in the yard and were now sitting there perfectly still, watching the house.

"They're always quiet before the bad stuff happens," Jadyn warned.

"YOU SENSED ALL THESE birds out here?" Christian asked as he stared out the window, spellbound.

"Yeah," Jadyn answered, unsure what he'd think of her little talent. She'd hinted at it earlier, but when he didn't seem to pick up on it, she'd dropped it. Before she could worry about it further, something odd happened in the yard. A vertical line of dark smoke appeared near the far edge and stretched into an oval shape about six feet tall. The birds, having done their best to warn her, took flight. "What is that?"

"That's dark magic," Christian answered, extracting his cell phone from his pocket.

"What do we do?"

"Pray," he answered. "And I'm calling for backup."

CHAPTER SEVEN

K iara gasped at the woman's revelation as she watched the conversation
unfolding through the vision pool. She gripped the stone rim encasing
the magical water to steady herself as she tore her eyes away from the
shimmering image of Christian and the woman to look at the Dream Teller.

"Who is this woman, Krystaline? What is she?"

Krystaline's mouth subtly curved upward at the edges. "You're the angel.
The all-knowing."

"We don't know everything."

"I know." Krystaline's smile grew wider. "I just love finally hearing one of
you admit to that."

"This isn't time for games, Krystaline. Who is she? She shouldn't be able
to see those crosses. They are there to guide the way of the most holy. She's
just a human."

"Is she, Kiara?" The slender woman let her blue-eyed gaze drift to the
image in the water. "You may not know everything, but you know enough.
Did you not sense trouble when she entered Christian's church? Maybe you
just don't want to admit to what you know."

"You're speaking in riddles." Kiara stared at the woman, her heart racing
as she noticed Christian's hand covering his chest. "He's regaining his
memory, isn't he?"

"He feels something, something very strange yet familiar to him. He's
grasping at it."

"His grace," Kiara whispered, rubbing the center of her own chest.
"Maybe now he can finally come home."

"He's been away a long, long time," Krystaline said, with a slight shake of
her head. "He may not want to return to Heaven."

"Of course he will!" Kiara's grip along the rim of the birdbath grew tighter, the stone threatening to crack. She loosened her fingers and took a calming breath. "Even as Christian, Aurorian has remained a good man. A protector of mankind. He can do so much more from Heaven where his power is far greater."

"Then why did he fall in the first place?"

Kiara bit her lip, biting back the words she wanted to say, words she wanted to scream from the mountain tops until someone finally heard her, but knew she couldn't. What she felt deep in her heart was something that could never be spoken aloud.

Krystaline watched her a moment longer, then sighed. "You are asking the right questions, Kiara. You even know some of the answers, whether you are afraid to admit to them or not. You know who is capable of creating the crosses. You know who is capable of seeing them. You know what you yourself did to make it so this woman whose name you can't bring yourself to utter has the abilities she has. You knew Aurorian, and what he was and wasn't capable of. Many of the answers you seek are already inside you. The others can be found if you only look."

"Find them where?" Kiara asked, running her finger over Christian's jaw, delicately so the water wouldn't ripple too much and destroy his image.

"They are all around you." Krystaline turned in a slow circle, her arms sweeping wide.

Kiara looked to see words glow from the trees in the garden, and light shine from the crevices of caves as far as her eyes could see. The dream realm was not just a place the Dream Teller brought special people to give them guidance. It was also the realm that housed prophecy, more than just the Blood Revelation. The prophecy that foretold of an angel giving his life to save a *drac chemare* was etched into a cavern wall within the realm. Kiara had read it eons before she'd been the one to drive her sword through the very angel who'd sacrificed himself for the demon caller he loved.

The young woman, Jadyn, grabbed her head and winced in pain, drawing Kiara's attention back to the image in the vision pool. She watched, her heart in her throat, as the pair opened the blinds to see birds of every size and color scattered over the lawn. "She is a guardian."

Krystaline nodded. "A lower level guardian, but her talent is immense. It's grown tremendously in the two years since the event."

A line of smoke opened in the yard, widening into an oval portal, and the birds flew away. Not very long after, shifters stepped through. "I have to help them."

Krystaline gripped her forearm. "Amuel has instructed you to stay here. It was not just a suggestion, and you know that. The only way to leave here is a way you can never come back from."

Kiara growled as she watched the enemies spill out onto the lawn outside of the small house one of her dearest brothers took shelter in. "Why am I not allowed to help him? He's unarmed, it's daylight, and he has a woman with him he will choose to protect over himself, a woman he hasn't told what he is for fear of her reaction. He is too vulnerable. He needs me." She swiped at something wet gliding down her cheeks, surprised to realize she'd swiped at tears. Actual tears. When was the last time she'd cried? When the news broke that Aurorian had fallen? When he'd been beaten? Turned? "I have to help him."

"If you do what must be done to go to him, you will be no help to him whatsoever," Krystaline warned her. "You must help him from here."

"How?"

"Find the truth," Krystaline said slowly before making a shooing gesture with her hand. "Christian has called for help and it is already on the way. He will survive this fight, but there may be a day he does not. I do not believe it was a coincidence Amuel placed you here at this moment in time. Go now, Kiara. Find the answers you seek and help your brother."

Kiara placed her fingers over Christian's image and took a deep breath, putting a halt to the flow of useless tears. "If you remember anything, dear brother, remember you are a warrior. You have weapons." She took one last deep breath, nodded at Krystaline, and left to find answers within prophecy.

"CHRISTIAN!"

"Yeah, I see them." Christian fought the urge to close the blinds, knowing it wouldn't be any kind of barrier between them and the enemies pouring out onto the lawn. They already knew they were in the small building, which wouldn't provide much resistance.

He had no weapons other than his own power, which with his age was more than the average vampire had at one's disposal, but that meant Jadyn was going to get a crash course in just how unhuman he actually was.

"What do we do?"

He looked over at the young woman and his chest constricted, seeing the familiar glossy fear he'd seen in her eyes the first time he'd met her a decade ago. Finding a decent set of family members to care for her should have been the last of that fear, but now she was with him again, her body overwhelmed with the emotion. He reached out and took one of her shaking hands in his, giving it a gentle squeeze before dropping it to return his attention to what lie beyond the flimsy walls separating them from the enemy. "I will protect you."

"How?" She looked at him incredulously. "Yeah, you've got a pretty good right hook, but there's so many of them! We need guns, knives... something!"

They had none of those things. Most of the boxes in the room had been labeled BOOKS, and the unlabeled one he'd opened earlier to find the deck of cards for Jadyn to amuse herself with while he slept held nothing remotely useful for battle. "I called for help. We just have to hold them off."

"We're somewhere in West Virginia. Your friends are back in Baltimore. You said yourself you didn't know exactly where you were headed when we left. How close can anyone be to help us?"

He grinned. "You'd be surprised, and I figured out where we're headed about the time I got here. Jonah isn't my only friend, and he's certainly not the most powerful. Just try to stay calm, no matter what you see. Remember I'm on your side."

"That sounds kind of spooky."

Christian looked over, saw the wary look in Jadyn's eyes, and shrugged. "Well, we established I'm not exactly normal. Just trust me. I'll keep you safe."

As the men and women stepped out of the portal, he counted them. They quickly surrounded the small building, forming a circle two rows deep. None were vampires, which made sense given the hour. They were shifters, and judging by the way some already had claws out but kept the rest of their bodies human-looking, there were lycanthropes in the mix. "Stay behind me no matter what. If they bite you, they will infect you."

"Infect me?" Jadyn's voice raised several octaves, almost hurting Christian's eardrums. She narrowed her eyes in concentration as she took a better look, gasping when she saw the clawed hands. "What are those monsters?"

"Shapeshifters," he answered. "Lycanthropes, to be exact." His whole body tensed as one last figure stepped out of the portal; a short, hooded figure reeking of power. "That's the worst monster right there. That's the one who created the portal, and that's the wild card. The lycanthropes will claw and bite, all brute strength. That one's a witch. She can do a lot more than they can."

"The dark magic you were talking about?"

"Yes. I'm somehow going to have to fight my way through all of them to get to her."

"You need help."

"It's coming," he said, bracing himself as the witch stepped into the center of the yard and raised her hands.

"You need help now," Jadyn clarified as she lowered her head and closed her eyes.

Christian cast a glance at her for as long as he dared take his eyes off the witch, noticing her hands tightly fisted at her sides. Her brow creased, and an indentation appeared in her jaw, showing her teeth were clamped tight.

The witch started chanting, ripping his attention away as the air around them shifted. The ground trembled, the beginning of an earthquake. Christian braced himself and tapped into the place he went inside him when he needed a power boost, wishing he'd drunk more blood before leaving Baltimore. The power boost was mostly a mental, almost psychic, power he possessed, but it drained overall energy and intensified his blood thirst. He inhaled, ready to absorb whatever the old hag threw at them and fling it back onto her and the army she came with, but found his breath expelled through a surprised exhale as a large hawk dove from the sky to attack the witch's head, breaking her concentration. Two more of the large birds quickly followed, joining in on the attack as the witch's power broke, sending a roll of dark magic vibrating through the ground before dying out as she fell to the ground, swatting at the killer birds.

Christian swung his head around to Jadyn, finding her in the same stance she'd been in before, face taut with tension. "Did you call the hawks?"

Eyes still closed, mouth clamped shut, she nodded quickly as more birds flew down from the sky, attacking the shifters. He stood still, his mouth hanging open as he watched the scene play out, suddenly remembering she'd said something about talking to animals. He'd thought she meant like in the way people spoke to their pets, but evidently, she had a talent with animals unlike anything he'd ever seen.

Realizing the witch wasn't going to do whatever they'd planned on, the lycanthropes charged, running toward the house with their heads down. They hit with enough force to rock the small building, and burst through the windows.

"Don't get bit!" Christian yelled over the noise, and ran toward the first attacker he saw charging toward Jadyn. He drove his fist into the man's face as it started to elongate into that of a werewolf, spun around, and kicked the next guy in the gut. The man swiped out with his claws as he fell backward, leaving four slashes down Christian's arm, shredding the sleeve of his sweater in the process.

Christian sucked back the pain, turned, and dove for a woman almost on Jadyn. He grabbed her around the waist and flipped her, tossing her body into three other approaching shifters to take them down like dominoes.

Eyes open now, and visibly tired, Jadyn looked around the room and screamed. "Christian!"

He turned to see a yellow-eyed man's open mouth coming toward his throat, two elongated fangs dripping what looked like acid. Christian drew his arm back but before he could throw the punch, he heard a roar and a blur of golden brown barreled into the shifter, taking him down. He watched in amazement as a brown mountain lion tore into the shifter's throat.

"Was that you?" he asked Jadyn.

She nodded, her mouth open as she breathed heavily, her chest rising and falling rapidly.

"It'll be all right," he told her as he reached out to steady her.

A loud whoosh sounded above them and he pulled her into him, ducking down to shield her from danger as the roof was ripped off the house and sent flying. The witch had managed to fend off the birds long enough to give him yet another disadvantage in the fight.

Jadyn was snatched out of his arms by a large man who'd partially shifted so that only his hands and face now resembled a wolf. She looked into the beast's face and screamed in terror, provoking a rage unlike any Christian had ever felt before in all his centuries. With a powerful roar of his own, he bared his own fangs and sank them into the wolf-shifter's throat, tearing out a chunk of flesh. The shifter released Jadyn, allowing her body to fall to the floor as Christian spit the chunk of meat out and picked the shifter up over his head. He turned and threw the creature at a group of others rushing him, knocking them down before they could reach him.

Claws sank into his shoulders before he could turn around to check on Jadyn. He went down to his knees, the sun burning his flesh as he braced himself for the bite he knew was coming. A blur of fur flew over his head and he was released. He turned to see the mountain lion shaking its head vigorously, the werewolf who'd gotten him from behind's throat now between its powerful jaws.

"Thanks," he told the animal as he looked for Jadyn. She was no longer by him. A scream came from outside the house and alarm slammed into his chest. She'd fled the building without him, or had been taken.

The sun leeched his energy, heating his skin to a painful degree in the process, but he forced himself to his feet and ran for the door, noticing mountain lions, foxes, and birds attacking his attackers as he sped past them.

He saw Jadyn in the middle of the yard, surrounded by foxes. They'd created a circle around her and bared their teeth at the approaching shifters as large birds dove down to peck them. Christian stumbled down the porch steps, but righted himself just in time to get knocked off his feet by a woman with yellow eyes and dripping fangs. He knew she and the man who'd attacked him inside the house were some kind of snake shifters who carried venom, so he grabbed her by the throat and squeezed, using every bit of his strength to keep her face away from his. He didn't want any of that venom to drip onto him.

The woman shifted completely, until he held a very large snake in his hands, its head grotesquely huge and too wide for his hands to effectively wrap around. Christian closed his eyes against the terrifying sight and called on the power inside him, scrounging deep inside for every bit he could find. His chest burned as if fire were coming alive inside him, and when he couldn't take it anymore, he let go, releasing the power in a blast that knocked every living being in the yard back several feet, including the snake who'd been more than ready to sink her fangs into his face.

Hot tears slid down his face as he slowly managed to get to his knees, sucking in air greedily. As a vampire he didn't actually need oxygen, but he couldn't fully function without it. Blood seeped out of the scratches on his arm and more across his chest he didn't even remember getting. Blood poured down his shoulders from the werewolf who'd clawed him deep before the mountain lion had jumped to his rescue.

Having all been knocked down by his power blast, the shapeshifters scrambled back to their feet. Beaten, bruised, and bloody, having been pecked at by birds, bitten by foxes and mountain lions, and blown back by Christian's power, they were truly pissed off.

"Christian!" Jadyn fell to her knees beside him. "Where are the keys? We have to go. You can't take much more!"

He looked at her. Finger-shaped bruises marred her throat, her hoodie was ripped, and the blood seeping out of various scratches on her body called to the hunger inside him. He gritted his teeth and pushed past it, checking for severe wounds. "Bitten?"

"No," she answered, relieving him by understanding the one word he'd been able to get out through the burning pain.

"Your skin is really red, Christian, and there's so much blood." She slipped her hands beneath his armpits and grunted as she helped him get to his feet. "Where's the keys?"

"Pocket," he said as he fought through a wave of dizziness and looked up to see at least thirty lycanthropes fully shifted into their large wolf forms. A line of foxes and half a dozen mountain lions stood between them and the enemy, and Christian knew the poor animals didn't stand a chance against the werewolves in their fully shifted state. Four large snakes slithered forward, protectively circling the witch. He couldn't see the woman's face, her hood effectively covering her, but he felt the pure fury rolling off of her and worse, felt the tremendous power she still had inside her while his was all but drained.

Jadyn's trembling hand slid into his front pocket and extracted the car keys. "Let's go," she said, her voice stressed under the weight of having to help hold him upright.

"No time," he said, his words coming out on gasps of air as he drew upon what strength he had left to stand straight and stare down the remainder of the army before him. "The witch will probably just blow the car up once we're inside. Your animals... will die. Send them away."

She whimpered softly, but he felt a pulse of something strange yet familiar in the air, and the animals turned to look at her before scattering away. The fire he felt burning in his chest flared and he stood stronger. He slid his fingers through Jadyn's and felt that fire blaze brighter.

"We were sent to retrieve you, not kill you," the witch said, her voice sounding dry and ancient. "If you weaken much more, you will die. Do not fight us."

The werewolves crept forward, heads lowered, ready to pounce if he made one wrong move. The snakes rose, watching him with their yellow eyes, bodies coiled to strike, and he knew they could cover the space between him and them in a fraction of a second if they wanted to.

"This isn't your fault," Jadyn whispered next to him as she squeezed his hand. "You saved my life once, gave me a decent chance at one, and I'll always be thankful for that. You've always been my hero. You're still my hero."

The flame inside him grew until the center of him was as hot as his sun-kissed flesh. "I'm still going to save you," he said as he closed his eyes, searching that fire inside him. It held secrets. He only had to find them. He focused on the sensation, following it, allowing it to take him wherever it wanted to lead him.

"Guide me, Lord." He opened his eyes, reached out and wrapped his hand around nothing, pulling a sword out of thin air. Jadyn gasped and stepped away as he turned his head to see the weapon he now possessed. The entire thing appeared to be made of crystal, but it burned brightly without harming his own flesh.

82

He carefully moved Jadyn behind him. "Neither of us will be leaving with you today, nor will we die," he announced, his voice much stronger as he rushed forward.

The lycanthropes rushed him in response, charging toward him with teeth bared. He swung the sword, effortlessly slicing through three as if they were made of butter before turning and slicing through another pair. He caught sight of the snakes rushing past him and turned to see they were headed straight for Jadyn.

"Run!" he yelled as he continued to swing the sword, trying to slice his way through the wolves who were trying to overpower him, his newfound strength quickly draining.

Jadyn's face morphed into a silent scream as she saw the large attackers headed toward her. Before she could turn to run, fire shot down from the sky, burning the large snakes until they resembled crispy onion straws.

Christian looked up, blinking when he saw a large dragon bearing down on them. He gave the sword one last good swing, slicing through the enemies closest to him, dropped to the ground, and rolled away as the dragon released a stream of fire, annihilating the wolves who remained. The large, blue-green beast turned and went after the witch, barely missing her as she ducked through the portal and it closed behind her.

"Christian!"

Christian struggled to get back up, the sword gone, just vanished from his hands, but could only manage to get to his knees. He fell forward, bracing himself by the palms of his hands, even the soft grass inflicting pain on the sunburnt skin there.

"We have to go!" Jadyn fell to her knees beside him, placing her hands on his back. Pain ricocheted through Christian, starting from the point where her hands had touched him, and quickly spread through his entire body, causing him to cry out. He smelled Jadyn's blood and growled as his fingers dug into the earth. The action caused him more pain, but if he didn't dig his fingers into the ground, he would use them to attack Jadyn, to get to the blood the beast inside him craved.

The dragon dove for them, disappearing into a shower of rainbow-colored sparkles before it hit the ground. A tall, slender, but powerfully built man, handsome with honey-colored eyebrows and rainbow-colored hair cut short, but a little on the shaggy side, stepped out of the sparkles to stare down at them.

"Back away from the vampire, sweetheart. He's looking mighty damn thirsty."

"Vampire?!" he heard Jadyn exclaim before the beast inside him took over, and he lunged for her.

CHAPTER EIGHT

Jadyn screamed as Christian lurched toward her, his mouth wide open, fangs clearly on display. He knocked her to the ground and dove for her throat, but before his elongated teeth touched her skin, the dragon-man yanked him away from her.

"Told ya," the stranger who'd come to their rescue said as he managed to get Christian into a choke hold and dragged him toward the Taurus. "I see that witch tore the damn roof off the house. Fucking bitch," he muttered. "I hate damn witches. Get those doors unlocked. We have to get him out of direct sunlight and get some blood in him, preferably a controlled sip, not the feast he was about to indulge in."

The man reached the car, turned, and glared at her. "Damn it, woman, move!"

Jadyn shook herself out of the shock she'd gone under seeing Christian lunge for her, baring fangs like some horror movie monster, like the other people who'd attacked them earlier, and ran toward the car, ignoring the pains shooting through her body. She clicked the lock release as she approached the car and opened the back door on the driver's side.

"Thanks," the man muttered as he crawled in and dragged Christian after him, until he had him lying across the back seat, his head resting against his chest.

Christian's skin was bright red as if severely sunburned, and he was growling, his eyes wide as they latched on to her. The mystery man kept him secure with one arm as he reached around with the other and placed his own wrist in Christian's mouth. "Here ya go. Take the edge off, buddy."

Jadyn's mouth dropped open and stayed that way as she watched Christian sink his fangs into the man's flesh and greedily slurp down blood. Her own pain and the fear of the attack they'd just been under faded away as she stared at the creature before her, the vampire, and tried to reconcile him with the man who'd saved her life a decade ago. He saved your life tonight too, she reminded herself, silently chastising herself for allowing even a sliver of doubt into her mind.

"Close the door. He needs out of the direct sun," the man told her. "You can sit in the passenger seat. I'll be driving you to a safe place once he stabilizes. If you can find a blanket real quick, that would be great."

"I'll look." Jadyn closed the door and looked toward the house. She'd checked it out while Christian had slept earlier. There were no blankets, not even a fitted sheet on the mattress that had been left behind in the bedroom. She unlocked the trunk and looked inside, finding a light blanket. "Bingo."

Casting a quick glance around to make sure no other portals were about to open, she closed the trunk and got in the car on the passenger side. "Will this do?" she asked, handing the blanket back to the man.

"Yeah, that's good." He took the blanket from her, apparently no longer needing to restrain Christian with his free arm.

Jadyn fastened her seatbelt and stared straight ahead at what was left of the house, deciding looking at it was better than watching what was happening in the backseat and trying to wrap her mind around the fact her superhero was drinking a man's blood.

"Is he going to be all right?" she asked, still worried about him no matter what she'd seen, no matter that he'd lunged for her. Before he'd done that, he'd gone up against a whole army of monsters to protect her. That deserved forgiveness.

"He's used a lot of power and being in the sun drained him even more. My blood is stronger than human blood. It, combined with the deep sleep, will heal him," the man said, suddenly appearing in the driver's seat within a burst of rainbow sparkles.

Jadyn yelped and grabbed the door handle, ready to run. The man's hand came down on her arm and squeezed. "Relax. It's just me. I'm one of the good guys. Burned the bastards trying to kill you, remember?"

"How? Who... But..."

The man's eyebrow rose as the corner of his mouth curved upward. "Pick a thought and run with it. That usually works best."

She turned to look in the back seat and found Christian half stretched across the seat, half slumped against the door, completely covered under the blanket. "You were just back there and practically under him. How did you just poof your way up here?"

"I'm awesome like that," the man said, starting the car. "And don't say I was under him. That's an image I don't want in my head." He peeled out of the small driveway, leaving a storm of flying gravel in their wake as he floored the gas and put them back on the road. "I probably should have burned the whole damn house, but there's lots of trees out here. I'd hate for the wind to pick up and catch the whole area on fire. The place is pretty secluded so Rider will probably have a cleanup crew in place way before the local police even catch wind something went on out here."

"Who's Rider?" Jadyn asked, gripping the dashboard as the dragon-man took a hard curve at way too fast of a speed. "And do you have to drive this fast?"

The man glanced at her, frowning before returning his focus to the road as they continued speeding down it. "Rider is my boss, the man Christian asked for help. I'm the help that got sent. Actually, there's more of us, but since there was an immediate threat, I flew in solo. I'm taking you to the others now. We're to keep you safe until your escort arrives to take you to The Midnight Rider."

"The Midnight Rider?"

"Rider's bar, his whole base of operations," the man explained, frowning again. He whipped around another curve. "It would have been easier to just fly Christian back, but he's really injured. Doesn't he have some of the special sunscreen Rider's vamps use?"

Jadyn sat still, just staring at the man as she let his question process. He noticed her silence and glanced at her, raising one of those honey-hued eyebrows again. Then his face changed, all hints of humor fleeing. "Shit. You didn't know he was a vampire, did you?"

"I didn't know vampires even existed, or the lycanthropes who attacked us, or ... whatever you are. What are you? Who are you?"

"My name's Daniel," he said. "I work for Rider Knight, who is a friend of a friend of Christian's. I'm a dragon shifter, as you saw, but I am not a lycanthrope." He slowed the car down and pulled over on the side of the road.

Jadyn's nerves kicked in as she looked around, seeing nothing but trees. "Um, this doesn't look like any place."

"This isn't our destination," he said, putting the car in Park and leaning toward her. "Don't freak out. I won't hurt you, but you have scratches and blood on you. I need to make sure you aren't carrying the lycanthropy virus before I take you back to my people."

"How are you going to do that?"

"Just relax. Trust me." He wrapped one of his hands around the back of her neck and leaned in close, sniffing her throat.

Jadyn gasped as she felt the beast inside him. Unlike the lycanthropes, she actually felt the animal inside him, felt its pain and sorrow, heard it call out to her. She grabbed his shoulders as he started to pull away. "Wait."

"Whoa." He pushed her away, carefully. "Honey, I was just checking to see if you'd been infected. I wasn't trying to hook up with—"

"Oh, shut up," she said, focusing as she sensed the story being revealed by the beast inside of him. Once it was done, she drew back on a gasp, her eyes wet as her heart ached for the poor creature who had been so wronged. "A dragon was slain, its soul forced to bond with yours?"

Daniel's eyes widened slightly before darkening, the already rare grey color of his irises turning a shade of deep steel, eclipsing the ring of brown around the rim. "What the hell are you?"

"I'm... wh...what? Why?" Jadyn sputtered, suddenly sure she'd said the wrong thing. "I'm a person."

"What kind of person?"

"A human?"

His nostrils flared as he studied her. "Care to be any more specific than that?"

"Uh, Asian and white?" she said, shrugging, unsure what more he wanted from her. "Female. Vegetarian..."

Shaking his head, Daniel put the car in gear and peeled out again, lurching back onto the road. His foot seemed to weigh a ton as it pressed the gas pedal. "I'm not sure what you are yet, but you're more than just a human," he said, continuing to defy the speed limit, "and your boyfriend back there is more than just a vampire."

HE OPENED HIS EYES to see shadows dance over the ceiling above him, cast there by the flames he sensed nearby. The warmth of the fire blanketed him, wrapping him in its embrace, but it wasn't enough to calm his racing heart. He listened carefully, only hearing the crackling of the kindling giving its life to provide warmth and light in the fire. He willed his heartbeat to slow and focused on the stillness until he heard it: the slow heartbeat of another, much too slow a heartbeat to belong to anything human.

"You are safe here," a melodious, yet masculine, voice said.

He lowered his gaze from the ceiling and turned his head toward the fire, and the man who stood near it, peering down at him, his face covered in shadow. The fire backlit the man, illuminating the reddish highlights in his hair. The color gave him a start, and he jerked into a sitting position as a memory assaulted him, but before he could grasp onto it, it fled, along with the moment of fear.

"Relax, young one. Whomever hurt you is not here, and your wounds have been mended."

He looked down at himself, vaguely remembering pain, and blood. So much blood. His arms were unmarred, as was his chest which appeared as nude as the rest of him under the thin sheet he'd been provided for cover. He was on a bed in a small one-room shack. A small table rested near a window, dark drapes blocking the view of anything beyond. He saw a washbasin and a few chairs, not much else. "Where am I?"

"A little sanctuary I found. There's not much, but it provides shelter. I will be moving on in a few nights. You are welcome to join me."

"Who are you?" He rubbed his head, remembering it had hurt before, but now he didn't feel anything there, and his fingers came away clean.

"My name is Eron. I found you abandoned, covered in blood and dirt. I brought you here, cleaned you, and allowed you much needed rest so your wounds would heal. Who are you, friend?"

He opened his mouth to answer, and discovered he had no answer. He had no name. No memory. Nothing. "I am not sure."

The man, Eron, lowered himself onto his haunches and peered closer at him, revealing crystal green eyes. "I know you feel strange. You had been bitten before I found you, and abandoned during your turning. You are a vampire now, but do not be alarmed. I will help you find your way. We do not have to be soulless monsters."

Vampire? He knew the word, but it felt strange. He couldn't remember his name, where he had come from, or even what he looked like, but he felt...wrong. He wasn't supposed to be a vampire. He was meant for something greater than that. He wasn't a monster. He wasn't a creature of the night. He was a creature of light and love. He was a servant.

"Do you have a name I may call you, my friend?"

He started to shake his head, but stopped. He did not remember his name, his family, or any friends he might have, nor did he remember where he had come from, what had led him to waking up in the strange place with the strange man, but he knew who he was at that moment as sure as he knew he was alive. "I am Christian, for I serve the Lord."

Eron's mouth curved into a smile. "I am glad to hear that the taint of this curse has not darkened your spirit. I am very pleased to meet you, Christian. I think we will be good friends."

CHRISTIAN'S EYES OPENED. He stared up at a bare white ceiling as thirst quickly made itself known, as did the presence of another paranormal being. It was not Eron, whom he'd left behind in his dream.

"Rise and shine, Sleeping Snarly."

The events of the previous night and day came to him in a rush as Christian sat up to find himself in what appeared to be a small office. He'd been asleep on a leather sofa, and apparently watched over by the dragon shifter who'd flown in to the rescue back at the abandoned house.

The man rose from his seat behind a large executive desk and carried a tall glass of blood over to him. "The girl is safe. We thought it best she or pretty much anyone else not capable of beating your ass not be within grabbing distance when you woke. You were pretty bad off before you went under."

Christian took the offered glass, and drank its contents, watching the man as he did. He remembered seeing him effortlessly shift from dragon to man and knew he was the Imortian Seta had told him about. He didn't look like the most professional guy, especially with the dazzling hoop in his nostril and the strangely colored hair, every strand a different color of the rainbow, but Rider Knight trusted the man enough to assign him to guard over his beloved. That meant something. "You must be Daniel."

The man grinned as he leaned back against the wall, lean but muscular arms crossed over his chest. "Good to know someone knows who's who. Your girlfriend didn't seem to know anything about us, and by us I don't just mean Rider and his organization. She didn't know you were a vampire, but she sure does now."

Christian grimaced. "I attacked her."

"No, you didn't, because I snatched your ass up before you could, but yeah, you went for her. Pretty sucky way of finding out your guy's a vampire."

"I'm not her guy. We're not in that type of relationship." But he was her protector and they were still in danger. Christian stood. "Where is she?"

"She's safe," Daniel told him, holding his hand out in a gesture meant to be calming. "Her scratches were taken care of and she changed into clean clothes. She was hungry so we fed her and I've been watching over her. I just switched out with my partner to watch over you about twenty minutes ago."

"How long have I been out, and who is we?"

"About four hours. You needed the healing. My blood is good stuff, but you were out there in direct sun without adequate sunscreen and used too much power too quickly. What the hell kind of sword was that I saw you wielding, and where did it go?"

Christian frowned, and looked at his hand that now held an empty glass where he clearly remembered a blazing sword. That hadn't been his imagination. He walked over to the desk and set the glass on its surface before turning toward the dragon. "Where is Jadyn? I want to see her immediately...unless...is she afraid of me?" His heart ached, imagining the young woman not wanting to have anything to do with him anymore, looking at him as if he were a monster.

"Maybe you should change first," Daniel told him, smirking, as he pointed at the change of clothes and a case of wet wipes atop the desk. "And you seem awfully concerned for a guy not in that type of relationship. She's fine. She was shocked, but overall, I think she took it pretty well, especially when you consider you went for her like a dog going for a meaty bone." His eyes narrowed as he angled his head to the side. "You know she's not just a human herself, right?"

Christian nodded, recalling her help in the attack. He quickly removed the ripped and bloody clothes he'd had on during the attack and replaced them with the black long-sleeved T-shirt and dark jeans the shifter must have found in his duffel, using the wipes to clean dried blood from his body. His actual wounds had been healed during sleep. "She has a gift with animals. She can speak to them, and they defend her when she calls upon them."

"I know. I think she spoke to mine."

Christian and the dragon shifter stared at each other for a long stretch, neither blinking. "You mean...?"

Daniel nodded. "I'm sure Seta told you about my kind, how we were created. Your girl out there didn't know anything about the paranormal community, especially not Imortians, but she knows I carry the soul of a dragon inside me. She communicated with it or something, without me even knowing it was happening. That's more than unusual."

Christian pondered this, agreeing it was unusual, but in a way it made sense. "She is still human and not familiar with our world. She must be in a state."

"Danni, Angel, and Ginger have been keeping her entertained. She seems fine, not that I've gotten close to her since we got here. I have to tell you the whole sensing the dragon's soul thing has me a little weirded out."

"Who are Angel and Ginger?" Christian asked, already knowing the Danni he'd mentioned was Rider Knight's girlfriend, and the reason Seta had been visiting the powerful vampire recently although the details of what their particular trouble was had not been shared with him. "Are we at The Midnight Rider?" he asked, trying to figure out how they would have traveled there so quickly.

"We're still in West Virginia. I brought you here by car, the car you were driving, actually. Angel is Danni's blood donor, and Ginger is my partner. We both watch over Danni to ensure she doesn't get into too much trouble."

Christian's nostrils flared as his blood warmed. "Blood donor?"

"Relax, superhero. Angel was saved from a really bad situation and is treated well. Danni has ...unique blood requirements. Angel helps with that."

Christian held the man's stare, feeling him out. Sensing no darkness in the man, he unclenched his teeth and forced himself to calm down, at least until he could get more information. "I am not a superhero."

"You are to that girl out there." He inclined his head toward the door as he opened it and led Christian through, "and when I saw you in battle you had a flaming sword. Man, that's badass superhero stuff right there. I wish I had a cool ass fire sword."

"You can actually make fire come out of your body," Christian reminded him, trying to avoid questions about the sword, questions he did not have answers to.

"Big deal. Any guy can make fire come out his body. All he needs is a couple cans of beans in his belly and a lighter handy, but a fire sword? That's awesome."

What would really be awesome would be knowing where the thing had come from to begin with, and where it had gone. "Where are we?" he asked as Daniel led him down a narrow hallway.

"Gruff's Bar and Grille," Daniel said, as he pushed through a door which led them to a room full of people. "That's Gruff," he said, nodding his head toward the burly, bearded man tending bar on the right side of the room. The rest of the room held tables, booths, arcade game machines, and signs indicated where the pool room and bathrooms were.

Christian felt the room with his senses, picking up on several shifters, including the establishment's namesake, who put out a strong wolf vibe. None felt like lycanthropes, which eased his mind.

"Rider owns this place," Daniel told him. "Gruff is part of his extended network of allies. The local paranormal community know all about this place, plus it's also popular with the non-paranormal locals and truckers. Gruff's aware of what happened earlier and if those bastards pop up on you here, Gruff and his people are good in a fight."

Christian nodded, appreciating the help, but his attention was focused on the circular booth in the corner where Jadyn sat in the center next to a pretty brunette who gave off an odd paranormal vibe, vampire and something else. A vampire with short, dark, spiky hair, dramatic eyeliner, and bright red lipstick sat on the other side of Jadyn. A teenaged Latina girl sat next to the brunette giving off the hybrid vibe. They talked and laughed, but the smile left Jadyn's eyes as her gaze landed on him, sucker-punching him in the gut.

"Ladies," Daniel said in greeting as they reached the table. "This is Christian. Christian, this is Angel," he said, starting his introductions with the young Latina on the right end and working his way around to the other side. "This is Danni, you know Jadyn, and this pain in the ass on the other end is Ginger."

The spiky-haired vampire flipped Daniel off and eyed Christian in a less than friendly manner. "So, I hear you're a minister," she said.

"I am." Christian nodded, wondering if that was why he sensed contempt from her.

"Are you a loving, all are united in God type minister or are you a judging, hateful, gays are evil and all Muslims are satanic terrorists type of minister?"

"I'm the type of minister who does his best to follow the Lord, which includes helping all people in need and knowing it is not my place to judge anyone."

She narrowed her eyes. "I like women. What do you have to say about that?"

"Not much." He smiled. "May I sit by you?"

She studied him a moment longer, then slid closer to Jadyn, allowing him room to slide in next to her. Daniel took the seat across from him, sliding in next to Angel. He shook his head at Ginger and smirked. "She takes some getting used to."

"I can see that," Christian said as the woman stuck her tongue out at Daniel. He looked at her T-shirt, noting the cartoon testicles being stabbed by a knife, and the words DANNI THE TESTE SLAYER written in a bloody red font.

"Cool shirt, huh?" she asked.

"It's, uh, interesting."

"Danni totally pulverized a wererat's nut so I had commemorative T-shirts made."

"Ginger." The brunette blushed as she directed a glare at the bold vampire before returning a much softer gaze to him. "He was a really bad guy."

"I'm sure he was," Christian told her, but he wasn't looking at her. He watched the young Latina as she ate a thick slice of apple pie. She seemed young, but he didn't sense any fear from her, or any indication she didn't want to be there. She appeared to be a healthy weight without any of the signs he'd seen in other humans who had been drained by vampires.

"Your reputation for saving children precedes you," Daniel told him, seeming to read his mind. "I assure you Angel is here by choice and not in any need of saving, nor is she a child."

The young girl looked up at him. "I'm eighteen," she said around a mouthful of apple pie before swallowing, "and Danni gave me a place to stay when I was on the street. She doesn't even drink from me that much. It's cool."

"I might stab a rapist in the testicle," Danni said, her tone holding a hint of anger, "but I'd never hurt a child."

"I'm not a child," Angel reminded them.

"Oh, hush and enjoy the apple pie that I can't," Danni told her, pouting for effect before sharing a grin with the girl.

"I'm sorry," Christian apologized. "I've witnessed a lot in my years. I've become suspicious by nature, especially when it comes to the welfare of the young and innocent. Seta wouldn't associate with Rider if he were allowing anything underhanded to go on under his nose though, and his reputation precedes him as well. I know he's aware of everything that goes on within his organization, and although he is not someone you want to anger, he's fair and a fierce protector of the innocent himself."

"It's cool," Daniel told him, "but you have enough on your own plate to worry about."

"Very true." Christian looked over at Jadyn, noting her intense focus on Daniel, before he glanced around the bar. "So, we're still in West Virginia. Is Rider here?"

"No, he's at The Midnight Rider, in Louisville," Daniel answered. "Danni's just recently joined us in the security field, and we were assigned a job out here. We were the closest when you sent up the bat signal so I was sent to retrieve you and we'll have your back until your escort arrives to take you to Louisville."

"I appreciate that." Christian said. "I was under the impression you were actually Danni's bodyguard, but the three of you work for Rider as security?"

"It's complicated." He grinned. "But fun. That, uh, battle I flew in on looked pretty intense. I smoked a lot of shifters, but there was a witch who appeared to be running the show. She got away through a portal before I could get her."

"She's not in charge," Christian told him. "She said they were supposed to take us alive, so someone's giving her orders."

"Any idea who, and what they want with you?"

Christian shrugged. "Initially I thought this was another case of human hunters discovering a vampire in their midst, assuming I was a monster and coming for my head on a pike. It's happened several times before, but they appear to be after Jadyn too, and a friend managed to drag it out of some that a vampire is involved. Now that a witch and lycanthropes are in the mix, I have no idea."

"Rider can help figure it all out once you reach him. In the meantime, we just need to keep you safe. Any idea how you were tracked to that house? I didn't find any kind of tracker on the car."

"Believe me, I've been trying to figure that out," Christian told him. "I know Rider was tracking me by my phone, but no one else should have been able to do that."

"Witches have tricks," the dragon shifter muttered before looking around the room. "You should be safe here. The two of you probably want to talk so we're going to do our security thing and let you have a moment. We'll stay close in case anything does happen. Just yell for us."

The Imortian jerked his head, indicating the others should follow him, and slid out of the booth. Christian stood to allow Ginger an exit. She stood and paused long enough to give him a long, hard look before subtly grinning. "I might like you," she said, and walked away.

"That's high praise," Danni told him as she and her young donor followed the brusque vampire. Daniel shook his head, laughing silently before leaving them.

Christian slid back into the booth, next to Jadyn, who stared at the cup of coffee her long fingers were wrapped around. He noticed the way they trembled slightly, and knew the caffeine wasn't the sole reason for that.

"I'm sorry I lunged for you back there, and I assure you that is not normal behavior for me. You must have a lot of questions."

"I do," she said, "but mostly I want to know why we're being followed by those monsters, and don't tell me you have no idea because I know you do. I know what you are, so you can stop hiding the truth from me. I'm in this with you so tell me right now what's going on."

CHAPTER NINE

Jadyn stared directly into Christian's blue eyes, fully aware she'd made a demand of a vampire who could easily suck her dry, but she knew he wouldn't. "I know you're a vampire now, and I was given quite the education about vampires, shifters, and witches while you slept. Yeah, I nearly wet myself when you lunged for me, fangs bared, but I forgive you. I know you're a good guy so don't abuse my faith in you by hiding things from me, especially something this major."

Christian stared back at her a moment before nodding. "We've both been keeping secrets from each other."

She blew out a sigh. "In my defense, I did tell you that animals spoke to me when I went to the church."

"True, but I had no idea you were being literal." He grinned.

"Well, it's not like they open their mouths and talk to me," Jadyn said and took a sip of coffee.

"How many cups have you had?"

"Uh, let's put it this way; I can hear color and see music." He laughed, drawing a small laugh out of her too. "I was worried about you, and I didn't know how long you'd be out. They told me the healing process can be quick during the day sleep and that you wouldn't sleep very long into the night, but given the damage you took, I found it hard to believe so I chose to drink mass amounts of coffee rather than risk falling asleep if you did sleep long. I wanted to be awake when you got up."

He moved his hand toward hers, stopping short before he cleared his throat and folded his hands before him. "It takes a lot to truly hurt my kind, but I appreciate your concern. You are much more fragile than me, and you were bleeding. How are you now?"

"I'm good." She scrunched her nose, remembering the peculiar first aid she'd received. "Apparently vampire saliva has pretty awesome healing properties. I don't have a scratch on me now."

"Did they lick you?" His voice had deepened, almost into a growl.

"No. Ew." She squirmed in her seat. "That would have broken the weird-o-meter, and although I'm decently cool with the whole vampire thing I'm not quite at the level where I want vampires licking my wounds. Just using the saliva as an ointment was gross enough, thank you very much, but it worked."

Christian looked around the bar, zeroing in on Angel, who'd moved over to the arcade games and currently entertained herself playing Ms. Pac-Man. "They treated you well?"

"Daniel is a little... aloof... but the girls are great. Danni's really nice, and although she speaks her mind, Ginger is nice too. She didn't seem thrilled to meet you, but I figured out pretty quickly she's had some run-ins with very judgmental church leaders in her time. Angel is in good hands. I got the impression Danni did for her what you did for me eleven years ago."

"I didn't feed off of you."

"No, but I was a child then. You almost fed from me today."

He lowered his gaze to the table. "I'm very sorry. I can't apologize enough, but I assure you I won't allow myself to grow that thirsty again."

"You might not be able to help it." She shivered a little, remembering the fight that seemed so surreal as it happened. Now, hours later, she almost had to tell herself it had happened, and she hadn't hallucinated the whole thing. "I could *feel* your power or whatever it was. It was almost suffocating, and the stronger I felt it the redder your skin grew, the more your eyes showed the strain of bearing it. Then you created that sword and it was like all the air got sucked into a vacuum. That's a part of vampire lore I definitely never heard of."

He looked at her, saying nothing, but he didn't need to. His eyes told her enough.

"Maybe because it isn't a vampire thing," she suggested, remembering what Daniel had said about Christian being more than just a vampire before he'd closed up on her. The dragon had definitely sensed something different in Christian, and that something might be part of the reason they were being hunted. "How did you make the sword? No more secrets," she prompted as he sat silent.

"I don't think I did," he answered, and ran a hand down his face as he leaned back in the booth and expelled a breath. He stared at a spot on the table for a long moment, seeming lost in thought before speaking again. "I have no idea where it came from, or how I knew about it. I saw you were bleeding and it spurred my protective instinct. I knew I couldn't lose, especially when you showed faith in me. I reached out ... and there it was."

"Reached out where?"

He shrugged, looking at her. "I'm not sure. It was instinctual."

"So, you just have this burning sword that appears when you need it, and then disappears when you're done with it?"

"I don't know. I've never used that sword before in my life, except..."

"Except," she prodded when he went quiet, staring off into space.

He shook his head. "I don't know. It felt familiar, if that makes sense. Honestly, it almost felt like an extension of myself, like it was designed just for me."

OK, she accepted the vampire thing and the shapeshifter thing. She kind of had to, considering the things she'd seen that day, but the mystery sword that looked like actual fire being something Christian hadn't even known existed was a bit of a stretch.

"How is that possible?"

He took a slow, deep breath, and met her gaze. "I'm trying to figure that out."

"Do you know of anyone else who has a sword like that?"

He shook his head. "It seems like something a witch could do, but I'm not a witch, or a warlock, I should say. I do have some psychic power, but other vampires of a certain age have that as well. I've never known of any who could pull a sword out of nowhere like that. It was burning. It should have burned me, but it didn't."

They held each other's gazes for a long beat, neither seeming to know what to say. The moment grew uncomfortable, prompting Jadyn to break off the eye contact and take a sip of coffee.

"Have you always been able to communicate with animals? I know you always loved them."

She swallowed the coffee and set her mug down. "No. You're right that I've always loved them, and I always wanted to protect them whenever I could, but I didn't start communicating with them so clearly until a couple of years ago."

Christian's brow creased as he studied her. "What changed in your life two years ago?"

Now it was Jadyn's turn to shrug, which she did, adding a shake of her head. "Nothing I can think of, except the animals suddenly started communicating with me. I thought I was going crazy at first." She laughed a little. "Heck, sometimes I still think I'm crazy. When I saw you on the news and noticed how you looked exactly the same, the oddity of that kind of gave me hope, especially when I went to the church and saw you in person."

"Gave you hope for what?" He angled his head, watching her intently.

"Hope that someone else out there could understand being different, having a gift no one else had. Even back then in New Jersey, when I was just a kid, I felt something in you. I didn't just have faith in you because you saved me that night. I felt something very special in you, something I've never felt in anyone else. You were different, more than human." She laughed. "Of course, I didn't know you were a *vampire*."

He grinned. "You were young and I rescued you from a very bad man. It was natural you would view me in an admiring light."

"It wasn't just that," Jadyn told him, looking straight into his ethereal blue eyes. "You gave me peace when my life was chaos and hell. Once I trusted you, just being around you gave me security, and I never forgot you or that feeling. Whenever I've been worried or afraid, I remembered you and I felt safe just knowing you were out there somewhere. I don't get that feeling from Danni or Ginger. It's not the vampire thing. You're something much more than that."

"I'm just a man."

"You have never been something as ordinary as a man. I've compared every other man I've ever met to you and they all paled." Jadyn's cheeks heated as she realized what she'd let slip, and how Christian could take it. He stared at her, his eyes warm, but giving away nothing. He sat perfectly still, possibly not even breathing. Jadyn wiped her suddenly damp palms on her jeans legs and shrugged out of her grey hooded jacket. "Um, do you think I could check in on my kits? I just want to make sure your friend understood my instructions and isn't having any trouble taking care of them."

Christian blinked, the request seeming to pull him out of some deep thought. "Yeah, sure. That shouldn't be a problem. I'll just call Marilee." He pulled his cell phone free from his pocket and scrolled through his contacts as he discreetly slid an inch away from her.

Great, Jadyn thought as her entire body warmed. She'd all but declared her love for the man, and made things incredibly awkward.

CHRISTIAN MOVED TO the back of the room where Daniel stood with arms folded over his chest, watching Danni where she sat at the bar across the room.

"Everything all right?" the dragon shifter asked, not taking his eyes off the pretty woman.

"Yes. I just thought I'd stretch my legs a little while Jadyn makes a call. When is this escort supposed to arrive?"

"Sometime tonight. Rider didn't give a specific time," Daniel told him, casting a quick glance over at Jadyn. "Ready to get out of here? The girl making you nervous?"

"What?" Christian looked over at Jadyn. "Why would you think that?"

"She makes me uneasy, although she makes me uneasy for an entirely different reason." The shifter looked at him for a moment before laughing. "Dude, you're kind of old to be scared of a cute girl, don't you think?"

"I'm not... She's not..."

"She's not cute?"

"I didn't say that. She's..." He looked over at the booth where Jadyn sat, speaking with Marilee on his phone. Her gaze never locked onto anyone in the busy room, her focus completely on the conversation about the care of the young animals she'd reluctantly given over to a stranger, trusting his word that Marilee would not harm them. The faith she had in him along with the generous love she showed the small animals warmed his heart, drawing a smile out of him.

The smile faded as he remembered the odd feeling her earlier statement had sent through his chest. He'd been told many times he was a handsome man so he wasn't unfamiliar with flirtation from women, or even deep admiration from those he'd helped get out of abusive relationships or just lent an ear to when they needed someone to really hear them. He provided comfort and guidance, but no more. He never returned the romantic interest. It simply had never been there for him, but the feeling inside him when Jadyn had told him she'd been comparing other men to him all this time and finding them lacking was ... new.

"More than cute?" Laughter practically coated Daniel's words.

"She's very pretty," Christian conceded, knowing as he said it that pretty was not a sufficient word to describe the young woman. Even in the red T-shirt and plain blue jeans she'd changed in to after the attack she was far from ordinary, and her green monolid eyes, fair skin, and nearly pitch black curls were more than merely pretty, but that had nothing to do with the pull she had on him. He'd seen thousands of aesthetically pleasing women in his extremely long life. They didn't give him the weird feeling inside. He was drawn to her, to something inside of her that called to something inside of him, and he had no clue why. "But I've never thought of women in that way," he said, pulling his gaze away from the woman.

Daniel frowned for a moment, then his eyebrows rose. "Oh. That's cool. I assumed you were into women, but, yeah, no judgment here. You might want to make sure the girl knows though. She seems a little googly-eyed for you."

"I am not attracted to men," Christian clarified, realizing the impression his statement had given.

Daniel's brow scrunched as he tore his gaze off of Danni long enough to give Christian a curious appraisal. "What are you, like, a furry or something?"

"I have no idea what that is."

"You're telling me you aren't attracted to women, but you're also not attracted to men? You have to be attracted to something. People, animals, vegetables, rocks, *something*."

Christian expelled a breath. "I can admire a woman's beauty without desiring her in a romantic or sexual nature."

"Nuh uh." Daniel shook his head adamantly. "Dude, that's not even a thing."

"I assure you it is."

The dragon shifter stared at him, eyes slightly narrowed. His nostrils flared a little, and he barked out a laugh. "Ya know, you might actually think you're telling the truth, but vampires aren't the only ones with gifts. You might not even realize it yet, but the two of you are definitely vibing."

Christian wasn't sure what Daniel was implying, but he didn't care for it. "I have treated her with the utmost respect and she has behaved appropriately."

"Appropriately? Dude, unstarch your shorts." Daniel clamped a large hand on his shoulder and guided him toward the bar. "You need a drink. It's on me."

"It's not wise for my kind to drink."

"Yeah, I know about the blood thinning thing. No worries. I know what your kind can handle." Daniel directed him to one of the vacant stools across from where Danni and Ginger sat at the other side of the bar and took the one next to him, snagging the bartender's attention in the process. "The usual, Gruff, and a very bloody mary for my friend."

The barrel-chested wolf shifter acknowledged Daniel with a grunt and deposited two long neck bottles in front of them before moving down the bar to chat up two attractive ladies.

"And now you know why he's called Gruff," Daniel said with a smile as he tipped back his bottle of beer, watching Danni as he drank.

Christian picked up his own, much darker, bottle and sniffed it. "It's blood," he said quiet enough no human in the vicinity could possibly hear.

"Yup. Your kind of people can order a very bloody mary in any drinking establishment Rider owns and get exactly what you need. He's still working his way toward Maryland, but he already does some security related business there."

"Where does the blood come from?"

"An artery?" Daniel grinned. "Seta vouched for Rider, didn't she? You really need to work on that suspicious nature of yours, bro. I promise you you're either drinking a murderer or a pedophile, or someone who was really bad off before they took a job donating."

Christian sighed. "I was asking if it was human or animal, but thanks for clearing that up. And yes, Seta did vouch for Rider, which was why I was headed his way when Jadyn and I were ambushed." He took a drink, not in grave need of it after drinking from Daniel earlier and topping off with another glass after waking up, but given his current threat level, staying tanked up wasn't a bad idea. "Thanks for feeding me, by the way. Your blood packed a wallop. It was spicy, which was kind of strange, but it was more than adequate to speed the healing process."

"Yeah, I get that a lot." Daniel took another drink. "Look, I know there's this whole vampire etiquette that no one is supposed to ask your age, but I have no desire to take your territory or whatever it is you guys are always on guard about so when I say I can sense you are freaking old and powerful as hell, don't take it as a threat that I'm out to get you, because I'm perfectly cool within my current status and have no reason whatsoever to want to kill you."

"Noted."

"Good." Daniel took a long pull from his beer, took an even longer look at Danni, and turned toward him, leaning in before asking in a low voice, "OK, so you're telling me you're like hundreds of years old and you've never desired a woman, but you're not gay."

"That is correct."

Daniel sat still, blinking at him for a moment before shaking his head. "I don't get it. My dragon can sense you're attracted to Jadyn, although I admit it's a weird attraction."

Christian frowned. "What do you mean, weird?"

"It's like... all flowers and butterflies, but no dick twitch."

Christian rolled his eyes. "It is possible for men not to be slaves to their libidos."

"Yeah, but we still have libidos," Daniel countered. "Whether we do something physically is about the only choice we have. We still lust for women we are attracted to."

"Something you know very well," Christian said, noticing Daniel's gaze moving back to Danni. "You can barely take your eyes off of Rider's mate. That has to be dangerous."

Daniel's entire body tensed as he paused with his bottle halfway to his mouth. "It's my job to watch her," he said firmly as he set the bottle down on the bar, flicking a quick glance the hybrid's way. "As old and powerful as you are, I know you picked up on her being a hybrid, if Seta didn't already tell you. She's got some issues that require her to be under constant supervision."

"I am not here to judge," Christian told him. "I am also good at picking up on things, little signals people are unaware they are transmitting. You care for her."

"She's the best friend I have in this realm, nothing more. Even if I was interested in her, her heart has already been taken."

"All right then." Christian nodded, deciding to let it go. From what he sensed in the dragon, his feelings for the hybrid woman were honorable, as honorable as could be considering her heart belonged to another man, but he also mourned someone. "You've been in love before."

"That's what men do. We lust and if we're lucky, we fall in love." He looked over at him and shook his head. "You've had to have loved someone in all the time you've been alive."

"I love my friends, who have become my family, actually."

Daniel laughed a little, swirling his finger over the rim of his beer bottle. "I'm not talking about that. You say you've never thought of women in that way, but what exactly does that mean? I mean, you've had sex."

"No."

Daniel's mouth dropped open and hung there.

"I have never been married," Christian told him. "I have never dated, never had a girlfriend. I have no desire whatsoever for men, so that has nothing to do with it. I see women I think are attractive, but I have never connected with a woman in a romantic way, at least not since I've been a vampire, and not that I have any memory of prior." He shrugged. "It simply has not been something I've longed for in my time."

Daniel closed his mouth and stared at him as he took a drink. "Correct me if I'm wrong, but you've been alive for centuries."

"True."

"That's not normal." He scanned the room before returning his attention to Christian. "Men are lustful creatures by nature, and vampires are even worse. No vampire could live as long as you and not lust for someone. I got a sense earlier that you were more than a vampire. What are you, man?"

"Thanks." Jadyn slid onto the empty stool on Christian's other side, and passed his phone over to him as he grappled with Daniel's question, a question he'd asked himself a lot, especially as of late. "I hope you don't mind, but I programmed Marilee's number into my own phone. She said it was fine."

"That's fine," Christian told her, happy she and Marilee had apparently hit it off, and glad for the reprieve from Daniel's questioning.

Jadyn smiled, a little shy, and looked around. "You know, I don't think I was done asking you..." She locked eyes with Daniel and went quiet, her mouth still open, but the words gone.

"I'm going to go check in with the others, maybe see if there's an update on your escort," the dragon shifter said, grabbing his beer as he stood.

"Daniel, please wait." Jadyn slid off her stool and stepped in front of him. She chewed her bottom lip, and for a brief moment Christian thought she was going to let Daniel pass, but she squared her shoulders and looked him straight in the eyes. "I know I clearly made you uncomfortable when I told you what the dragon inside you told me, and I'm sorry, but the dragon wants to say something else. To you."

"The dragon wants to tell me something?" Daniel's jaw clenched as he swallowed hard. "It's aware of me? Everything?"

Jadyn nodded. "I think so. He's trying to talk to me, but he's so anxious to speak he's all jumbled. Can I?" She raised her hand, splaying her fingers out as her palm hovered over Daniel's chest.

The dragon scanned the room, ensuring no one was watching them, and nodded on another hard swallow.

Christian watched, spellbound, as Jadyn placed her hand over the center of Daniel's chest, closed her eyes, and inhaled deeply before slowly releasing the breath with the barest whisper of sound. She clasped her free hand over her mouth as her eyes, now wet, opened. She sniffed, lowered both hands, and smiled.

"He doesn't blame you or hold anything against you," she told a rapt Daniel. "He knows you were as much a victim in the bonding as he was, and he said that if he had to be bound with an Imortian, he's glad someone like you was chosen."

Daniel's taut shoulders relaxed, his breath leaving him on a wave of visible relief. His gray eyes glistened. As if aware how close he was to showing his emotion in the form of tears, he sniffed and straightened his shoulders again. "Why?"

Jadyn stared at his chest again, her head slightly tilted, listening. "Because you know loss," she said. She listened a moment longer and laughed, the action putting an indescribably beautiful sparkle in her eyes. "And he says you might be a cocky jackass with an often-immature sense of humor, but you are a fierce protector, just like him, and you have a heart as beautiful as imortium." She frowned. "He's showing me a jagged chunk of silver."

"It's imortium," Daniel explained, taking a deep breath, fighting not to show emotion. "Only those who have been to Imortia or are of Imortian blood can see its true beauty. To anyone else it looks silver." He pointed to his nose ring. "This is imortium."

Christian watched Jadyn nod in understanding, and felt dizzy. "Jadyn, what does Daniel's nose ring look like to you?" he asked, steadying himself.

"Silver, just like he said."

"What does it look like to you?" Daniel asked him, his tone implying he already knew, but couldn't quite believe it.

"Not silver." Christian swallowed, and found his mouth dry. "It's a beautiful metal, or crystal. I'm not sure what it is, but it's unusual. It's almost translucent, but I see a lot of colors. They change depending on how the light hits the hoop."

"You're not Imortian," Daniel said. "I would feel it. Have you been to my realm?"

"I never even heard of it until your queen was defeated and many of your kind came here, not that long ago."

"Dude, seriously, what the hell are you?"

CHAPTER TEN

A shrill scream came from the other side of the bar. Christian was surprised to discover it came from a rather large man whose genitalia had been caught in the tightly clenched hand of one furious hybrid.

"And that's one of the reasons why I watch her like a hawk," Daniel said. "I took my eyes off her for like one second, damn it." He quickly moved toward the other side of the bar, the rest of the patrons and staff not appearing to want to get involved as they watched the incident play out, and if Ginger's laughter was any indication, she was enjoying it too much to step in.

"Oh, you don't like it when it happens to you?" Danni asked, nearly shouting.

"I didn't even touch you, you crazy bitch!" the man cried, dropping to his knees as he wrapped his meaty hands around Danni's small wrist and tried to pry her off of him, but failed.

"You touched her!" She pointed at a blonde woman in tight jeans and a fitted leather jacket who currently stood about a foot away from the man, glaring down at him.

"Release the man's testicles," Daniel ordered, reaching her, "or what's left of them."

"He called me a bitch."

Daniel looked down at the crying man, whose face had grown as red as his flannel shirt, and grimaced. "You've taught him a lesson and made sure he'll never reproduce. Now let him go." He shot a dark look at the vampire standing behind her. "A little help here, Ginger?"

"I want to see if they pop," the devilish woman told him.

"If they do, you're cleaning up whatever gets on the floor," Gruff said, not seeming particularly bothered that a customer was being brutalized in his own establishment.

"Stay," Christian ordered Jadyn, who stood next to him watching in rapt fascination, and made his way over to the other side of the bar. He reached them just as Daniel grabbed Danni's arm. The woman reacted instantly, growling at him as her eyes flickered red.

Acting on instinct to what he now sensed inside the woman, Christian stepped between her and Daniel. "Do not rise."

Danni gasped, releasing the man's crotch as she stepped back, almost backing over Ginger in her haste to get away. Her eyes flickered once more, then bled back to their normal green color. Braced by Ginger's hands on her shoulders, she stood trembling as she stared at Christian. "What was that? You scared it."

"What the hell just happened here?" Daniel asked, moving to where he could look between the two.

"Show's over!" Ginger yelled to the gawking patrons before lowering her voice. "Yeah, I want to know too."

"Somebody clean that pile of jackass up," Gruff barked, refilling drinks.

Christian waited until a burly wolf shifter he'd seen bussing tables earlier hefted the still crying man over his shoulder and took him out the front door, presumably to dump him somewhere, and the remaining people in the room settled back into what they had been doing before Danni had grabbed the man by the testicles.

"Thanks for that," the blonde said to Danni before dropping a few bills on the bar. She grabbed her purse, her red-headed friend next to her, and the pair left.

"I knew you were a hybrid, but I didn't know what the other half of you was," Christian told Danni, "until just then when your other half started to rise. You're part demon."

"Succubus," she muttered. "I know it's still bad, but it sounds a little less evil."

"You're not remotely evil," Daniel told her before turning his attention back to Christian. "What did you just do? Usually when her eyes go red all hell is about to break loose and there is no calming her, not that damn easily."

"I've been known to destroy demons," Christian told him. "She's part demon, or succubus," he corrected, feeling how bothered the woman was by what she carried inside her, "so I commanded that part to behave."

"How?" the Imortian asked.

"With faith."

All three stared at him, dumbfounded.

"Can you ... destroy that part of me?" Danni stepped forward, no longer needing Ginger's hands supporting her. The hopefulness in her eyes tore at Christian's heart. "Make me all vampire?"

He shook his head sadly. "The succubus is half of what you are. Destroying it would kill you, and I will not do that."

She nodded slowly in understanding as her eyes glistened with unshed tears, then abruptly turned and left, headed toward the bathrooms. Ginger gave Christian a long, curious stare, and followed her. Angel breezed past, apparently noticing her friend's distress from where she'd been watching from the arcade games.

"Dude..." Daniel began, that one word full of questions.

"You said she is your best friend," Christian reminded him, not wanting to answer anything he might say next. He didn't have answers. "She is clearly upset. Go to her."

The dragon narrowed his eyes a moment before finally nodding and parting ways, headed in the direction the women had gone. Christian looked across the bar to see Jadyn sitting where he'd sat earlier, watching him.

"I feel like I'm missing a whole lot," she said a moment later as he approached her, taking the empty stool to her left, at the corner of the bar.

"A feeling I can relate to more than you could possibly know," Christian murmured.

She watched him for several beats before speaking again. "When I came over here, I was going to remind you that I'd asked why we were being hunted and you hadn't answered, but I got distracted by Daniel's dragon."

"You gave that man a tremendous gift," Christian told her, remembering Daniel's struggle to contain his emotion. "I sensed a great weight taken from his shoulders."

"All I did was deliver a message."

"You have a very special gift, and you were generous to share it with someone very much in need of it."

She placed her elbow on the bar and supported her head with her curled hand as she looked at him. "You have gifts too. Is that why those men were at your church? Were they at my apartment because of my gift? Are we being hunted for what we can do?"

"Those are good questions," Christian told her, wishing he knew the correct answers to those, and the many other questions he himself had. Why had they both been targeted? Who was the golden-haired woman? What was the weird feeling in his chest that seemed to expand when Jadyn was near? Why had she started communicating with animals two years ago? Why could they both see the glowing crosses? Why had he sensed Khiderian before the attack? Why, during all this, had he dreamed about the night he first woke as a vampire, and where in the universe did he get that sword, and where was it now? "I am telling you the truth when I tell you I do not know why we're being hunted. At first, I thought I was being targeted because of my friends, who are very special people themselves, and somehow through some use of dark magic you got caught up in this by chance, but now... I don't know if these latest attacks have anything to do with them. Glowing crosses led you to Baltimore, the same glowing crosses I've seen for centuries, crosses that led me to New Jersey when I rescued you, and led me to Baltimore, only to lead you there later. Wait... you said you started seeing the crosses again about two years ago?"

Jadyn nodded.

"And that's when the animals started speaking to you?"

She nodded again. "My cat had been really sick, and I tried so hard to help her. I paid a small fortune for medicine, took her to the vet constantly. She had cancer and eventually ... she asked me to let her go." Jadyn's eyes watered and she wiped away a tear just as it started to spill over, then took a deep breath, blinking back the remaining moisture before continuing. "At first, I thought it was all in my head, the grief and the long struggle finally breaking me, but I kept hearing her begging me to give her peace and just let her close her eyes and drift away painlessly. I took her to the vet and let them end her suffering. Later that day, a bird flew down from the sky, landed right on my shoulder and I saw her in my mind as I heard the bird telling me she thanked me."

"That was in New Jersey?"

"Yes. After that day I started hearing animals all around me, either I'd hear their actual thoughts or I would see images. I helped dogs who'd gotten lost find their way back home, rescued baby squirrels who'd fallen out of trees, fed hamsters whose owner had gone on vacation, leaving them behind without enough food and water, and yes, I broke into the guy's apartment to do it, but I don't care, I'd do it again."

Christian smiled. "Given the circumstance, I can't blame you."

"It was overwhelming, but I didn't mind. I was able to help animals more than I'd been able to before, because they could tell me what they needed. I could sense them, even when they were in a different apartment or three streets over. Then I started seeing the glowing crosses. They led me to Baltimore, where I continued helping animals, scraping by, working temp jobs because holding a fulltime gig was impossible, what with animals randomly sending up the bat signal whenever and wherever."

"And you have no idea why the crosses led you to Baltimore?"

"None."

Two years ago. Christian pondered that. She'd started communicating with animals and saw the crosses two years ago, out of the blue. "And there were no other life changes then? No medical issues? You didn't hit your head, have a surgery, anything? Anyone new come into your life? Anything different at all?"

"Nothing I can remember." She laughed. "And I think communicating with animals and being led to another state by glowing crosses is enough different for any one person."

"Yes, but there has to be a reason for it," he murmured, wishing he knew what had caused Jadyn's ability to kick in at that exact time, and what they shared in common to enable both of them to see the crosses. "Do you attend church?"

"Not regularly," she confessed, blushing. "I do believe in God and have a personal relationship with Him, but my church attendance has been hit or miss. Sorry."

"No need to apologize. Believing and following are the two most important things."

"So then why did you ask?" she asked suspiciously.

"Not to scold you if you said no," Christian answered with a grin, finding her suspicious face adorable. Adorable? When had he ever thought that about a woman?

"So why?"

"Huh?" He snapped out of his thought. "What?"

"Why did you ask me?"

"Oh." It took him a second to even remember, so baffled by the fact he found Jadyn's suspicious face adorable. "I'm just trying to figure out what it is about the two of us that makes us see the glowing crosses. I've been around a very long time and no one has ever seen them but me, and now you. They're crosses so I've always thought I was being guided by a holy source, that they were created by the power of my faith, even though I've known others with strong faith who have not seen them." He shrugged. "I have no answers. Only questions."

"I thought they were signs from a guardian angel. The first one I saw was on your church when you saved me so when I started seeing them again, I actually thought of you." She released a shy laugh. "I always thought you were my guardian angel."

"That's a kind thought, and I try my best to be a good servant, but sadly I am something very far from an angel." The center of his chest burned, causing him to wince as he placed his hand over the spot.

"Are you all right?" Jadyn leaned forward; her brow furrowed with concern.

"Yeah, I'm good." Christian picked up the bottle he'd been drinking from earlier and took a sip, knowing blood and sleep were the best fixes for his kind. "This must be what humans call indigestion. Not sure what would give it to one of my kind, although Daniel's blood was awfully spicy."

Jadyn laughed. "A dragon with spicy blood. Go figure."

"You're taking the whole vampires, witches, and shifters thing very well."

"I can hear animals thinking." She shrugged. "Some would find that even crazier."

Christian started to respond, but noticed Daniel walking toward them. "Is Danni all right?" he asked as the shifter approached.

"For the most part." Daniel stopped next to them and shoved his hands into his jeans' pockets. "You remember how I told you earlier that Danni has unique blood requirements?"

Christian nodded. "I'm guessing because she's a hybrid, and not just any type of hybrid?"

"Right. How much do you know about..." He cast a wary look at Jadyn before continuing "... her other half?"

"You can trust Jadyn not to judge her. She's not a judgmental person," Christian advised, even though he hadn't actually seen the girl in over a decade and was still getting to really know her. He knew that much though, could sense it.

"It's not that." Daniel shifted his feet. "She's not a hybrid mix anyone's really heard of, and Rider is super protective, and with good reason. Who knows what certain information in the wrong hands could lead to?"

"And you trust me?"

"We kind of have to, and you figured out what she was all by yourself."

"True." Christian took a drink before continuing. "You can trust Jadyn. I give you my word, and Seta will vouch for my word. Now, what can I help you with? You have the face of a man asking a question he's not sure how to ask."

"Yeah, I'm sure I do." Daniel ran his hand through his uniquely colored hair and scratched his head. "All right, so here's the thing. Her two sides are always battling each other. The vampire side is the side we want to stay dominant for reasons I'm not going to go into. Giving her a specific blood cocktail helps mellow out the side we don't want overpowering the vampire side. To keep her two sides harmonious, she alternates bagged and fresh blood straight from the tap, and that blood needs to be male and female."

"Angel supplies the live female blood," Christian said, figuring out the issue.

"Yes, but there's no permanent live male donor because that's a little trickier."

"Because of the effect her other side's bite can have on a man."

"Exactly." Daniel cast another look at Jadyn before continuing. "Rider was her main source of that because he's powerful enough to fight off the effect, and I've fed her a few times without incident, but it's a crapshoot any time she feeds straight from a man, especially now that she's not with Rider."

"Are you intending to ask me to feed her?" Christian skipped to the point.

Daniel bit his lip. "Yeah, man, I am. I know it's a big ask, but you seem pretty damn powerful yourself, and, uh, from our talk earlier, I think maybe you might not be that susceptible to the venom if it's there. Unfortunately, we can't tell until she has her teeth in a guy."

"Wait." Jadyn held her hand up. "What's the deal here? I have no clue what this other half is you're talking about, but venom never sounds good."

"She might not even have it," Daniel said, irritation coating his tone. "But her eyes did flicker red earlier, so her other half was close to the surface, which is why I'd really like for her to get some fresh male blood in her system, calm down a bit. Christian, you spoke three words to that part of her and it backed off. You're the safest bet in this building."

"I'll do it," Christian said, not having to give it much thought. Someone was in need and he was in position to help. There wasn't anything to think about. He swallowed down the rest of the blood Daniel had ordered for him, and stood.

"Hold on." Jadyn came off of her stool as well and grabbed his arms. "This sounds dangerous. Why does she have venom and what can it do to you?"

"Danni is half succubus," Christian explained. "A succubus is basically a sex demon. Their teeth carry a venom they inject into men when they bite them. The venom ..." He felt himself blushing as he searched for the right words to describe the effect without offending her.

"It turns men into rutting pigs," Daniel cut in, having no such qualms. "Succubi seduce men and kill them, and it's easy because the men are so damn horny they don't even care that they're being murdered."

"You can't let her inject him with that!" Jadyn turned on Daniel with a dark glare, and attempted to lower her voice, but it came out as a rather loud stage whisper. "He's a minister."

Daniel fought back a laugh. "No worries, sweetheart. If she does have the venom in her fangs at the time of bite and he's affected I'll make sure his virtue stays intact."

"This isn't funny, and how exactly will you ensure nothing will happen? It sounds like the men have no choice."

"Christian is powerful. I'm not even a vampire and I can feel that. I think he's actually the real deal too, not just blowing smoke about faith and all that, and the succubus part of Danni actually seemed afraid of him when he stepped in earlier. He might not be affected at all, but if he is, Ginger will be in position to handle Danni while I handle him."

"Handle him how?" She stepped toe to toe with the six-foot-tall dragon shifter and squared up, not seeming to realize her five-foot-four inch frame was no match for his height and muscle, or she just didn't care.

"I'll stab him until he comes out from under the spell."

Christian saw the anger flood into Jadyn's eyes and grabbed her before she launched herself at Daniel. "It'll be fine," he assured her in a calm voice, positioning himself between her and the dragon. "I've been stabbed more times than I can count, and Daniel won't be trying to maim me, just redirect my attention."

Jadyn's mouth opened and closed as she sputtered unintelligible word fragments, too worked up to focus enough to create an actual sentence. He waited until she worked through her rush of anger to finally take a breath.

"I don't believe he'll need to, but if he does, I'll survive."

"I don't like it."

"It'll be fine." He fought back a grin, touched by her concern. "I'd rather not leave you out here alone so you'll be with us."

"You bet I'll be with you." She looked around him to glare at Daniel. "I might be small, and just a human, but I can call a pack of wolves. Real ones."

Christian turned to see Daniel smiling ear to ear, clearly amused, and shook his head. "Let's do this."

"Follow me." Daniel led them toward the bathrooms, turning right after entering the hall. They passed the bathrooms and continued on until they reached the office Christian had woken up in earlier, and entered to find Danni and Ginger sitting on the desk. Angel was asleep on the couch.

Ginger's eyebrows raised as they stepped inside and closed the door. "You said yes?"

Christian nodded.

"Were you told what could happen?"

"I am aware."

"And you still want to do it?"

"Someone is in need and I can help. I have faith I will be fine, and if not, Daniel will ensure nothing inappropriate happens."

Daniel snorted as he moved to stand beside him. "Inappropriate. You're so stuffy, it cracks me up."

"He's a minister," Danni said as she stood and wiped her palms on her jean-clad legs. "Maybe this isn't right. I should just drink from you or someone else."

Jadyn shifted her feet behind Christian and he heard her take a breath, about to speak. He looked back at her and shook his head, stopping her before she said something to make the obviously bothered hybrid feel worse.

Once sure Jadyn wouldn't say anything, he stepped toward Danni and opened his senses wide as he focused on her, searching until he sensed the succubus part of her. "Give me your hands."

He held his hands out and Danni hesitantly placed hers in his. He stood still, willing his strength into her until her hands stopped trembling, and gave her a reassuring smile before staring straight into her eyes and speaking to the part of her that shamed her. "I am sharing my blood freely. You will not attack me. My faith is stronger than any dark power you think you may have." He squeezed Danni's hands before letting go and held his wrist out in offering. "Take what you need."

Danni looked at Daniel nervously as Ginger moved in close to her, and Daniel removed a switchblade from his pocket before positioning himself at Christian's side. Christian cast a quick glance back at Jadyn and subtly nodded, letting her know all was well. The young woman stood with her back to the door, watching warily.

"It will be fine," he assured the hybrid, turning his attention back to her.

"I apologize in advance if anything happens," she nearly whispered and tentatively took his wrist in her hand before lowering her mouth to it. He felt her fangs cut through the skin and then she began to drink.

"Well, you're not humping her leg, which is a good sign," Daniel said after Danni had swallowed a few times. "How do you feel?"

"Geez, Daniel, even I wouldn't say that like that to a minister," Ginger scolded the shifter.

"It's all right," Christian assured them, used to such language. They had nothing on Jacob Porter, or an angry Seta. "I feel fine."

Danni gasped, and backed away, dropping Christian's wrist. She nearly toppled backward, but Ginger braced her.

"What's wrong?" Daniel asked, moving forward as Christian placed his wrist in his own mouth, healing the wound Danni hadn't sealed before backing away so quickly. He stood where he was, unsure if his blood had caused her distress.

"It was too much." Danni raised her hand to her chest, breathing rapidly as she moved to the desk and sat on it, her knees shaking. Ginger sat next to her, offering support.

Daniel and Ginger eyed Christian curiously. "What do you mean it was too much?" the dragon shifter asked.

"It was..." She moved her other hand in a circular rotation, searching for the right word.

"Overwhelming?" Christian suggested, sensing the unease of the succubus part of her.

She nodded. "Your blood packs a punch, just like Rider's, but it was different. I swear I felt like I was floating on air, and then it just overpowered me, and part of me really didn't like it. Yet, I wanted more at the same time."

"And you didn't feel anything at all?" Daniel asked him as he stood next to the hybrid, one arm protectively draped over her shoulder.

"No, but I sensed the succubus part of her and kept my focus on it, ensuring it behaved."

"How do you do that?" Ginger asked.

"My faith is strong," he explained.

A loud vibration came from Daniel's pocket. He reached in and pulled out a cell phone, checking the screen. "Your escort is here to take you to The Midnight Rider," he said, texting a response before looking down at Danni. "Are you all right?"

She took a long, deep breath and nodded as she expelled it slowly, visibly relaxing. "Yeah, I'm good. I think the really dark part of me doesn't like him, but his blood still qualifies as live male, so I should be good from any flare ups for a while."

Daniel ruffled her hair playfully and stood straight. "Then it's time to say goodbyes. These two have somewhere to be."

"I hope everything works out for you," Ginger told him. "For a really religious type of guy, you're cool enough, even if you're kind of strange."

"You're the one with an impaled cartoon testicle on your shirt," Christian reminded her, grinning.

She smiled back. "Yeah, well, you hang around Danni long enough and brutalized testicles become the norm."

"Sad but true," Daniel murmured as he extended his hand.

Christian gave it a firm shake. "Thank you for your assistance, Daniel. If there's anything I can ever do to return the favor, you need only ask."

"I might do that," the shifter replied, "but first you need to figure out why you have an army of evil bastards after you and get that mess cleaned up." He walked over to Jadyn. "You freak me out a little," he told her, "and you threatened me, but I still think you're all right. Can you tell the dragon I'm sorry?"

"You just did," she replied, "and he already knows."

"Thanks for everything," Danni told Christian as she stood from the desk, appearing much steadier than before, and hugged him. "This is weird, but I have the urge so just go with it."

He laughed as he released her. "I am not bothered. I'd like to think I've made a new friend."

"Even if she's part demon?"

"A true demon wouldn't be so loved," he told her. "Who we are is far more important than what we are."

The women said their goodbyes to Jadyn, wished them well, and stayed behind in the office with the sleeping teenager as Daniel walked them out.

"Don't forget your sweatshirt," Daniel reminded Jadyn as they passed the bar and Gruff held the hooded sweatshirt out to her.

"You left it in the booth," he told her.

"Thanks." Jadyn grabbed the sweatshirt and slid her arms through the sleeves before zipping it up. She eyed Christian's long-sleeved T-shirt. "You're going to be cold outside."

"I'll be fine."

"Your escort is waiting outside," Daniel told them as he led them to the front door and pushed it open.

They stepped out into the cool night air and saw a pretty coffee-skinned woman with long dark hair highlighted with purple streaks, dressed in tight black leather pants and a matching jacket that fit her like a second skin. Stiletto-heeled boots stopped at mid-calf. She stood in the center of the parking lot, feet apart and arms folded over her generous chest.

"There's my sexy dragon boy. When am I going to get the chance to take *you* somewhere?"

Daniel laughed and shook his head. "This is Rihanna," he told them, "and she's very friendly. Rihanna, this is Jadyn and Christian. They were under a pretty bad attack earlier so the sooner you get them to Rider, the better."

"No problem, cutie." She looked them over. "I will be teleporting you to The Midnight Rider. If you have any luggage, grab it."

Christian took the car keys from his pocket and walked over to the Taurus. He removed his and Jadyn's bags, locked the keys in the trunk, and walked back over to the group. "We packed light."

Rihanna looked at the car. "Rider will make arrangements for the car later."

"It belongs to a friend of mine, who is also a witch. She'll be able to retrieve it herself. It has a locator spell on it."

The ground shook and a long line of dark smoke appeared ten feet away from them.

"Christian!" Jadyn grabbed his arm. "They're back!"

"Oh, not tonight, bitches," Rihanna growled as she flung a ball of light at the portal, disintegrating it before it could open, then wrapped her arms around both of them. "Time to go."

CHAPTER ELEVEN

One moment they were outside of Gruff's Bar and Grille, and the next, before Jadyn could even blink, they were standing in an office. Black bookshelves full of aged books lined the gray walls, a black leather couch sat along the wall next to the closed door, and a very attractive man in a dark blue long-sleeved button down shirt sat in a black leather office chair behind a large black lacquer desk, his fingers steepled as he watched them. Like Christian, he had black hair, blue eyes, golden skin, and even while sitting she could tell he was tall, lean, but powerfully built. Unlike Christian, his hair was long and pulled back into a ponytail at the nape of his neck, and he didn't give off the same peaceful vibe. His vibe was much more predatory.

"A portal almost opened, but I destroyed it and immediately teleported us here," Rihanna told the man as the three of them split from the huddle they'd formed before she'd transported them. "Depending on how these two are being tracked, it may reopen or they may sense these two are gone and not bother. Even if they do, it will take a while for them to create the portal again."

"Will the warding here prevent a portal from opening?"

"This building is warded against that type of intrusion. Whoever is after them will have to come in by foot, if they can figure out how to track them here."

"Do you know how they are being tracked?"

The witch looked over at them and shook her head. "Dark magic is involved. If whoever it is has access to their blood or anything else physical, that could be used. Of course, with dark magic, there are other ways. It's hard to say, but the portal didn't appear until they were outside of Gruff's, indicating the warding on the building worked, and will work here too."

"Very well. Thank you, Rihanna."

"No problem, Rider, honey. You know how to reach me any time you want to line my pockets." She blew him a kiss, winked at Christian, and left the room, leaving them alone with the man they'd heard about. Rider Knight.

Christian stood at Jadyn's side, his back straight, hands loose at his sides, but despite his relaxed appearance, she sensed his body was coiled, ready to strike if need be. He stared straight ahead at Rider as if awaiting instruction. The other vampire remained seated, staring back over his steepled fingers. He paid her no attention at all, his focus on the man next to her. He closed his eyes for a moment and when he opened them again, they glowed. The air in the room became thicker, seeming to push out of him.

Christian's jaw clamped and the air shifted again, a wave of it coming from him. They seemed to be pushing against each other with their energy or power, testing each other. The room became so thick with it, Jadyn grew lightheaded, and nearly stumbled. She quickly righted herself, and tried to take a deep breath, but couldn't.

"Stop," Christian commanded. "She can't breathe."

Rider looked over at her and the thick air snapped back into both of them. She rocked back on her heels, and Christian's hand shot out to grab her bicep, steadying her.

"What was that?" she asked.

"A test," Christian answered. "Kind of a way vampires get to know each other sometimes."

"Oh. Like dogs sniffing each other's butts?" She felt heat flush her face, and instantly regretted what she'd said.

"Uh, something like that." Christian smiled before returning his gaze to the other vampire, whose mouth had been turned up the slightest bit at the corners before straightening back out.

"You are very powerful," the man said, his eyes no longer glowing.

"So are you," Christian responded, "but I expected nothing less from an old friend of Seta's."

"If I'm being honest, your power is more than I expected." He gestured toward the two chairs before his desk and waited for them to sit. "Welcome to The Midnight Rider. I am Rider Knight. I run this territory, and provide security services across multiple states."

"I'm Christian, and this is my friend, Jadyn Lee."

Jadyn frowned, wondering why Christian hadn't given a last name. He'd never given one when she'd been a child either. It was one of the reasons it had been so hard for her to track him down.

"I've been in contact with Daniel," Rider said, looking between the two of them. "Your friend can communicate with animals, and you ...are very interesting."

"I am as interesting as any of my kind."

Rider's eyes narrowed a fraction. "I have to say I've never known any of our kind to wield a flaming sword, and he says you are able to see imortium, but you have no recollection of ever setting foot into Imortia. And you are not Imortian."

"All true."

They stared at each other long enough a nervous sweat trickled down Jadyn's spine. She had no idea what was happening between them, but it was starting to make her uncomfortable.

"Seta spoke very highly of you, and I do owe her a great debt," the vampire finally said. "I'm not thrilled about bringing danger to my people, but we will help you. I ask that when you leave, you tell no one of what you learn here. That goes for both of you. Also, I expect complete honesty at all times. Nothing less will be tolerated when I am using my people and resources to aid you."

"Understood, and appreciated," Christian said. He reached over and threaded his fingers through Jadyn's, giving her hand a reassuring squeeze. Butterflies fluttered inside her belly, but she quickly reminded herself he was her guardian angel, her childhood hero. He was simply reassuring her that everything would be fine. It would do her no good to get excited about such an innocent gesture, and get her hopes up for something that would never happen because the man was on the run. He wasn't thinking of anything other than keeping them alive.

Rider gave a quick, firm nod. "First things first, we need to figure out who and what we are dealing with, and why this is happening to you now. Seta was of the mind you'd merely been discovered by vampire hunters, but after communicating with Daniel, that doesn't seem to be the case. He said you'd been attacked by lycanthropes and a witch."

"True," Christian replied. "And whoever is behind this sent a human team to my church first, and another human team had been sent to Jadyn's apartment at the same time. They were intercepted by two of my friends, one of which was able to determine they worked for a vampire, but she couldn't get any more information than that."

Rider's eyebrows rose. "And the two of you have had no communication with one another since you rescued her as a child over a decade ago?"

"Correct."

"Do you have any idea who would want the both of you?"

"None," Christian answered. "And I'm not sure they actually want both of us. If dark magic is involved, they may have somehow figured out Jadyn would be arriving at my church and used her to locate me. It wouldn't be the first time I've heard of a dark witch using a psychic vision to track someone through someone else."

"Seems a bit farfetched," Rider murmured. He looked at Jadyn, and her mouth went dry under his scrutiny. "Do you have any other abilities besides communicating with animals, and controlling them to some degree?"

She shook her head. "And even though I can call upon them, I don't control the animals."

"It's all telepathic?"

"Pretty much." She felt Christian's hand squeeze gently around hers, and was grateful to have him there to calm her nerves. Rider didn't seem mean or hostile, but he intimidated her all the same. "Sometimes I speak to them, just because it feels natural, I guess, and they understand me, but when I hear them it's in my head."

"Can you move objects with your mind? Do you get visions?"

"I can't move objects, and the only visions I get are pictures that pop into my head sometimes while sensing or conversing with animals. I can see their thoughts sometimes."

"Tell me about the fire sword," Rider ordered, returning his attention to Christian. "Daniel saw you wielding it, and it disappeared before he hit the ground. Where did it come from, and where did it go?"

"I don't know."

Rider's eyes darkened. "I asked for complete honesty."

"And you're getting it." Christian's tone was respectful, yet firm. "I have no idea how that sword got in my hand or where it went. I just reached out and it was there."

"You've never done that before?"

"Not that I can remember."

"Not that you can remember?" Rider unsteepled his fingers and leaned forward. "How would you forget a thing like that?"

Christian looked down and took a breath before releasing Jadyn's hand. He folded his hands together and looked Rider Knight directly in the eyes. "I don't know how old I am or where I came from. I don't know my blood family, my birthplace, or even what name I was given at birth."

Jadyn's mouth hung open as she stared at Christian, his mysteriousness making greater sense.

"Why is that?" Rider asked, his tone much softer.

"My earliest memory is of waking up covered in blood, in the middle of nowhere. I was beaten severely, so severely my memory was lost."

Jadyn gasped, her hand automatically covering her mouth as her heart ached, imagining the scene Christian described. She wanted to reach over and hold his hand, give him the comfort he'd given her moments ago, but was unsure if it would be too bold of her. He glanced over at her, gave her a small, gentle smile as if to say it was all right, he'd survived, and turned his attention back to the other vampire listening intently.

"A kind older woman gave me shelter, tended to my wounds, and fed me. I was with her a short while before I was attacked again. This time I was turned. I hadn't remembered anything before the first beating, and when I woke as a vampire my memory was even more damaged. With time, I remembered the kind woman and the very short span of time between the two attacks, but I never have been able to remember anything at all before the first beating."

"Who turned you?" Rider asked, his eyes dark, nostrils flared.

"I do not know that either. I was jumped so quickly I never saw anyone. At least I can't recall seeing anyone. I woke up and there was a vampire with me by the name of Eron. He was not my sire, but he'd found me and took me under his wing since I had been abandoned during the actual turning."

"Seta's Eron?"

"Yes."

"He's a good man, from what I've heard about him." Rider leaned back in his chair and studied Christian. "Even if your sire left you, you would feel a connection if he or she were alive."

"I have never felt the connection. I suspect my sire was killed before I made it through the turning."

"Adaptation to the vampire world is hard without a sire's guidance. We have that in common," Rider told him. "Where did the name Christian come from?"

"Eron asked my name. I had no idea what my name was, and the woman who'd helped me after the first attack had never called me anything. I didn't know who I was, but I knew what I was. A man of God, a follower of Christ."

"So you named yourself Christian."

He nodded.

"And all this time, you've remembered nothing of your life before the first attack?"

Christian started to shake his head, but paused mid-movement, his brow furrowing. "I do not recall ever using that sword, but it felt familiar in my hand, and there was a woman who helped us outside the church. She felt familiar, but I have no idea where I would know her from, if not before."

"Seta told me you had been attacked at your church, but didn't mention any woman helping you there. Daniel didn't mention that to me either."

"So much has happened in such a short time," Christian said, shifting in his seat. "I don't think I even mentioned her to Daniel at all. I've mostly been focused on our attackers, trying to figure out who they are and what they want with us. The mystery woman who appeared out of nowhere to help us has mostly just been a niggling thought in the back of my mind. It almost feels like I dreamed her, but Jadyn can attest to the fact she was really there."

"Yeah, she was," Jadyn muttered, recalling the too beautiful to be real woman who'd swooped in to help them. She tried to imagine where Christian would know her from, and didn't like the ideas filling her mind. She clearly wasn't human, and if she helped him there was a chance she cared for him. If she was from his past ...she could have been a very important person in his life. Someone he loved, who loved him back. Someone who could remind him who he was and take him away.

"Was she a vampire?" Rider asked.

"No." Christian shook his head adamantly. "She was definitely not mortal, but I didn't sense a drop of darkness in her. She was ..." He smiled. "She was ethereal. Pristine, strong, and too perfect for this world. And somehow, I felt like I knew her."

Jadyn chewed the inside of her lip and fought against the thoughts creeping into her mind, recognizing them as jealousy. She was better than that, or at least she aspired to be. The mystery woman had helped them and she knew she should only be thankful.

"What happened to her?" Rider asked.

"Two men I could describe the same way I described her appeared, grabbed her, and disappeared after she helped us. They were all extraordinarily beautiful, powerful, and pristine in the whitest clothing I've ever seen."

Jadyn quit chewing her lip, relief flooding her system. He thought the men were beautiful too? She'd seen them, and would agree, but knowing he thought so gave her a little hope he wasn't enamored with the golden-haired woman's beauty, but had simply noticed it as he had the others.

Rider steepled his fingers again and studied Christian. "Did they have swords?"

"Not that I recall. I was actually fixated on the woman's eyes too much to notice more than their unique gold color, her matching hair, and the uber white clothing. Her eyes were very familiar to me."

"Did you notice swords?" Rider asked her.

"I was busy trying to not get kidnapped," Jadyn answered while trying not to be bothered by Christian's fixation with the woman's eyes.

"I can't say I've heard of anyone fitting that description," Rider told them. He narrowed his eyes on Christian, studying him. "Nor have I known of anyone before you who could pull a flaming sword out of nowhere. Is it possible this familiarity might be because you are one of whatever the woman is?"

Christian's eyes widened. He appeared to think of the possibility, and quickly shook his head, his shoulders slumped. "I couldn't possibly be. It almost seems blasphemous to even think I could be whatever it is that she is."

"Yet, she is familiar to you and you have no idea who or what you were prior to the attack that robbed you of your memory." Rider rubbed his chin. "You are not just a vampire. It can be argued your power has come with age like most of us, but vampires don't wield flaming swords and even I can't affect Danni's succubus side the way you did. My life, and hers, would be far simpler if I could, but that is not a vampire power. You do not seem to struggle with lust the way most of us do either."

"I am a servant of the Lord. My faith keeps the darkness in me manageable."

Rider's eyebrows rose. "I respect your faith. Lord knows I've run across too many of our kind who lose it quick and give in completely to the pull of the beast inside. Still, I would like for you to have a thorough examination."

"An examination?"

"Yes. Both of you, actually." Rider glanced at Jadyn. "A non-shifter who can communicate with animals is as unheard of as a vampire who wields a flaming sword, and there's the fact you can see imortium. Daniel is sure you're not Imortian, but I'd like to do an actual medical test."

Christian frowned. "A medical test? On a vampire?"

"My personal physician is a vampire and the underworld hospital ward I fund combines medicine with magic. I know Seta's group keeps it old school, but there are advantages to embracing technology and human science. For starters..." Rider opened a desk drawer, removed a white plastic bottle and tossed it to Christian. "Slather that on any time you have to go out in the daylight. It's far more effective than regular sunscreen created for humans. How have you been getting your blood?"

"Bagged, through a shipping service I believe you have a hand in," Christian answered. "Of course, there's the occasional ingestion sometimes when capturing a pedophile or other sex offender."

"So you haven't been drinking living blood often?"

"Not frequently, although Daniel fed me recently."

"You are extremely powerful for a vampire whose diet primarily consists of bagged blood." Rider's eyes narrowed. "You can order a very bloody mary at the bar any time you need it. It's on the house while we're sorting this all out." He looked at Jadyn. "There is food on the bar menu, but not the most nourishing. I'll arrange to have food for you. It's best the two of you stay here while we're figuring this all out. If whoever is after you can track you and open up portals, you're not safe anywhere that isn't warded. Do you have a problem staying here?"

"In a bar?" Jadyn asked, confused. Where exactly would they sleep? On the office couch?

Rider stood. "Follow me, and remember... tell no one what you learn here."

Jadyn shot Christian a questioning look as they rose and followed the vampire out of the office. Christian gave her a reassuring nod and placed his hand along her lower back, his touch feeding the sense of security into her as they fell in step behind Rider, following him down a hallway.

Jadyn heard music and talking coming from the right, but they went left, through a door that led into another hallway. This small hallway had a staircase leading up, and a door on each side of the room. They passed the staircase and took the door on the left, which opened to another set of stairs. They took the stairs down one flight and stepped through a door Rider unlocked by placing his hand on a control panel to the left of it.

A long black table occupied the center of the room and supported the weight of ten computers, five on each side. Each computer was manned by a man or woman whose fingers flew over their keyboards. An assortment of men and women in black clothing, most of them armed, stood near the back of the room watching as information populated on a large plasma screen taking up the front wall. There was another door to the side of the table, and a man stepped out of it, checking a gun before sliding it into his web belt, leading Jadyn to believe it was some sort or armory.

"This is where my tech team does remote surveillance," Rider explained, gesturing toward the plasma screen. "They can tap into security and traffic cameras, in addition to hacking computer systems and tracing phones. That's how we traced your location. I actually had an escort en route by vehicle, but when you texted you were in more immediate need of assistance I sent in Daniel to retrieve you and get you to a more secure spot, then sent Rihanna to pick you up once she was available. Teleportation was a safer way of retrieval given the fact you're being tracked by someone who can create portals. The tech team is currently monitoring for portals."

"They can do that?" Christian asked.

"Combining technology with paranormal skills is as effective as mixing modern medicine with magic. Magic leaves a trace, and my tech team knows how to use technology to track it." Rider started walking left and they followed as he led them down a long hallway. Glass ran the upper half of the left wall, allowing them to see into what appeared to be a gym where men and women of various sizes ran on treadmills and lifted weights inside. Doors labeled for men and women were on the right side of the hall, indicating bathrooms or locker rooms. They passed another door on the left and went through a door at the end of the hall, on the right.

Jadyn looked over at Christian as they descended another set of stairs, but he didn't seem bothered by the fact they were now going two sublevels beneath The Midnight Rider, or was it all The Midnight Rider? Jadyn realized she had no clue. When Danni and Ginger had told her about the place, she'd imagined a bar. She knew Rider lived there, and assumed that was where the staircase they'd passed on the ground floor led to, and that the building served as his base of operations, but she hadn't suspected the whole sublevel tech center and gym.

Rider placed his hand over another panel when they reached the bottom of the stairs, opening a heavy metal door. They stepped through and Jadyn noticed the atmosphere was different. It seemed darker, almost foreboding. Part of that may have been the armed guards posted throughout the area, watching them as they passed.

"You will not come down here without an escort," Rider told them as he led them straight back and took a hall on the right. They passed several doors with small windows, continuing until they reached the door at the very end of the hall. This one didn't have a security panel, and opened with a simple twist of the knob. Rider stepped in and stood aside, gesturing for them to enter.

A hospital bed rested near the back wall. To the right were counters with a sink, microwave, and a mini refrigerator. An open door revealed a small bathroom. A couch sat against the wall on the left, and a small table and chairs were positioned in the corner to the right of the door.

"It's not much," Rider said, "but it's a safe place to sleep until we get to the root of who is threatening you and wipe them out. Hopefully, you won't be here long, but if it does take longer than we hope, you have a place to rest.

I have someone out now getting food so you always have something available if you don't want what's in the bar, but you are more than welcome to order from the bar any time you want, on the house. You can go ahead and put your stuff in here."

Christian looked down, seeming to have forgotten he still carried their duffel bags in one hand. He walked over to the table and set them on top before turning to look at her. Jadyn looked over at the one bed and bit her lip.

"I'll sleep on the couch," Christian offered, seeming to sense her discomfort.

"I can see about getting another bed put in here," Rider told them, "or I can put one of you in another room. This is the only one available with a bathroom. In another room you'd only get a place to sleep."

"This is fine," Jadyn said, knowing she'd never sleep in a room by herself. It wasn't that she thought Rider was a bad guy, but he put off the vibe of a man who wasn't above killing to get what he wanted and there was something definitely unsettling about sleeping two levels below ground, in an area guarded by armed men and women, especially when she knew those men and women were probably vampires or some sort of shifters.

"Good. Hopefully you won't have need of it long. I'm not thrilled that someone is using dark magic to hunt vampires and whatever it is you are. The less time that someone is allowed to hunt you two and do who knows what to anyone else, the better." He stepped back out into the hall. "First, we need to find out what you two are. I've arranged an appointment at the underworld hospital ward. After some poking and prodding, we might just get some answers."

"How much poking and prodding?" Jadyn asked.

"However much is required in a normal dissection," Rider answered, looking down at her.

"Dissection?" Alarm slammed into Jadyn's chest and came out loud and clear in her voice.

"Well, how else are we going to find out what you are unless we cut you open and take a look around?"

CHAPTER TWELVE

"He's teasing you," Christian said, stepping forward. He placed his hands on Jadyn's shoulders and squeezed while giving the vampire a hard look. "No one is going to dissect us, and no one is going to lay one finger on you in my presence."

He felt Jadyn relax as Rider stared at him over her head. The vampire didn't smile, but his eyes twinkled with amusement before he lowered his gaze to meet Jadyn's. "I couldn't resist, but Christian is correct. No one is going to cut you open. Both of you are under my protection and I take that seriously. I'm not sure what exactly the examination will entail, but no harm will come to you."

Rider turned and started down the hall. Christian moved beside Jadyn, threaded his fingers through hers, and followed, smiling down at her as they walked. "I know he and everything about this place is probably scary for you, but I wouldn't have sought his help if he wasn't a good ally. He's on our side."

"Why is the bed a hospital bed?" she whispered, her eyes full of worry that tugged at his heart.

He squeezed her hand and fought against the urge to smooth the frown lines between her eyebrows with a kiss, an urge no woman had ever made him feel in any of the centuries he could actually remember. "He has a lot of security guards. I imagine sometimes they need to recover after getting injured, or he could use those beds for people like us, who need a place to hide out from killers on their tails. If Rihanna hadn't teleported us here when she did, we might have arrived bloody and in need of medical care."

"That's a better idea than where my mind went," she said.

"Evil medical experiments?" Christian smiled wide, unable to control himself. When she looked up at him and narrowed her eyes in annoyance at his amusement, something inside him fluttered. Without thinking, he kissed her forehead and felt the oddest sensation flood his body. Looking into her eyes, he knew she'd felt it too.

Christian tore his gaze away to see Rider standing by the door to the stairwell, looking back at them. The vampire let his gaze roam over them a moment, but said nothing as he opened the door and led them up the stairs to the first sublevel. They walked past the gym in silence, and into the area his tech team occupied, where he stopped by the table with the computers and turned toward them. "Give me your phones. They need to be checked to ensure no one other than my team has been tracking you through them."

Christian withdrew his from his pocket and handed it over, nodding at Jadyn when she questioned him with her eyes.

"You'll get them back after they've been checked," Rider promised, and handed them to the young man sitting at the computer station next to him. Christian had already opened his senses earlier in the room and knew the young man was a vampire. Everyone in the room was a vampire or a shapeshifter.

Rider closed his eyes and Christian felt his power pulse. He knew the vampire was communicating telepathically with his nest and realized since he himself had recently fed from a live source he could tap into his own telepathic power that lie dormant when he drank solely from bagged blood. He reached out with his mind, feeling for the link with Seta. He came up empty and knew she'd either chosen to close herself off or had traveled beyond his reach. He prayed wherever she was, she and her family were safe.

"Transport is in place," Rider said, opening his eyes. "Follow me."

They followed the vampire up the stairs to the ground floor, and stopped before the door opposite the stairwell as Rider turned to face them. "Whoever is pursuing you cannot track you while you are inside this building or create a portal on this property. Once we step outside of the protection of The Midnight Rider, all bets are off. You will be vulnerable. I need to create a bond with you so we can communicate telepathically should the need arise."

Christian nodded, understanding the importance of telepathic communication if they were attacked while out. He released Jadyn's hand and straightened his shoulders. "You may create the bond with me. It is not necessary to create the bond with Jadyn."

"If we are separated..."

"You can communicate with me. Jadyn will be with me at all times." He looked down at her and saw the confusion in her eyes. "She is not to be bitten by anyone at any time."

Her eyes widened with understanding, and she moved in closer to his side.

"Very well, but I am not responsible if she gets separated and we have no way of communication with her."

"It will take more magic than these predators have to separate us," Christian claimed, knowing it was a bold statement given he had no clue who was after them, but he did know he meant every word. He would not leave Jadyn's side, and he would not allow anyone to put his or her mouth on her.

He raised his wrist in offering, and stood still as Rider bit into the skin, taking a small drink of blood. The wound was quickly sealed and Rider placed his fingers at his temples. A moment later, he sensed pressure inside his head.

"You're sure about this?" the vampire asked. "We don't yet know who is after you or what they are capable of. The bond can add an extra layer of protection."

"I'm sure," Christian answered, looking over at Jadyn. "Unless she wants—"

Jadyn quickly shook her head, her face paling as she wrapped her arms protectively around herself.

"All right then." Rider opened the door, revealing a garage with three vehicles: a Ferrari, an SUV, and a motorcycle, all shiny and black. A musclebound man with no discernible neck stood beside the SUV. Dressed all in black like the men and women posted in the sublevels, Christian figured him to be part of Rider's security team.

"This is Hank," Rider said as he approached the SUV. "He will be riding with us. Two more vehicles are in our convoy, in case we run into any surprises on our way to the underworld ward."

The large man opened the back door and stood by for them to get in as Rider rounded the vehicle to slide into the driver's seat. Christian helped Jadyn inside before sliding in next to her, giving her hand a reassuring squeeze. Hank closed the door behind him, got in the front passenger seat, and Rider hit a button on a remote to open the garage door. They backed out into a narrow alley and turned. Christian noticed an SUV ahead of them at one end of the alley, and another SUV at the other end, quickly moving in behind them. They followed the SUV in front out of the alley and onto the street, Rider's eyes scanning constantly as they headed to their destination.

"Where are we going?" Jadyn whispered.

"The underworld ward," Rider answered, his vampire hearing easily catching her question. "It's a section of the hospital dedicated to the paranormal community and is not a place often shared with humans. I'd appreciate if its whereabouts are not shared with the general public. It would be very bad for any foolish humans who try to catch a peek inside."

"You can trust Jadyn," Christian advised before turning his head toward her. "Our kind has managed to survive this long by staying under the radar. Yes, there are books and movies, and myths and legends of pretty much every paranormal being, but as long as the non-paranormal world thinks that is all fiction, we can continue to live among them."

"I don't think anyone would believe me even if I did tell them," Jadyn laughed, quickly sobering as she looked up and caught Rider's gaze in the rearview mirror. "But I promise no one will hear about any of this from me. I mostly speak with animals anyway."

"Can you sense the animal spirit inside Hank?" Rider asked, his gaze returning to the road and the SUV leading their way.

Jadyn's brow creased as she stared at the hulking man sitting up front, her eyes narrowed in concentration. Christian had already sensed the man was a shifter when he'd first stepped into the garage. Opening his senses wide now and concentrating on the man, he was surprised to discover the man was a wererhino, not a were he had ever come into contact with before.

"There is no animal soul inside him," Jadyn said, her brow smoothing back out as she relaxed in her seat. "I don't sense anything."

"Interesting," Rider murmured. "Not entirely surprising though. Hank can take on the shape of his animal, but he was not created in the same way Daniel was. He was born a shifter, and is not Imortian."

"What kind of shifter are you?" Jadyn leaned forward, her interest piqued. "If that's all right for me to ask."

"I'm a wererhino," Hank answered, his voice as gruff as one would expect a man of his size to speak.

Jadyn's eyes widened as she turned toward Christian.

"He is not a lycanthrope," Christian advised, and she visibly relaxed. "While I'm sure there are some decent lycanthropes in the world, I have yet to come across any who are. They become shifters from lycanthropy, a disease they carry in their saliva as well as pass on to their children. They tend to be more violent by nature, less in control of their animal side, especially those who are born with the disease. There are different types of shifters. Some are therians, created through ritual magic, and you met Daniel, an Imortian. Shifters from Imortia are considered to be weres, and you know the awful way they were initially created, although they also pass the trait to their children. There are other weres, like Hank, who are born as what they are, but cannot pass the trait to anyone other than their children who inherit the gene."

"What types of shifters are there besides wolves, dragons, snakes, and rhinos?"

"One of my friends is part pantherian, which is what it sounds like."

"Panther?"

He nodded, but said no more about the half vampire, half panther hybrid, realizing it was best Rider not know anything more about his friend. Nyla was Jake's mate, and the mother of one of the three children born as part of the Blood Revelation. Seta trusted Rider to help them, but they were all in agreement that it was best the prophecy remain their secret.

They remained silent the rest of the trip. Jadyn stared out the window, watching the buildings and streets pass, and Christian entertained himself watching her until they pulled into an underground parking garage and went down the ramps until they reached the lowest level, where they took the three parking spaces next to the elevator. Christian had a feeling those were Rider's personal spots.

"So far, no problems," Rider commented. "The underworld ward has warding too so we should be clear of surprises until we head back out again."

Rider and Hank exited the vehicle, and the wererhino opened the door for them as vampires and shifters emerged from the other two vehicles. Christian slid out and helped Jadyn, who held on to his arm as they moved to join Rider and the others at the back of the SUV.

"Hank and Juan, you're with me. The rest of you stay alert for anything out of the ordinary," Rider instructed the men in black before moving over to the elevator. Christian and Jadyn followed, Hank and the slender man who must be Juan following them.

Once all were inside the elevator with the doors closed behind them, Rider pushed the basement button three times in quick succession and the car started its descent. Christian opened his senses, discovering the tall, slender, but strong man coming along with them was a werewolf.

The elevator came to a stop and the doors opened to reveal what looked like any floor on any normal hospital floor. As they passed the waiting room, it became clear it was not part of the regular hospital. Every person waiting gave off a paranormal vibe and the buzz of magic hung heavy in the air.

A petite woman with delicate features, short pink hair, and big brown eyes looked up as they approached the check-in desk. Her wide eyes grew even bigger as she saw Rider. She quickly grabbed a clipboard and stepped around the desk to greet him. "Good evening, Mr. Knight. We have rooms set up for you."

"We only need one examination room," Christian said.

Rider turned toward him, one eyebrow arched. "Is that so?"

"I'm not leaving her alone." he replied, sure not many dared to overstep their bounds with Rider, but as powerful as the vampire was, he wasn't going to put Jadyn through any sort of test Christian didn't approve of first.

The vampire gave a quick nod before turning his attention back to the young woman. "One examination room will do, Arianne."

"Yes, sir." The small woman who practically trembled with nerves led them to an examination room down the hall and around the corner. "Nannette will be right in as soon as she finishes up with her current patient."

It had been a long time since Christian had been in an examination room, only having need for hospitals when one of the humans he helped were injured worse than he could fix himself, but it looked like any other examination room. White tile floor, white tile walls, medical equipment here and there, a refrigerator he assumed held medicine, or given the clientele here, blood?

"Who is Nannette?" he asked as Jadyn took a seat on the examination table. He opted to stand at the head of it, his back to the wall so he would see whoever entered the moment they stepped through the door.

"She is a nurse here, and a highly trusted member of my nest," Rider answered as he gestured for Juan and Hank to stay posted outside the room and closed the door behind them.

"Vampire?"

"Yes."

"Your fledgling?"

"No," Rider answered.

"So the hearsay is true. The majority of your nest is comprised of vampires you've rescued from abusive sires and rogue shifters you've taken in."

"For the most part." Rider leaned back against the opposite wall, taking a spot to the side of the door. "I checked in with Daniel and so far, no one has reopened another portal there."

"Good," Christian said, relief filling his chest. "I wasn't happy thinking I may have left them a mess to deal with. I know we came to you for help, but I'd like to actually be in the battles being fought for us. Otherwise, it feels as if people are being used. I can't say it's a feeling I care for."

"My people are used to danger, and the types of predators after you need to be exterminated for the good of us all anyway."

"Be that as it may, I get the impression you'd rather Danni not be caught up in this. Why else would the people she works with be assigned to watch over her as well?"

Rider watched him for a moment before replying. "Danni is a part of my security team, but she still has her training wheels on. You are aware of what she is, and can understand why she would need to be monitored."

"She seems like she can handle her own. She nearly castrated a man with her bare hand, in fact."

Rider grinned. "She has a thing for neutering men."

Christian knew the two were romantically involved and thought the idea of his girlfriend neutering men was an odd thing for Rider to find amusing, but what did he know about romantic relationships? He decided to change the topic. "We left a mess back there in West Virginia."

"I was told. The witch ripped the whole roof off the house?"

"Yes, but I was more concerned with the dead bodies left littering the ground."

"No need to worry. I keep Rihanna on retainer." The vampire sighed. "That woman is going to bankrupt me one day, but she's damn good at what she does. She's no Seta, but she's a pro. Not one speck of blood will be found there."

The door opened and a tall, slender woman with rich brown skin, big brown eyes, and dark hair shaved close to her scalp entered. She wore a long white lab coat and immediately picked up the clipboard the woman who'd shown them to the room had left on the counter before studying Jadyn and Christian, then nodded at Rider. "You brought me more lab rats?"

"Careful with your words, Nannette. The woman is new to our world, and skittish."

Nannette looked at Jadyn, her brows slightly arched. Christian reached over and squeezed Jadyn's shoulder, reminding her he was there, and she was safe.

"You are safe here," the woman told her. "I am Nannette, and you are..." She looked at the clipboard. "... interesting. You communicate with animals, but to your knowledge you are only human."

"To my knowledge?" Jadyn looked at Christian. "I think it would be obvious if I was something other than human."

"Can other humans communicate with animals in the way you do?" the nurse asked.

"None that I know of," Jadyn answered.

"Then you are not just a human, yet that doesn't appear obvious to you." The nurse turned as an Asian woman entered the room and set up supplies on the counter. "Thank you," she said to the woman after she finished and left, then walked over and retrieved items for a blood-draw and a small jug of blood.

"Drink up. I'll be drawing blood," she said as she tossed the jug to Christian and set the blood-draw supplies next to Jadyn on the examination table.

Christian drank the blood while he watched Nannette tie a tourniquet around Jadyn's arm and search for a vein. She inserted the needle with great skill and quickly withdrew enough blood to fill two small vials before pressing a cotton ball tight against the small puncture wound. By the time Christian finished the jug off, she'd labeled Jadyn's blood and set it aside.

"Your turn," she said as she walked over to Christian with a needle. Being a vampire, his blood was thinner and easier to draw so no tourniquet was necessary. Neither was the cotton ball. Christian raised his arm to his mouth once she was done, quickly sealing the puncture with his own saliva.

"What are you expecting to find in our blood?" he asked. "I wasn't aware blood tests could reveal vampirism, or anything else of the paranormal variety."

"You'd be surprised to know what can be revealed when magic and medicine mix," she answered as she labeled his blood and set it on the counter.

She picked up a stethoscope and walked back over to Jadyn. "Relax," she told her as she gently pulled the collar of her T-shirt away from her body and placed the chestpiece underneath. After giving a few instructions on breathing, she moved behind Jadyn and inserted the chestpiece under the back of her shirt and repeated the process. Once done, she walked to the end of the table, hooked the rolling stool there with her foot and kicked it over to Christian. "Your turn. Sit."

"I'm a vampire," he told her. "You might as well use that thing on yourself for all the difference it will make."

"Christian, I think you know yourself that you are not like other vampires," Rider said. "No one in my nest could have done what you did for Danni, not even me, and I'm her sire."

"Fine," he said, taking a seat, although he felt silly. Vampires didn't need checkups, and for obvious reasons.

"Breathe normally," Nannette instructed as she attempted to pull his collar away from his skin far enough to slide the chestpiece under. "Your shirt is too snug for this. Remove it, please."

Christian did as told, hearing a soft gasp as the material left his body. He looked over at Jadyn and saw where her gaze had fallen as Nannette moved to look at his back.

"Wow," the nurse said. "That's some serious ink."

"It was a gift," he explained.

"You were given a tattoo for a gift?" Jadyn asked.

"After the attack that left me unable to remember my past, the woman who helped me said it would help me find myself. She wasn't a witch, but she practiced divination. She said the image came to her in a dream and it would help me discover who I am." He shrugged. "That was centuries ago and I still do not remember anything from before the attack. Maybe it would have worked if I hadn't been turned into a vampire shortly after receiving it."

"Two violent attacks so close to each other could have caused irreparable damage to your memory," Nannette murmured, looking over the information on her clipboard. He assumed it was full of the information Rider had given to her when arranging the appointment. With the nurse part of his nest, he could have been feeding her information telepathically the whole time he'd been with him and Jadyn.

Nannette put the clipboard aside and used the stethoscope to listen as he breathed. While she did that, the same woman who'd brought in supplies earlier returned and took the vials of blood out of the room.

"How did you calm Danni's succubus side?" Nannette asked as she finished and placed the stethoscope back on the counter.

"Succubi are demonic. I have called upon my faith in the past to destroy demons. This was the same, but less. If I destroyed the succubus part of her, she would die, so I only forced it back."

"How?"

"By calling upon my faith," he said, slowly.

"How?"

"I just told you how," he responded, baffled as to why no one ever seemed to understand what he was talking about when he explained how he destroyed demons.

Nannette and Rider shared a look before the nurse shook her head and turned her attention to Jadyn. "When did you start communicating with animals?"

"About two years ago," Jadyn answered. "And no, there were no sudden changes in my medical history or life around that time." She looked at Christian and he knew she was thinking about the crosses, but she kept that to herself. "I wasn't struck by lightning, bitten by a radioactive bug, or anything else odd. One day I just heard my cat's thoughts and then I started hearing other animals. Or catching images of what they were thinking."

"Does anyone else in your family have any special gifts or talents?"

"I come from a long line of drunks and losers. I don't think any of their talents are what you're referring to."

"Well, I didn't find any abnormalities in your heart rates or breathing patterns. Your blood will be tested for anything interesting. I'd like to run another test on both of you. We have a machine here that is very similar to an MRI but far more advanced, and attuned to the peculiarities of paranormal beings."

"You're saying you can scan people and see whether they are vampires, shifters, witches, or other paranormal types?"

"I'm saying if there's anything magical or biologically odd happening inside you I may be able to tell from what is scanned through the machine. Also, the two of you are being tracked and you know whoever is doing the hunting dabbles in dark magic. If the witch they're working with is skilled enough they could have put a magical tracker in you. This machine has been used before to find such trackers."

"Well, that sounds like a useful test," Christian said, pulling his shirt back on. "Let's definitely do that one."

"Finding out if you're being tracked magically is useful," Rider agreed, "but finding out what you are is even more useful. Have you ever thought that maybe whoever is doing the hunting knows something about you that you don't?"

Christian stood and sighed. "Of course I think knowing more about myself is important, but I've been this version of me for a long time. Seta has worked every spell, consulted every book, and she has no answers. Not even the Dream Teller has been able to tell me who I was before my attack. I'm having trouble believing your medical tests will give me answers that not even the Dream Teller can give."

"You've actually seen the Dream Teller?" Rider frowned. "I thought she was a myth."

Christian quietly scolded himself for even mentioning the Dream Teller and hoped mentioning her would not lead to any questions that would in turn lead to the Blood Revelation prophecy. "She's real."

The room grew deathly quiet as the three vampires stared each other down. It didn't take psychic skill to know he'd just blown the other two vampires' minds and they now questioned why he'd seen the Dream Teller and they hadn't. And poor Jadyn just sat still, watching them, clueless to what was going on.

"Show me the sword," Nannette finally said, breaking the silence.

"What?"

"Daniel said you held a flaming sword and it disappeared. You told Rider you just grabbed it, not even knowing about it. Do that now."

Christian looked down at his hand and the air around him as he shifted his feet awkwardly. "I don't think I can just grab it."

"Have you tried since the attack?'

"Well, no."

"Then how do you know?"

He thought about that. "I don't think I grabbed the sword so much as it came to me. It was instinct that I reached for it. I don't feel anything now."

"Try it," Rider said as he stood straight and folded his arms. "Let's see what happens."

He looked over to see Jadyn watching him as intently as the vampires, and sighed. With a shrug, he reached out and grabbed at nothing, getting nothing in return. After a few attempts of this, he felt like an utter fool and waved his hands through the air. "See? Nothing there. I don't know how I did it."

"Interesting," Nannette murmured. "Let's get both of you in the machine and see what it tells us. From what I hear, Seta is a master of magic and just being a badass in general, but applying a little medical science might just get you some of those answers you've been seeking. A man of such faith shouldn't give up so easily, especially before trying all avenues." She inclined her head toward the door, silently suggesting they follow before she opened it and stepped through.

Nannette led them down the hall, Juan and Hank following close behind until they reached another white-tiled room with a machine inside that did look very similar to an MRI machine. The security detail remained outside as the rest of them stepped into the room and assembled in the center.

Nannette looked them over. "I need any metal you have on you before you get in."

Jadyn removed the small gold hoops from her ears and handed them to the nurse. "We can do this fully clothed, right?"

"Yes," Nannette answered as she set the earrings on a table next to a computer. "This procedure works similar to a CT scan or an MRI so it is a very simple process. You simply lie down and remain still while the machine scans your body. Jadyn, we'll do you first."

Christian remained with Rider as Nannette showed Jadyn how to lie in the machine and walked back over to the computer. She pushed some buttons on her keyboard and the machine started scanning.

"It doesn't seem very magical," Christian commented.

"Trust me, the magic is there," Rider replied. "This machine was used on Danni to find out how she was being tracked by someone using dark magic. I believe Nannette is doing a more thorough scan on the two of you, given the oddity of your abilities."

After about ten minutes passed, the machine completed its scan and Nannette advised Jadyn she could get up. Christian walked over and helped her up before they gathered around the computer to see what seemed to be holding Nannette and Rider's interest on the monitor. Both of them eyed Jadyn curiously as they approached.

"What is it?" Jadyn asked, a slight quiver to her voice.

"You seem to have a small trace of some sort of energy in your center," Nannette said, pointing to an image on the screen.

Christian looked at the image, but wasn't sure what he was looking at. It looked like an ultrasound image but with far greater detail. As Nannette had said, there did appear to be something in the center of Jadyn's chest, a sliver of bright white color that appeared to glow. "What is it?"

"I'm not sure," Nannette said, shaking her head. "From the glow, I would definitely say it is a source of power or energy. It doesn't appear to be carved in, but is an actual part of her. Jadyn, have you ever felt anything odd in the center of your chest, like an energy pulsing out, or a burning sensation, anything at all?"

"No." Jadyn shook her head slowly. "Should I?"

Nannette opened her mouth to answer, but didn't, looking at Christian instead, and he realized he was rubbing the center of his own chest, right where he'd felt the strange sensation that had started around the time he reconnected with Jadyn. "Christian, do *you* feel something like that?"

He dropped his hand and took a breath. "Yeah, actually, I have felt something like that. In a way I always have, much like any vampire with any amount of psychic ability. We all feel power in our core, but since we've been on the run from whoever it is after us, I've felt a difference, a spike, I guess you could say. The energy is more intense than usual."

"Since about the time you came back into contact with Jadyn," Rider commented.

"Get in the machine," Nannette ordered, rapidly pressing keys on the keyboard.

Christian walked over to the machine, not having to be told twice. He lay down and relaxed his body the best he could, not the easiest feat as his mind raced with thoughts. Could this machine actually discover something inside him that could lead to answers no other source had been able to give him. Could it really be that easy?

He willed himself to remain calm, to not set himself up for disappointment if the machine didn't turn up anything. After all, Jadyn wasn't the same as him. The fact the weird energy was found in her might very well mean he would come up negative for the same thing. He closed his eyes and focused on quieting his mind as the machine hummed and began to scan his body.

The machine's hum turned into a strange groaning sound as his body was fully pulled through, and that groan became an ear-splitting crack of thunder as he opened his eyes to see nothing but blinding white light as if a giant flash bang had been set off and he was the unfortunate soul inside it.

CHAPTER THIRTEEN

As the white light receded, Christian realized he could see through a crack in the machine to the ceiling above. The machine no longer groaned, hummed, or made any noise. There was no noise at all. The world around him had become unnaturally quiet. He pushed at the walls around him and they fell without a sound.

He quickly sat up, relieved to find he could. He felt no pain other than the throbbing in his ears, but his heart was filled to the brim with fear. He saw Juan and Hank enter the room, panic etched into their faces, but ignored them, quickly swinging around to look for Jadyn and the two vampires who'd been in the room with him.

Relief replaced the panic as he saw Rider on his haunches, protectively shielding Jadyn with his body, and Nannette hunkered down beside him. They both were wild-eyed with shock as they came out of their crouches, revealing a trembling Jadyn. Tears streamed from her eyes, but otherwise she appeared fine, if not completely terrified. She broke away from Rider and met Christian halfway as they both ran for each other, coming together in a tight embrace.

More people rushed into the room, mouths moving, but he heard nothing. He saw Rider point to his ears and realized they'd all been deafened from the blast. Behind him, the machine was broken in half, smoking, completely beyond repair.

An older woman with long gray hair entered the room and a path was made for her as she moved straight to Rider and cupped his ears with her hands. Light escaped through her fingers as she spoke words Christian couldn't hear and Rider soon nodded, relief flooding his eyes. The woman repeated the process with Nannette.

You will be able to hear again in a moment, Rider's voice spoke into his mind as the vampire stared at him.

Christian nodded his head, saying nothing as he rubbed Jadyn's back, trying to comfort her as she continued to tremble, and waited for the woman, obviously a witch, to restore his and Jadyn's hearing.

Once Nannette nodded to the witch and spoke, giving confirmation she could hear, the woman moved to him. He gently moved Jadyn back, making sure she could see what the witch did so she wouldn't be alarmed when her turn came. Her eyes rounded in wonder as she watched the witch work her magic on him and understanding what she'd done, didn't recoil when the witch covered her ears to do the same.

The sudden noise rushing in the moment the magic worked was a little jarring after the dead silence, but a relief all the same. He could have lived without sound if he had to, but living with the knowledge he'd caused physical harm to Jadyn and the other two would have been a painful pill to swallow.

"Everyone out!" Rider commanded, his voice firm, but not hostile. "There is no danger here. Thank you, Marigold," he said to the witch as she bowed slightly in respect and left with the other members of the security team. Juan and Hank were the last two out, and they watched Christian warily until they exited the room, pulling the door closed behind them.

"You broke my machine," Nannette said as she tapped at her keyboard. "I loved that machine."

"I'll pay for it," Christian offered.

"Appreciated," Rider said, moving toward the broken machine to survey the damage, "but not necessary. It's insured. Fortunately, we use an agency operated by vampires. We'd have a hell of a time explaining this to a human-run insurance agency."

"What happened? I heard the machine groan once I was completely inside and then it just..."

"Damn near exploded," Rider offered. "There was a thunderous crack as it split down the middle and then bright white light everywhere. I thought we were about to all be obliterated."

"I'm trying to get a good image," Nannette said, tapping furiously at the keyboard. "I was watching through the monitor as it happened and I saw the same white energy show up in the center of your chest, but it wasn't a sliver like Jadyn's. It was much wider, and clearly more concentrated. Damn it, the images that were actually captured are just whiteness. It's as if the energy inside you sensed it was being studied and didn't like it one bit."

"You're telling me I have some strange energy inside of me, and it attacked the machine?"

"Energy, power..." Nannette said, shrugging as she gave up on the images and stepped away from the computer. "Whatever it is, it is one hell of a force, and yes, I think it felt threatened, or maybe it felt you were threatened, and it lashed out, destroying my favorite machine."

"I'm sorry," Christian apologized again, sincerely meaning it.

"Don't be. That was one of the most amazing things I've seen within these walls, and I've been in this field for a long time."

"And we definitely know you are not just a vampire now," Rider said, walking back over to them. "Nannette has used that machine on a large variety of paranormal beings. No one has ever done anything close to that."

"Why didn't I break it?" Jadyn asked, speaking for the first time since the incident. She stood at Christian's side, her arms folded protectively in front of her as she leaned into him, sheltered by the arm he draped protectively around her shoulders. "You said I had the same energy. Even if it wasn't as concentrated, wouldn't it have reacted the same way?"

"Not necessarily," Nannette answered. "Think of it like poison. A person could be given a drop of poison every single day and never get more than sick, but a whole cup of poison? Instant death. Or chemistry. A little bit of a particular chemical in a beaker of solution can make a stink, but pour in too much and you set fire to the lab. I believe the two of you have something similar inside you, but Christian's is a higher concentration."

"Or it is purer," Rider suggested. "Jadyn hasn't even been alive three decades. Christian has been around much longer. It makes sense that her bloodline could have been diluted."

"Excellent observation," Nannette said. "That is very possible."

"I cannot communicate with animals in the way she does," Christian reminded them. "If I have a higher concentration of whatever this is inside us, shouldn't I have the same abilities she has in addition to whatever I have?"

"Not necessarily," Nannette said. "Some vampires without any psychic power at all can sire fledglings with a great deal of psychic power. Witches come with a variety of talents. The source of your power can be the same, but still give you different talents. Jadyn can communicate with animals. You pull flaming swords out of thin air."

"Clearly, both of you are protectors," Rider commented. "Her power is more nurturing, however, and attuned to animals, whereas yours is more that of a warrior. Maybe you're right about the sword. It came to you because the power in you called to it."

"Why now?" Christian asked. "All this time, all the times I've found myself in danger or needed to protect someone else, and I never drew that sword until this last attack."

"You were with her," Nannette murmured, looking at Jadyn.

"Could their energies have reacted to each other?" Rider asked, rubbing his chin as he studied them.

"It's possible." Nannette nodded, continuing to stare at them as she processed this new concept. "For whatever reason, her power was dormant until two years ago so they wouldn't have reacted to each other, at least not strongly enough to be noticed, when they'd met during her childhood, but now that they've reconnected..."

"The connection is making them stronger," Rider finished.

"Fascinating," Nannette said softly, agreeing. "Hopefully their blood will tell us more so we can figure out what exactly they are."

"I haven't heard an explosion from the lab so I'm guessing their blood isn't as volatile," Rider said dryly.

"The power seems to be centered in their core, so no, their blood wouldn't react the same. Thankfully, I should say, since it would have probably knocked me on my ass when I drew it." Nannette studied Jadyn; her eyes narrowed in thought before she moved her gaze to Christian. "You're a minister, and you work with humans?"

"Yes," Christian answered. "I welcome all to my churches."

"So you have to move constantly." She looked at Jadyn again. "What state did you two first meet in?"

"New Jersey," Christian answered. "I left a couple years after I secured a new family living arrangement for Jadyn. I was in Baltimore from then until the night of the attack. I had actually just packed up to leave when it happened."

"And that was when the two of you reunited? Jadyn, you came to Baltimore later without knowing Christian was there?"

Jadyn nodded.

"Why?"

She looked at him, seeking approval.

"We can trust them," Christian told her. "I don't see any reason why we should be secretive about the crosses, and maybe they can help us to discover more about them."

"What crosses?" Rider asked, his eyes lit with suspicion. "I told you I expected complete honesty."

"We have told no lies," Christian assured him. "I have seen crosses lighting my way various times I have found the need to relocate without much notice. Jadyn saw the same crosses around the time she started communicating with animals. Those crosses led her to Baltimore two years ago."

"What kind of crosses?" Nannette asked.

"Glowing crosses only we can see," Christian answered. "I usually see them on buildings, and I've always taken them to indicate shelter. I saw one on the house we took shelter in after we fled the church. That was the only time I've been attacked while staying in a building marked with one."

"I saw one on Christian's church the night he rescued me," Jadyn added, "but after that night I never saw them again until two years ago, like Christian said. I saw one on the bus station and when I went inside, I looked at the destinations and Baltimore shone brighter than every other city listed. I saw one on the bus and on the signs leading to the city. That was two years ago. I didn't see another one until I reunited with Christian."

Nannette and Rider looked at each other, bemused. "That definitely sounds like someone guiding them," the nurse said.

"Crosses are religious symbols," Rider added. "He is a minister, so it makes sense for him."

"So, what, they have a guardian angel, like, a for real guardian angel?"

"Demons are real," the vampire said. "The idea of angels isn't any crazier. I believe there is a God. The bible speaks of angels."

"But have you or anyone you've ever known actually seen one?" Nannette countered.

"I have," Christian said.

All three heads turned toward him. Jadyn's mouth fell open. "You've actually seen an angel?"

"A fallen one," Christian said, "but I met him after he was no longer an angel. He was turned after falling, but he's not even a vampire anymore now. It's a long story and there was a prophecy involved, but he sacrificed himself to save the life of the woman he loved. That woman is Marilee."

"Holy crap," Jadyn said, the words barely a whisper.

"After the sacrifice, he was given a chance at life, as a human."

"This fallen angel, have you asked him about the crosses?" Nannette asked.

"He claims he doesn't remember anything from when he was an angel," Christian told them as he removed his arm from around Jadyn's shoulders and shoved his hands into his pockets. The image of Khiderian he'd seen at the house before the attack flashed through his mind again.

"Claims?" Rider raised an eyebrow. "You don't believe him?"

"I've never had reason not to," Christian answered despite the memory of his image niggling at the back of his mind. Why had he seen it when he'd opened his senses to Jadyn? Why had he thought of him after seeing the golden-eyed woman?

"Where is this fallen angel now?"

"He works with a friend in Baltimore, doing surveillance and security work," Christian answered. "He's on assignment. I don't know where."

"Find out. He may have answers. Maybe you just need to coax them out, or I could take a stab at it. I can be very convincing." Rider moved behind him. "Let me see this tattoo again."

JADYN HELD HER BREATH as Christian grabbed the hem of his shirt and peeled the black material from his body, revealing the tattoo that covered his entire back. As Nannette moved closer, she took a step back, staying between but behind the two vampires, where they, hopefully, wouldn't see the blush she felt creeping into her cheeks.

She'd had a crush on Christian since the moment he'd rescued her, natural given he'd literally been her hero, and he was a very attractive man. Actually, he was beautiful, a word she'd never used to describe a man, but handsome wasn't quite sufficient, not with those perfectly proportioned lips, a Greek nose so flawless it could have been carved from marble, and crystalline blue eyes almost too pure to be real. She'd known he was a gorgeous man, but she'd had no idea his body was also a work of art. She'd gasped when she'd first seen the tattoo, but despite the shock of the image, her reaction had mostly come from the surprise of Christian being built like a man who spent a lot of time at the gym, not the church. He was lean, but he was all muscled, golden perfection. Not even the black ink etched into his skin could be considered an imperfection.

"What do you know about the woman who gave you this, other than what you already told us?" Nannette asked.

"I told you pretty much everything I remember about her," Christian said, his voice almost sad. "I can't even remember what she looked like, to tell the truth. I can't remember her name. I only know she was kind; she gave me shelter and sustenance, and I remember her giving me this."

"I bet," Rider murmured. "It had to hurt like a sonofabitch."

"I slept through it."

Rider raised a disbelieving eyebrow and Nannette snorted. "With my medical knowledge, as well as my knowledge of how tattoos used to be created, I am willing to bet by 'slept through it' you mean you passed out from the pain?"

Christian turned his head to look at the nurse. Jadyn could see a grin curving his mouth from that angle. "Either way, I was unconscious."

"Men," Nannette muttered as she traced her fingertips over the tattoo.

Jadyn's fingers curled into fists as she bit her tongue, but said nothing, instantly feeling ridiculous for the little spark of jealousy. Nannette was a medical professional. She knew better than to think of the woman's exploration as anything other than an examination, even if her own fingers wanted to reach out and trace every line of the tattoo, and her reasoning wasn't the least bit medical. Not trusting herself to be able to focus if she touched the gorgeous man before her, she followed Nannette's fingers with her eyes as they moved over the lines.

The tattoo had been created with only black ink, which may have been the only ink available during the time Christian had received it. Her knowledge of tattoos wasn't vast, and she'd never been much of a historian in general either. A figure had been drawn in the center of Christian's back. A man, bald, his face turned up toward the sky. His body was muscular, giving the sense of great strength, his arms spread wide, but low enough he didn't appear to be challenging. He almost seemed to be offering himself. She could picture him kneeling, opening his arms as if giving himself to the heavens, but the figure had no legs.

Two giant wings joined at the base of the figure's torso, stretching out to cover Christian's back from the base of his spine to over his shoulders. Some of the feathers along the top were tall enough to reach the back of his neck, and had she ever paid attention before, she was sure she'd have seen them peeking out over the back of his collar.

"Interesting design," Nannette murmured. "I can't quite tell if the wings belong to the man, or if they belong to Christian and the man is merely trapped inside them."

"I noticed that," Rider agreed. "They look like they could start at Christian's shoulders, but they also look like they belong to the man in the tattoo."

Jadyn had noticed this as well. She peered closer, trying to pinpoint where the wings began, but couldn't. The man could be using the wings to fly, or he could have been wrapped inside of them with no connection himself. Maybe the man and Christian were connected *through* the wings. "Maybe the wings belong to both," she said. "The man has no legs. His body seems to stop beneath the torso."

"It's like he's bursting out of him," Rider said, studying the design. "The woman said this would help you understand who you are?"

"Yes," Christian answered. "Unfortunately, she never gave any further information. She had a dream and saw this image, saw that it would tell me who I am, where I came from, but it has only served as another mystery."

"Did she tell you who the man is supposed to be?" Nannette asked. "Is he supposed to be you?"

"She didn't say, and I was turned before I ever saw the healed tattoo. Honestly, I forgot its existence until Eron saw it and questioned me. Maybe it would have triggered something had I seen it before the second attack. Maybe the turning wiped out any chance I ever had of discovering its meaning. Seta tried revealing spells, but the tattoo wouldn't give up its secrets to the magic."

"The man doesn't look like Christian," Jadyn stated the obvious. "He is strong though, very powerful. He almost looks like..."

"If Christian had no skin," Nannette said, drawing grimaces from the rest of them. "Sorry," she apologized, with a small laugh. "The figure almost looks like the figures you would find in any anatomy book. If this tattoo had color, it would almost look like a drawing of the musculoskeletal system."

"Why would he have an image like that on him?" Jadyn asked. "What could that mean?"

"It's art," Rider said. "Art isn't always literal. Sometimes it's symbolic." He leaned forward, narrowing his eyes. "If this is a drawing of the musculoskeletal system then the man could represent man in general. This could mean Christian himself, or it could mean humanity."

"His humanity?"

Rider glanced at her and nodded before returning his focus on the tattoo. "You know, between this image, the power inside him, and the glowing crosses thing, I'm thinking angel isn't too crazy of an idea."

"No." Christian abruptly stood, pulling his shirt back on in the process, but not before he turned, giving Jadyn a clear view of rock-hard abs. She might have drooled over them a bit, if not for the anger in Christian's eyes. He shook his head adamantly. "That is not a possibility."

Rider folded his arms and pinned Christian with a steely gaze. "You have some sort of power source inside you that neither of us has ever seen or heard of despite our years, a source so powerful it destroyed a machine designed to withstand any paranormal forces, you see glowing crosses that people around you do not see, you have giant wings on your back, and you pulled a flaming sword out of nowhere."

"I am not an angel."

"You spoke to the demonic force inside Danni, and it was afraid."

"Faith is a powerful thing."

"That is true," Rider agreed, "but I bet that faith is a thousand times more powerful when it comes from an angel."

"Not a fallen angel," Christian snapped. "Don't you understand?"

Rider nodded. "To be an angel on earth, you would have had to fall."

Jadyn's mouth parted as her eyes burned with the threat of tears, realizing why Christian seemed so upset at the thought of being an angel. A man of his faith would see the act of an angel falling from Heaven to be the greatest betrayal any being could ever commit.

"Christian, think about it," Rider said softly, his body braced in expectation of a possible assault as Christian's eyes darkened, his shoulders tensing. "Is it possible that you do not remember the first beating because you were not beaten by men, but instead injured yourself in the fall?"

"No," Christian growled, his head bowed, fists clenched.

"You're overlooking something," Jadyn quickly jumped in, afraid Christian would lose his temper and lunge at the powerful vampire if Rider kept pushing him with an idea he clearly didn't accept. "You said Christian and I have the same energy or power source, or whatever, inside us. I have no memory loss, I have never suffered any sort of major head injury, and trust me, I don't come from people remotely angelic. I would know if I was an angel, even part angel, and whatever he is, I have to be a little bit of too, right?"

"She has a point," Nannette said. "Their energy appears very similar and they have a connection. Her abilities started two years ago. I don't think people suddenly just become angels, nor would I think of it as a recessive gene humans are harboring."

Rider looked at her and sighed. "Well, then, I got nothing."

"As I said earlier, hopefully their blood will tell us more. I will notify you immediately with anything I learn, and I will reach out to colleagues to see if anyone knows anything, discreetly of course."

"Very discreetly," Rider warned. "Not knowing what the hell they are means we also don't know who all could be after them. Hopefully my tech team can find something on who attacked them earlier and we can figure things out from that angle. With any luck, I'll have one of the bastards in interrogation soon."

"You think the people after us will reveal all they know to you?" Christian asked.

Rider shared a cold grin with Nannette. The gleam in his eyes sent a chill down Jadyn's spine. "When I get someone in interrogation, they spill everything."

Rider moved toward the door. "We've done all we can here. Let's get back to The Midnight Rider. The two of you can eat, drink, rest, whatever you need to do." He opened the door and led them through, giving the two men he'd left outside a silent instruction with a simple head gesture. They fell into step behind them as they moved in the direction of the elevator.

The ride up to the parking lot was silent and a little uneasy. He no longer looked like a raging bull about to charge, but Christian's shoulders hadn't relaxed since the possibility of being an angel had come up. Jadyn ached to reach over and hold his hand, offer some small form of comfort, but didn't feel comfortable. Sure, he'd draped his arm over her shoulders after the machine had broken, but he was a protector. Draping his arm over her shoulders could be as innocent as a bird sheltering a smaller bird under its wing. She cautioned herself not to read too much into the action, or the gentle kiss he'd pressed against her forehead. A real kiss would have been on the lips. For all she knew, he looked at her and still saw the child he'd rescued in New Jersey. He might never see anything more than that child looking back at him.

Despite being a normal human, or mostly normal, at least biologically, and not sharing the telepathic bond Rider had spoken of earlier, Jadyn felt the shift in the air between the men as they exited the elevator and got into the SUVs, and know they were communicating with each other, all of them on guard against attack, which fortunately didn't come.

Once again, she and Christian rode in the back of one SUV as Rider drove, Hank next to him in the passenger seat. Another SUV led the way while a third followed behind them. Christian stared out the window on his side, his chin resting on his hand as he rubbed his fingers over the skin, pensive. Rider glanced back at them through the rear view mirror every few minutes, but said nothing, and Hank appeared to be on alert, continuously scanning the streets for signs of danger.

Jadyn took the opportunity to analyze everything she'd learned in the underworld ward as they continued on in silence. She and Christian both had some sort of power inside them, something similar. Whatever it was, Christian had more of it. She could totally buy the angel explanation with him, if only it didn't mean he had fallen. The man who'd saved her life would have never done that. He was far too noble, far too good. Even if he was literally a blood-sucking vampire, he was the kindest, most genuinely *good* man she'd ever come across. The kind of man whose heart would shatter at the thought of betraying his heavenly father.

With that thought, she reached out and squeezed his hand, her heart skipping a beat as he lightly squeezed hers back. Then her heart skipped several more beats as images quickly flashed through her mind along with the sound of flapping wings and warning cries.

"You might want to step on the gas," she told Rider as she looked around and recognized a few of the buildings as being close to the bar. "Someone is following us."

CHAPTER FOURTEEN

Kiara froze as a garden loomed before her. It was beautiful, bright, and sunny with flowers of every color, the clearest sky, and a sense of warmth that wafted over into the cerulean forest she'd just reached the edge of. It was also very familiar. It had to be the way.

She moved forward into the garden where the sound of birdsongs engulfed her, the beautiful sound welcome after the seemingly endless silence she'd trekked through to reach this place. She passed a large tree with multicolored vines spiraling up its trunk, knowing she would see a waterfall before she took the turn left.

She turned full circle, sensing her whereabouts. No, she had not stepped into Heaven, but this place was a close replica. She could only think of one reason why this part of the dream realm would mirror a garden she'd spent time in before, a garden Aurorian and she had frequently visited before he'd left their home.

"You know what I seek," she spoke aloud, knowing the realm was not just a place. In a sense, it too lived and breathed. "Where can I find what I need?"

She stood still, listening, but the answer did not come as easily as she had hoped. The bird's song did not change, the flowers did not move, the waterfall flowed exactly as it had before. She did not sense a change in anything and no words appeared. She closed her eyes and looked inside herself. Krystaline knew the dream realm better than anyone and had told her she already knew the answers she sought before sending her on this journey. What did she already know?

"I know Aurorian." She opened her eyes and looked around. "I know he loved this place. He loved Heaven. He loved, *loves*, our Father. He has never truly left ..." She looked up, past the waterfall where she knew she would find a ledge. "He never truly left us."

She ran past the waterfall, toward the place she knew answers would be found.

"FOLLOWING US HOW?" Rider asked, sending out a pulse of power as he communicated with his team. All three vehicles sped up.

Christian looked over at Jadyn, noticing the strain in her face as she squeezed her eyes closed and barely breathed. "She's focusing on the animals. They must be able to detect the magic before one of those portals open. Birds warned her before the first portal opened."

"Those kinds of birds?" Rider pointed up.

Christian ducked a little for a better view at what Rider looked at through the windshield. A dark blanket of birds briefly covered the moon before diving down to light upon buildings. His vampiric sight allowed him to tell they were assorted breeds and sizes, ranging from small robins to large hawks, even owls. None of the more predatory birds appeared to care about the smaller prey among them, almost as if a truce were being drawn while they helped Jadyn.

"Yes. If a portal opens up here it'll be really bad. Dozens of shifters came through last time. This area is nowhere near as secluded as where we were in West Virginia."

"We're almost to The Midnight Rider." The SUV in front of them took a hard left and Rider followed suit, raising his hand to click the remote door opener as they entered the alley behind his bar. He slowed a fraction to allow a turn into the garage before parking and clicking the remote to lower the door.

"Will the others be all right?" Christian asked, noting that the garage seemed to only be for Rider's personal vehicles.

"Those portals seem to only be opening for you," Rider answered as he turned the ignition off. "One or both of you appear to be what they're homing in on. They shouldn't have any trouble with whoever is after you. If they do, they're trained to kick ass. How's she doing?"

Christian looked over at Jadyn, saw her rubbing her temples, and reached over to squeeze her shoulder. "Are you all right?"

She nodded as she expelled a breath, opening her wet eyes. "Yeah, I'm good. It's a lot of noise when so many of them start speaking at the same time. They could feel a shift in the air, sensed a predator circling, and they were afraid."

"Can you still hear them?" Rider asked.

"Yes, but they are calmer. Still nervous, but they know we are safe now. Apparently, they can sense we are protected inside here."

"The bird early warning system may come in handy," Rider said, nodding to himself as he opened his door. "Come on."

Jadyn looked over at Christian with raised eyebrows. He shrugged, not sure what the vampire was up to, but he trusted him so he quickly got out of the vehicle, waited for Jadyn, and followed the man out of the garage and through the door across the hall from it.

"If we're lucky my tech team may have picked up on something. We were close to the building when we got the warning from the birds and they always have this general area under surveillance anyway," Rider explained as he descended the stairs at a fast clip. "If any dark magic spiked in the area there's a good chance they caught it."

Rider placed his hand on the access panel and opened the door, entering the room where his tech team busily tapped away on keyboards, their gazes alternating between the large plasma screen at the front of the room and their own screens.

"We picked up on strange energy circling you as you left the hospital," a thin woman with dark hair styled in two ponytails at her nape said, immediately rising from her workstation to cross over to the plasma screen.

She wore a corduroy skirt, a navy and green sweater, and clunky shoes with thick knee-high socks. Christian opened his senses and was surprised to discover the woman was paranormal, but nothing he'd ever come across before.

"We got a minor blip before you reached the hospital," she continued as they met her at the front of the room and watched as surveillance footage of their convoy pulled up. "All was quiet while you were inside, except there was a huge surge from the hospital itself. We checked in and Juan informed us what had happened there." She eyed Christian curiously for a moment before turning her attention back to the screen. The footage had been sped up and now showed them leaving. "Not long after you left the protection of the hospital things got weird. We noticed a large amount of birds, even birds that should have long been asleep, closing in on you. Around this same time we picked up dark energy right here."

The woman fiddled with a remote in her hand, freezing the image on screen and panning out to what looked like a dark cloud hovering in the middle of the street. As she moved in closer, Christian recognized it as looking very similar to the portal in West Virginia before it opened.

"Can you track it?" Rider asked, his gaze never leaving the screen.

"We're working on it. We know it's dark and powerful." She shuddered. "Very powerful. It would have been very bad if that had opened."

"Yes, downtown Louisville is not a good spot for an all-out paranormal battle," Rider agreed. He turned and eyed Jadyn. "If whoever is behind these attacks is brazen enough to even consider opening a portal in an area so highly populated by humans, maybe we should bring the fight to them, ensuring a location that won't risk discovery."

"How do you propose to do that?" Christian asked, moving close enough to Jadyn to feel her body heat pressing against his front.

Rider's gaze shifted to him. "Bait, but relax, I won't use her ...unless you turn out to be a dud. We haven't yet figured out whether they're tracking one of you or both of you. I will, however, definitely use her access to the animals to warn us when we're about to be attacked."

"What's he talking about?" Jadyn turned toward Christian, eyes wide.

"He thinks he can dangle me out in the open and get one of these portals to open," Christian explained. "It's not a bad idea as long as the situation is controlled, and as long as Jadyn stays out of harm's way," he added, holding Rider's gaze. "Despite her incredible ability, she's still a human with all the fragility that comes with that."

"Understood, and I have no intention of putting her in danger."

"You know if one of these portals opens up all the way, a whole lot of trouble will spill through, the kind of trouble you're going to have to kill. We have no idea how deep that well of trouble runs."

"I only need to keep one alive for questioning," Rider said with the confidence of a man used to winning as he turned his attention back to the woman with the ponytails. "Any indication how they're being tracked?"

The woman glanced at Christian before answering. "The energy that flared while at the hospital was extremely powerful. A disturbance like that gets noticed, especially if whoever is after them already knows it exists. They could be scanning for it just as we're continuously scanning for their dark energy. The portal didn't open immediately, but it started to open close enough after you left, I wouldn't be surprised if they already had the area pinpointed and were just waiting for the source of that energy to come out into the open."

Rider took the remote from the woman and pressed a button, unfreezing the screen. They watched in silence, watching themselves return to the shelter of Rider's property. The partially formed portal disappeared soon after. The vampire fast-forwarded until surveillance showed the property in real time. Panning out, they still saw several birds perched atop buildings, including The Midnight Rider and surrounding properties.

"Unless they're completely ignorant, it won't be hard for whoever is after you to figure out where you are, even if the warding here blocks out whatever signal it is you're sending out," Rider said, speaking aloud the very thought that had just entered Christian's mind upon seeing the footage. "Those birds are like a neon sign pointing right to this building."

"I can tell them to leave," Jadyn said.

"No." Rider frowned at her. "Don't do that."

"But you said whoever is after us will know we're in this building. They'll swarm us here like they did at the house in West Virginia."

"They wouldn't dare," Rider assured her. "I might not know who we're dealing with ...yet, but there's no way they don't know who they're dealing with now. They won't attack you while you're inside my building. They'll send in a spy, someone they expect to fly in under the radar."

"And that's a good thing?" Jadyn asked.

"That's a very good thing," Rider answered with a slow spreading grin. "Like I said, I only need one."

"Hopefully it isn't the one who likes to tear roofs off of buildings," Jadyn murmured before worrying her bottom lip with her teeth.

"I think it's a safe bet to say The Midnight Rider can withstand a great deal more than that rundown house we took shelter in," Christian said, nudging her with his arm. "My actual home beneath the church was warded against fire and intrusion. I'm sure Rider has had his property bespelled as well."

"Some areas more warded than others," Rider said, "but Christian is right. There will be no ripping the roof off my building and no burning us out. As you can see, my tech team is surveilling the area, and my staff is predominantly nonhuman and more than capable of sensing other nonhumans that may come sniffing around. Humans attacked at the church so we know whoever is doing this is working with them. That's who they will probably send in to scout around, thinking they won't set off any bells and whistles, but my people are trained to know when someone's shady. I'll be in the bar tonight myself, watching."

"I'll be with you," Christian told him. "I've seen some of these people."

"So have I," Jadyn reminded him.

"I'm aware of that, but you'll be safe in the room Rider provided, getting the sleep you have to be craving by now."

"I'm fine."

"You haven't slept since last night."

"I said I'm fine." She folded her arms and stared at him. "All I need is coffee."

"We have plenty of that upstairs," Rider cut in, seeming to sense Christian wasn't going to win the argument. "Follow me."

Jadyn shot Christian a smug look and followed Rider. Christian trailed after them, shaking his head. He knew Rider wouldn't be lax in security considering security was his whole business, but he'd feel better if Jadyn was tucked away below the bar, not right in the area accessible to the general public.

They took the stairs up to the first floor and passed the garage and the staircase leading up to the second floor. Christian glanced up the staircase, seeing a door to the left, nothing to the right.

"That's my private quarters," Rider said, noticing. "The Midnight Rider is through here," he added as he continued forward toward the sound of music, and stepped through the door he'd used when leading them from his office to the garage earlier. This time instead of taking a right and going to his office they went through to the actual bar.

"Welcome to The Midnight Rider," Rider said, stretching his hand out in a sweeping gesture.

Christian stopped next to him, positioning himself so Jadyn was behind and between them, and looked around. The room was a decent size with the actual bar sitting dead center. It was a square bar with one bartender, an Asian man who gave off a feline shifter vibe, tending all four sides effortlessly. Booths lined the walls and tables filled in the rest of the room, with exception to a small space near the jukebox, a decent size for dancing. To his left, he saw the signs for the bathrooms, and to his right, a kitchen area he imagined servers coming in and out of with stacks of onion rings and chicken wings dripping with barbecue sauce during the busier hours. At the current late hour, the bar appeared to be packed with people wanting alcohol and alcohol only.

"That's the only way in or out," Rider said, nodding toward the front door which was guarded by two hulking shifters. "We have an emergency exit, of course, due to fire safety laws, but an alarm will ring loud enough to wake the dead if it's even breathed on."

"What about the way we just came in?" Christian asked inclining his head toward the door they'd walked through. "The garage leads into that back hallway."

"No one can get in through the garage without the access code which is now only shared with three people including myself."

"Now?" Christian asked, picking up on something in Rider's tone. "You had a security issue before because of that access code, didn't you?"

"An employee shared it with a hunter, which is why it is now regularly changed and only I and two very trusted employees know it. The employee who betrayed me was taken care of."

"Fired?"

"Beheaded."

"No wonder you and Seta work well together," Christian murmured.

"We get the job done." Rider scanned the room with hawk-like eyes. "I'm surprised she isn't more involved in this. Whatever she's dealing with right now must be huge."

"She thinks you're sufficient enough for this job," Christian said, afraid the man was fishing for information. "And you owed her favors. Knowing her as well as I do, I know it was easier for her to call in that favor on my behalf than to ask for help for herself."

"True." Rider's mouth curved up at the edges for a brief moment. "That woman would be covered in her own blood and barely holding on to life before admitting she couldn't handle something. Still, she is very protective about those she holds close and I've heard enough to know you are pretty much family to her."

"We are family and she would be by my side in a flash if she felt the situation grave enough. This may be the first time I've pulled a sword out of the air, but it isn't the first time I've been run out of a church and stalked." Christian shrugged. "I haven't told her everything. Like you, she has collected her fair share of enemies. Until I know whether whomever is after me wants me for me, or because they know I'm a way to get to her, I'd rather leave her out of this."

"For what it's worth, I'm sure they want you both for whatever that energy is you have inside of you, but I respect the fact you don't want to bring danger to your friends. Loyalty is worth more than gold." Rider frowned. "That reminds me, we still haven't figured out why you can see imortium. I'm going to dig deeper into that. I'll contact the agency that has been working with the Imortians transitioning to this realm and see if they have any idea. Maybe you were there prior to losing your memory. If that's the case and we get lucky, someone may remember you. Imortians are people of great magical power. Some of them are even immortal like us. Even those who haven't leveled up to immortality age much slower once they reach their peak physical age."

"Daniel didn't seem much older than he looked."

"Daniel hasn't reached his peak physical form yet. The jackass," the vampire muttered under his breath.

Christian knew there was a story there, and couldn't help but think it had to do with the fact Daniel had been assigned to watch over the woman Rider loved. Rider wasn't the type he'd expect to feel jealousy given the man's off the charts confidence level and reputation for being a ladies man, nor would he expect the vampire to assign someone he felt threatened by to guard his most prized possession, but he knew very little about the kind of love between Rider and his fledgling. He looked over at Jadyn and knew in his heart if putting someone he felt threatened by in charge of her was the best thing to keep her safe he would do it. He frowned, wondering where that thought came from. Before he could ponder it much longer, Jadyn released a good-sized yawn.

"You should get some rest," he told her.

Her eyes narrowed. "I missed the part where you adopted me and took charge of my schedule. I'm getting coffee and I'm staying up here with you."

Rider chuckled. "Why don't you two take that corner booth in the back? It's the perfect vantage point to see all areas of the bar at once without sticking out like a sore thumb. I'll grab her that coffee, and something for you?"

"I'd appreciate that," Christian said, deciding to stay tanked up in case things went sideways unexpectedly, and added through their telepathic link, *Make that coffee decaf.*

The vampire nodded, barely suppressing a grin as he moved over to the bar, leaving them.

Christian looked down at the small woman. "You can be a bit bratty, you know that?"

She stuck her tongue out at him, earning a smile. He couldn't help it. She was cute. He placed his hand along the small of her back and guided her to the corner booth, allowing her to sit first before sliding in next to her, positioned so he could see everything.

"Why does he need a phone if he can talk to people in their heads?" Jadyn asked, nodding toward Rider who stood at the bar speaking on a cell phone.

"That only works if a link is established and the other party is within range."

"So, West Virginia is in range of Kentucky? He's been speaking telepathically with Daniel all this time, hasn't he?"

"He has. They have a strong bond. I believe Daniel is part of Rider's nest and there may also be other things going on between them. Different types of bonds get different results as far as telepathic communication goes."

"Nest," Jadyn said, seeming to try out the word on her tongue before giving her head a small shake. "I'm not sure this will ever stop being weird."

"You're handling it all rather well for someone who had no idea any of this world existed."

She shrugged. "I talk to animals, and even before I could do that I was always the weird girl in school. My classmates weren't my friends. My friends were a family of opossums that lived in the tree outside my bedroom window. I guess I'm accustomed to weirdness."

"I'm sorry to hear that. From what I remember, you were a good kid. A little shy, but bright and warm. I can't imagine why kids didn't adore you."

She blushed a little as her heavy-lidded gaze dropped to the table. "You know what my childhood was like before you rescued me. After that, I didn't have actual parents in my life anymore. I lived with my aunt and uncle, who were great, but didn't have a lot of money so I didn't wear the best clothes. I had no athletic ability, spent all my time with animals, even volunteering to clean up their poop at the zoo, and let's face it, I didn't fit in aesthetically either. I was a pasty half-Asian kid with a mop of curls and green eyes. I didn't fit in with the Asian kids who at least knew about where they came from. My mother never taught me anything about our culture. The Asian kids thought I wanted to be white because I knew nothing I should have known, and the white kids made fun of me because they said I looked weird with my eyes that were too slanted to be white and too green to be Asian. I've always been a freak so I guess this just doesn't faze me very much."

Christian felt his nostrils flare as he looked at the woman next to him and imagined the younger version suffering under the weight of hurtful words piled upon her by ignorant people, words that clearly still affected her.

"You have never been a freak, and you never looked weird. You were unique then and you still are. It's that uniqueness that makes you stand out from the rest. Combined with the warmness of your heart, and the loving nurture you give to those in need of your help, you are easily one of the most beautiful women I have ever laid eyes upon in all my years."

She turned her bright eyes, now coated in a sheer film of water, to him and opened her mouth, a slight parting of soft pink lips, but said nothing, the words seeming to die as their gazes locked. Christian lowered his gaze to those inviting lips and felt a pull to do something he'd never desired to do before.

CHAPTER FIFTEEN

"**O**ne coffee and one very bloody mary."

Christian almost jerked back, Rider's voice snapping him out of the almost dream-like state he'd fallen into. He looked up to see the vampire staring down at him, the hint of a grin tugging at the corner of his mouth.

"Did I interrupt anything?"

"No," he and Jadyn both said quickly. Too quickly. He picked up the dark bottle that had been set before him and took a drink of the warm blood, giving himself something to do as he gathered his wits. He felt heat creeping into his cheeks and the knowing look on Rider's face didn't help to diminish it.

"I made a call to the Moonlight Agency," the vampire said as he slid into the opposite side of the booth and scanned the room. "My tech team is sending them your picture now. They'll check with their contacts in Imortia and see if anyone knows who or what you are."

Christian started to ask how Rider had obtained a picture of him, but a quick look around showed cameras strategically placed around the room. Between the expensive vehicles in his garage and the fact Rider ran his security business in multiple states as well as bars and other businesses, bringing in multiple streams of income, Christian knew the man could afford the best technology which included cameras capable of getting a clear image good enough for identification.

Jadyn made a sound close to a gag as she set her coffee mug on the table, her mouth puckered. She directed a dark look at him. "This isn't decaf, is it?"

"No," Rider answered in his place to help him avoid having to lie. "Hey, we're vampires. Coffee isn't really what we drink so ours might not be the best, but it helps sober up humans who drink more than they can handle."

Jadyn held his gaze a moment, searching for signs of deceit, but Rider Knight had an impressive poker face. She finally gave up, her nose wrinkling as she looked down into the mug. "Good thing you run a bar and not a coffeehouse."

Rider's eyes almost twinkled with mischief as he shared a look with Christian before returning his gaze to the woman at his side. Christian looked over at her, noting how heavy her eyelids appeared to be growing.

You'll have her in bed where you want her in no time, Rider spoke into his mind. Christian delivered a cutting glare to the man, but the powerful vampire only grinned before redirecting his attention to the room. "I'm going to move around so this isn't so conspicuous. It's mostly humans in here right now, most inebriated enough I know they have nothing to do with whoever is after you. We might not even get lucky tonight. They may wait until we close and reopen during the day, thinking we'll be weaker and a human won't be noticed as much."

"What's the plan for that?" Christian asked, knowing he'd need sleep at some point himself. "What's daylight security like?"

"The majority of my staff are vampires or shifters with a small amount of other paranormals mixed in, and a few trustworthy, capable humans. I actually sent one of my best human guards to meet you in West Virginia and escort you here, but you needed assistance sooner. He and the shifter I sent with him are on their way back now. I have plenty of manpower available for all shifts. Besides, I don't sleep too well lately." Rider's gaze took on a faraway look, touched with a hint of sadness. "Get as much rest as you need during the day and don't worry. I'll be up, and during the short time I may actually sleep myself, I have people in place. Pity the dumbass who thinks a daytime strike will get them any kind of advantage in one of my properties."

"There will be guards outside our room?" Jadyn asked, setting her drained mug on the table. She made a face as the taste of her last gulp worked its way through her system, and Christian picked up on her fear, realizing she wasn't determined to stay awake due to stubbornness alone.

"There will be, for your protection as well as for my own peace of mind. I generally do not have people outside my organization within the sublevels of The Midnight Rider, at least not people I intend to allow to continue to exist. If I didn't trust Seta as much as I do, I wouldn't be so accommodating. I want you to feel welcome, but I also need to feel secure. No one should be able to get past this room anyway, but yes, there are added layers of protection. You will have privacy inside your room, but you will be monitored every second you spend out of it, as will be anyone who sets foot into The Midnight Rider."

"And we'll be allowed to continue to exist?" she asked, eyes wary.

"Yes. Otherwise, I would have shown you to interrogation, not the room I've offered. You'll find the room has been stocked with groceries and toiletries since you first saw it, by the way. Not much since I hope to get this whole mess resolved quickly, but enough to hold you over for a few days and nights if you want anything to eat that hasn't been fried, or just want to stay in the room." He looked around the bar and stood. "Reach out if you need anything. Otherwise, try to rest and relax. Security is my business, and I'm good at it. Even if you don't see me, I see you. I see everything."

"He's not bragging," Christian told her as the powerful vampire walked away, crossing the room to mingle with staff, appearing casual as he continually scanned the area. "He has cameras all over this building and the surrounding area, as well as tricks the non-paranormal community wouldn't dream of. Honestly, part of the reason why he's so good is because most everyone who has ever heard of him is too afraid to cross him."

"Because he beheads people?" She shuddered. "Are you sure he's one of the good guys?"

"I'm sure. The bad guys do much worse."

Her eyes widened, but only briefly. The weight of her eyelids proved too great to hold open long. She looked at her coffee mug through the narrowed slits she struggled to hold open. "I think you gave me decaf. This coffee is doing nothing for me."

"I didn't give you anything. Rider brought you that, and I think you know you need sleep, but you're scared to sleep downstairs alone."

"Of course, I'm scared. You just told me the bad guys do worse than behead people and in case you forgot, the bad guys are after us."

"The bad guys won't get you."

"How can you be so sure Rider will keep us safe when none of us know who is after us?"

"I think he's good at what he does, but I don't need to know who we're up against to keep you safe. I only need to stay between you and them."

She held his gaze for a moment before her mouth curved into a slight smile. "You're very kind, and I know I told you you've always been my hero, but I'm not a little girl anymore. You don't have to feel obligated to protect me, especially if it puts you in danger too."

"I'm aware you're not a little girl anymore." His gaze narrowed on her lips and he began to wonder if they would feel as soft as they looked, and if kissing was as exciting as people made it look. Would he do it well or fumble awkwardly? Realizing where his thoughts were going, he turned away, dropping his gaze to the table. "Friends still need protection, even adult friends, and we are friends, aren't we?"

"Oh." She seemed to deflate next to him. "Yes, we are friends."

Sensing disappointment, Christian risked a glance of the raven-haired beauty. She turned her coffee cup with the lightest touch of her fingertips, and although she stared at the cup, her gaze seemed elsewhere. Her mouth turned down at the corners, her pretty face overwhelmingly sad. Had he disappointed her? His chest ached. Being the cause of her frown didn't sit well.

"Jadyn?" He reached out as she turned her green eyes toward him, placing his fingertips beneath her chin. Her eyes widened on a gasp, and he quickly dropped his hand. "What did I do?"

"Dog!" She pushed at him as she made to exit the booth.

"What?" He nearly fell out of the booth, too shocked to hold his ground.

"There's a dog in trouble." She brushed past him, headed for the front door.

"Oh." Relief flooded through Christian, realizing she hadn't reacted badly to his touch, but had sensed an animal in distress. Then he realized she intended to leave the protection of the building. "Wait!"

Rider was at his side by the time he caught up to the determined woman. "Problem?"

"She senses an animal in trouble."

"Animal in trouble? Kind of a perfect trap, don't you think?" Rider stepped in front of Jadyn, halting her progress toward the door. Behind him, the guard stepped in front of the exit, picking up on the situation.

"Move!" Jadyn commanded.

Rider raised an eyebrow, staring at Christian over her head. Christian gently took hold of Jadyn's arm as he cast Rider an apologetic look, knowing most who talked to Rider in such a tone on his own property in front of his people didn't tend to fare well. "Jadyn, this could be a trap to get you outside in the open."

The look she turned on him threatened to burn through his skin. "Whether it's a trap or not, there is a dog out there that needs me. I will not let it suffer."

"Where is the dog?" Rider asked. "I will retrieve it."

Jadyn closed her eyes a brief moment before shaking her head. "I don't know this area so I can't tell you where it is. I can only sense it. I need to go to it. Now." She tried to move, but Christian's hold on her arm kept her in place. She glared down at his fingers wrapped around her bicep. "Let me go."

"We're vampires," Rider reminded him. "We could easily stop her."

"That's true," Christian said.

"But you're not going to, are you?"

Christian looked into her fiery eyes and sighed. "No. I'm not."

"And if I stop her, we're going to have a problem, aren't we?"

Christian looked directly into the eyes of the vampire legendary for killing powerful masters and taking control of their nests, a man rumored to have removed organs from people just for pissing him off. "Yes, I'm afraid we will."

The two held each other's gazes until all the air seemed to leave the room. "I don't feel like a pissing contest at the moment and I'm too intrigued by what you are to kill you now," the vampire finally said. "We do this quick. Find the animal, get it and the two of you inside immediately. Understood?"

"Understood."

"One second." Rider's energy pulsed through the room and they were quickly joined by Hank and Juan as the shifter who'd been guarding the door stepped aside, back to his post. "Let's do this. Quickly."

The vampire turned and moved toward the door. Christian relaxed his hold on Jadyn's arm, but didn't let go completely as they followed Rider out into the cool night air. Rider moved aside, allowing Jadyn to lead the way as they flanked her. Juan and Hank covered their backs.

"This way." Jadyn winced, and covered her heart with her hand as she picked up speed, leading them down the street.

Christian kept his senses wide open, alert for any sudden attacks. He had no doubt Jadyn honestly sensed a dog in pain, but he also knew whoever hunted them wouldn't be above hurting an innocent animal just to draw them out if they knew of Jadyn's ability. Seeing the birds still lining the rooftops of the buildings around them, there was a chance they may have figured her gift out even if they'd had no clue before.

After covering three blocks, Jadyn took a right turn into a dark alley where four silhouettes were illuminated in the moonlight. Three men circled a medium-sized dog as it cowered in fear. Its pitiful whine could be heard over their raucous laughter. One of the men grabbed the dog by the scruff and brandished a pair of scissors.

Christian barely heard the man announce to his friends that he was going to give the dog a makeover before Jadyn broke free of his grasp and barreled into the man. They'd barely hit the ground before her fists started pummeling him.

"What the fuck?" the man screeched before shoving Jadyn off of him and balled his hand into a fist.

The man's fist crunched inside Christian's hand before the punch could be thrown. He kicked the man in the face to stop his pain-filled screaming and turned to see Jadyn soothing the whimpering dog. The other animal abusers were bloodied and battered on the ground, courtesy of Rider and his men.

"Shit," Rider said, nodding his head toward something beyond Christian.

Christian turned to see the dark line of smoke indicating a portal was about to be opened. He reached down for Jadyn, but she shrugged him off.

"I can't leave this dog. He's hurt bad!"

"Take the damn thing with us," Rider growled as he scooped the dog into his arms and moved toward the opposite end of the alley. "We don't want this fight until we're the ones calling the shots. Let's go!"

Christian clamped his hand around Jadyn's arm and followed Rider, both vampires using bursts of vampiric speed to get them to the back of Rider's building before the portal could open.

Rider quickly input his code as Juan and Hank caught up to them, and ushered them inside as soon as the garage door started to rise. Once in, he lowered the door and moved them across the garage to the hallway behind the bar.

"You should be off their radar now," he said as he lowered the dog to the floor and kneeled beside its head. "Damn, those bastards did a job on this poor guy. His nostrils flared, as did Christian's, but not from the scent of blood seeping out of the dog's many cuts.

"I should have broken more than that man's hand," Christian said as he lowered himself onto his haunches to really take in the damage done to the dog. Jadyn had already dropped to her knees across from him to gently rest her hand on the animal's shoulder. Silent tears spilled from her eyes.

"I should have ripped all of their spines out," Rider murmured as the dog released a sad whine and stretched its neck to lick Rider's hand.

"He likes you," Jadyn said. "The man you took out was his actual owner. He abused him all the time, and you saw what he let his friends do. They were about to cut his ears again." She moved her hand from the many cuts on the dog's side to lightly touch the scarred edges of its ears. She took a deep breath and gasped as her hand started to glow.

"Jadyn?" Christian looked at her, seeing the same surprise in her eyes that he felt inside. Rider and his men all watched her, more curious than surprised.

"I don't know what's happening," Jadyn said, breathless, as she used her free hand to clutch at the center of her chest before she moved it to hover over the dog's side.

"Do you feel the power inside you?" Rider asked. "The power Nannette found with her machine?"

She nodded as the light shone brighter. Christian's chest tightened and burned as whatever inside him reacted to what she was doing. He looked over to see Rider watching him and knew the vampire picked up on it.

"I've never felt this before," Jadyn said, her voice strained. "I can sense every wound and I know I can fix him, but it's not working. I don't have enough..." She looked up, met Christian's gaze and held her hand out to him. "Give me your hand."

Christian placed his hand in hers and was almost knocked back as energy arced between them. He held his ground and watched as Jadyn's body vibrated with power. Her eyes turned completely white, glowing with the same light that spread from the fingers she still held over the dog's ear. The light washed over the dog's body, closing wounds and erasing scars, repairing the damage that had been inflicted on the poor animal.

As he watched, the ears regrew their shape, the animal's body filled out, the blood disappeared and fur filled in the bald spots caused by what looked like burns. Before their eyes, the mangled dog whose breed had been unrecognizable developed coloring and features revealing it to be a cross between a shepherd and a Doberman, and a young one at that, judging by its overall size.

Once the dog's wounds healed completely, the light snapped back into Jadyn and she fell forward into Christian's arms, unconscious.

CHAPTER SIXTEEN

Jadyn opened her eyes and panic immediately set in as her gaze settled upon the rail of a hospital bed. She sat up quickly and took a deep breath, willing her heart to slow down as she recognized where she was. She was safe. She was at The Midnight Rider, in the guest room beneath the bar Rider had provided to them. She wasn't actually in a hospital, and she wasn't alone.

Christian rested on the couch, his eyes closed in sleep. One hand rested over his brow, the other over his stomach. His feet hung over the arm of the couch, making her feel guilty she hadn't demanded to take the couch herself. She frowned, wondering how she'd ended up in the bed anyway. She didn't remember...

The dog!

She looked down at her hands, recalling the light that had seemed to form in her core and flow from her fingertips to heal the poor dog. She had no idea how she'd done it. One moment she'd touched the dog, and the next thing she knew something inside her seemed to come alive. She'd acted on instinct, letting her hands hover over the dog's wounds, and when she sensed what needed to be done but couldn't get up the power to do it herself, she'd held her hand out to Christian, knowing she could draw from him what she needed to heal the dog. The moment they'd touched she'd seemed to fill with power, almost bursting at the seams with it, and then the power itself took over. She vaguely remembered thinking how beautiful the dog was once he'd been repaired, before the lights had gone out. She must have passed out from the ordeal, she realized.

But how had she done it? She looked at her hands again, studying the palms that had produced light. Healing light. What was it? What was she? She looked over at the vampire sleeping on the couch, the vampire whose power had strengthened hers. They clearly shared the same source of that power, but what was it?

A quick study of Christian's form revealed him to be in the deep sleep stage she'd learned about, his chest completely still. She swung her legs over the edge of the bed and moved toward him. Now aware of the deep stage of sleep vampires went through, she wasn't alarmed to see him frozen like a statue. She took the opportunity to study him more thoroughly than she would dare while he was awake, watching her.

She lowered herself onto the couch, sitting on the very edge of the cushion, her hip touching his, and lightly rested her hand over his heart. After a while she felt the barest flutter. After a few minutes she deduced a vampire's heart beat three times per minute in the deep stage of sleep. It was fascinating. He was fascinating... and he was beautiful.

Her hand slowly slid up his chest and, unable to stop herself, she ran her fingers over his face, tracing the lines. His skin was flawless, golden, and full of youth. Not one single wrinkle lined his eyes or creased his brow. His dark eyebrows arched perfectly, his lashes were pitch black and lush, and his lips were silky smooth, she discovered as she lightly brushed her thumb over the bottom one. Her breath caught in her throat as she imagined lowering her mouth to cover his, but she wouldn't dare. She shouldn't even touch him like this, she realized. Not while he was oblivious. Not even if she only dared to get so close because he was unaware and she was far too cowardly to touch him like this while he was awake, looking back at her in all her paucity. Even with the strange power they seemed to share, she knew he was so much greater than her. She could heal a thousand animals and still not be nearly as amazing as him. She wouldn't have even been able to heal the dog without drawing strength from him.

She forced herself to withdraw her hand, missing the feel of his perfection under her fingertips the moment she broke contact, and stood. Christian had placed their bags on the table when they'd initially been shown the room. She walked over to them, glancing toward the mini-fridge as she crossed the room. True to his word, Rider had provided food for her. Fresh fruit had been placed into a bowl on the counter between the mini-fridge and the sink, along with a few other things, and she knew she'd find perishable items inside the little refrigerator. Her stomach grumbled, but she ignored it as she unzipped her duffel and rooted around for clothes, wishing she'd packed something a little more appealing than jeans and T-shirts, not that any of it could be seen under her bulky hoodies. But she hadn't so she silently chastised herself for worrying about such things while she and Christian's lives were in danger, grabbed clothes and the few necessary toiletries she'd brought with her, and stepped into the bathroom to take care of immediate needs and clean up.

Christian was still asleep when she stepped out of the bathroom fifteen minutes later in a fresh pair of jeans and T-shirt, her slightly damp hair pulled back in a ponytail. She looked down at her worn sneakers and frowned. She wouldn't win any pageants, but she was clean and she could run if needed to. Remembering how quickly Christian had moved her from the alley to the back of the building, she didn't think she'd really have to do much running if they found themselves in trouble though. Her stomach grumbled, reminding her she hadn't eaten since Gruff's the night before and she'd slept well into the day. Also, she felt a bit woozy, no doubt from whatever she'd done to heal the dog.

She'd healed the dog. She marveled over that as she looked inside the mini-fridge and checked out what had been set out on the counter. After looking through everything she grabbed a small bottle of orange juice and a banana before moving over to the table. As she ate, she closed her eyes and searched for the dog, unsure what had happened to it. She'd healed the poor thing's wounds but had passed out before ensuring its safety. She doubted Christian would abandon the animal, but for all she knew, he'd followed her into unconsciousness. She'd drained power from him too.

She smiled as she sensed the dog nearby, still within the building to be exact. He didn't seem hurt or even afraid, which was a good sign, especially since he was in a building with vampires, wererhinos, and who knew what else. *Hey, buddy, how are you doing?* she thought, sending her thought to the dog.

Love him, came back the dog's thought along with a clear image of Rider. *Stay here. Stay please. Stay.*

"Oh boy," she said around a mouthful of banana. Rider hadn't seemed happy in the image she saw, and he didn't strike her as the type of guy who'd adopt a dog. Even if he would, she wasn't sure he could provide the best environment, and she feared what would happen to the poor thing if he or any of his people got thirsty. She scrunched her nose. Would they feed from a dog?

She finished eating and downed the rest of the orange juice, cleaned up, and moved over to Christian. He still slept. It was daylight and he'd been through a lot. He'd probably sleep through most of the day. The dog's overwhelming hope for a new home with the daunting vampire washed over her and she knew she couldn't wait for Christian to wake up before leaving the room. Rider had told them they could go to the bar. He'd never said they had to go together. She watched Christian a moment longer, hoping he was all right, but reminded herself that whatever the power was inside them, he had more of it, and he was a vampire. He was stronger than her. If she woke up after using her gift to heal the dog, he'd wake up too. Watching over him made no sense. No one would hurt him. Rider was too intrigued by him to allow him to be hurt, and she was pretty sure Rider wouldn't allow anyone to hurt her either. As for the dog, she wasn't willing to risk it.

She crossed the room and opened the door to find a lithe blonde in tight black pants and a fitted shirt leaning back against the wall, twirling a switchblade. She lifted her bored gaze. "Leaving, or do you need something?"

"Um..." Jadyn glanced behind her, hoping to see Christian sitting up or behind her, but he still rested on the couch with his eyes closed. She squared her shoulders and looked the woman in the eye. "Rider said we were allowed to go up to the bar."

"Sure." The woman straightened as she closed the switchblade and slipped it into a side pocket. "Follow me."

Jadyn closed the door behind her and followed the woman as she led her down the hall and took a left. Once they cleared the hall, she noticed other people dressed in black walking around or standing outside doors, piquing her curiosity as to what lie behind those doors. The woman led her to the stairwell and placed her hand over the panel, unlocking it.

"You will be met at the top," she said, opening the door.

Jadyn studied the woman, then looked back toward the direction she'd come from, where she'd left Christian.

"You'll be safe, and so will he," the woman said, seeming to read her mind.

Jadyn studied the woman, taking in her curves and seductive brown eyes, and almost turned around, but she couldn't. She needed to check on the dog, and if Christian woke up, saw the blonde, and went gaga over the sexy woman she doubted her presence would stop him from being attracted to her. She had no chance with him anyway, let alone a claim.

"Please make sure no one bothers him. He needs his rest," she muttered as she passed the woman and took the stairs up to the next floor. The door opened as she reached the landing and a burly man in black motioned for her to step out.

"Are you going into the bar or did you want to see Rider?" the man asked, his deep voice coming out a heavy rumble, as he slid his thumbs into his web belt.

"I..." Jadyn lost her train of thought as a door opened and two men rolled a gurney out with the unmistakable shape of a person atop it, wrapped in a blood-stained sheet.

The man stepped to the side, blocking her view. "That doesn't concern you."

She cast a mental net out, searching for the dog again as she fought not to show fear. She located the dog, again feeling its hopefulness. "I need to see Rider."

The man turned and watched the men moving the body until they and the gurney disappeared around a corner, then led her down the hall without a word. They passed the tech area and she couldn't help but pick up on the nervous tension. One of the stations had been abandoned, and the remaining techs seemed overly focused on their screens, almost as if scared to look up from the monitors. One tech did cast a quick glance her way, but immediately snapped her gaze back to her workspace.

The guard led her up the stairs in silence and continued to Rider's office. He knocked and opened the door before stepping aside to allow her to enter.

Rider sat behind the desk, working at his computer. He looked up with clear annoyance in his blue gaze. "Good. You're awake," he said as the guard closed the door, leaving them alone, and flicked a glance at the floor next to him. "You can do something with this dog now. Damn thing hasn't left my side."

Jadyn walked to the side of the desk and peered over, not wanting to encroach on the irritated vampire's personal space. The dog stretched out on the floor next to him, watching the vampire with big, pleading eyes. "He likes you."

"So you told me before you healed him and passed out." The vampire tapped a few keys on his keyboard and leaned back in his chair, folding his hands over his stomach as he stared at her. He appeared to have showered and changed into dark pants and a new black shirt since she'd last seen him. "How do you feel?"

"Physically fine," she said as she stepped back, patted her leg and made kissy noises, drawing the dog to her so she could check him over.

"And mentally?"

She kneeled on the floor as the dog moved to her and rolled onto its back, accepting her loving belly rub. "Better than the person who was rolled out on the gurney. What was that about?"

Rider didn't answer immediately and she worried she'd pushed her luck with him, but he finally spoke. "I have this whole area under surveillance. There's a camera in that alley where the dog was hurt."

Jadyn recalled the vacant computer as she passed Rider's tech team. "Your techs monitor those feeds."

He nodded. "The dog had been kicked, punched, and cut multiple times before we reached it. It was all on camera, yet only you notified me it was happening."

Jadyn's stomach rolled. "One of your techs saw it happening, and didn't say anything."

"He thought it didn't matter because it was just a dog. I won't have someone who thinks like that work for me."

"You could have just fired him."

"That is the way I fire people." His computer beeped, snagging his attention. He pressed a key, read something, tapped a few more keys and returned his attention to her. He watched her for a moment before speaking again. "I abhor animal abuse. I'm glad we rescued the dog and you were able to heal him, but now he needs to go."

The dog whined and looked up at her, aware of the intent in Rider's statement.

Jadyn continued to rub the dog's belly, and hoped she didn't have to break his little heart. He'd been through so much and now that she knew just how against animal abuse Rider Knight was, she wasn't so hesitant to allow the dog to stay there. "This guy has had a rough life. You actually killed the man who punished him over and over again for no reason other than pure meanness. He trusts you. He'll have a very difficult time trusting someone else."

"But he will."

"Maybe, maybe not." Jadyn shrugged. "If I'm correct, he's a mix of German shepherd and Doberman pinscher, and he's going to be very big in no time at all. A lot of people want purebreds. A lot of people are also afraid of large dogs, especially certain breeds like shepherds and Dobermans. Then there are the people like the type who owned him before, the ones who like big dogs because they want to make them attack dogs or they want to use them for dogfights. I don't think the shelter is a good idea for this guy. Even if someone nice does adopt him, he won't trust them, and he'll probably be returned. This will cause behavioral problems, making it harder for him to find a good home."

"Jadyn."

"Seems a crime to put a good dog through all that when he could have a perfectly good home with an owner he trusts and already loves."

"Jadyn, I'm a vampire."

"You're a vampire who killed a man for allowing this dog to be harmed," she said, raising her head to meet Rider's gaze. "I'm not saying I condone murder, but I don't really have a lot of soft spots for animal abusers or those who simply don't care about animal abuse. I recognize people who should and shouldn't have pets. You're a vampire, but you're a good man to belong to a dog."

His mouth turned up a little at the corners. "Don't you mean a good man for a dog to belong to?"

"A good owner belongs to a dog just as much as the dog belongs to him. This dog has claimed you whether you like it or not. Do you really want to break his heart?"

"Oh, come on, I—"

"This dog loves you. He has been abused, broken, and psychologically scarred, but he still found something in you to trust. That's a pretty big deal. If you give up this dog you will set him so far back he may never recover. He may never be able to trust anyone enough to allow him the chance at a loving home."

"I think you're exaggerating in order to get me to cave. He seems to like you enough."

"He knows I understand him," Jadyn advised, "but he loves you. He wants to stay with you, not just because you made sure his former owner could never harm him again, but because he wants to help you."

Rider's eyebrows raised in amusement. "How exactly would he help me?"

"Dogs sense things in people. He knows you're sad and lonely, and he can help with that."

Rider's eyebrows lowered as he sat forward, all trace of amusement leaving his face. He opened his mouth to speak, but a knock on the door stopped him.

A large black man dressed in a Louisville Cardinals T-shirt and jeans stepped into the office, mouth open to speak. He froze as he looked down and saw the dog. "There's a dog in here."

"This is Rome," Rider said, gesturing toward the man, "the genius I sent to retrieve you and Christian before plans changed. Rome, this is Jadyn. Christian is still resting."

"Whassup?" The man greeted Jadyn, but kept his gaze on the dog. "I was told the woman talked to animals but nobody told me there was a dog in here. Is that a dog-dog or did a new shifter join the team?"

"It's a real dog," Rider said, his voice heavily laced with irritation.

"Whose is it?"

"His," Jadyn said at the same time Rider said "No one's."

Rome crouched down and patted his big knees. "Here, dog. Come 'ere boy."

The dog, who'd already rolled onto its paws once the large man entered, lowered its head and growled as it scooted back.

"What's wrong with him?" Rome asked, slowly getting back up.

Jadyn looked at Rider until he raised his gaze to meet hers, and arched one eyebrow. "This is exactly what I was telling you about. He fears people, except for you. He is going to be aggressive in self-defense, which will lead to all sorts of problems. He may like me, but I'm currently on the run from who knows how many shifters and witches and God knows what else, and I don't even know if I have a home anymore. I barely have enough money to feed myself, let alone a big dog who is going to eat a lot. You have a home, you have money for vet bills and dog food, and this dog wants to be with you."

"You going to keep the dog, boss?" Rome's eyes lit up. "He's a nice-looking dog, and gonna be big as hell too. Man, he might scare some bitches off before we even have to do anything to them."

"Yeah, he'll scare them off once he stops shaking and backing away from them," Rider muttered as he got up from his seat and walked over to the dog. He lowered himself onto his haunches and rubbed one of the dog's ears, quickly earning a few licks and an extremely excited tail wag. "What's his damn name?"

Jadyn fought to hide her smile as she communicated silently with the dog, reading through his thoughts and memories. "Ugh, his original owner named him Satan, which he hates, of course, because that man was horrible to him."

"What about his other name? Does he have a name that his mother gave him, something dogs call him? They don't use the names we give them, do they?"

Jadyn struggled not to laugh. "Well, they do, but they speak in barks. I'm able to understand animals through their thoughts and memories, but something like that would still be in the animal's language, which he can't translate to me. You don't want to name the dog a bark sound, do you?"

Rider rolled his eyes. "What does he want me to call him then? Tell him to pick a name."

"You know he's right here," Jadyn reminded the testy vampire. "Dogs are brilliant animals, and they understand way more than humans realize, even if they can't talk to us in the same language. He's still a dog though. Choosing a name for himself is a bit too difficult for him. Just choose a name, or you can have Danni choose one for you if you like," she said, having figured out the woman was very important to the surly vampire, and the reason why the dog sensed so much sadness in him.

Rider grunted. "No damn way. She'd name the thing Dean Winchester. I'm not calling him Dean Winchester."

"Uh, boss?" Rome raised his hand like a kid in elementary school might. "If I can make some suggestions, uh... no offense but white folks can't name dogs."

Rider and Jadyn shared a look before the vampire turned toward his employee. "What the hell are you talking about?"

"I'm just saying, man, white people always wanna name their dogs Buffy, Bob, Max, Rex, Rover, or Muffin. There are twenty-six letters in the alphabet and y'all only use three of them. You gotta use some other letters, man. Branch out a little."

"Fine. What do you think he should be named?"

Rome studied the dog, turning his head to take in all angles. "He's gonna be big and tough. He needs a strong name. A manly name." His mouth slowly curved into a big smile. "I got it. Name him... Notorious D.O.G."

Rider pointed to the door. "Get the hell out of my office."

"What? That name is lit, man."

"Out," Rider ordered again, "and change. You're going to be on security detail. Black shirt and pants."

"All right." The large man's shoulders slumped as he turned for the door. "Don't name that dog no stupid white name like Bobo or Maximillian Bon Muffinbutt. He don't deserve that bullshit, dude. He's a man."

"He's a dog."

"He's a big dog. D-A-W-G," Rome said, pointing at the dog as he stepped out of the office and pulled the door closed behind him.

Rider sighed and scrubbed his hand down his face. "See what I deal with? You really think throwing a dog into the mix is a good idea?"

"I think it's exactly what you need," Jadyn said, allowing the smile she'd been fighting to break free. She had him. The moody vampire was on the hook, right where she wanted him. Now to reel him in... She gave the dog a mental nudge and he quickly rolled over, presenting his belly to Rider as he gazed up adoringly into his eyes.

Rider glared at the dog, but the corners of his mouth twitched and the look softened as he gave the dog a good scratch and stood. He moved over to his desk and sat on the corner. The dog scooted over and rested his chin on

Rider's foot, drooling a little on his black leather shoe, but the vampire didn't seem to mind. Sensing all was well, Jadyn moved back to the couch.

"It's pretty amazing how you healed this dog," Rider told her. "Any idea how that happened?"

Jadyn shook her head. "I don't know. I mean, I know it has to do with whatever this energy is that Nannette found inside us, but I don't know what it means. I didn't even know I could heal animals. Instinct just took over, and I think being close to Christian helped. I drew from the power inside him when it became clear mine wasn't going to be enough."

"And you've never felt a desire to heal an animal like that before?"

"Well, of course I've wanted to. I held my cat in my arms as she died. If I could have healed her, I would have in a heartbeat. I don't know if it's just that I can only heal injuries, or that my ability to heal is brand new, or..."

"Or your proximity to Christian has strengthened the power inside you."

"Yeah." Jadyn chewed her bottom lip as she looked around the room, noting all the old, leather-bound books on Rider's shelves. A few had been removed and were open on his desk. "You know, I'd really believe in your angel theory if I wasn't part of it. I could totally see Christian as an angel."

"Even though he's a vampire?"

"I was a runaway when he saved me from a man who was about to pimp me out. He was a guardian angel then, for sure. He could have hurt me. He could have hurt a lot of people during his lifetime, but I really don't think he ever has."

"Oh, he's hurt plenty," Rider assured her with a grin, "but if all the stories are true, he has never actually killed a human and he has never harmed a child. He has destroyed demons too. Rumor has it, he once destroyed a demon with prayer alone."

Jadyn sat still, blinking at the man for a moment. "You mean, he just prayed and the demon died?"

"Supposedly, he just prayed and his prayer blew the demon's ass up." Rider stood, careful to nudge the dog's head aside, and rounded the desk. Instead of taking his seat, he stood and leafed through one of the open books. "I've been looking through some old books, searching for explanations for what I've been witnessing from both of you. The ability to heal the way you did is an angelic power, and I can't think of any other being who could destroy a demon with prayer alone. Then there's the sword Christian drew from out of nowhere." Rider picked up the book and brought it over to her.

Jadyn stood and looked at the page he'd opened the book to. She saw a beautiful painting of a white-robed winged woman holding a sword that appeared to be on fire. Her palms grew sweaty as she noticed the pure golden color of the woman's eyes and long hair. She couldn't read the words written on the other page. They were written in an unfamiliar language. "This looks a lot like the woman who helped us outside Christian's church, except I didn't notice a sword, and she wore a dress, not a robe."

"I imagine angel clothing changes with the times just like it does for us, and according to what is written here, an angel's sword is an extension of their power. Just because the woman you saw didn't have a sword you could see doesn't mean it wasn't right within her reach."

"Like Christian's."

"Exactly like Christian's." Rider closed the book and moved back to his desk, setting it on top of others. "More and more, Christian seems like an angel to me, but he won't accept it because it would mean he fell. For a man like Christian, I can't imagine learning a worse thing about yourself."

"Could it be anything else?" Jadyn asked. "He doesn't have golden hair or eyes, and then there's me. I know my family line all the way back to my great-great-grandparents and none of them could have possibly been angels, fallen or otherwise."

"I have a theory on you, actually, but I won't even speak it until I get a few questions answered. Also, that painting of an angel was just one representation. There's hundreds more of angels with different hair and eye col—" Rider stopped talking and cocked his head to the side, his eyes narrowing. "Table this discussion," he said a moment later. "Someone who may prove to be very helpful just entered my bar."

CHAPTER SEVENTEEN

Christian sat up, instantly aware something was wrong. He looked at the bed where he'd lain Jadyn to rest before stretching out on the couch for his own much needed recuperation. She was gone. He quickly stood and crossed the room. The bathroom door was open so he looked inside, coming up empty.

He crossed over to the door in a few quick strides and opened it. A blonde woman stood outside, playing with a knife. She jumped a little, but quickly gathered herself. "She asked to see Rider. She's upstairs."

Christian studied the woman. "Are you psychic?"

"No, but your face is screaming, 'Tell me where my woman is or everybody's getting a free ass-kicking today' so I took a wild guess."

Christian stepped out and pulled the door closed behind him. "Take me to her now."

"Yes, sir." The woman straightened and pushed off the wall she'd been leaning against. "Right this way."

Remembering he'd bonded with Rider earlier, Christian expanded his senses, searching for the vampire. He sensed him upstairs. The vampire wasn't afraid, but he definitely gave off a predatory vibe. Knowing Jadyn had gone to see him, Christian's unease spiked.

Good afternoon, Rider spoke across their newly formed link, sensing him. *Jadyn is with me and she is safe. We're viewing the security feed from the bar, and there's someone very interesting in my building.* The vampire withdrew from his mind.

Christian forced himself to blow out a pent-up breath as he continued to follow the woman, surveying his surroundings as he did. There were armed security guards on the floor, but they didn't look as if they were expecting any action. They almost appeared bored. Christian pushed his senses out, allowing them to wash over the whole level. He counted heartbeats and energies as he counted guards. He ended up with one heartbeat too many and that heartbeat had a very strange energy attached to it.

The blonde, who he picked up shifter vibes from, unlocked the stairwell door by placing her palm over the access panel and led him up the stairs without a word. They passed the tech room where he sensed nerves in abundance coming from Rider's techs, and continued on without a word. Christian glanced up at the door to Rider's private quarters, wondering if the vamp had gotten any rest since they'd arrived.

Music could be heard as they entered the narrow hallway that ran between the bar and the rest of Rider's building, but instead of leading him to the bar, the blonde stood back and pointed down the hall. "They're in Rider's office."

The woman backed through the door leading to the bar, leaving him alone. Christian covered the distance in mere seconds, a little of his vampiric speed kicking in to get him to Jadyn as quickly as possible.

He knocked once and opened the door, not waiting to be invited in. Rider sat behind his desk with Jadyn standing at his side. She appeared to have showered and changed into light jeans and a gray T-shirt. Her hair was pulled back into a tight ponytail. The style, along with her makeup-free face reminded him just how innocent the woman was. Innocent and precious. Christian ignored the vampire and crossed the room to grab Jadyn.

"Are you all right?" he asked as he ran his hands over her arms, checked her eyes, her pallor, and listened to her heartbeat, timing it. "Did you eat? Did you drink? How did you sleep? Do you feel light-headed? Any pain?"

"Good grief, Christian, would you let me answer a question before asking twenty more?" She laughed nervously as she grabbed his hands and forced him to stop pawing at her. It was then he realized she'd been sputtering, trying to keep up with his questions, but he'd never given her a chance to answer a single one. "And I'm fine. I slept well and I had a decent brunch."

"You think he's bad now, you should have seen him after you passed out," Rider said, but he didn't lift his gaze from the monitor in front of him. "Take a look. Jadyn just confirmed this is the man who tried to snatch her at your church."

Christian willed his own heart to calm and moved in a little closer, careful not to step on the dog stretched out on the floor behind the desk. Sure enough, the man who'd tried to abduct Jadyn sat at the bar, his thick fingers wrapped around a bottle of beer as his shifty eyes scanned the room. A blonde slid onto the stool next to him and leaned in.

"That's your guard, the woman you had posted outside our room," Christian said, recognizing the blonde. Jadyn tensed beside him, but said nothing when he looked at her. She stared at the woman, eyes narrowed.

"That's Lana," Rider told him. "She's new. After sending Daniel off with Danni and Ginger, I decided to try out another Imortian. She's going to chat this guy up a bit, then bring him to interrogation where I'm going to get some answers."

"You mean where we're going to get answers."

Rider looked at him. "You can wait in the observation room and watch if you'd like. I'm good at this. I'll get what we need to know, and if you have questions to ask, we're linked."

"I'm going to be in there, Rider. This guy is after me, and he's after Jadyn. This is our battle."

"It became my battle when you came to me for help. That bastard is sitting in my establishment. I'm in this now, and whoever is behind this knows I'm in this, or they will soon enough. There's a reason why I always get answers in interrogation. I can't have a boy scout in there trying to hold me back." Rider stood, grunting as he had to wait for the dog to lift its head off his shoe and move away, and stood before him. "Let me help you so we can get this over with, and get Jadyn back to a nice, safe life."

Christian grit his teeth. Rider knew what button to push to get to him. He wanted to question the man. If he were being honest, he wanted to break the man in half for touching Jadyn. Anger he didn't often feel bled through his body, infecting his every thought with the desire to make sure the man would never have the chance to harm her again. But he needed to do whatever was best to get Jadyn out of harm's way as soon as possible, and if that meant allowing Rider to do what he specialized in, then he had to do it.

"Fine, but you should know I broke that man's hand. I heard the bones crunch, and that was before I threw him across a parking lot. He doesn't appear broken now. Whoever he's working with, they have powers."

"Dark powers," Rider said, turning to look at the monitor. "We knew they were working with black magic, but healing like that indicates they're pretty damn good at it, pretty advanced. Maybe even satanic." He looked at a stack of books on his desk. "You ever hear of something called a Blood Revelation prophecy?"

Christian's breath slammed to a stop as he looked from the stack of books to Rider's calculating eyes. He knew, or at least he suspected Christian's involvement. He thought over everything he'd said to the vampire, trying to figure out where he'd slipped up, but couldn't think of anything he'd said or done other than mentioning the Dream Teller. He knew Seta wouldn't have told him anything. Seta was the one who cautioned him not to reveal what they knew. He looked at the stack of books again, wondering what information the vampire had stumbled upon. "I've heard of it, but I don't see what that old prophecy would have to do with any of this."

"A group of vampires versus Satan's wrath." The dog whined, and Rider shushed it. "I wasn't talking about you. No one's calling you that name again."

Christian looked over at Jadyn and found her hiding a grin behind her hand.

"Whoever is after you is skilled in the dark magic," Rider continued, having settled down the dog. "Could be a sa... a cult of people who follow the devil. I stumbled onto some interesting information about the Blood Revelation prophecy while researching."

"Researching what, exactly?"

Rider opened his mouth to answer, but his attention was caught by the action on his monitor. "Lana's on the move. We can discuss this later after I finish my nice little chat with this asshole."

Christian backed up, allowing room for the two of them to move around the desk. Jadyn followed him and Rider grumbled as he walked around the desk with the dog close to his legs.

"You stay," Rider told the dog and pointed to a spot on the carpet. The dog jumped up and barked, its tail wagging at an almost dizzying speed. Rider looked at Jadyn. "Tell it to stay."

"No it. He's a he," Jadyn said. "Don't call him an it. That's just rude. He's a person too."

"He's a ..." The vampire shook his head. "Forget it. Look, interrogation can get really ugly. It's not a place for a dog, especially not a whiny one like this."

The dog growled and barked with ferocity.

"I think you made him mad," Christian said, not sure why the dog was still there, but Rider didn't appear to be getting rid of it any time soon.

"Did you feed him?" Jadyn asked.

"Yes, I gave him meat in the kitchen, and water too."

"Um, we're going to have to discuss proper nutrition," Jadyn said before squatting down so she was on the dog's level. "Did you get a leash for him?"

"No, I didn't get him a leash. He wasn't my dog."

"Did you at least allow him to use the bathroom?"

"Yes, I took him out back in the alley four times. He should be all piss and crapped out by now."

Jadyn stifled a laugh. "Well, that's good, at least. He needs a leash so he can be taken on walks. I wouldn't recommend leaving him in the office while you're doing this interrogation thing. He might chew everything up out of anxiety. I believe you said something about an observation room, which is where I intend to be with Christian. I'll watch him there."

"If you watch the interrogation, there's a good chance you're going to see things you can never unsee."

"You should stay here and watch the dog," Christian suggested, despite not wanting to be so far away from Jadyn. Rider's reputation for being violent and merciless warned him the vampire wasn't exaggerating what she might witness if she chose to observe him in action though. He didn't want her to suffer nightmares from what she saw, or worse, be afraid of vampires after witnessing how brutal they could be.

"I want to observe," she said. "That man tried to take me. Who knows what he would have done with me if he'd succeeded? Trust me, I don't care what you do to him to get information if it means stopping whoever else is after us. I'm not that little girl you rescued years ago, Christian. I'm a grown woman. I can handle whatever it is Rider's going to do."

"You have my sympathies," Rider said to him as he crossed over to the door. "She's got that same damn stubborn streak as Danni. Let's go, then. Lana should already have him down in interrogation by now."

Between the fire in her eyes and the steely determination in her clamped jaw, it was evident Jadyn would not be swayed by words alone, and he didn't want to physically restrain her from entering the observation room, so Christian followed Rider down to the interrogation room.

He noted again the nervousness as they passed the tech team, the way the techs kept their heads down, refusing to make eye contact with Rider as he passed. The vampire did pick up their fully charged cell phones and hand them back, advising they found no magic or tracking technology other than his own on either phone.

Christian checked for messages, and finding none, slid his phone into his pocket. They passed the interrogation room and Rider opened the next door for them. "You will wait here in observation."

Christian allowed Jadyn to enter first, then followed her in. The dog plopped down right next to Rider and barked.

"Please convince this damn dog to stay in here. I can't have him weaving in between my legs in there, and the last thing I want to give that bastard is a target. If he even tries to touch this damn dog, I'm going to kill him before I find out anything."

Smiling, Jadyn lowered herself down to her haunches and called the dog over. Christian saw her close her eyes and felt the subtlest hint of power, and knew she was communicating with the animal.

"He'll be a very good boy," Jadyn promised, ruffling the dog's fur between his ears as she opened her eyes.

Rider grunted and looked at Christian. "You make sure you're a good boy too. Stay put."

Christian rolled his eyes as the vampire left them, closing the door behind him. The room was dark and without décor. A table and two chairs sat before a one-way mirror which allowed them to see into the interrogation room without anyone in the interrogation room being able to see them.

"Can he see us?" Jadyn asked as she stood rigidly before the table, looking through the mirror to where the man who had tried to abduct her sat at a table in the center of the room. It, too, was an unadorned room. Simple white walls and floor like any interrogation room seen on television, except this one had a drain in the floor, which Christian imagined was to help clean up the messes Rider made in there.

"No," he answered as he moved next to her and turned her to face him, away from the stocky, freckled man with the stubby nose and short brown hair who sat in the other room, looking in their direction, legs shaking, hands clamped together before him. "It's a one-way mirror. He can't see us, and he can't touch you. He will never get near you again."

Jadyn nodded before looking through the mirror again. She shuddered and turned her face away.

"You don't have to stay here," Christian said softly as he gently gripped her arms just above the elbow. "I've heard a lot of rumors about what happens in Rider's interrogation room. He doesn't want me in there because he's afraid I'll try to stop him. He knows I don't care for unnecessary violence. No one will think less of you if you opt out of watching this."

"I can handle it," Jadyn said, voice firm as she raised her head and stared directly into Christian's eyes.

Her eyes were full of determination, but her body trembled. Christian couldn't take it, but there was nothing he could do, short of tossing her over his shoulder and packing her out of the room, but she'd be upset with him. Knowing the type of childhood she'd had, the last thing he wanted to do was force her to do anything she didn't want to do, even if what she didn't want to do was save herself from a gruesome scene she'd never be able to scrub out of her memory.

The dog whined, capturing Christian's attention. He looked down to see it sitting beside them, pawing at Jadyn's leg. She scratched his head absent-mindedly.

"So why can't Rider say Satan around the dog?" he asked, earning a whine.

"The jerk who owned him named him that," Jadyn explained, rubbing the dog's ear, something the animal seemed to enjoy. "He doesn't want to be called that name anymore. Rider hasn't chosen a name for him yet."

"Rider? He's keeping the dog?"

Jadyn nodded. "It's what the dog wants."

"Rider? Rider Knight? He's keeping the dog and you're fine with that?"

"He killed the tech who watched this poor thing get abused right on his camera feed and didn't do anything to help it. I think a man who does that cares more than he wants to admit."

"Or he just likes to kill people," Christian murmured, looking at the dog. He chuckled as the young dog growled at him. "But he's not a bad guy overall. I doubt he'll drink the pup."

Jadyn playfully slugged him in the rib. "That's awful."

"Yeah, but it got you to quit trembling." He walked her to the table and pulled out a chair for her, then took his seat next to her. "Just promise me that you won't try to be a hero. You have nothing to prove. If this gets too rough, you can leave, or at least put your head down."

She held his gaze for a moment, then nodded. "All right."

The door to the interrogation room opened, and Lana stepped inside, followed by Rider.

"I was promised sexual favors, but I don't do guys," the man who'd tried to abduct Jadyn said, glaring at Lana. "Where are my sexual favors, bitch?"

"I gave them to your mother," the blonde said as she moved to the corner and leaned back against the wall where she began to study her nails as if already bored.

Rider tossed a folder onto the table and sat across from the man. He opened the folder and read from the papers inside. "Charles "Chuck" Lester, twenty-eight years old, jobs ranging from fry cook to gas station attendant, and a multitude of arrests for fighting and domestic disturbances. Nothing remarkable about you, Chuck."

"How do you know all that?" Chuck's eyes widened. "What kind of bar is this?"

"Did the monsters you're working for bother to tell you anything at all about the arena they were throwing you into before tossing you in here, Chuck?"

"I don't know what the hell you're talking about," Chuck said, his complexion growing ruddy. "I came in here for a drink and this bitch came on to me, asked if I wanted to go somewhere private, if you know what I mean."

"Look at her, Chuck. Look at yourself. In what reality would a woman like her come on to you because she actually wanted to have sex with you?"

"Women love me, you pretty-boy jackass. I was captain of the football team."

"You're twenty-eight years old, Chuck. Nobody gives a shit about your high school sports accolades. Nobody gives a shit about you at all. That's why you were the one sent in here alone. There's no use trying to pretend you're just some random guy stopping in for a drink. We were already expecting you."

"Bullshit."

"You tried to abduct a woman out of a church parking lot after helping burn down the church itself, and attacking the minister, who then broke your hand and tossed you aside like a ragdoll."

Chuck Lester sank down in his seat as his eyes darted around the room.

"Let me guess. They told you this would be a simple job. No one would suspect a human of infiltrating my bar. You were supposed to come in here, find the woman, maybe the man, not real clear yet on who your true target was, either lure them out or just report back with a verification they were in fact here. Did they even tell you about me, Chuck? Do you have any idea who the hell's doghouse you just stuck your fool neck into?"

"Just another mongrel who's going to die soon," Chuck said, leaning forward, full of false bravado. Christian could hear his heartbeat racing. "Is this the part where you reveal you're a vampire and I piss my pants? That's not going to happen. I know all about vampires. I've killed some, and I know one of the scariest vampires who ever lived, or whatever the hell it is you all call what you do. You're going to give me the vampire and the woman, and you're going to let me walk out of here, or he's coming and he's bringing hell with him."

Christian reached over and took Jadyn's hand, knowing things were about to take a dark turn. He couldn't see his face, but from the set of Rider's shoulders, he was getting bored with merely talking. He also knew the vampire didn't allow people to speak to him in the way Chuck Lester just foolishly had. The only reason why Chuck's neck hadn't been snapped yet was because Rider still needed answers.

"Really?" Rider finally said as he stood from the chair and slowly walked around the table, circling his prey. "You're paraphrasing *Tombstone* quotes to me? So, Wyatt Earp's a vampire now?"

Chuck sneered. "Jaffron is a bigger badass than Wyatt Earp could have ever hoped to be."

Rider looked at Christian through the mirror, sensing where he sat. *Jaffron? You know that name?*

Christian let the name tumble through his mind. It was familiar, yet he had no memory of meeting anyone with that name. Then it came to him. *Jacob Porter was ensnared by sirens. A vampire named Jaffron was behind it. He worked with sirens, lycanthropes, weres, and witches as well as pranic and non-pranic vampires.*

Rider's eyebrows rose. *Jacob Porter as in Jake Porter, legendary slayer?*

Yes.

This Jaffron got the drop on Jake Porter?

He used sirens to do it. Apparently, even a slayer can be snared by them.

And Porter didn't kill him?

Again, he was ensnared. Khiderian was involved in his rescue. Things got hectic really fast. They didn't stick around to track and kill Jaffron.

Rider's eyes narrowed, and Christian knew he was trying to figure out the connection. He was as well. Was it possible this was all about Jake? If so, he needed to warn him. He pulled out his phone to send a text, but saw he'd received one from Jonah.

JUST HEARD FROM JAKE. SAID THE WOMAN YOU DESCRIBED SOUNDED A LOT LIKE THE ANGEL WHO TRIED TO GET HIM TO KILL MARILEE. I HAD TO TALK HIM DOWN FROM FINDING YOU. HE NEEDS TO STAY OUT OF THIS.

"Christian? Are you all right?"

Christian realized he'd squeezed Jadyn's hand in reflex. He let go so he wouldn't accidentally hurt her and slipped the phone back into his pocket as he nodded. "I'm fine," he reassured her. He wasn't fine. Thoughts overran his brain, scattered and confused.

An angel. He pictured the woman again, the golden eyes and hair, the power. Even the men who'd come to take her had given off the same intense power within the blink of time they'd been there. Maybe this wasn't about Jake, or Rialto, or the Blood Revelation at all. Maybe it was about him, and Rider had been right. But if he was right...

Ask if he's after me or Jake.

Rider subtly nodded and continued circling Chuck. "You attacked the minister, then tried to grab the girl. Who was the actual target?"

"I'm not telling you shit. In fact, I'm leaving." The man leapt forward, having drawn a knife from his pocket.

Rider raised an arm and sent the man flying backward into the wall without touching him. His eyes glowed gold.

"How did he do that?" Jadyn asked.

"He's very powerful," Christian answered. "That's just the tip of the iceberg of what he can do."

"The hell?" Chuck Lester gasped out as he slid down the wall, landing roughly on the floor.

"My name is Rider Knight," Rider told him, standing before him with his hands clasped behind him. "I am very old, and as you can see, very powerful. You thought any vampires you encountered here would be weakened by daylight, weakened enough that you would actually have a chance with that blade you dipped in hawthorn oil. You thought wrong. You already failed at grabbing the vampire in Baltimore. Now you've completely screwed yourself because I'm a hell of a lot meaner than he is. Do yourself a favor, Chuck. Answer my questions and your death doesn't have to be as bad as I normally prefer it to be."

Chuck looked between Lana and Rider. "Jaffron will kill you. He'll destroy all of you."

Rider's power flooded the room, the force so strong Christian felt the edge of it in the next room. Chuck's face grew cherry red as he struggled to breathe. Rider released the power, and Chuck gasped in air.

"I can handle Jaffron," Rider advised. "I'm getting annoyed, Chuck. I need you to answer my questions now. If you refuse one more time, I'm going to let Lana eat you. Now would be a good time to prove your usefulness."

Chuck looked over at the blonde. "I'm not afraid of her."

Rider looked over at Lana. The Imortian nodded as she quit studying her nails and pushed away from the wall she'd been leaning on. The air around her shimmered and suddenly a giant anaconda stood in her place, ready to strike.

"What the hell is that?" Jadyn asked the same moment Chuck Lester started to scream.

"That's an Imortian," Christian answered, "and a very terrified man who is going to spill his guts whether he wants to or not."

CHAPTER EIGHTEEN

Rider grabbed Chuck Lester by the front of his shirt and slammed him onto the chair he'd left, then shoved him face first into the table. "You can answer my questions now or after Lana eats and regurgitates you. What's it going to be?"

"I'll answer! I'll answer! I'll tell you whatever you want to know!"

Rider nodded to Lana and she returned to her human form in a shimmer of colors before returning to casually leaning against the wall, bored.

"Who was the target when you went to the church?" Rider asked.

"The minister was the one Jaffron wanted," Chuck said, his cheek pressed against the table as Rider leaned over him with his elbow in his back. "The woman was just something a little extra. She was supposed to lead us to him."

"How did Jaffron know she would lead you to him? Why did he want him?"

"I don't know the exact details. I'm not exactly in his inner circle. I just heard stuff."

"What stuff?" Rider dug his elbow further into the man's back. "Tell me everything."

"All right, all right! I heard Jaffron talking to this old hag he keeps around. I think she's a witch, like a real, actual witch. Jaffron had been looking for this vampire for a long time. He said he was promised to him, but he got away. Something in him shields him from Jaffron so he can't claim what's his."

"What do you mean claim what's his?"

"You're a vampire, man. Figure it out. Jaffron turned the guy and he got away from him somehow."

Every vein in Christian's body ran cold as his mouth fell open. Rider looked up, looking directly at where he sat, but said nothing. Christian doubted he would hear the vampire even if he did speak into his mind, not with all the blood rushing into his ears. Jaffron was his sire. All the centuries he'd lived, he'd thought his sire must have died shortly after turning him, but he hadn't. The strange power inside him had protected him from the vampire, a vampire who had tortured one of his best friends over and over.

He felt Jadyn's hands on his shoulders, vaguely heard her voice, but couldn't focus on one thing with the million cascading thoughts and questions tumbling through his mind. Then her hand gripped his jaw and his head was turned. His gaze connected with hers and all the noise went away.

"Are you all right?" she asked.

He nodded, still too stunned to speak, but he could focus again.

"So none of this had anything to do with Jake Porter?" Rider asked the man in the next room.

"I don't know who Jake Porter is," Chuck answered, free to sit up now as Rider had returned to circling the table. "All I was told was the girl would lead us to the vampire Jaffron wanted. We were to follow her and get the vampire. If we didn't get the vampire, we were supposed to snatch the girl so he'd come for her. They have some kind of connection or something."

"How does Jaffron know about her and the connection?"

"Witches and wizards, and magic and shit. I don't know how they know half the stuff they know, but they're really leveled up in the dark arts. This was like my way in. I get the vampire, and they turn me into one of Satan's right hands."

"You're a devil worshiper?"

"Hell, yeah," Chuck said. "There's a war coming. It's going to be epic and when Satan wins, I'm going to be right there standing with him, safe from the pain and torture he's going to fill the earth with."

"A war?"

"Yeah, man. The ultimate battle. Jaffron is recruiting for Satan, building up our army. I heard once he gets this vampire under his command like he's supposed to be our power will triple."

Rider was silent for a moment, letting the information soak in. "Where is Jaffron now?"

"He's everywhere, man." Chuck laughed. "He's here. He's there. He's everywhere! He's everything!"

Rider snatched the man from the chair, his hand squeezed tight around his throat. "How do I find him?"

"You... don't. He...finds...you," Chuck managed to get out past the tight vise of Rider's hand.

Rider flung the man back into the chair. "What was your exact mission today?"

"Come in, look around, see if I spotted either of them. Report back with what I saw. They're coming for him. Even if you keep me locked up here, they'll know it's because he's here and they'll come. They'll save me and give me my prize, and they'll kill all of you before leaving with him."

"Chuck, Chuck, Chuck..." Rider shook his head. "It pains me just how stupid you are. They sent you in here because you're expendable. We're not going to lock you up. I'm going to kill you because, you see, that's the big rule in my interrogation room. No one ever survives interrogation."

Chuck's eyes widened. "I told you everything. You owe me."

"Yeah, no. You tried to abduct an innocent woman and kill a vampire who is now under my protection. I believe you when you say you don't know who I am, because you're no one, but this Jaffron bastard knows exactly who I am. He didn't just send you in here to look around. He sent something with you. Congratulations, Chuck. You get to meet the devil now."

Rider's hand shone with the same golden hue as his eyes as he grabbed Chuck by his shirt, slammed him on top of the table and shoved his bare hand through the man's chest, digging around until he pulled free a small black orb that radiated energy, and crushed it before he began to quench his thirst on the man's blood.

Jadyn gagged and ran to the nearby wastebasket where she fought not to throw up. Christian left his chair and went to her, nearly tripping over the dog as it moved toward her to offer comfort.

"It's all right," he assured her as he rubbed her back. "It's over now. Honestly, that was way less bloody than I expected. I think he held back because he knew you were watching."

She turned to look at him, her face slightly green. "Are you serious?"

"Very. That was tame for him."

"That was disgusting." She gagged again, and clamped her hand over her mouth. "Change the subject."

"The dog's urinating in the corner."

She looked over where the dog had raised his leg in the far corner of the room. "Lovely."

Christian helped her stand, careful to use his body to block her view of the mess in the interrogation room. He led her toward the door, but it opened before they reached it.

Rider stood there in a blood-soaked shirt, using a towel to wipe more from his face. "You and I need to talk now. Alone. Lana can take Jadyn back to your room." He looked over at the corner of the room, where the smell of urine permeated the air, shook his head, and stepped back, allowing them to exit.

Jadyn cringed and gripped his bicep as the Imortian woman stepped forward to lead her to the room.

"You'll be safe," Christian assured her.

"Honey, I've rarely actually eaten a person," Lana told her, "and to be honest, I don't even care much for snakes, but this was the hand I was dealt. Come on."

Jadyn looked up at him, and Christian gently ushered her toward the woman. "You know I wouldn't let anyone hurt you," he reminded her.

"I believe him," the Imortian told her as she started to lead her down the hall toward the stairwell that would take them back to their room. "He looked pretty dangerous when he woke up and found you missing. Hey, are you good with nails? I could use a manicure."

"We have a lot to discuss," Rider said, turning the opposite way to lead him and the dog who'd remained toward the opposite end of the hall. As they neared the end, a dark-skinned man appeared, dressed in the security uniform of black shirt and pants.

"Rome, the dog pissed in the observation room. Clean that up and then come to my office for a list of things I need you to get him."

"You're really keeping the dog?" Christian asked as they passed the grumbling man.

"I don't think I have a choice. If I refuse, your girlfriend might sic a flock of birds to peck out my eyeballs." He looked down at the dog, sighed, and led Christian up the stairs to the first floor. "I like you, Christian, but you've seen how I get when I have to wait too long for answers. I have questions for you and I highly suggest you answer them."

KIARA REACHED THE EDGE of the cliff and looked down. The sky above her and the puffy clouds below her grew bluer, reminding her that no matter how familiar this all looked, she was still in the dream realm. She was not in Heaven where an identical cliff could be found, a cliff Khiderian had voluntarily fallen from, the same cliff Christian was rumored to have taken the same fall from. Rumored? She nodded. Yes, rumored. She didn't believe it. She never had, not in her heart. Why would Christian fall? He loved serving the Lord. He loved what he was.

"He loved me, and all his brothers and sisters."

So why was she here? What was the realm trying to tell her? She turned, looking for clues, but nothing stood out. No glowing words, no books of prophecy, no cave wall drawings. Only the cliff, the cliff that had drawn her ... and what the clouds covered beneath. She looked over the edge again to where the puffy clouds awaited her.

"This is not Heaven and I am not falling," she declared in her strongest voice. "I am only seeking the truth."

She took a deep breath, and jumped over the edge of the cliff.

CHRISTIAN LOOKED UP as Rider entered his office, freshly showered and dressed in clean, dark clothes. The dog trailed behind him as he closed the door and rounded his desk to sink down into his leather desk chair. "Sorry for the delay. I was getting sticky."

"I can imagine."

Rider's mouth curved a little. "No condemnation?"

"The man professed to wanting to be in hell's army. Even I have limitations to my sympathy." He used to, but if Christian were being completely honest with himself, he'd been struggling with his own moral compass lately.

Someone knocked on the door and it opened, revealing the man who'd been assigned to clean up after the dog in the observation room. "This a bad time, boss?"

Rider ripped a piece of paper from a notepad on his desk and stretched his arm out. "Get everything on this list at the animal store."

"You, uh, mean pet store, boss?" the man asked as he approached and took the list.

"Whatever. You've been apprised of the latest security protocol?"

"Yes, sir. I'll take three men with me, and we'll stay alert."

Rider nodded and the man left. "That was Rome, one of my most trusted employees."

"He's only a human."

"Yeah, but he's a big human." Rider leaned forward and grabbed a few of the books on his desk, turning them to face Christian. "Enough small-talk. I haven't slept since you got here. I've been researching. That healing thing Jadyn did? That's an angelic power. That sword you drew out of nowhere? That's an angelic weapon. So far no one from Imortia has claimed to have ever seen you, but an angel has access to all realms so it's possible an angel can see imortium."

"Jadyn can't see imortium," Christian reminded the vampire. "Whatever I am, she is too, remember?"

Rider raised a finger. "Yes, and no. I have a theory on her. She started to heal the dog, but she couldn't fully do it, not until she touched you and drew from your power. I believe you're an angel, Christian. A full angel. Jadyn has some grace, or angelic power, but she is not a full angel. She inherited her power from her family line. She is, according to what I've found in my research, what is considered a guardian. Specifically, she is a guardian of beasts."

Christian stared at the vampire in front of him, blinking, trying to find a way to poke holes through his theory. "If that were true, why is she just now able to heal?"

"Being in your presence strengthens her, and when you first met her, the angel whose grace eventually went to her was still in possession of it. The small trace of grace she had in her blood at the time wasn't enough to do much of anything. Something changed two years ago, and I think I know what."

"So enlighten me."

"Where were you two years ago?"

"Baltimore. We've been over this."

Rider held up his finger again. "If my assumption is correct, you met someone around the time Jadyn's grace spiked. Who did you meet two years ago?"

Christian thought back. He wasn't the greatest with dates. As long as he'd been alive, the years kind of blended together. He'd been with the same group of friends for as long as he could remember, although since Rialto had met his soulmate, Aria, new friends had been joining their tight little group. Jake, Nyla, Jonah, Malaika, Marilee, and ... "Khiderian."

Rider nodded, appearing quite pleased with himself. "I don't know the exact details, but you said Khiderian had been a fallen angel who turned vampire, then sacrificed himself to save the woman he loved. He became human. Did that sacrifice occur roughly two years ago?"

Christian thought back, and nodded. "I think so."

"His grace didn't just disappear. At some point between falling and becoming a vampire he impregnated a human woman and a trace of his grace was carried throughout the family line. When he sacrificed himself, losing the grace that remained in him, it increased in the worthiest person in his family line."

"You're saying Khiderian is Jadyn's ancestor?"

The vampire nodded. "I know it seems kind of crazy, but I've seen crazier. You can do the research yourself if you want, but I figured it best if I just give you the summary so we can move ahead. You're an angel, Christian, or at least you were. Somehow you ended up here with us worthless bastards, and somehow you became a vampire. According to the idiot I just killed, you were promised to Jaffron. That's kind of an odd thing for him to have said, don't you think?"

Christian fought down the urge to vomit at the thought of being an angel and throwing such a gift away. "It was all odd. How could my sire be alive and I never sense him? How could he not easily locate me? And how could I have been an angel and toss away such a blessed gift?" He rose from the chair and paced the floor, shaking his head. "I couldn't have. I don't know who I was before the attack that took my memory, but I know who I never could be. I could never be the type of disrespectful—"

"So maybe you didn't fall."

Christian stopped and met the vampire's gaze. "How else could an angel end up where I am?"

Rider opened one of the books and pointed. "I didn't just research angels. I ran across the Blood Revelation, a prophecy I believe you and all your friends are very familiar with, seeing as how you have seen the Dream Teller. I trusted Seta with something pretty damn huge. I'd think she could trust me with this."

"I'm familiar with the prophecy," Christian admitted as he moved back over to the desk and took his seat. "I don't know what it has to do with anything Chuck Lester said in your interrogation room or why I'm being hunted to be returned to my sire."

"He said you were promised to Jaffron. Maybe I'm just going off lack of sleep and a blood-high here, but I think that sounds pretty damn strange. Whether or not you're on board or not yet, I'm convinced you were an angel before you were turned. Now, who do you think would promise an angel to a vampire?"

Christian shook his head, not even wanting to go there in his mind. "You're the man with all the ideas. You tell me."

Rider held his gaze for a stretch, nostrils slightly flaring, before he spoke again. "I may not be in your inner circle, but I have history with Seta. I know when she's hiding something, and I have eyes and ears everywhere so it's pretty hard to get shit past me. I'm known all over the paranormal community for being one of the last vampires you'd ever want to mess with, and even I wouldn't want to end up on Jake Porter's radar, so I found it very interesting when rumors started circulating about him being in the same building as you when you blew up a demon, yet you and all the other vampires walked away. Then I heard he wiped out a vampire-infested town with a little help from Seta, and there are whispers he's married to a vampire now, and his brother is married to a witch. When he was caught by Jaffron, Khiderian rescued him. A vampire rescued one of the most dangerous slayers to ever walk this earth."

"And?"

"And I can't imagine why any of you would allow him to live, or why he would allow any of you to live, unless you were all working together." Rider tapped the book with his finger. "The Blood Revelation. Vampires and other immortals working together to save the world from Satan's wrath."

The dog whined, and Rider shushed it. "Chuck Lester spoke of an epic war. It sounded an awful lot like this prophecy, and according to him, Jaffron is recruiting for the other side. Jaffron even captured your buddy, Jake Porter. This vampire, this recruiter of satanic servants, sired you. He was promised you. That sounds an awful lot like some traitorous shit to me. Maybe someone from the holy side wasn't so holy. Maybe you didn't fall. Maybe you were traded."

Dizziness set in, and Christian took a breath, willing it away. "You think I was an angel, and another angel made a deal with a vampire to turn me?"

Rider slowly nodded. "I can see you as an angel. I can't see you falling, but I can see an army of assholes who worship the devil making a deal to nab themselves an angel to turn. According to this, it adds up."

Christian took the book Rider pushed toward him and read from its pages, translating the ancient language the best he could. "In this great war, some cursed ones will rise above their darkness, and some who are blessed will fall to the evil. Deals will be made between the light and the dark to gain power. A holy one will be put through trial. The lives of the chosen will be at risk if the trial is failed." Christian's hands shook as he pushed the book back toward Rider. "You think this is me? You think I'm this holy one put through a trial?"

Rider had sat back in his chair, and now stared at Christian over steepled fingers. "I told you I was going to ask questions, and I wanted answers. This prophecy speaks of chosen ones, children born to immortals, children who will battle the devil and save the world from his wrath. I can help you, but I need to know what I'm really dealing with in order to do that so tell me right now, do you know who those children are?"

Christian held Rider's hard gaze as his heart thumped. Seta had told him not to tell anyone about the children, and he understood why. The more people who knew of their existence, the more danger they were in, but Rider had figured out a lot on his own. As much as he didn't want to admit it, the vampire's theory made sense, and if it were all true, he needed help. He couldn't ask Seta to leave Rialto and her grandchild. He couldn't draw Jake away from his son either, especially not if asking for their help would mean bringing them closer to a vampire who very likely was working closely with the devil and wanted nothing more than to locate and destroy the chosen ones.

Rider could help, but he needed to know he could completely trust the vampire first. He remembered the extra heartbeat he heard when he left his room earlier. "If you want to know the answer to that, you're going to have to give up something yourself so I know I can trust you."

The vampire's eyebrow raised. "Such as?"

"I found the amount of security you have on the basement floor a little excessive for just Jadyn and me. I did a little investigating of my own as I left the room this morning. I counted security guards and heartbeats. I picked up an extra heartbeat, one with a very strange signature. Who, or what, are you hiding here?"

The vampire's nostrils flared and his steepled fingers tightened. After a moment, he lowered his hands and straightened in the chair. "I see Seta kept her promise of secrecy. She's well aware of who I'm hiding, because she worked the spell to do it."

Relief flooded Christian's system. If Seta helped Rider, what he was doing couldn't be nefarious. "Seta always keeps her word. I know she's been visiting you recently, helping with something, but she didn't tell us what exactly."

"I asked her not to. You've met Danni. I've tried keeping my affection for her under wraps to make her less of a prize to my enemies, but clearly, I fail at every turn because everyone seems to know how precious she is to me."

Christian nodded. "I imagine it's very hard to hide a love that strong."

"It is, and it's also hard to do anything that displeases her, which is why I turned her sister after she was shot. I knew damn well her sister would be a bad turn, but I feared losing Danni if I didn't do it."

"Things went bad," Christian guessed, recalling how Rialto had been forced to kill his first love after turning her. The woman had been through a horrible ordeal, her heart and mind filled with vengeance during the turn. She'd awakened a bloodthirsty monster.

"She tried to kill Danni. She needed to be put down, but Danni, of course, didn't want that. You figured out what Danni is when you met her. I imagine you know enough about succubi to know they have certain needs a woman of high moral standards would object to."

Christian's face flushed with heat as he realized what Rider was alluding to. He nodded, not wanting to risk saying anything that could be perceived as a judgment against the woman Rider loved.

"Danni was bitten by a very powerful incubus. I tried to save her by biting her right after. I'd hoped to redirect her turn so she would become a vampire. As you've already discovered, that didn't work. She became a hybrid. She serves two masters and the other is equally as powerful as I am, meaning he has a strong hold over her when her succubus side takes over. She was going through a cycle called the Bloom. Basically, she went into heat. It would have been fine if she only craved sex. I could have kept her with me until the Bloom ran its course, preventing her from doing anything she couldn't forgive herself for, but as you know, succubi like to kill the men they have sex with."

"She tried to kill you."

Rider nodded. "I barely made it through the first Bloom. I probably wouldn't have made it if Seta and Malaika hadn't arrived just in time to work some magic and lessen the incubus's hold on Danni. It wasn't much longer after that when her sister was shot and I turned her. To make a long story short, Seta has been working with me, trying to come up with a way to free Danni of the incubus's threat completely. In the meantime, we've developed a work-around for the Bloom. I didn't kill her sister. Instead, Seta worked a spell that has suspended her. You could say she's in a magically-induced coma. Part of the spell included allowing her to carry out the Bloom for Danni."

"You mean... when Danni would normally go through the Bloom, her sister goes through it instead?"

"Yes, but she's in a coma-like state so she doesn't suffer from it like Danni would. Maybe someday after we destroy the incubus we'll figure out how to wake her without her trying to kill Danni again. Until then, we keep her in the coma and help Danni in the process. Very few people know about any of what I just told you. I'd appreciate if you would keep this to yourself, for Danni's sake."

"Of course," Christian said.

"Do I have your trust now?"

Christian nodded, not able to blame the man for what he'd done. The love he had for Danni was evident, and wasn't the selfish love of a villain. The fact he'd allowed the woman the freedom to be away from him although he clearly worried about her spoke volumes as well.

"I revealed my secret. Now it's your turn. Do you know who the chosen ones are? Have the children been born?"

Christian sighed as he nodded again. "I think you've already figured it out. Seta's son and his wife are the parents of one. Jake Porter and his wife are the parents of another. According to the prophecy, there will be a third child born. That one, we don't know about yet."

"Jake Porter is the father of one of the chosen ones." Rider blew out a breath as he raked a hand through his hair. "That's ... I'm not sure there's a word for that. I'm assuming Jaffron grabbed him because of his child?"

"Jaffron has been working with witches and others who've been in league with the devil. We're not sure they know the children have been born, but we're fairly certain they've somehow figured out my people are involved, possibly myself as well."

"Jaffron sired you. That grace of yours that you can't seem to wrap your mind around has somehow hidden you from him all this time, but he's clearly figured out a way to track you. That orb I took out of Chuck Lester was a hex orb. It was supposed to break through our warding, but I anticipated something like that so I had Rihanna in the bar the whole time, making sure our warding stayed in place. They very likely would have stormed in here during his interrogation had I not. They're going to come for you, Christian, and it's going to be bad. He left you after he turned you, most likely to feed since I imagine turning an angel took a lot out of him, and apparently your grace shielded you. I suspect more than just your grace was at play though. I don't think it was a coincidence Eron just happened upon you. Someone's been watching over you, and you've seen the crosses to prove it."

"If someone's been watching over me, why haven't they given me my memory or warned me about any of this?"

Rider shook his head. "I don't know. It's probably all a part of the prophecy, and prophecy can be a mess. I don't think they're going to just drop down here and help you out now either. You're going to have to get through this without turning to the dark side."

"I'd never—"

"You have no idea what it's like to be controlled by your sire. Yours stepped away while your body was still going through the turning and you were taken away from him. The grace protected you, but make no mistake about it, once you are in that vampire's presence his power will be strong enough at that range to bend your will. You are his fledgling. You won't be able to fight against him, especially if you're not ready to claim yourself as the angel you are."

"I drink blood for God's sake!" Christian slammed his hand down on the desk, startling the dog. He rarely lost his temper, but this was too much. "If this is all true, if I was an angel, I still allowed this to happen, or I was tricked at the very least. I don't deserve to call myself an angel. I'm a vampire. I am far from holy."

Rider sighed. "Yeah, I figured that would be the way you'd feel about all this. There's one other way I can help you so you don't become that bastard's puppet, but you're going to have to really trust me."

Christian took deep breaths, willing himself to calm. He couldn't lose his cool now, not when Jadyn's life and the lives of his friends depended on him. He might not have known his sire, but he knew enough about them to know Rider wasn't exaggerating the power a sire held over a fledgling. He couldn't risk allowing someone as evil as Jaffron to control him. "What did you have in mind?"

"Pledge your allegiance to me. I couldn't fully turn Danni because the incubus who turned her is the same age and level of power as I am, but I had my tech team do some digging, and I know I outrank the evil sonofabitch who turned you. Give yourself to me, become a part of my nest, and I will become your master. Jaffron can't control you if you're mine."

CHAPTER NINETEEN

Jadyn held three queens and two nines in her hand. She pushed three Oreos to the center of the table. "All in."

Lana studied her cards from where she sat across the table, chewing her lip as she decided her next move.

The door opened and Christian entered, paler than he'd been the last time Jadyn had seen him. He paused for a moment to take in the poker game happening between her and the Imortian, then crossed the room, squatting to open his duffel bag she'd set on the floor to make room for the game. "I'm taking a shower. I didn't get to earlier."

"OK. Are you all right?" she asked, noticing the light shadows under his eyes and the tense set of his shoulders.

"Fine," he said, a little snippish, as he withdrew clothes and entered the bathroom, closing the door hard behind him.

"What crawled up his nuts?" Lana asked, looking over her cards.

"He's a minister," Jadyn advised. "We shouldn't be talking about his... personal areas."

Lana laughed. "Personal areas? What are you, five? What the hell, I'm in." She shoved forward her remaining cookies and set her cards down, revealing three aces, a king, and a ten. The hopefulness in her eyes fled as Jadyn revealed her cards. "Damn."

"I'm very lucky today," Jadyn said, reaching for the cookie pile as the shower turned on in the bathroom. Her face flushed as her head filled with images of Christian standing in the stall, the water sluicing down his bare skin.

"You all right over there? You look like you're having a hot flash."

"I'm fine," Jadyn quickly said as she gathered the cookies. "Shuffle."

"Jadyn!" Christian called sharply from the bathroom. "Get in here!"

"Well, that sounds like your lucky day's about to get even luckier. That's my cue to give you some privacy." Lana set the cards down and excused herself from the room, giving Jadyn a sly wink before she closed the door behind her.

Jadyn turned her head toward the bathroom door as it opened, and Christian stepped out, covered only in a towel tied around his waist. He moved toward her in two quick strides, grabbed her hand and pulled her into the bathroom before turning so he could see his back in the large mirror that hung over the bathroom counter.

"Is that what my tattoo looked like when you saw it earlier?"

Jadyn forced herself to raise her eyes from Christian's abs and look at the tattoo image reflected in the mirror. She blinked, sure she was seeing something wrong, but the image didn't change. She looked directly at the tattoo on his back, and reached out, touching the image with her fingers, half expecting it to smear. It didn't, but it was not the same exact tattoo she'd seen in the hospital. It was larger, and more detailed. The man's muscles had been covered in smooth flesh, and he seemed to be coming out farther. The wings were somehow bigger, possibly with more feathers. "I don't understand."

"What did it look like when you saw it earlier?"

"Similar, but it seems to be growing bigger, and the man was mostly muscle. He's more fleshed out. He... he looks like you. Christian, has this tattoo changed before?"

"Apparently. I haven't looked at it in a long time, but these wings weren't so big the last time I looked at it, and the man wasn't the way he is now. It does look like me."

"How have you not looked at it?"

"How often does a person look at his own back?" Christian answered. "I've never owned a mirror this big in my life so I don't catch glimpses that often. I looked at it a lot after it first healed, and for decades after that, but I got so frustrated not knowing what it meant so I quit. I don't go around others with my shirt off a whole lot either. If it's been changing no one's really had the opportunity to notice."

"You said the woman who gave you this wasn't a witch, but this has to be some kind of magic, doesn't it?"

"I don't know. I don't know what she was. I don't know what I am." He gripped the counter and growled as he lowered his head. "I don't know what's happening!"

"Christian..." Jadyn noticed the mirror starting to fog as her hair started to frizz from the steam of the shower, and turned the water off. She turned from the shower to find Christian in the same position, his hands clenched so tight around the edge of the counter she feared he would break the granite. "Hey..."

She cautiously rested her palms over his shoulder blades, and when he didn't shrug her off, rubbed his back. "We'll figure it all out. Talk to me."

He made a strangled sound in his throat that might have been a laugh wrapped in disgust. "I've been trying to figure this out for centuries." He raised his head and stared at himself in the mirror, his lip curled. "I have tried so hard to live the way a man of God should. I've fought against this dark beast that was put inside of me; I've fought against human nature. I've fought, and prayed, and searched, and fought harder and prayed harder ... and it probably never mattered."

"Christian, don't say that. You don't mean it."

"You don't know that. You don't know me. I don't even know me."

"I know you."

"You know the person I pretend to be." He stood up straight, causing her hands to drop away from him. "I pushed down every desire, every craving, fought so hard against what I really am, trying to be something better, something worthier, but I never was. I should have just given in to all my wants. I'm no better than anyone else. I'm becoming more of a common, lustful, greedy man every day, just like this man inked into my flesh. One day I'll look in the mirror and there won't even be wings left."

"I know you, Christian, and you don't have any darkness in you. You drink blood. So what? You're still a good man. You could take everything you've ever wanted and still be a good man because it's not in you to be a bad one."

He turned toward her. "So I should just take what I want?"

"Go for it." Jadyn straightened her shoulders, determined not to cower under his hard gaze, to be strong for him. "You're not selfish or greedy. No matter what you do, you're still going to be the bes—"

Jadyn gasped as Christian pulled her against him, covering her mouth with his before he backed her against the wall. The edge of the counter dug into her hip, but she barely felt it as Christian's tongue delved inside her mouth to explore and his hands gripped her backside, pulling her tighter against his body, where the hardness of him pressed against her. Her hands traveled down his back, hesitating when her fingers met the terrycloth wrapped around his waist.

Christian's mouth left hers to travel down to her throat. She felt the scrape of teeth against her skin. With a growl, Christian tore his mouth away and leaned over her, eyes closed, breathing heavy as he braced himself with a hand against the wall on either side of her head. "I should have asked before I did that."

"It's all right." Jadyn reached up to cup his cheek, and tried not to feel too bad when he flinched from her touch. "I always wanted to do that with you."

"I never wanted to do that with anyone, until these last few days. I'm being tested. I'm failing." He opened his eyes and pushed himself off the wall, away from her.

"What do you mean?" She tried to keep the hurt out of her voice as she reached for him.

He backed away. "Please don't touch me. If you touch me, I don't think I'll be able to stop myself."

"Christian?"

"I can't, Jadyn. I just can't." He moved forward, grabbed her bicep and pushed her out of the bathroom before closing the door.

"Christian?" Jadyn stood outside the bathroom, staring at the closed door, unsure what had just happened, or what she'd done. Or what Rider Knight had done, she thought, wondering what the vampire had wanted to speak to Christian about in private. What had he said to him to upset him so much? She'd seen Christian in full protection mode before and hadn't felt so much anger in him.

She started to ask through the door what the vampire had said, but heard the water come back on. She moved over to the table and cleaned up the cookies and cards used in the poker game with Lana, busying herself while Christian showered.

When Christian came out of the bathroom fully dressed ten minutes later, she stood in his way with her arms folded over her chest. "What did Rider say to you?"

Christian walked past her. She grabbed his arm, and he shrugged her off, causing her to stumble, but he quickly caught her and pulled her close enough to press a kiss against her forehead. "I need to be alone."

He walked out of the room, leaving her to stare at another closed door between the two of them.

KIARA FELL TO THE GROUND with a grunt. She looked up to see Krystaline sitting on a ledge, her gnarled hands folded calmly in her lap while her sightless eyes seemed to pinpoint Kiara's exact location within the small cave. The image shimmered, allowing the angel a glimpse of the young beauty underneath the façade. "You seem upset."

"I've been falling for four hours."

"Eh, more like four minutes. Did you find the answers you sought?"

"You already know I did." Kiara stood and dusted her dress off, a mostly symbolic gesture as dirt wouldn't dare touch her pristine clothing. "Just like you knew I already had some of the answers, but didn't trust myself enough to believe in them. Aurorian didn't fall. He was betrayed. We were all betrayed."

"Yes." Krystaline nodded.

"I didn't see by which of my brothers or sisters, but I have my suspicions. I need to warn him."

"My dear, you know you cannot do that without falling yourself. You have been banished to this realm by your superior. This is Aurorian's trial to pass or fail on his own."

"This isn't right!" Kiara's voice echoed off the jagged walls. "Amuel isn't answering me. No one is answering me or even listening, not even our Father. I've been completely cut off while the traitor is out there plotting with Jaffron. Aurorian has been fighting against the darkness forced on him for so many centuries..." Hot tears trailed down Kiara's cheeks. "He didn't fall.

He didn't make that choice. He shouldn't have to suffer the consequence. He shouldn't have to go through this alone."

"You know very well he is never alone."

"I have heard his prayers for centuries, Krystaline. He's not alone, but despite the strength of his faith, he is struggling. He loves the humans he calls family. He loves that woman. He will choose them, and he will lose everything, that's if he even survives."

Krystaline cocked her head to the side. "You think he won't survive?"

"I saw everything. Griana fell, but she had enough grace left to heal him and give him the gift of that tattoo. All these centuries and he never figured out what it meant, because he is in denial. His faith has kept him strong, but he's broken now that he knows what he was. I saw what happened when he was betrayed, what's happening now, and what's coming next. He needs someone to help him."

"He has friends."

Kiara rolled her eyes. "Rider Knight and that clueless guardian? Is she going to sic squirrels on his attackers when they come for him? It won't just be Jaffron and his mongrels."

"I know," Krystaline said softly. "I know *all* that he is battling."

"Then you know he needs someone to remind him who he is, who he *really* is. He needs his sister!"

"You can't go to him unless you fall, and you already know he cannot be told anything directly from any angels. That's the rule. He cannot receive any information *directly* from any *angelic* sisters or brothers, and neither can the guardian."

"I know, I know." Kiara lowered her face into her hands. "You don't have to stress..." Kiara gasped, and looked up to see Krystaline grinning slyly. "He can't receive information directly from any of his angelic sisters or brothers. That was stated very clearly."

"Very clearly," Krystaline agreed.

"Aurorian is not Aurorian down there. He is Christian. Christian has a family, and they are all far from angels."

Krystaline nodded. "Keep going."

"I can tell someone who can tell him, someone he trusts, someone who will get through to him and restore his faith now that he needs it the most, and somehow who can fight at his side. I don't have to fall to tell this person because you can bring him to me right here in this realm." She smiled, new hope filling her chest. "Bring me Jacob Porter."

"FUCK ME SIDEWAYS," Jake Porter said as he opened his eyes to find himself standing in a clearing ringed with tall trees. Everything for as far as his eye could see was tinted blue by the cerulean moon hanging overhead. Cool air whispered across his skin.

"Always so eloquent."

"You know me," he said, turning to see the Dream Teller. She stood four feet away from him, dressed in the same hooded cloak she always wore, long, white hair poking out from underneath. She looked at him with sightless platinum eyes that always seemed to see everything. "Now I know why I was so damn tired. You lured me to sleep so you could get me here."

"Sorry about that, but you know I can only bring you to this realm while you're asleep or otherwise unconscious."

"Yeah, I know." Jake's stomach twisted. He'd been on edge due to recent events and wasn't that surprised the old witch had brought him to her realm. "I know Christian's in some kind of mess and Seta's taken her family into hiding so if this is about them or my family is in danger just skip to it and tell me who the fuck I have to kill and send me on my way."

"Killing isn't always how you save someone, although you may still get to do some of that," another voice said as a figure emerged from the tree line behind the Dream Teller.

Recognizing the woman with the golden eyes and matching hair, Jake lunged forward, but the angel raised her hands and blasted him back ten feet.

"I told you he'd do that," the Dream Teller told her as the angel stopped at her side.

"You tried to get me to kill my own sister, you bitch. I'll kill you right in your fucking face," Jake growled as he stood.

"I told you he'd say that." The Dream Teller raised her hand, palm out. "Jacob, please. Christian needs your help. Calm yourself."

"This bitch—"

"This angel had a direct order to kill your half-sister, but instead, Kiara devised a plan that ensured not only would Marilee survive, but cured her of her curse in the process."

Jake stilled and looked between the old witch and the angel. "You knew what would happen?"

The angel raised a shoulder. "I saw an opportunity and hoped for the best. It worked out. I am not your enemy, Jacob."

He glared at the woman. "I still think you're a bitch."

"That's fine. You're far from my favorite person, but you're useful. If you can refrain from trying to kill or maim me, I'd like to tell you a story."

"That's nice, but there's this little thing called the Blood Revelation happening so I don't have a lot of time for story circle."

"Listen to her, Jacob." The Dream Teller waved her hand and knocked Jake back. He landed on a ledge inside a small cave, the clearing no longer there. "You know I don't bring you here unless you or your loved ones are in danger."

"Fine," he said, looking up at the witch and the angel who both stood in the center of the cave. "Tell me this story, but make it quick."

"The vampire you know as Christian is in desperate need of help," Kiara said.

"The vampire I know as Christian?"

"Christian is the name he gave himself after he lost his memory many centuries ago and was attacked, turned into a vampire. Before that, he was an angel." Kiara paused, frowning when he didn't say anything. "You don't seem surprised."

"I saw the dude blow up a demon with a prayer and he has more faith than any non-vampire I've ever known. He goes out of his way not to kill despite being a vampire, and I don't even think he's ever been laid. Christian being an angel isn't that crazy to me," he responded, shrugging. "It takes a lot more than that to surprise me. I once killed a demon dog with three dicks."

"Thank you for that image." Her lip curled in disgust.

"Oh, I didn't give you the image. The dicks were on its—"

"Jacob." The Dream Teller shook her head.

"Fine. Whatever. Go ahead."

"As I was saying..." The angel huffed out an irritated breath and told him the story of how Christian had been betrayed, attacked, turned, then tested for centuries afterward and what he was going through, having figured out a little of the truth.

"And some bullshit rule won't allow any of you feathered fuck-wads to help him?"

"Is that really called for?"

"Hell, yes. You're angels. You're supposed to help people and you've left one of your own hanging out to dry for centuries. Hell, one of you fucking betrayed him. Now I understand why I've never seen a halo on you. You can't fit it over your damn horns."

"We've never worn halos. That was some artist's interpretation of the halo of light around us when we reveal ourselves and it caught on." She took a deep breath and Jake caught a glimpse of water in her eyes. "I don't think my brother has been treated fairly either. I attempted to help him without revealing anything to him and I was banished here where I can't do anything unless I fall. I don't expect a human to understand how abhorrent the concept of falling is."

"I think I can imagine." Jake shook his head. "This is so fucked up. So what do you need from me?"

"I'm not allowed to directly interfere, nor can the Dream Teller, but I can put you near Christian. More than anything right now, he needs a friend, a brother. I think you're close enough to that. He is very fragile. Even though the suspicion of betrayal is there, he blames himself for not being strong enough to fight against it. He questions his worthiness."

"So, I'm supposed to give him a pep talk?"

"It wouldn't hurt, but that's not it. He was betrayed by an angel. That angel will go to any length to keep that betrayal under wraps. That angel will want Christian dead before the truth gets out."

"An angel is going to try to kill him?"

"There is no definite outcome to this, but there are definite possibilities. If Christian gives in completely to the darkness he has fought all these centuries, he will fail his trial and the dark side will gain in power, which endangers the chosen ones. If he kills in a way that is not righteous, he will never be permitted back into Heaven. He needs someone to help him emotionally and in battle. Rider Knight is not close enough to him for that, and in helping him, may have done some damage. The guardian has genuine love for him, but his feelings for her... confuse him."

Jake raised an eyebrow. "Are you telling me Christian has the hots for a woman?"

Kiara frowned. "He is an angel. Get your mind out of the gutter, and do not encourage him. Leaving Heaven and becoming a vampire were not his choices. What he does with his mind and body are. The trial is nearing its end. His human wants and desires are stronger than ever before. The woman is a temptation. She can ruin everything for him."

"Don't let him get his freak on with the chick with the sprinkle of angel power. Got it. Anything else?"

"If the angel who betrayed him resorts to trying to kill him, Christian may not defend himself. He will hesitate to destroy a holy being, even if that being is a traitor to Heaven. You will need to destroy the angel, but only if the angel tries to kill Christian in a way that is clearly murder and not self-defense, otherwise you will be cashing in a one-way ticket to Hell."

"Of course."

"Do you understand what is being asked of you, Jacob? Can you do this?"

"If Christian goes dark the chosen ones are in danger. One of those chosen ones is my son." He stood. "And Christian is my brother. Hell yeah I can do this."

Kiara reached out and a flaming sword appeared in her hand. "Killing a pure angel isn't easy. You will need an angel's sword. I will loan you mine in case Christian is unable or unwilling to draw his."

"Awesome," Jake said, and genuinely meant it as he watched the sword appear to burn.

"An angel's sword is an extension of the angel it belongs to. In order for you to wield mine without burning yourself I will put a little of my grace into it, and put a little grace into you. Hold still." She raised the sword, narrowing her eyes as she stared at the center of his chest.

"You're going to stab me with that thing, aren't you?"

"It's how I inject the grace into you." She grinned.

"I really don't like you at all."

"You don't have to like me. You just have to accept my grace and save Christian. Are you still in or not?"

"I'm in, I'm in. Wait. What the hell is Christian's real name anyway? Shouldn't that be part of what I tell him?"

Kiara stilled. "No. You can tell him what he is, but the moment he relearns his true name he will have all the knowledge of Heaven. He isn't allowed that unless he passes the trial."

"Man, you guys suck." Jake braced himself. "Come on then. Get this shit over with. Lord knows *someone* needs to actually help Christian."

CHAPTER TWENTY

Jadyn opened the door to find Lana leaning back against the wall with her arms folded over her chest. The Imortian glanced at her watch. "Twenty minutes. I expected you to go running after him a lot sooner."

Her face warmed. "Did you hear us?"

"I'm here to guard your door and escort you between floors, not snoop. I could tell from the look on his face when he left here he wasn't happy. It was easy to guess the two of you had a spat in the bathroom instead of a quickie."

"Where is he?" Jadyn asked, opting to ignore the quickie comment. She didn't think reminding the shifter Christian was a minister would make any difference in the way she spoke of him.

"In the bar. Word around the lobe is he's been downing a lot of blood."

"The lobe?"

"Telepathy." Lana pointed to her temple. "You want me to take you upstairs?"

Jadyn nodded as she stepped out of the room. Christian had always been a considerate man. She doubted he would raise his voice to her or cause a scene if she tried to talk to him in the bar, but her palms still sweat as Lana led her to the stairwell and placed her hand over the access panel to allow her to leave the lower floor.

"Rider's working on arrangements to draw out the vampire who's after Christian," Lana said as they took the stairs up. "If all goes well you might be able to get out of here soon, get back to your life."

Jadyn didn't respond. Sadness hung heavy in her heart. What life did she have to get back to? What would Christian do after they were cleared to leave the protection of Rider's building? Would he stay with her or leave her behind?

"You don't seem excited about that," Lana commented as they exited the stairwell. "Rider and his security are really good so try not to worry too much. The other guys don't stand a chance. I mean, not to brag, but I'm on your side and I'm Imortian. I can slay all day."

Jadyn forced a small closed-mouthed smile, hoping to stop any further questioning before the tears she felt burning the backs of her eyes welled up and spilled over.

Lana guided her to the door leading to The Midnight Rider and opened it. "There he is," she said, standing back to allow Jadyn to enter. "Good luck."

Jadyn offered another hint of a smile, the best she could do, and crossed the floor toward the booth where Christian sat. He'd chosen a booth along the wall, near the front, but still in shadow. He faced the front door so she couldn't see his face as she approached, but the set of his shoulders and way his head hung forward told her he was still upset. As she passed the actual bar in the center of the room, an Asian bartender nodded toward her before glancing Christian's way, seeming to know who they were. She supposed she shouldn't be surprised. Everyone in the bar was probably some sort of vampire or shifter with a direct mind-link to Rider and each other, except maybe for the guy she remembered from Rider's office. Rome. He stood by the front door with his muscular arms folded, his feet in a stance that said he was ready to jump in if anyone got rowdy. He nodded at her and offered a warm smile before his face shifted back into an intimidating mask.

"Can I sit here or do you still want to be alone?" Jadyn asked softly as she reached Christian's booth.

He looked up from the bottle he held loosely with both hands and gestured toward the other side of the booth with his head, inviting her to sit.

"I'm sorry," he said as she slid into the seat across from him. "You didn't deserve the way I behaved, or to be left behind. I just..."

"You needed some space," she finished for him when he seemed lost for words. "That's perfectly fine, and I'm not mad at you. I just want to help."

"I don't think you can. I don't know that anyone really can." He took a pull from the bottle and set it back down on the table top, next to two empty ones.

"You look better," Jadyn advised, noticing his color had returned and the dark circles under his eyes were gone. "What happened with Rider? You were so upset after speaking with him. What did he say?"

Christian opened his mouth to speak, but paused as a woman in jeans and a black shirt came by and set two fresh bottles in front of him before picking up the empty ones and setting them on her tray. "Would you like anything?" the woman asked Jadyn. She was pretty with brunette hair and light green eyes. She looked like a normal woman, except for the tips of her ears, which were a little pointy.

Jadyn shook her head. "Thank you though."

"All right. Just holler if you need anything," the woman said and left them.

"Is that a normal amount of blood for you to drink?" Jadyn asked, eying the bottles.

"I'm tanking up." Christian lightly gripped the top of one of the bottles and turned it slowly. "You remember what that man, Chuck Lester, said during Rider's interrogation? About Jaffron?"

Jadyn's stomach rolled a little as she remembered what had happened to Chuck Lester. She forced the mental image away and focused on the actual information they'd learned prior to Rider deciding to kill the supplier of that information. "He said the man behind all this is a vampire named Jaffron, and Jaffron is the man who turned you into a vampire."

Christian nodded. "One of my friends in Baltimore was abducted by that same vampire and he was tortured mercilessly. Jaffron is part of a very large group of paranormal beings who worships the devil. For your own safety, I can't give you a lot of details, but I'm part of a group who has been trying to wipe out Jaffron's group, and other groups like his."

Jadyn let this information sink in, starting to realize why Christian would be so upset about learning about Jaffron. "I can imagine how horrible it would feel knowing you were turned by someone that awful, but it wasn't your choice. You were attacked and turned without any agreement on your part. It wasn't your fault."

"No, that turn wasn't." He picked up one of the bottles and tipped it back, taking a long pull. When he set it down, he curled his lip in disgust. "Jaffron sired me. That makes me his fledgling. Sires have the ability to control their fledglings. They can make them do anything they want. I was spared all these centuries because..." He sighed and let out a small, strangled laugh that sounded anything but merry. "I know you and Rider had a discussion in his office earlier and you saw some of the books he'd researched from. Rider believes I am, or I was, an angel. As much as I don't want to believe it, he made a good case."

Jadyn reached across the table and took Christian's hand. "Hey... you're a good man."

"Man," he muttered. "Yeah, just a man, but with a little angel protection I don't even deserve. Rider thinks this energy inside us is grace. Mine was enough to somehow block me from Jaffron all these centuries, but he's found a way to track it, to track me. He wants to find me so he can control me. At close range, my grace wouldn't be enough to protect me from being his puppet. He could use all my power to hurt those I care about the most."

"Oh, Christian..." Jadyn squeezed his hand. "That's scary, I know, but Rider has a lot of power too, and his security is impressive. I'm sure he's thinking of a plan to—"

"He thought of a plan." Christian pulled his hand away and raked it through his hair. "I did it. I made a choice. This time I allowed the darkness in."

Jadyn frowned. "What do you mean?"

Christian's eyes glistened as he lowered his hands to the table and tightened them into fists. "Rider is powerful. With him as my master, Jaffron can't control me. I pledged myself to Rider. I let him drink from me and I drank from him, creating a powerful bond. I didn't choose to allow Jaffron to force this dark beast on me, but I willingly accepted Rider's mark. He's a decent guy, for a vampire, but he's still a vampire and I pledged my loyalty to him."

Jadyn's mouth dropped open. It made sense now. His paleness, the dark circles. Rider had probably drank a lot from him to form the bond. Christian was tanking up to replenish what he'd lost, and he was torn because of what he'd done. He was ashamed. "Jaffron would have controlled you, made you turn on your own people. You said it yourself. You didn't have a choice."

"I had a choice. I chose this." He took a drink of the blood, grimacing as he finished and placed the bottle down harder than necessary. "Rider said he couldn't see me falling, thinks between his own suspicions and what was said in the interrogation, someone might have betrayed me. An angel. He said it like this cleared me in some way, you know? It wasn't my fault what happened. I didn't turn my back on Heaven. I didn't fall. I was pushed, but I still chose to accept him as my master. That was *my* choice."

"You are being way too hard on yourself."

"No, I'm not being hard enough. I'm supposed to be better than this."

"Because you were created as an angel? You have no memory of any of that." She sat back, realizing he'd mentioned their grace, and remembered Rider telling her he had a theory about her, but he'd never shared it with her. "You said our grace. If I have grace inside me too..."

"Khiderian, the fallen angel I mentioned before, sacrificed himself to save Marilee two years ago. Rider believes Khiderian may have impregnated a woman prior to his turning and a small amount of grace carried through the family line, so small it wasn't even detectable, but when he sacrificed himself and became human two years ago, this strengthened the grace in his most worthy descendant."

"Me? So I'm like, what, a nephalim?"

Christian shook his head. "The small amount of grace you have makes you a guardian. In your case, a guardian of beasts, judging by your abilities centering around animals. You're not exactly an angel, but you have a little angelic ability. You were never in Heaven so you don't carry the burden of maintaining angelic purity."

"The purity you're trying so hard for? You may have been an angel at one time, Christian, but if Rider's right and you were pushed out, attacked, and turned, how can you be expected to still attain those standards?"

"Because it's what an angel is. An angel is a servant of the Lord, not a creature with selfish needs, a creature who lusts, or a creature who accepts a vampire as his master. An angel serves, no matter what."

"Christian, you were already a vampire when you created this bond with Rider. You were doing what you had to do to protect the people you care about. Is that so wrong? Are the people you care about not worthy? What about me? Jaffron's men were tracking me to get to you. They can track my grace too, what little I have. They could still try to get me. Am I not worthy enough to be protected?"

"You know how I feel about you."

"No, I don't. You saved me when I was just a girl, but you saved a lot of kids. I wasn't special. You've protected me during all this, but I know you'd protect any woman who happened to walk into your church at that moment and got caught up in this mess."

"I wouldn't have kissed any woman," he said. "I've never felt that desire with anyone other than you."

"Yeah, you kissed me," Jadyn agreed. "Then you pushed me out of the room and closed the door in my face."

"Jadyn... I was seconds away from sinking my fangs into your neck, and desiring more than just your blood."

Her face heated as she realized what he meant. She forced herself to ignore the warmth in her cheeks and hold his gaze. "I told you before that I've compared every man I've met to you and they all came up lacking. That's true. I care a lot for you, I always have, but what you're talking about is something I won't do until I'm married so I would have told you to stop, and you would have. You're a good man. You were a good man before you fell, or were shoved out, or whatever happened. You were a good man when you saved me the first time. You were a good man when I found you again, and you're still a good man now. You wouldn't have taken anything from me that I refused to give willingly so there was no need to push me away." She looked at the bottles in front of him. "As for my blood, I would have given you that if you needed it."

"I know you would, because you are a very loving and giving creature, which I think is what draws me to you." His mouth curved upward, but the expression was too weighted with sadness to be called a smile. "You are a guardian of beasts, which is what I am. I am a blood-sucking beast, a parasite that feeds off what gives others life. I went without fresh blood for so long, but in recent years it's been harder and harder to ignore the heartbeats around me, to say no to the taste of hot blood flowing freely straight from the vein. I lived peacefully, avoided violence, but that has become harder as well. I still say I abhor it, but those words are a lie. There was a time I would have stopped Rider from killing Chuck Lester. I would have valued that human life, even though the man had chosen to follow the devil. I would have forgiven him."

He lowered his head, but not before Jadyn saw the tears rimming his eyes, and sniffed. "I'm finding it harder to care for all life. I'm picking and choosing, like a hypocrite. I'm becoming an increasingly darker version of myself. If it's true, if I was an angel, it doesn't matter whether I fell or was betrayed, because there's no angel left in me. If anything, I am an abomination."

"Dude, say some more self-pitying bullshit like that and I will punch the stupid out of you."

Christian's head came up, his eyes filled with recognition, before Jadyn could turn her head fully to take in the man who'd just intruded in their private conversation. He was tall and well-built, but not overly so, with short tawny hair and a chiseled jaw. Green eyes glanced at her before refocusing on Christian. He wore jeans and a dark T-shirt under a leather jacket, and appeared to have a sword strapped to his back. He reminded Jadyn of someone, but she couldn't quite place who.

"Jacob!" Christian rose from the booth and embraced the man, who stiffened before reluctantly returning the hug.

"Man, this is killing my image," the man complained, but grinned before separating. He glanced around the bar and that was when Jadyn noticed a lot of the people in the bar looked at him very unfriendly.

Christian looked around too, seeming to pick up on the atmosphere. "Join us. I'm sure Rider will be out soon"

"Yeah, if none of his people attack me first."

"They sense what you are, just as you can sense them."

"Yeah, I know." The man looked down at Jadyn again, the corner of his mouth curving upward before he removed the scabbard and placed it on the tabletop with the sword inside, and slid in next to her. "I'm Jake. You must be Jadyn."

Jadyn raised her eyebrows and turned toward Christian, who had taken his seat across from them.

"Jonah is Jake's brother," Christian explained. "He would have told Jake about you when they spoke."

"Oh." She looked at Jake, trying not to stare as she tried to think of who he reminded her of. "You came all the way here from Baltimore? That's a long drive."

"It wasn't as much of a drive as it was a poof," he said, reaching across the table for one of the dark glass bottles. "I'm just going to take this off your hands."

"Oh, that's—"

"I know," he said, cutting Jadyn off before he took a long drink and set the bottle down in front of him.

"Jacob, why are you here? Your family needs you with them," Christian said, his tone mildly scolding.

"You're family too, jackass, and you're in a pretty messed up situation." Jake looked up at the exact moment Rider Knight stepped through the back door of the bar, as if he'd sensed the vampire coming, and muttered, "This should be interesting."

The bar became uncomfortably quiet as Rider crossed the floor, his gaze locked onto Jake. The air seemed to thicken, and as Rider approached the table, Jadyn noticed the golden glow in his eyes.

"I'm here to help my friend, not raid your nest, so you can ease back on the vamp power," Jake told him, voice low. "Word is you've been helping him. I appreciate that and as long as I don't see any vampires or shifters killing humans for no good reason, we won't have any issues."

Rider's eyes bled back to blue and he took a seat next to Christian, placing him directly in front of Jake. "I never thought I'd see the day Jake Porter would call a vampire his friend."

"Well, our boy here isn't any ordinary vampire, is he?"

"No, he's not, and you're not any ordinary slayer." Rider eyed the bottle in front of Jake. "A slayer who drinks blood. What exactly does that make you?"

"Dangerous, and extremely hard to keep dead. I wouldn't recommend trying."

"If the two of you are done," Christian said, "I believe we are all on the same side."

Jake and Rider stared each other down for a long, tense moment. During that time, Jadyn became aware of distress coming from beyond the bar. She sensed Rider's dog clawing at his office door, trying to get out. She closed her eyes and focused, sending the dog the message that Rider had not left him, and would be returning. After a moment of whining, the dog calmed down and although she sensed him sulking, she also sensed he would wait patiently.

She opened her eyes to see all three men staring at her. "What?"

"You made a little ... sound," Christian told her.

"You barked," Jake advised.

"It wasn't a bark," Christian said, giving Jake a dark look before returning his attention to Jadyn, whose cheeks were aflame. "It was like a little growl. It was cute."

"Oh." She lowered her gaze to the table. "Rider's dog was clawing at his door, trying to get out. I was telling him Rider would be back, and to calm down."

"You have a dog?" Jake asked the vampire. "Like a pet?"

"Apparently," Rider answered, not sounding too thrilled. "That's not important right now. Why is this sword on the table?"

"I didn't want to sit with it strapped to my back and stab myself in the ass."

"That's not exactly what I was asking."

"Where did you get this sword?" Christian asked, looking at the weapon strangely. Jadyn really looked at it for the first time, and saw it appeared to be made of glass, or crystal, similar to the sword Christian had used before.

"The Dream Teller called me to the dream realm where I had a chat with her and the same angel who tried to get me to kill Marilee, an angel who thought I might need to use this if shit really goes south." Jake narrowed his eyes, looking between Christian and the sword. "Touch it."

Christian looked over at him. "Why?"

Jake shrugged and took a drink of blood. "I heard you have one similar to it. I'm wondering if this one responds to you since it belongs to someone claiming to be your sister. She's a real bitch, by the way."

Christian glared at Jake disapprovingly, but for only a moment before his face softened. "So, it's really true?"

"That you were a whole-ass angel? Yup. Wings and all, I guess, whenever you wanted to sprout 'em. One of your brothers or sisters wanted you out of the picture so he or she started making deals with Lucifer's ass monkeys."

"*The* Lucifer?" Jadyn asked. "As in Satan?"

"Satan, Lucifer, Beelzebub, the devil, whatever you want to call him, that's the guy." Jake continued telling Christian what he'd learned. "Anyway, whoever wanted rid of you got hold of some really dark magic that sucked your feathered ass out of Heaven, stripping most of your grace, and making it look like you chose to fall. The angel already arranged to have a group of men in place to beat the hell out of you. They were promised riches beyond their wildest dreams if they beat you to death. They failed to bludgeon you to death, but they beat you senseless, giving you amnesia in the process."

"That, I remember, although I never knew the attack had been arranged."

"I'm pretty sure you also didn't know who the woman was who took care of you after that, because she, too, was an angel."

Jadyn's mouth dropped open. She looked over at Christian to see he was stunned. "The tattoo. That's why it's changing. She must have used her grace or something to create it."

"What do you mean, changing?" Rider asked, looking between the two of them.

"I caught sight of the tattoo earlier before stepping into the shower," Christian told him. "It's changed from when it was given to me. Apparently, it's changed a little since Jadyn first saw it too. I never noticed before that it was changing because after decades of looking at it and not figuring out what the message was, I quit looking at it."

"The woman was actually a *fallen* angel. She fell long before you were screwed over. It turns out there was a prophecy about an angel betraying another angel. She was aware of it. She knew who you were. I don't understand why the angels weren't allowed to just tell you what happened or why the hell their all-powerful asses don't just know who did this to you, but you know how this prophecy shit works. The tattoo was the best thing the fallen angel could do, I guess. She imbued it with her grace. I know she told you it would help you find yourself, but it also protected you."

"How?" Christian asked.

"The angel attempted to nurse you back to health. Since you didn't truly fall, your grace could have replenished itself with enough time. Your memory should have come back with it. The angel who betrayed you knew this and got scared. A direct attack would have revealed him, so he went another route and pulled in more help. An angel was a prize Jaffron couldn't resist.

He was told where to find you and just as you were starting to really get your health back, before your grace could come back, he made sure that didn't happen. He turned you into a vampire and did even more damage to your memory because you apparently fought pretty hard against him. He beat the hell out of you before he could turn you, adding even more boo-boos to your melon. He was also told about the former angel who'd helped you. After he turned you, he left you to feast on her before killing her. The very last trace of her grace went into that tattoo along with her prayer that it would shield you, and that tattoo has shielded you from Jaffron ever since. Her name was Griana, and you have carried a part of her on your back all this time."

Christian reached back and touched his shoulder blade, where the tattooed wings would be beneath his dark sweater. His eyes glistened with unshed tears as he clenched his jaw. "I remember her face now, the sound of her voice. She told me this image came to her in a dream."

"And who do we know who lives in a realm where prophecy is stored and has the ability to visit people in dreams?"

Christian looked directly into Jake's eyes. "The Dream Teller, who never bothered to share any of this before."

"Yup. Your betrayal was predicted long before it happened, long before Griana fell and was conveniently in place to help you when the time came. As usual with this prophecy stuff, the Dream Teller gives us only a little, only when it suits her reasons."

"What about the angel?" Christian asked. "This one who speaks of me as a brother? Why didn't she tell me anything? It seems she knew."

"I told you she's a bitch." Jake took a drink. "She claims she actually wasn't allowed, none of them were allowed to. It was like some order on high or something. Even Khiderian, who had fallen, was told to never speak a word of it."

"So he knows too?" Christian's eyes darkened.

"He knew you were an angel who had fallen, which was the story all the angels knew. He knew he wasn't allowed to tell you. Of course, that was before he sacrificed himself for Marilee and became human. His memory of all that is about as bad as yours now. He knows he was an angel but can't remember crap."

Jadyn rubbed her temples. "This is insane."

"Welcome to the world of prophecy," Jake muttered before continuing. "Your, uh, sister or whatever, she says she wanted to tell you but the punishment would be severe. Still, she watched over you, sending you images of glowing crosses to guide your way when you were in trouble, and she popped down into that parking lot when your church was attacked, trying to help."

"The men who grabbed her, they were angels," Christian said.

Jake nodded. "She was banished to the Dream Teller's realm because of her interference. While there, she went looking for answers and found some. She found the prophecy. She couldn't see the angel who betrayed you though, but she knows what he did. I'm saying he because she thinks it may be an angel who has steadily tried to talk her out of watching over you, but she's not definite. She knows that the angel who betrayed you sent Jadyn to Baltimore, using the same glowing crosses to guide her way, and while she was banished to the dream realm, that same angel guided both of you to a house where Jaffron's people attacked, and she believes that angel will come for you if he feels his identity may be blown."

"Wait..." Jadyn's stomach dipped. "The angel who betrayed Christian led me to Baltimore? Why was a bad angel leading me to him?"

The look Jake gave her didn't do anything useful for her stomach. "Like I said, the angel couldn't attack him directly without revealing himself. He was too afraid to make direct contact with Jaffron again, but he knew Jaffron wanted the angel-vampire he'd created and would never stop looking. Do you know how you became a guardian?"

"Rider thinks I'm descended from Khiderian, and when he sacrificed himself, I became a guardian of beasts."

"You also became a beacon. Jaffron had been working with witches for decades, tracking every hint of grace they detected through their dark magic, searching for Christian. I know Christian rescued you when you were a little girl. The tiny little grace inside you then reacted to him, and the angels saw it, but Jaffron couldn't. When you became a guardian, the one who betrayed Christian knew your grace was then strong enough for Jaffron to track."

Jake looked at Christian for a moment before meeting her gaze again. "Jaffron's mark was distorted by Christian's grace so he couldn't locate him through the normal sire-fledgling link. Christian's grace was hidden by the tattoo Griana had gifted him with. The prayer of protection she spoke upon dying stayed with the grace she'd imbued in it, and canceled out Christian's ability to be traced by the dark spell. However, once you became a guardian your grace was strong enough to be traced, and the angel who betrayed Christian knew Jaffron would be tracking you so he led you to Baltimore. Then, he waited until you just happened to stumble upon Christian again."

"And once I did, Jaffron's minions had visual confirmation of Christian."

Jake nodded, and handed her a napkin, which was when she realized she'd shed a few tears in silence. They'd suspected she'd led Jaffron's men to Christian, but knowing it had been planned so far in advance, and by the very angel who betrayed him, made it feel even worse.

"This isn't your fault," Christian told her, his voice firm.

"Christian's right," Jake agreed. "It isn't your fault. This is part of a very old prophecy set in motion before you were ever born, but it's only part of it. Christian, this ties in with the Blood Revelation. Jaffron is working for Satan, recruiting for his army. You were his fledgling and he isn't done trying for you. If he succeeds in getting you, he'll have all your knowledge. He'll have access to all you know about the Blood Revelation, including the children."

"I know. Rider found warning of this in his books." Christian looked at the vampire, who sat quietly, taking in everything. "We've made arrangements so Jaffron shouldn't be able to control me."

"Yeah, The Dream Teller saw and told me, but leading Jaffron to you isn't Jadyn's only part in all this. You've been feeling things over the last couple of years, going through changes, feeling temptations. If you give in to temptation enough, you could lose every bit of angel you have left in you." Jake looked at Jadyn, and her blood ran cold under his scrutiny. "Jadyn isn't just a beacon for your enemies. She's your greatest temptation, and has the potential to be your greatest downfall. The two of you probably shouldn't even be near each other."

CHAPTER TWENTY-ONE

C hristian's heart plummeted just as fast as Jadyn's face fell. He fixed a hard glare on Jake. "That's ridiculous, and completely uncalled for."

Jake held his hands up. "Dude, I'm just the messenger."

"Relay the message without being so cruel."

"He's just telling the truth," Jadyn said softly. "I mean, an angel told him, right?"

"Thank you," Jake said as he reached across her and picked up a small rectangular menu propped between condiment bottles. "Man, I'm starved. If you don't mind, I'm going to eat something."

"Order whatever you like," Rider told him, crooking his finger as he got the pointy-eared server's attention. "On the house."

"Awesome. Ooh, pie. Love me some pie," Jake murmured.

"Dean Winchester," Jadyn said, her voice still holding a trace of sadness. "That's who you remind me of."

"What?" Rider's eyes darkened, focused on Jake as the slayer groaned.

"Why do people always say that? I'm nothing like that douchey character."

"You do favor him," Rider agreed, his voice a growl. "Stay away from Danni Keller."

"Who?"

"Are you ordering?" the server asked as she approached the booth.

Jake looked between Rider and Jadyn, frowning before he set the menu back where he got it. "Yeah, I'll take the bacon cheeseburger basket, chicken tenders, a basket of onion rings, and a big slice of whatever pie's the best. Oh, and whatever these guys want."

The woman raised her eyebrows and looked at the others. Rider shook his head, as did Jadyn.

"I'm good with this," Christian said, raising one of the bottles of blood in front of him. "Jadyn, you need to eat."

"I have food downstairs. I don't want anything greasy at the moment."

"All right. I'll put that order in," the woman said. "How about a beer while you wait?"

"Awesome." Jake smiled at the woman and she blushed before leaving them.

"Fae?" Jake asked.

Rider nodded. "I don't employ a lot of fae, but Hazel's not exactly a representative of the more peaceful ones. She has a mean streak when provoked."

"If you'll excuse me, I think I'll grab something to eat downstairs."

"Jadyn." Christian reached across the table, but Jake had swiftly moved out of the booth, allowing her to exit.

"Let her go," Rider said softly. "You know she's safe here, and even I can sense she needs a little space right now."

Christian watched her leave, moving quickly across the bar as if restraining herself from outright running away from him. He didn't like to hurt people's feelings. Seeing the hurt in Jadyn's eyes wounded him as well. He turned his gaze back to Jake, who'd repositioned himself in the center of the seat across the booth. "You are my friend, but I have the strongest urge to punch you directly in the center of your face right now."

"Awesome," Rider mimicked Jake with the gleam of dark amusement in his eyes.

The slayer gave the vampire an unfriendly look before sighing. "Dude, I'm not forcing the two of you apart. As far as I'm concerned, people can do whatever they want with each other as long as it's consensual, but I was given this information for a reason. You should at least know what you're risking with her."

"Do you think I didn't already know? You didn't have to say anything in front of her. You've hurt her feelings."

"I'm sorry for that. This is prophecy shit. Someone always gets hurt at some point." He nodded politely at the fae server as she deposited a mug of beer in front of him and left. "Tell you what, give me the same understanding I'm giving you for telling Count Gucci over here about my kid. Yeah, I know about that, which is why I even mentioned the prophecy in front of him in the first place. The Dream Teller's blind ass sees all. Sometimes you just have to risk saying things in front of people."

Rider looked down at his black silk shirt. "Count Gucci?"

"Just take it as a compliment," Christian told him. "He calls most people a whole lot worse." To Jake, he said, "I'm sure the Dream Teller also showed you that Rider figured out most of all this himself. He has a lot of ancient texts in his office and appears to be very knowledgeable. It's no wonder Seta works with him from time to time, and if Seta trusts him, you know he's trustworthy."

"I suppose." Jake narrowed his eyes on the brooding vampire. "I've heard your name pop up from time to time. Word is, you can just yank people's insides out of their bodies."

Rider shrugged. "I can do a lot of things."

They stared at each other until Hazel arrived with a tray of food, and set it all in front of Jake. He grinned with genuine merriment, always happy to eat, and pushed the sword closer to Christian, allowing more room for his personal buffet. "Touch the damn sword."

Christian sighed, and waited for the fae to leave them before he touched the tip of the sword. Golden color shimmered over the blade, and faded away, leaving the sword as it had appeared originally.

"Well, that was disappointing," Jake mumbled around a bite of cheeseburger. "But not surprising. This is why I was sent here. You have the angel juice, but you don't believe in it so it's just sitting there, doing nothing. First, you were in denial because you thought it meant you had fallen, then when GQ McFang over here figured out the traitor angle, you still didn't want to believe it because you had all this guilt about how you've been craving blood straight from the tap since you drank from me like five years back." He swallowed the last of the burger and picked up an onion ring before pointing at Christian. "Still a dick move, by the way."

"You survived, and we saved Jonah."

"Yeah, yeah." Jake ate the onion ring and continued. "Then this woman comes back in your life. You already cared about her, but she's not the little girl you saved anymore. She's all grown up now, looking good to you, and she starts giving you twitches where you've never twitched before."

"Jake." Christian lent a little growl to his tone.

"What?" The slayer laughed before devouring a chicken tender dipped in barbecue sauce. "We all got dicks and we all wanna put 'em in someone, but you're all hung up on the angel thing and feeling guilty as hell, which is screwing with your head. Am I right?" He looked at Rider for backup as he scarfed down another chicken tender.

"He does have a point," the vampire agreed, "and some sauce on his chin."

"We all have points, but only Christian tortures himself over acknowledging his wants some action," Jake said as he grabbed a napkin and wiped his chin. "Bitchy McBitch-Wings was adamant that you not do that, but, dude, you can't be hating on yourself for wanting to. You were an angel, but another angel got the drop on you. That's not your fault, and it says nothing about your worthiness. Why the hell do you think an angel would do that to you anyway?"

Christian frowned. He'd been so focused on how he could have allowed such a thing to happen, he'd never even wondered why another angel would go to such lengths to get rid of him. "I don't know."

"Yeah, you probably don't, because you don't have a devious bone in your body no matter how much you try to tell yourself you're... what was that bullshit again? An abomination?" Jake finished off his onion rings, took a swig of beer, and pulled the large chunk of apple pie toward him, his eyes gleaming as he picked up the fork. "Clearly, you were worthy of something pretty damn great and that jealous asshole saw it. You weren't tossed down here with us losers because you weren't worthy of Heaven. You were betrayed because you were too great. If you quit licking your wounds like an abused mutt, you could be great again."

"Not with the angel who betrayed him in the picture," Rider said, "but first we need to get Jaffron squared away."

"Oh, you leave that red-headed sonofabitch to me," Jake said, looking up from the pie he'd halfway devoured. "We have history."

"I don't care who takes care of him as long as they wipe him from existence," Rider said. "Of course, with you here now, I can make a very good alteration to my plan that will give you a face to face with Jaffron."

Jake set his fork down. "I'm listening."

"Jaffron is working with at least one witch. Whenever they track Jadyn, they open a portal and he sends his army through. So far that army has included a witch, some werewolves, and other shifters. At night I'm sure it would include vampires as well."

"So you're going to use Jadyn to draw them out after you find the perfect location?"

Rider nodded. "I've found the location. It's a secluded area, a good place for a battle we don't want seen by human eyes. So far, Jaffron hasn't come through the portal. I believe he's wherever that portal is opened from though. I was going to jump through it."

"No." Jake shook his head. "You stay with Christian, and I assume you'll have your own army of men and women. Stay with them. I'll go through the portal and gank Jaffron's ass."

"I'll send one of my men with you. I know you're a slayer, but a little backup never hurt anyone."

"Fine." Jake picked his fork back up. "Make it a woman. That bastard has worked with sirens before. I'd rather have backup who can't get ensnared in case he's brought in more."

"Wise. I'll make sure the women with us on the battlefield are aware sirens may be in the mix so they'll take them down immediately if they come through the portal."

"When is this going to happen?" Christian asked.

"Jaffron already sent in a spy today," Rider said. "I'd rather strike before he sends in anyone else. Frankly, I'd like to take care of this matter as quickly as possible and get back to business as usual."

"You're a vampire and you run a business where you employ a wide assortment of paranormal beings, from what I can tell," Jake said. "I doubt you ever have business that could be considered usual."

"True, but dealing with angels is beyond the realm of unusual, even for me."

"Yeah, I'll give you that." Jake shoved a chunk of pie into his mouth, and barely chewed before swallowing. "With Jaffron out of the picture, the angel will be forced to reveal his hand if he wants to wipe out Christian. Hell, he might have to whether we kill Jaffron or not. Angels can see all kinds of shit.

He probably knows we've figured out that you didn't actually fall and it's just a matter of time before you start to remember more. You remember who did this to you, and it's all over for him. He'll try to kill you out of pure spite then."

"If I remember. Listening to the two of you telling me what happened to me... It's like listening to a story of someone else's life. I can't picture it."

"You don't want to picture it," Jake said, voice sharp, as he finished off the pie and shoved the plate away. "You have all the juice, man. I know you pulled out one of those angel swords when you were defending Jadyn at that house. Khiderian couldn't do that shit. He was angel enough to save Marilee through a sacrifice and he had some cool psychic power, but he wasn't on your level. You didn't fall, not for real, and yeah, you got turned, and I know about the arrangement you worked out with Rider." He looked over at the vampire. "You'd better not take advantage of my boy."

"Your boy will be fine. Jaffron could have puppeteered him if he managed to get to him. With my mark on him, he won't be able to bend him to his will. You're welcome."

Jake narrowed his gaze on the vampire and held it for a moment before continuing. "The Dream Teller knows what you did, and so does your bitch-ass sister. They know it's made you doubt yourself even more, which is the only bad part of what you did. You were already a vampire, and that was done to you without your consent, but you have fought harder against that beast than anyone I've ever come across. The vampire part of you never killed the angel, not completely. You still have a lot of grace, and you can do some amazing shit with it, but you have to have faith in yourself, brother."

Christian looked down at the weapon peeking out from the scabbard. It was a beautiful piece of art, and he sensed its power. He imagined the golden-eyed woman swinging it, slicing through demons with little effort. Again, some vague memory of her pressed against his mind, but stayed just beyond reach. "The angel. What is her name?"

Jake stared at him for a moment before speaking. "She warned me that learning her name might bring back some, not all, of your memories. It might be jarring at first. Are you ready for that?"

Christian stared at the sword and nodded, bracing himself. "I've been in the dark far too long. What is her name?"

"Well, I call her Bitcherella, Queen of the Winged Bitch-Brigade, but—"

"Jake."

"Her name is Kiara."

PLASTER FELL FROM THE crack in the wall as the angel grunted. Pain spread from his tightly gritted teeth to his temples. Another chunk fell.

The door opened. Boots attached to thick legs in dark pants emerged at the top of the stairs. The man walked down the stairs. It was another shifter. Another disgusting creature who had chosen to dedicate its life to the dark.

The man smirked at him as he passed the pentagram confining him to the dank basement floor, grabbed the chair the last guard had vacated, and straddled it. He unwrapped the wrapper from a long strip of beef jerky and ate it with his mouth wide open.

"I see manners aren't one of your virtues, nor hygiene." He curled his nose as the monster's stench reached him.

"Bite me, Clarence."

"That is not my name."

"It's from a movie, dipshit."

The angel rolled his eyes. He was starting to prefer the lycanthropes to the wereanimals. They didn't try to be witty. They weren't as smart, either.

"Where is Jaffron?"

"Still sleeping. He won't wake up until almost nightfall. Why?" The shifter laughed. "You got somewhere to be?"

"Once my brethren discover you've trapped me here, they'll come in, swords blazing."

"For a traitor who set up one of their own?"

"They'd never suspect me, and I'm clearly here against my will."

"This whole room is warded. Angels can't find you. You're completely lost to them."

"Maybe I'll just come over there myself and take care of you."

"Yeah, maybe if your ass wasn't glued to that pentagram. You fucked over the wrong vampire, Clarence. You're not going anywhere until he gets what's his, and once he gets the ingredients he needs he's going to take your grace and turn your ass too."

The angel roared, using his anger as a cover as he pretended to try lunging out of the pentagram's hold. His body couldn't get past it, but enough of his energy could if he really pushed.

The shifter laughed at him before removing a cell phone from his pocket and pulling up a game. The angel narrowed his eyes on the animal and growled, straining to draw up as much energy as he could and push it out beyond the painted lines on the floor.

He discreetly glanced over at the crack running down the wall, the crack he'd been working on for hours. It was almost to the floor. Once he got it to the floor, it was only a matter of time...

JADYN SAT UP AS THE door opened. Christian stepped inside, and paused. "You don't have to get up."

She swung her legs over the side of the bed. "Why are you here?"

"I was going to nap, keep my energy up. I need to be at my best when we draw out Jaffron's army. Rider wants to do it just before nightfall."

"You can have the bed." She stood and moved toward the door. "I'll go upstairs."

Christian sidestepped, blocking her exit. "You don't have to do that. Stay here. Rest. You should know Rider wants to take you to the location he intends to draw Jaffron's army to."

"I figured as much." She laughed, the sound of it strangled. "I'm a beacon, right? I draw everything bad."

"Don't say that."

"It's true." She looked up into his blue eyes, noting the weariness, and cupped his cheek. "You need to rest. You're closer than ever to finally finding out who you truly are, to regaining everything you've wanted for as long as you can actually remember. I won't get in the way of that."

"You're not in the way, and I was hoping to spend some time with you, talk before I fall asleep."

Because he would be leaving her soon? She lowered her hand, letting go, and steeled herself against the sadness threatening to leak out of her eyes. "You heard Jake. We shouldn't be together."

"I'll risk it."

"I won't. I've loved you since I was a little girl. You were the boogeyman." She laughed. "You slammed a man onto the hood of your car, nearly beat him to death in front of me, but you fed and clothed me. You were dark, mysterious, and dangerous, but you never harmed me. I felt safer with you than I ever felt with anyone else. I know you think I care about you because you were my guardian angel, but I didn't know about the angel stuff when I fell for you then, or when I fell harder for you this time around. I only knew you carried a heavy darkness inside you, and you still had more good in you than anyone I'd ever known. I love all of you, even the darkness, but I know you loathe it. If I'm a temptation, if I make you feel things that make you less of the type of being you want to be, then I need to stay away from you, because you didn't fall, and it sounds like you might actually have a chance of regaining everything you lost. I won't take that from you."

"Jadyn."

He reached for her, but she turned away and left the room, fleeing before she caved, because she wanted to talk with him before he fell asleep. She wanted to watch over him while he rested, just to spend time with him before he left, but she'd meant what she said. She cared too much to risk causing him to lose what he really wanted, and what he wanted was to be with the angels he'd been taken from, not her. He only desired her because of some prophecy, some prophecy that had sent her to ruin him.

Lana wasn't outside their room so she walked down the hall and turned toward the stairwell. A man she didn't recognize was there. He nodded politely and activated the access panel before opening the door. "Rider is in his quarters and asked not to be disturbed, but you're welcome to go to the bar or use the gym if you'd like."

"The bar will be fine," she said, opening her senses until she locked on to the dog. She caught an image of him lying beside Rider's bed, waiting for the vampire to fall asleep so he could climb up with him.

The man escorted her to the bar, leaving her on her own once she was through the door. She saw Jake sitting in the same booth she'd shared with him earlier. He nodded to her by way of greeting. Deciding she'd rather not deal with him at the moment, Jadyn moved over to the bar and slid onto a vacant stool far enough from other people that she didn't think she'd be bothered.

"What can I get you?" the Asian man bartending asked as he placed a small bowl of peanuts near her.

"A black coffee, please."

"Coming right up."

The coffee had barely begun to cool before a plate with a slice of pie was set on the bar top next to her, and Jake Porter took the seat on her right side.

"Well, if it isn't Dean Winchester. Here to warn me off of Christian? Don't worry. I heard you the first time."

"I really wish that show had never been created," he muttered. "I don't look that much like the guy."

Jadyn looked over at him and begged to differ. "You do, and you have the same attitude, and Dean loves pie."

"Yeah, well, I love all food."

"Very Dean."

He rolled his eyes and grunted. "I came over here to check on you, and to apologize if I was too blunt. I'd just had a load of information dropped on me by a bitch who once tried to get me to kill my own half-sister, and I arrived just in time to see she really wasn't stretching the truth about the shape Christian was in. I needed to get him all clued in so I could work on building his ass up, get him to have a little faith in himself. He'll fare this upcoming shitfest a lot better if he isn't full of doubt."

"You want anything?" the bartender asked Jake as he approached, his tone not nearly as nice as it had been with her.

"I'm good, but I'll let you know." Jake gave him a big fake smile, and received a dirty look in return before the bartender topped off her coffee and left them alone.

"You aren't very popular here."

"I'm a slayer. I sense paranormal beings and it's in my genetic makeup to want to kill them all. They can sense me too. We have a nice predator-prey thing going on."

"A slayer, like Buffy the Vampire Slayer?"

He grinned. "Really? I went from Dean to Buffy? You really don't care for me."

"Hey, Buffy's cool, and Dean Winchester is a very attractive bad-ass. Being compared to him isn't bad."

"It is when you get mistaken for Jensen Ackles by a bunch of screaming girls, which has happened to me, and it sucked balls." He shook his head. "So, are we good?"

"Sure." Jadyn sipped her coffee. "So, Marilee is your half-sister?"

"Yes."

"I spoke with her on the phone not that long ago. She's taking care of my kits while I'm... whatever this is I'm doing."

"Kits?"

"Baby skunks. I rescued them after their mother was killed. I'm caring for them until they can be released, or I was."

"Marilee's taking care of baby skunks." Jake chuckled. "Yeah, that sounds up her alley."

Jadyn glanced over, noting Jake didn't have the sword he'd entered with. She looked back over at the booth and saw a server wiping it down. "Where's the sword?"

"Rider offered to keep it until it's needed. It was conspicuous. Most of the employees here are paranormal, and even some of the customers, but there's a lot of clueless humans here for the drinks and onion rings."

Jadyn scanned the bar, trying to discern who was what, but gave up. "Tell me the truth. What's going to happen tonight, and how bad could it be for Christian?"

Jake pushed his pie away and leaned on the bar before turning toward her. "Rider has a location in mind. Wide open, and no people nearby. We're all going to go there and get in position, including Christian. Once we're in place, Rider's witch associate will teleport you there. This should almost immediately cause Jaffron to send his people through a portal. Then we fight to the death, hopefully of them."

Jadyn's stomach sank. "Could Christian die?"

"Not on my watch. The dork means a lot to me. He's like a brother. So far, Jaffron's been sending his people ahead and hanging back, so if he does that this time, I'm going through the portal to root him out and kill him."

"And if he comes through?"

"I kill him on this side."

"What about the angel who betrayed Christian? You weren't given an angel's sword to kill a vampire."

"No, I was given that to take out an angel if necessary. The hope is that Christian will angel-up and defend himself if that angel shows up. If he doesn't, I have the sword as a back-up. Apparently, it's the only thing that can kill an angel."

"What does the prophecy say will happen to Christian?"

"Prophecy can be vague, but from what I've gathered, he can either remember himself and become his true self once more, or go dark and put all of us in grave danger, and by all of us I mean the whole freaking world because this prophecy is tied in with another about Satan's wrath, but I won't go into all that."

"I could make him go dark?"

Jake's brow creased. "You know, I honestly don't know. Apparently, he never actually fell so it sounded like, if I understood correctly, he actually has a shot at going back, but he can't know that so don't tell him. This thing is so tedious. He has to find his true self, and I can tell him he was betrayed, and that he has all his angel mojo if he quits the self-doubt and draws on it, but if he goes back, it'll be because of the purity of his heart. If he knows he has a shot at actually going back to heaven, and makes decisions based off that it takes away from the purity. That make sense?"

"I think so. You're saying he has to make choices based off what's in his heart, and what's the right thing to do, just because he wants to, not because he's trying to work his way back into Heaven?"

"Right. Basically, he has to be as angelic as possible, and it has to be natural."

"And an angel wouldn't fall for a human, not even a guardian." Jadyn quickly picked up her mug and took a drink, hiding the trembling in her bottom lip.

"I guess so. Honestly, Kiara seemed more hung up on the him staying away from you thing than the Dream Teller was. I'm not so sure if your presence turns him dark or just keeps him from going back home. Jaffron controlling him may have been what the prophecy was talking about when it mentioned him going dark. If so, hopefully Rider knows what he's talking about when he says his mark is strong enough to prevent that from happening."

"Who's Kiara?"

"The angel. I still say she's a bitch, but once I said her name to Christian and he remembered her, he said she was a good person, full of righteous goodness and blah, blah, blah." He shrugged. "I still say nope, don't completely trust her."

"Wait. He remembered her?"

"He didn't tell you?" Jake frowned. "Yeah, she said that saying angel names could bring back some memory, but not all. He remembered talking with her, fighting at her side, that sort of thing, but in the memories he only saw her. Dude can't even see himself as an angel. He needs to get past that. I told him the name of the angel she thinks betrayed him. Zaccharus. That name didn't ring a bell. You'd think he'd remember the guy who screwed him over."

"If he ever had the opportunity to see the face of the angel who betrayed him." Jadyn chewed her lip a bit as she remembered the gorgeous woman who'd helped them at the church. "This... Kiara. So, she was like a sister to Christian? Nothing romantic?"

"Ew. No." Jake shuddered. "From what I gather, they're like actual family. He definitely said he felt a brotherly relationship with her."

"Oh." A small smile escaped.

"You were jealous of her?"

"She's very beautiful," Jadyn said defensively. "Besides, I kind of wondered if Christian was really drawn to the grace in me, not me, myself."

"You're a guardian, which sounds like something similar to like a twentieth cousin thrice removed or something, not really a blood relative, and no, I don't think the little grace in you has anything to do with Christian's attraction to you. I don't think grace works like that."

"I guess it doesn't matter, since I'm either his downfall or just a way to ensure he doesn't get back into Heaven." She sighed. "So... we have to get him into Heaven. He deserves it."

Jake stared at her, his mouth gently curving. "You really love him, don't you?"

"I do."

"But you'd let him not just go, but leave this world completely?"

"He's an angel, Jake. He's an angel who was betrayed and turned into a vampire, yet still clung to his loyalty to God through all that, with no knowledge whatsoever of who he actually was. He still doesn't know his own name." She grabbed his arm. "Did Kiara tell you his name?"

"No. Once he recalls his name he regains all the knowledge of Heaven. He can't have that until he believes he's worthy and allows himself to be the angel he's supposed to be."

"I love him too much to see him here when he aches to be there."

"Then we get our boy his wings."

"Then we get him his wings," she agreed. Even if it meant she gave up her own heart in the process.

CHAPTER TWENTY-TWO

"**A**waken."

Christian opened his eyes, feeling the pull of Rider's power tugging him out of unconsciousness. He sat up and rubbed his eyes, blocking out the view of the vampire standing next to the bed. "*Awaken?* Were you purposely trying to sound like some old Hollywood cliché of stuffy master vampires?"

"It amuses me. I could have told you to rise and become one with the night, but that was a little much, even for me."

Not really sure how to respond to that, Christian looked around the room, hoping to see Jadyn, but it appeared to just be him and Rider.

"She's upstairs. My people tell me Jacob Porter has been keeping her company while you rested. I've told my nest to allow him peace, but I don't want him to know too much about me. He is not allowed beyond the bar."

"You can trust Jake," Christian advised, biting down on the disappointment Jadyn hadn't returned. "He could have killed me several times, I'm sure."

"He may be part of the Blood Revelation, married to one of us, and even the father of another paranormal being, but he's still a slayer. It's a hard thing for one to fight against their DNA. You know that. I'll trust him a little, but never completely. You might be family to him. I am just a vampire his genetic makeup says to destroy."

"Fair enough," Christian murmured, knowing Rider had a point. Usually, Nyla kept Jake in check, using her empathic ability to calm the beast inside him when his lust for the shedding of paranormal blood started to get out of control, but she wasn't able to leave their child to be at his side. He'd forgot to factor that in, and they were about to put him into battle. "It's time?"

"Yes. Rihanna has transported most of my people to the location already. Jadyn will be the last one since she's the beacon who will bring the army to us." Rider clasped his shoulder. "I thought you might want a moment alone with her first. Once she's transported to the site, things will move very fast. Depending on what happens, you may not get much of a chance to tell her whatever you need to say."

"Thank you." Christian stood from the bed and pushed up his sleeves. He'd gone to bed fully dressed, and was ready to go. Physically, anyway. His heart was no longer sure what he wanted. "I'm as ready as I'm going to be."

"I hope that means you're prepared to pull your sword out if needed," Rider said as he turned for the door. "No pressure, of course."

"Of course," Christian muttered as he followed the vampire upstairs, noting the diminished amount of security left behind. "Most of your nest will be in this battle, won't they?"

"I will leave behind just enough to continue to conduct business here and maintain security in place, then there are others who are on assignment elsewhere. I would have liked to have Daniel for this, but I'm not drawing Danni into this fight. She's not ready, and I'm not leaving her vulnerable where she's at. Other than that, yes, I have a large group in place."

They reached the top of the stairwell and exited onto the ground floor. The human security guard, Rome, stood in the room behind the bar, Rider's dog connected to the leash in his hand. The dog whined, and Rider shushed it. "Silence, Kutya. You cannot go with me."

Christian grinned at the newly-named dog, the brief interaction between vampire and adoring pet a small amount of much needed amusement. He'd been in many fights, and the lives of others he cared about had been on the line before, but none of those battles seemed as important as the one he was about to step into. This wasn't just a fight. This was a battle that could change everything he ever knew. He sensed he could gain everything, or lose it all, and he didn't know which outcome would be worse.

They stepped through the door, leading to the narrow hall that ran between the bar and the rest of Rider's property. Rihanna stood there, next to a portal.

"I'm going through," Rider told him. "Jadyn is in my office. Say what you need, and Rihanna will bring you through. Once we are all in place, she'll bring Jadyn and we can finish this."

Christian nodded and watched the vampire step through the portal, disappearing on the other side. Once gone, he nodded an acknowledgement to the witch and moved down the hall to Rider's office, where Jadyn awaited.

He stepped through the door to find her pacing the floor, her arms folded over her chest as she worried her bottom lip with her teeth. Ready for the oncoming battle, she'd bundled up in jeans and a thick hooded sweatshirt. She stopped mid-stride as he entered, lowered her arms, and practically threw herself at him, embracing him in a tight hold he didn't want to relinquish, but he allowed her the space to move back as she pulled away. "Be careful out there."

"I will be." He kept his hands at her waist, relishing the closeness. "I need to ask a favor of you."

Her brow creased, but she nodded. "Whatever you need."

"It's what Jake needs, actually. He'll be fighting with us. You know he's a slayer, right?"

"Yes. We spent some time talking while you rested. He explained it to me."

"It's in his genetic makeup to want to kill all paranormal beings. He fights against his nature, much like I fight against the beast inside of me, but when he gets caught up in battle, the bloodlust can be too much."

Jadyn's eyes widened. "Should he be out there?"

"A slayer is a very powerful ally to have at your side in battle, as long as he can control the desire to kill everyone. His wife is an empath. She usually fights at his side and lays her hand on him when he starts to lose control. She takes the edge off, helps him focus so he only goes for our enemies, but she's not here and we can't bring her here. She's needed where she is."

"So how are you going to keep him from losing it?"

"What's inside of him is similar to what's inside of me. It's a beast. If he gets too bloodthirsty, see if you can calm him. At the very least, try to talk him down if you can't reach through to the slayer in him using your gift. You're only a guardian, so you're still very much human. Even at his worst, he will be compelled to protect you, maybe only you."

Sadness entered Jadyn's eyes and he realized what he'd said, his poor choice of words. "Sure. I'll do my best."

"Jadyn, you're not *just* a guardian. That's not what I meant. You are no lesser than I, or any of us."

She nodded, her eyes tearing up. "Now I'm going to ask a favor of you. I want you to remember what you just said, and know it holds true for you too. You have searched for centuries for who you are, chasing after something always out of reach. You've been told now that you were an angel and you can't bring yourself to see it. You drink blood, call yourself a vampire, but you fight against it, believing that's wrong too. Neither fits, because neither is you. You may have been an angel. You may have been turned into a vampire, but those are parts of what you are, not who you are."

She placed her hand in the center of his chest and the grace inside him seemed to react, spreading warmth from his core to the rest of his body.

"You have always had the answer to who you are. Who you are is right in here. You're an angel, a servant of the Lord, a protector of mankind. You are a vampire, a dark beast who drinks blood. Both of those entities are you. No matter what your name once was, you are Christian now. You have been Christian as long as you can remember. We are ever-changing, all of us. You, right now, are who you are supposed to be in this moment. You are no greater or lesser than any vampire or angel you've compared yourself to. Remember that when you get out there. You have gifts to protect you and others. They are there for you for the taking. Use them. Believe in yourself and who you are. Know yourself as you are now, not what you think you should be, and you will make the right choices. If you get lost out there, then look for me. I know who you are, and I believe in you enough for the both of us."

Christian gasped as heat flooded his body along with images of himself. He saw himself fighting with a legion of angels, drinking from the throats of humans, watching over humans as an angel and as a vampire. He saw himself serving, worshiping on bended knee as an angel, and ministering in one of his many churches as a vampire. He saw himself as two different entities, yet the same.

Jadyn firmly pushed him away. "Now go. Your army is waiting for you."

His army. A group of people who mostly didn't know him, but put their faith in him. He looked at the woman doing the same and nodded before he stepped forward, grabbed her, and kissed her. He didn't know what was going to happen, or even if he would survive, but he knew Jadyn had just given him the greatest gift of all. She'd given him her complete faith.

He stepped back and gently released her. "I had to do that. No matter what happens out there, I'm thankful I met you. I love you."

Then he left the office before his heart glued him to the floor. He wanted to stay with her, but he knew that would be selfish. An injustice had been done centuries ago, and needed to be rectified, and he needed to wipe out the evil that dared threaten the woman who'd reminded him what love and faith really meant.

He walked past the witch, and stepped through the portal without a word, coming out into a wide clearing. The sun was almost completely gone. Vampires, shifters and other non-humans from Rider's nest formed a circle, braced for battle. The master vampire and the nurse who'd ran medical tests on him stood to his right, along with Hank and others he recognized from around Rider's building. Jake stood to his left with the angel sword strapped to his back, Lana at his side.

"You ready to do this, brother?"

Christian nodded as the portal closed behind him. Fangs descended from his gums and his fingertips tingled, his sword calling to him as the power inside him warmed his body. "I'm ready."

Jake's eyes widened, seeming to pick up the change, but he didn't say anything. The slayer turned his head to face the center of the circle, sensing something. Jadyn appeared there with Rihanna at her side. She turned and looked at Christian before a dark line of smoke formed a few feet before her.

"Here we go," Jake said, palming a dagger in one hand, a gun in the other, as Rihanna grabbed Jadyn's shoulders and teleported her to the edge of the circle as the line of smoke became a portal.

"Bring it," Christian said, reaching for his sword as the first wave of lycanthropes spilled through the portal.

"HE DREW HIS SWORD!" Jadyn exclaimed, grabbing the witch's shoulders. She barely restrained herself from shaking the woman in excitement, knowing the witch needed to focus.

Rihanna looked over at Christian. "Yeah, he looks like one pissed off warrior I wouldn't want to fuck with. What did you say to him?"

"I just reminded him who he is," she said, forcing herself to be happy for him. She had no doubt if given the choice, Christian would rejoin the angels in Heaven, leaving her and any hope she'd had of them being together behind, but after talking with Jake, it had become clear to her that loving Christian meant letting him go. Otherwise, he would always be a broken bird, and she was a guardian of beasts, not a collector.

Jaffron's lycanthropes spilled through the portal, immediately charging toward Christian. Rider and his people charged forward as well, cutting the shifters down before they could reach their prize. Christian joined them, refusing to stand by and allow himself to be protected. He was one with Rider's nest, using his fiery blade to slice through the bodies of his enemies.

Jadyn watched, mesmerized, as both sides clawed, cut, and shot at each other. A web-like film of silver netting was thrown over the witch who'd stepped through the portal with the lycanthropes. It seemed to trap her power inside her, disabling her ability to defend herself as one of Rider's men executed her. Rider's eyes glowed with power that spread over his body. He forced his glowing hand into the chest of a large man from Jaffron's army and yanked his spine out, tossing it aside as his victim's body hit the ground, and he moved on to his next opponent, all the while keeping his eyes on everything, ensuring his people's safety.

Jadyn gasped. "I didn't know vampires could do that."

"Rider is more powerful than most vampires. He has tricks others don't," Rihanna explained as she threw a fireball at a group of vampires rushing them, stopping their assault before they could get too close. "Jaffron knows Christian is here. He'll keep sending his people here to attack. I'm taking you back to The Midnight Rider."

"No!" Jadyn pointed toward Jake. He moved through the crush of shifters and vampires, Lana on his flank as he sliced, punched, and shot his way closer to the portal the enemies still poured out of. "That man is a slayer."

"Yeah, believe me, I know a slayer when I sense one, especially the legendary Jake Porter. Hotter than I would have pictured him, but still a killer."

"Exactly. You know what he's capable of. Christian asked me to keep an eye on him. Jake's a good guy, a rare breed of slayer from what I understand, but all this bloodshed can overwhelm him. He can lose control and just start killing everyone, no matter whose side they're on."

"And what are you supposed to do?"

"I'm a guardian of beasts, remember? I'm supposed to calm him, or at the very least, block him. Christian said I'm the only one here he won't want to kill if he loses control."

"Shit," Rihanna muttered. "I was supposed to take you back. Rider's going to be pissed if you get hurt."

"Yeah, I won't be too thrilled about it either," she said, folding her arms. She hadn't asked where the clearing was located, but it was chilly. Unlike the others who were actively fighting, she was standing still, being guarded by the witch, feeling the full effect of the cold. She tried to focus on what was happening around her to take her mind off the numbness in her fingertips.

Christian moved swiftly through the crowd of shifters and vampires, alternating use of his sword with his fangs. He seemed to prefer the sword, but didn't hesitate to rip a foe's throat out with his fangs if they got too close. Rider seemed to be sticking close to him, flanking him on one side as Nannette brought up the other side. She, too, appeared to be a skilled fighter in addition to a medical professional.

Rihanna cast a wave of green fire out, taking out more of Jaffron's men as they approached them, drawn to her. Christian may have been the target, but she knew she was a prize too, if only because Jaffron knew Christian would protect her.

As the green wave of fire burned out, leaving behind a row of charred bodies, Jadyn saw the bartender who'd poured her coffee earlier. She noticed he seemed to prefer fighting with his hands as he pulverized his way through anyone daring to get in his way. She wondered what he was, her curiosity soon answered as a man from Jaffron's side shifted into a weresnake and lunged toward one of Rider's women, its mouth wide open. The bartender quickly shifted into a tiger and lunged, catching the snake's body in his massive jaws, just below the weresnake's head. He took a chunk out of the snake, allowing its intended victim to bring her blade down between its eyes. The snake shifted back into a man as it died, the man's body pinned to the ground. The woman yanked her blade from his head, said something to the tiger and continued to fight.

"Look!"

Jadyn turned her head to where Rihanna pointed, and saw Jake slip through the portal, Lana right behind him.

"Now you're going back to the bar."

"No, he's going after Jaffron, but he'll be back and he could come back filled with bloodlust. You might not have time to get me back here in time of that happens. I need to stay here," Jadyn warned, trying to convince the witch not to zap her back to the bar. She watched Christian as he sliced his way through three men and flipped one over his back who'd tried to get him from behind. She couldn't leave Christian in the middle of the battle. She'd go mad with worry if she couldn't see that he was all right.

"Fine," the witch said, flinging another fireball toward Jaffron's men, "but there's only so much power I can use before I wear myself out. That slayer better take care of Jaffron quick and speed this shit up."

CHAPTER TWENTY-THREE

Jake saw his chance, and leapt through the portal, gun in hand. He knew more of Jaffron's men would be on the other side so he came through shooting. The specially crafted UV-filled, silver coated bullets tore into the shifters and vampires attempting to swarm him, mowing them down before they could gain the advantage. Unfortunately, Jake spent his last bullet, and more enemies remained.

The Imortian Rider had assigned as his backup came through the portal behind him, shifted into a giant snake and swallowed the lycanthropes remaining. Her snake-body constricted, and he heard bones crunching before she regurgitated the broken bodies and shifted back into her human form.

"You're disgusting," Jake said as he holstered the gun and waited for his stomach to settle.

Lana flipped him off and looked at the bodies littering the floor. They were inside a dark room that reeked of mildew and blood. Jake figured the blood was new, and their fault.

"This appears to have been the tail end of who he intended to send through, but I'm sure there's more here."

"Oh yeah. The jackass definitely has protection for himself. That witch he sent through wasn't the one who attacked Christian and Jadyn before. She wasn't powerful enough. That bitch is still here, protecting Jaffron." Jake inhaled, smelled the blood seeping out of what was left of the bodies around him. His hand tightened around the handle of his gun.

"Are you all right?" the Imortian asked, eying him warily.

Jake nodded, and took a deep breath. Imortians were new to him, and had a different feel to them. He wasn't as drawn to kill them on sight, at least not Lana, but the more blood he shed, the more he wanted to keep shedding it until only humans remained. "Let's get Jaffron and get back to the others. If we're lucky, they stop fighting when his body drops." And he wouldn't be pushed to the point of wanting to kill every last paranormal being on that field.

He squinted, allowing his eyes to adjust to the low light, and located the door. "This way."

He led the way through the open door, opening his senses wide. As a slayer, he sensed vampires, shifters, witches, and any other paranormal beings before he saw them. It was part of the protection in his genetic makeup. It was damned hard to creep up on a slayer, but not impossible, so Jake kept his guard up and his senses on alert. They crept down a hall, and noticed a section of wall missing. Jake stepped through what appeared to be a wide crack and cursed, seeing the crack had spread to the floor and worked its way across, splitting through a pentagram that had been painted onto the floor in blood. The hollowed-out carcass of what had once been some kind of male was spread out on the floor near it. It appeared the man had been burned from the inside while sitting in a chair that had toppled over near his body.

"This doesn't look good," Lana said.

"No, it doesn't. Something was trapped here," Jake told her. "Something that got loose. I don't even want to think about what an evil bastard like Jaffron would trap, or how powerful it had to be to break through a trap like this."

"Maybe it was something good. Jaffron's evil, remember? If he's evil, wouldn't it make sense he trapped something that could hurt him?"

Jake looked at the pentagram. He'd been held captive in a basement by Jaffron and his minions himself, but his gut told him this was something different. His gut, and the evidence that someone had blasted through a man with power capable of literally blowing out the inside of a human being. "No. This is bad. We need to find Jaffron now and get back to Christian. Whoever got out of this is probably headed toward him."

Jake took the stairs up and went through the door that appeared to have been blown off its hinges. His heartbeat increased as he went down the hall, seeing littered bodies with every step.

"Clearly, whoever they had trapped was pissed off about it," Lana said as she followed him. "Are we sure Jaffron is still alive?"

Jake held his hand up, requesting silence, and closed his eyes. He stretched his senses to the limit until he picked up cold, slow-beating hearts, the scent of lycanthropes, and the unmistakable hint of dark magic. "He's alive. The witch is protecting him."

Jake moved through the decrepit building, walking quickly. His slayer sense told him danger was near, but he didn't run from it. Jaffron had captured him, tortured him, tried to get him to reveal information that could have endangered his wife and son. That bastard deserved death and he was going to give it to him, no matter what he had to go through to do it.

"If he has sirens here, he'll use them against me. Kill me if you have to, just make sure that fucker dies too."

"Kill you?" Lana looked at him incredulously.

"He'll use sirens to force me to kill you, and then capture me. As a woman, they have no power over you. Kill me if you have to. I'll be all right."

"Yeah, sure, because that makes sense."

"It does, but I don't have time to explain it right now. Good luck." Jake rounded a corner, sensing the danger that waited beyond it. He drew the sword, figuring it was as handy on vamps and shifters as it was for angels, and rammed it through the first shifter that lunged for him. The sword seemed to come alive, igniting inside the shifter's body, burning him from the inside. Jake kicked out, knocking the shifter back, then spun around, ready to take on the next lycanthrope to lunge for him.

He fought side by side with Lana as they moved farther into the room. A rookie mistake, he realized as more lycanthropes and vampires entered the room through doors he should have noticed, but didn't, his mind preoccupied with thinking about who had escaped that pentagram.

"Get down!" he yelled as they quickly became surrounded, and he swung the sword in a circle, effectively beheading those closest to them and buying them room to maneuver.

He continued using the sword as Lana zipped and zapped around the room, her Imortian shapeshifting ability giving her the advantage of being able to hold her body in a mist-like state long enough to move from one place to another without actually having to shift into her other form. She zapped herself into place to lob off a vampire's head from behind, then zipped over to her next victim in a shower of multi-colored sparkles.

As their enemies started to thin out, a redheaded vampire entered the room, closely followed by an old hag of a woman, both focused on him.

"Jake Porter," the vampire growled, his skin paling, emphasizing the scar running down the side of his face.

"Ginger Spice," Jake replied, yanking the sword out of a vampire's chest. He flexed his hand, knocking the heart he'd pulled out of the vampire off the sword's tip. "What up, bitch? Been looking for you."

Jaffron moved aside and the witch raised her gnarled hands. She shot a blast of dark fire at him. Jake raised the sword, and once the witch's magic hit it, it reflected back onto her. She screamed and stumbled backward, her skin on fire.

Jaffron ran, and Jake went after him, leaving Lana to finish off the rest of his minions. She seemed to be holding her own, and he couldn't let the vampire escape.

"Face me, you coward!" Jake chased Jaffron into a room and skid to a stop as the vampire grabbed a sword from the wall and turned, blade in motion.

Jake raised his sword, clashing fiery crystal against metal. Jaffron was a coward who used others to fight the majority of his battles, but Jake had to give him credit. He knew how to use a sword.

"You'll never get Christian," Jake growled.

"Jake Porter, legendary slayer," Jaffron taunted him as they continued to maneuver around and charge each other, their blades clashing with a force that sent echoes ricocheting off the walls. "All this concern for a blood-sucking vampire?"

"Christian's not just a vampire," he said. "Or an angel. He's my brother."

Jaffron opened his mouth to respond, but froze as his eyes widened in pure fear. Jake felt indescribable pain and the blistering heat of fire spread through his body. He looked down to see the tip of a sword very similar to the one he, himself, still held on to emerging from the center of his chest.

He'd never sensed the enemy coming, because the enemy was a being even a slayer couldn't sense.

"Fuck!" Jaffron cried, and ran away as quickly as his vampiric speed would carry him.

The sword was drawn out of Jake's body, and he fell to his knees. He tried in vain to cover the hole left in his chest and looked up as his attacker stepped around and looked down at him.

The man was dressed in blindingly white pants and a button-down shirt. He glowed with power, as did the flaming sword in his hand. "Sorry, Jacob Porter, but I can leave no one behind who may save the man you call your brother." Wings folded out from behind the man, and he flew away, chasing the vampire who'd just escaped.

"Jake!"

Jake fell forward, bracing himself with his palms on the hard floor as he coughed up blood. The Imortian woman fell to her knees before him and gripped his shoulders. Still holding the sword, his hand tightened around it, aching to drive the sword through the woman, to kill every non-human in existence.

"Jake!"

He shook his head, growled as he fought down the dark beast inside him. "Christian," he said, and coughed up more blood as his vision went blurry. "The angel... Jaffron... on their way. Get to... the portal." He coughed again, pain nearly blinding him as more blood came up. "Go!"

"Jake!"

He heard her roar with rage before her footsteps quickly carried her away. Good, he thought as his body began to shut down. He'd catch up to her later.

CHRISTIAN KICKED OUT, knocking a vampire back before the woman could sink her fangs into him, and swung his sword, decapitating her. He caught movement toward the portal and saw a redheaded vampire emerge. He'd hoped Jake had succeeded in taking Jaffron out of the equation, but his hopes were dashed when the vampire stood straight and zeroed in on him.

Between the long, red hair and the scar down the vampire's face, he knew who he was looking at.

The vampire quickly made his way to him, cutting and biting his way closer. Once he had closed half the distance, he grinned. "Come to me!"

"No," Christian yelled back, ducking a meaty lycanthrope claw before punching the shifter in the face.

The vampire's mouth dropped open, his expression of surprise almost comical before his face screwed up in anger, a mottled red hue spreading across his skin. "I said come to me!"

"He doesn't belong to you!" Rider yelled, leaping over a pile of broken bodies, two daggers in hand.

The two vampires squared off, fighting with blades and fists, as Jaffron's remaining army continued to try for Christian. He caught sight of movement by the portal again and saw Lana come out, her body curled into a ball. She rolled to a stop, quickly stood, and looked around until she locked eyes onto him. Then she disappeared in a cascade of colors and reappeared at his side just in time to grab an approaching vampire and break his neck in a quick snap.

"Jake's dead," she said, tears in her eyes. "He went after Jaffron, and I had to stay behind to finish off the witch and the rest of Jaffron's people. I saw a winged man flying away. I couldn't save him."

"This is bad," Christian said, swinging his sword through a werewolf as it lunged for him in wolf form. "His bloodlust will be out of control when he gets here. Get to Jadyn and make sure she's ready to calm him."

Lana ducked a blow from a muscular man, sliced through his midsection, and looked at Christian in bewilderment. "Did you hear me? Jake is dead."

"Yeah, Jake dies all the time. He'll be all right," Christian assured her as he pushed her in Jadyn's direction to give himself some more room to maneuver while also keeping his eye on Jaffron and trying to stay alert for an angel attack. "Get to Jadyn now, and keep her safe!"

JADYN'S FINGERNAILS dug into her palms as she clenched her fists and shuffled, her body full of nervous energy. Jaffron's army had lessened, but there were still plenty left to do damage. Men and women on both sides were slowing down, the toll of fighting wearing them out. Rihanna wavered where she stood, the magic she'd been using taking its toll on her as well.

And now Jaffron was on the field. Her heart sank as she saw the redheaded vampire appear and quickly deduced who he was. At least he appeared to have failed in controlling Christian, but his presence still concerned her. Where was Jake?

Lana came through the portal as Rider fought Jaffron, keeping the vampire away from Christian as he and others from Rider's nest dealt with the vampires and lycanthropes swarming them. Jadyn held her breath, looking toward the portal, waiting for Jake to appear, but he didn't come out. She thought she saw tears on Lana's cheeks before the Imortian disappeared, reappearing at Christian's side.

"Where's Jake?"

"He may not have made it," Rihanna said, her voice giving away her tiredness. "If Jaffron had this many to send over here, who knows how many he has on the other side, and Jake clearly didn't kill him." The witch saw a group of werewolves in wolf form running across the field, headed toward Christian, ready to tear through him and Rider's people who were aiding him, and flung a fireball in their direction, knocking them back and setting one on fire. She groaned and stumbled backward.

Jadyn grabbed the witch's shoulders and lowered her to the ground. "You need to rest."

"No shit," the witch said, groaning. "I should have taken your ass back when I first thought to."

Jadyn yelped as someone appeared next to her and drew her fist back reflexively, but quickly realized the person was Lana. "Where's Jake? What happened?"

The Imortian shook her head as she crouched down next to her. "I don't know. I saw him die, killed by a man I'm pretty sure was an angel, but Christian says he'll be fine and told me to protect you and make sure you're ready. He thinks Jake is going to come through that portal ready to kill everyone."

Jadyn swallowed past the ball in her throat. "But... you saw him die?"

"With a hole clear through his chest and coughing up blood." Her jaw clenched as she turned her head to watch Jaffron and Rider fight. "There's no way he's coming back from... What the hell?"

Jadyn followed the Imortian's gaze and saw Jake Porter, bloody, pissed off, but whole, standing in front of the portal he'd just come from, sword in hand. He scanned the field, roared with rage, and lunged for the first paranormal being he saw. Fortunately, it happened to be one of Jaffron's women, but Jadyn could tell by the bloodlust in his eyes, he hadn't actually chosen that victim. He intended to kill everyone.

"He's Dean Winchester, back from the dead," Jadyn said, as she stood. "Get me to him now."

The Imortian reached for her as Jake finished off the woman and turned for Jaffron. The Imortian had the ability to zap herself across the field, but apparently couldn't do that with Jadyn, and Rihanna was far too weak to teleport her, so they ran, Lana slicing through anyone who tried to stop them. The whole time, Jadyn kept her gaze on Jake, watching as he tore into Jaffron with a vengeance she'd never seen. Even Rider seemed transfixed as he backed away, giving the slayer space as he repeatedly stabbed the sword through the vampire's face, not caring the vampire had died several stabbings ago.

Finally seeming to realize there was no life left in the vampire, Jake stood and locked his sights on Rider. His lips drew back in an animalistic snarl as he stepped toward him.

"Jake, no!" Jadyn screamed as Rider appeared to brace himself, preparing for battle against the slayer. Jadyn knew enough about both of them to know a fight between them would be a fight to the death, and if Rider killed Jake, she didn't think he'd leave anything left for the slayer to regenerate. If Jake killed Rider... Well, she didn't know what would happen to his nest, but she did know she didn't want to find out.

She skidded to a stop between them as Jake drew the sword and charged. Acting on impulse, she flung her arm up and grabbed Jake by the throat. "Stop!"

She opened her senses, searching for the beast inside Jake, praying Christian was right about him having one, and right that she possessed the ability to calm it. She latched onto something dark and hungry inside him, and pushed her energy into it, the same power from inside her she'd used to heal Rider's dog.

"Shhh," she whispered as Jake's eyes widened, then softened, the rage inside them bleeding out. His shoulders sagged, the anger left his body, and his knees buckled. She followed him to the ground and wrapped her arms around him, cradling him. "It's all right. It's over now."

"Well, that could have gone really bad," Rider said, above her.

Lightning streaked across the sky, thunder boomed, and a winged man in pristine white landed on the field.

"Fuck. Spoke too soon. Shit is definitely going to go really bad now."

CHRISTIAN DREW HIS sword out of the vampire he'd just killed and stepped over his body, his gaze steady on the man who'd just joined him in the clearing. Jaffron's men had all fallen. Rider's remaining men drew back, none daring to get between the two men left standing on the field.

The man stared at him, silver eyes full of loathing. His midnight hair stood out starkly against his golden skin and pristine white clothing. The wings stretching out behind him were at least four feet wide, each. The sword in his hand burned bright.

"So you finally show yourself?"

The angel shrugged. "I have nothing left to lose."

"You had everything you would have ever needed. Heaven. Our Father's love. Why did you throw it all away just to turn on your own brother? Why did you do this to me, Amuel?" Christian asked as the angel's name came to him along with memories, memories far beyond the recollection of the same angel taking Kiara away when she'd tried to help him. He remembered training with him, fighting at his side. He remembered battling Lucifer with him.

"Because you were the favorite. You were the fastest, the strongest, and the bravest. You desired nothing, but to serve. You desired nothing for yourself." Amuel's lip curled. "You were going to rule over us and you didn't even care about that. The greatest of archangels, and it meant nothing to you. The honor belonged to someone who could appreciate it, who craved it!"

"Power? Ego? That's what this is all about?" Christian shook his head. He tried to scrounge up anger, but couldn't. "We were brothers, Amuel, and you betrayed me for a title. A job."

"I deserved it. I worked harder than anybody to earn my rank."

"And what good has that done? You've revealed yourself here, out in the open for Heaven and all to see. Everything is about to be stripped away from you."

Amuel's mouth curved into a sneer. His eyes gleamed, moonlight reflecting off the silver. "As long as you never take my place, I will have won. With your blood on my sword, I will have peace."

"You are still my brother. I don't want to fight you," Christian said, memories of better times with the angel steadily flooding his memory. "Throw down your sword and I will forgive you. I will speak on your behalf and request leniency."

"No, brother." Amuel shook his head. "Lucifer was right. Sometimes you have to take what you want and destroy anyone who gets in your way, even if they call themselves family."

The angel spread his wings and leapt into the air, before diving toward Christian.

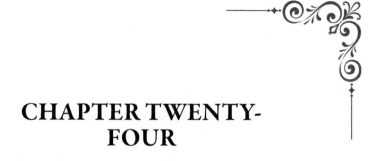

CHAPTER TWENTY-FOUR

"**F**ather, forgive me," Christian prayed as his brother barreled toward him, sword raised. "I do not want to destroy your creation, but he has to be stopped."

Christian braced himself, raising his sword as Amuel descended upon him. The burning blades struck each other, creating a sonic boom as a wave of power rippled out from the point where they connected. Christian was blown back several feet. He barely had time to look for the others and see the blast of power from the two weapons connecting had just narrowly missed hitting his friends. He and Amuel were inside a scorched circle, his loved ones just beyond the edge of burned grass, and already, Amuel was nearly upon him.

"Stay back!" Christian yelled, hoping Jadyn and the others listened as he rolled, narrowly avoiding Amuel's blade as the angel brought his sword down over him.

Christian sprang to his feet and switched hands, his palms slick with sweat. His heart thumped against his ribcage, the sound of it beating filled his ears. Amuel charged him and he jumped away, looking to the heavens for help. Amuel had revealed himself. Where were his brethren? Why had they forsaken him to fight the angel alone?

He jumped out of the way as Amuel's sword swung toward him again, crying out as the fiery blade scraped his arm, leaving a gash. There were many gaps left in his memory, but he remembered enough to recognize Amuel had ranked up to archangel since he'd been betrayed. Amuel had power and years of continued training that he'd missed. And the man was quick.

Christian continued to avoid Amuel's blade the best he could, swinging his own whenever an opportunity presented itself, but Amuel alternated between the sky and the ground, coming at him from all directions.

"You're weak," Amuel taunted him. "You've forgotten who you are because you were never worthy! You've allowed yourself to become one of these creatures you now call your family! You have no power against me!"

Christian raised his sword to deflect the blow as Amuel dove for him again. The force of the weapons connecting ricocheted down his arm, knocking him back. He nearly lost his footing. Christian struggled to remember more of himself as he continued to block Amuel's attacks, his body growing weaker as doubt engulfed him. Had he been a great warrior? Was Amuel right that he'd been the more deserving of the two?

Pain engulfed him as Amuel's blade sliced through his side and a sweep of the angel's legs sent Christian falling onto the ground. He looked up as the angel stood over him, smiling. "You're not even worthy of this death, but I will give it to you all the same," the angel said.

Christian's heartbeat pumped away in his ears as the skies opened up in a theatrical show of thunder and lighting. Amuel raised his sword, and above all the noise came a voice, the most beautiful voice, full of faith and love, screaming as loud as it could.

"Christian! I believe in you! I know who you are, and so do you! Believe in who you are!"

"I am not the angel you once knew," Christian said, staring directly into Amuel's eyes, seeing his own power reflected in the silver orbs as they widened in surprise. "I am ever-changing."

He looked to the skies and inhaled deeply, drawing in the lightning. He released it on a whoosh of air, blowing Amuel back several feet, and stood. His back burned, the tattoo he'd been gifted with no longer needed. His sire was dead, and he'd found himself. The tattoo burned away from his body, and in its place, two massive wings emerged, spreading six feet wide on either side. "Look at that," he said as Amuel picked himself up from the ground. "Mine's bigger than yours."

Amuel charged forward with a rage-filled roar, and leapt into the air. Christian joined him there, wrapping his body in lightning as he blocked Amuel's blows and delivered his own, and when the opportunity presented itself, he lowered his fangs and tore a chunk of flesh out of the angel's throat, a move he never saw coming.

He tossed Amuel to the ground and landed next to him, continuing the battle, putting every ounce of his strength and power, both angel and vampire, into the fight. He continued, never letting up, switching between blade, fangs, and lightning, until he'd pinned the angel to the ground, his foot pressed into his chest as the shocked man held his bleeding throat, staring up at him with shocked defeat in his eyes. Christian raised his flaming sword.

"Do it," the angel said. "What are you waiting for?"

Christian stared at his brother and allowed the anger to evaporate from his body. "I am an angel. I am a vampire. I am your brother. I know exactly who I am, and I am not a monster who destroys out of vengeance." He released his grasp on the sword, and it disappeared, drawn back into him. "Heaven will decide your fate. Not I. This is over."

He turned to walk toward Jadyn and his friends who awaited him along the rim of scorched earth that had served as the angels' arena. He'd made it only a few feet before he felt Amuel rise behind him and draw his sword.

Lightning streaked down from the sky. By the time Christian turned, all that remained of Amuel was smoke and ash.

When he turned back around, Kiara stood before him.

"That wasn't the one I suspected," she said, looking at the pile of charred angel behind him. "I owe Zaccharus an apology, and you. I'm sorry this happened, and that I could not help you. I wanted to."

"I know, and you did try, at the church. I hope your punishment was not severe."

She shook her head. "I was unharmed, just locked away where I couldn't interfere. We had to allow this all to play out, to let you earn your way back. You did it, brother. You resisted the temptations that have increased steadily as this moment drew closer, made all the right choices without the advantage of your heavenly knowledge, and you even spared your brother's life after he betrayed you. You can come home now."

"After all this, I can come back?"

"Yes. You've earned it." Kiara smiled, but it faltered as she followed Christian's gaze to the young woman at the edge of the clearing. "You, of course, have to say goodbye to all earthly desires, forever. To be worthy."

"Right." He stared at the woman who still cradled the slayer she'd stopped from killing, using only the goodness inside her, the woman who had believed in him when he'd needed it most, who had aided him in battle without even knowing it.

"Brother? You've redeemed yourself. Don't throw away your chance to come back home now."

He tore his gaze from Jadyn to look at his sister, and saw the fear in her eyes, the fear that he would throw away the greatest opportunity he could ever imagine, that he would throw it away for something she couldn't possibly understand.

"I can talk to our Father?"

"Of course." Kiara straightened, seemingly pleased. "Are you ready to come back home?"

He directed one last longing glance toward Jadyn, wishing he could wipe away the tears he saw spilling from her eyes as she watched him, knowing he was going to leave, and wished the best for him despite her own sadness. "I'm ready to see our Father."

She reached out to him. "Take my hand... Aurorian."

Power washed over him and he felt himself transforming as all the knowledge of Heaven crashed into him. He placed his hand in Kiara's, allowing his sister to take him home.

HE WAS GONE.

Jadyn sat in the booth where she'd last sat with Christian, staring at the place he'd once filled, fighting the urge to cry.

"You need something stronger," Jake said, sliding in next to her. He used the mug of beer he'd brought over to nudge aside the coffee that had cooled over an hour ago. He took a long drink from the bottle of blood in his hand, and set it on the table.

"I don't drink," Jadyn told him as she looked around the bar, wondering if she should start. Rider had called in another witch he knew to clean them up and get them all back. Rihanna's magic needed time to recharge. Jadyn imagined the witch was home, sleeping or doing whatever witches did to recharge their magical powers.

Nannette was at the hospital, caring for those who had been injured beyond what magic alone could fix. Some had died, which was expected in any battle, but the knowledge of that didn't make those losses any easier.

Rider was arranging burials for them. The bartender who'd turned out to be a tiger shifter was off duty, sitting on the other side of the bar, drinking. A somber air hung over the bar, unnoticed by the human patrons who'd come in for drinks, having no idea the employees had just been in what she considered a war between good and evil.

The sword Kiara had loaned Jake disappeared with her and Christian, taking all trace of angels with it, leaving them with only sad memories.

The only one in Rider's nest who seemed happy was his dog, who was just thrilled Rider had returned.

"Maybe it will help you forget."

"I don't want to forget him."

"That's not what I meant. I don't think you ever could forget him. I meant the horrors. There was a lot of blood and violence." He took another drink. "Thanks, by the way, for bringing me back to myself. The slayer part of me goes a little crazy sometimes, especially when monsters like that traitorous angel kill me and piss me off."

"Yeah, are you going to explain that?" she asked. "Lana said she saw you die, with a hole in your chest and everything."

"I've died a bunch of times, but as long as I drink blood, I come back. No, I'm not a vampire, and it's kind of a weird story, but let's just say a mad scientist kind of did me a favor and made it really hard for me to be taken off the playing board permanently." He took another drink. "You know, Christian was kind of Thor out there, all wrapped up in lightning and flying. All these years I've known him, I knew there was something special about him, but damn. Never saw that coming."

Jadyn nodded as she remembered the wings spreading from behind him, and the way he'd seemed to transform into his true angelic form as he made the decision to leave. Golden light had covered him, a white streak had spread through his hair, and his clothes had morphed into pristine white pants and a long-sleeved shirt. He'd become what he'd longed to be again. "He was beautiful, wasn't he?"

"He was freaking amazing." Jake looked at her, his gaze softening. "I've known Christian a good while. I've never seen him so much as look at a woman, not before you. Don't take his leaving as any indicator he didn't feel something mighty damn strong for you. I mean, it's *Heaven*, you know? I can't imagine anyone given the shot at going to Heaven would pass it up. Of course, someone like me can't even imagine coming close to getting that kind of offer."

Jadyn squeezed his arm. "Hey, you're not a bad guy. You protect people from a lot of monsters."

"Actually, I was thinking of my old porn collection when I said that. I had some DVDs that on their own would make sure I never set foot through the pearly gates."

Jadyn snorted a laugh, and shook her head. "I guess you need to leave soon too?"

"Yeah. Very soon, actually. I need to get back to my family." He lightly chucked her on the chin. "I just wanted to make sure you were all right first. Christian would zap my ass with lightning if I didn't take care of his woman."

"You think he's watching over us?"

"I think he's watching over *you*," Jake said, and slid out of the booth. "It's a long drive back home so I need to get started. Fucking angel-bitch was able to get me here to do her bidding, but stranded my ass. Are you staying here? I can drop you off somewhere, or take you back to Baltimore with me. Whatever you need. I can extend the rental agreement on the car if needed."

Jadyn looked around the bar, thinking of the idea that had been forming since before Jake came over. "No, but thank you. I'm going to stay here a while."

Jake stared at her for a moment, but eventually nodded before pulling a pen out of the inside of his jacket and grabbing a napkin. "I know you have Marilee's number, but here's mine. Call me if you need anything. I mean it."

She took the number and thanked him. "I'll be fine. Go take care of your family."

He nodded, reluctantly, and turned away.

Jadyn watched Jake until he left the bar, took a deep breath, and got up. She crossed the room, went through the back door, and turned down the narrow hall. She continued until she reached Rider's office and knocked on the door.

"Come in."

She entered the office, and was immediately greeted by the dog, who seemed to sense her sadness. Rider looked up from whatever he'd been doing on his computer, and frowned, seeming to also sense her emotions.

"Jadyn. How are you?"

"Been better, been worse," she said, wondering if she'd ever really been worse. She felt hollow inside, but she didn't want to tell Rider that. She hadn't entered his office in search of a pity party.

"What can I help you with?"

She sat in one of the chairs in front of his desk and rubbed her sweaty palms on her jean-clad legs. "I was wondering if you needed any help in the bar?"

His eyebrows raised a little. "Are you asking me for a job?"

She nodded. "I was already behind on my rent and about to get kicked out when this all happened and I had to leave with Christian." Her voice broke on his name. "I don't have any money, or anywhere to go. I only have what I packed with me. I was thinking I could work for you in the bar, and sleep in the room downstairs. You wouldn't have to pay me. I just need something to eat and—"

"Jadyn." Rider took a breath and leaned forward, his eyes softening as he stared at her. "I'll have Rome escort you downstairs. Try to eat something, and try to sleep. Tomorrow we will get you set up in an apartment and figure out the best job for you, along with pay and benefits."

Her breath hitched. "Really?"

"You stopped a slayer that even I don't want to go up against from attacking me. Giving you a job and an apartment is the least I can do."

"Thank you!" She ran around the desk and hugged the vampire, realizing what she was doing as his entire body tensed. "Oh, sorry!"

She backed away. "Sorry. You won't regret this, I promise."

"I might, especially if you try to give me any more dogs, but I'm doing it anyway. Go now." He motioned toward the door.

"Yes, sir." She backed out of the door and turned to see Rome approaching, apparently having been called to the office via telepathy.

"You need to go downstairs?" he asked.

"Yes, thank you."

She followed the large man down the stairs and thanked him as he left her in the room. After he'd left, she moved toward the food on the counter, but her gaze stuck on the couch where Christian had slept, then to the bed she'd given up to him earlier that day. The food forgotten, she crawled into the bed and inhaled his scent wafting off the pillow his head had rested on earlier. She tried to focus on the good things. Rider was giving her a job, and a place to stay... The happiness she'd felt only a moment ago disappeared as tears poured from her eyes.

A job and an apartment were good, but nothing would ever be good enough without Christian.

CHAPTER TWENTY-FIVE

J adyn rolled over and yelped, startled by the figure looming over her bed.

"Sorry," Rider said, his hands shoved into the pockets of his dark slacks. The dog who'd claimed him sat next to him. "You've slept most of the day. I thought we'd go ahead and figure out what's next for you. I was going to take you by the tech team first, get your security clearance so you don't need an escort to get through the doors."

"Oh, OK." Jadyn sat up and rubbed her scratchy eyes, still irritated from the tears she'd shed as she'd cried herself to sleep. She realized she'd gone to sleep in her clothes from the previous night. "Do you mind if I wash up first?"

"Not a problem. Take your time. I'll just wait out here since you'll need an escort getting upstairs to the tech team anyway."

"Thanks." Jadyn grabbed a pink T-shirt and a pair of jeans from her duffel, fighting back the urge to start crying again as she saw Christian's bag next to hers. At least I'll have some of his things to remember him by, she thought to herself, determined not to break down into a blubbering mess in front of Rider Knight. It was bad enough she'd hugged him. The brooding vampire didn't exactly give off the warm and friendly teddy bear vibe.

Jadyn took her things into the bathroom and quickly put herself together, washing up, changing clothes, and brushing her teeth. She sped through the tasks, not wanting to keep the vampire waiting when he was being more than kind in helping her. She stepped back out of the bathroom, prepared to apologize for keeping him waiting, but paused as she caught sight of him grinning from ear to ear.

"Change in plans," he said. "Follow me."

"What's going on?" she asked as she followed him out of the room, noticing the smiles on the faces of the security guards they passed.

"I was just informed we have a special guest. I think this guest will cheer you up."

Jadyn doubted it, but didn't want to seem unappreciative, so she didn't say anything as they continued up, passing the tech team, and going up another floor until they reached the room behind the bar.

There, her heart slammed to a stop as she stepped out of the stairwell to see an angel dressed in dark clothes standing beside the staircase leading up to Rider's private quarters. His blue eyes gleamed with joy as his mouth curved into a smile. He looked a little older than he normally did, less boyish, a lot wiser, and a streak of white ran through his short, dark hair. Otherwise, he was exactly as she'd last seen him, minus the wings, lightning, and power glowing all over his body. "Christian?"

"I'll give you two some privacy, but I expect you in my office once you're done," Rider said. "Both of you."

Unable to stop herself, Jadyn ran into Christian's waiting arms as the vampire and his dog left them alone.

"Did you really think I would leave you?" Christian asked, eyes sparkling as they stared down into hers.

"I... I don't understand. You left. You went... You went to Heaven, didn't you? Your sister took you home."

He nodded. "I needed to see my Father, to sort out some things."

"By Father you mean..."

"Our Heavenly Father, yes. Although I don't exactly remember it now, I do know it was a wonderful conversation."

"What? I don't understand. Are you saying you're back to not remembering who you are?"

"Oh, I know exactly who I am." He kissed her forehead. "You helped me realize that. I was born Aurorian, and I was a very powerful angel, on track to becoming an incredibly powerful archangel. I was betrayed by one of my own brothers, and turned into a vampire. I spent centuries fighting against the darkness in me, sensing I was supposed to be someone else. I was so busy trying to remember who I used to be, I never accepted who I was, until you told me we are all ever-changing, that I was the darkness in me, and the light, and you loved both of those parts."

He released her and took her hands in his. "Kiara told me I had redeemed myself when she welcomed me back. Redeemed, as if I hadn't been betrayed, as if I'd done something wrong to have caused all that happened. I love her. I love all of my brothers and sisters, but I was only worthy to them as an angel. They wanted Aurorian back, not me. I would have never even won that battle had I only been an angel. I was scared. Amuel was stronger than me, more powerful. He was winning. Your words and your faith gave me the strength and power I needed to fight him. I pulled from everything inside me, even the vampire part of me, and I won, and I still did it with a pure heart."

"Of course you did. You've always had a good heart."

He nodded. "It's easier to do the right, moral thing when you are designed to. Still, Amuel harbored the sins of jealousy and greed inside him while I continuously fought against sin as a vampire. I don't have to be an angel to be worthy of Heaven. No one does."

"Christian... are you still an angel?"

"I haven't been an angel in centuries," he answered, "and that's what I told my Father. Aurorian ceased to exist when Christian was born. Christian was a vampire with grace. Christian fought to be a good person, despite every obstacle thrown in his way, and Christian helped a lot of people. He made good friends, even helped other vampires who became his family to control their darkness better. I can't go back to being Aurorian. I can't leave behind all that I love here. Or *who* I love."

Jadyn gasped, struggling to comprehend, afraid she was misunderstanding and hearing what she wanted. "You said Christian was a vampire with grace. Aurorian was an angel. Who are you now?"

"Still Christian, but I fell. This time it was done with a blessing. Our Father always loves us. He knew what was in my heart, and that what I desired came from a place of pure love, not lust or greed, or even selfishness. He allowed me to fall and stand as a man, free to make his own choices, no longer ruled by prophecy. Any prophecy. Jadyn, I'm not a vampire anymore, either."

Jadyn sucked in air before releasing it with a squeal and kissing Christian, overcome with happiness the beast inside him he'd struggled with so long had been purged, and he was back on earth, with her. "Wait... Christian, you gave up Heaven."

"Not necessarily. We all have a chance at getting there eventually, and I'm fine with the decision I made. I still have a lot of memories so I won't be walking around wondering where I came from or missing a part of me, like I'd done for so many centuries already. I no longer have all the knowledge of Heaven, and I know I was given this chance by my Father, but I have no memory of His face or voice. That wouldn't be fair. If other humans have to depend on faith alone to believe in His existence, so should I. I already know I was an angel before so I've reached my quota on unfair advantages."

"But... *Heaven*."

He smiled. "I tell you what... You marry me, and we'll make our own Heaven right here."

RIDER SAT BEHIND HIS desk, looking between them. "So, you're still a guardian?"

Jadyn looked down at the dog and sensed its happiness, getting a flash of Rome sneaking him a treat he wasn't supposed to have because Rider didn't want a fat dog. "Yup."

"And you're no longer a vampire or an angel, just a normal human?"

"I wouldn't go so far as to say normal," Christian responded, grinning. "But I am human. I no longer need to drink blood. I will age, and I will die, just like any other human."

"And I'm assuming you're going to marry Jadyn?"

"That obvious?" Christian asked.

"A man doesn't give up Heaven because he really likes the baseball and chicken wings here. He does it because he loves a woman." The vampire shook his head. "All right then. I was going to put you into an apartment today, Jadyn. I'll still do that, and Christian can live with you or stay here until the marriage if you're going to be traditional."

"That's very generous," Christian told him as Jadyn's heart swelled, touched by how nice the vampire was being.

Rider shrugged. "I take care of my people. You might not be a vampire anymore, but as far as I'm concerned, you're still under my protection. You're a good man. The pastor at our local church is getting on in years. I'll look into getting you a job there. I assume you still intend on being a minister?"

Christian nodded. "It's still my calling."

"I figured, and don't look so surprised," he said to Jadyn. "If Christian could be a minister when he had fangs, you shouldn't be surprised that I go to church from time to time."

She laughed, not realizing she'd been gawking. "Sorry."

He grunted. "You can work in the bar like you asked, but we all know your talent is with animals. You're going to school to become a veterinarian."

"I can't pay for that," she reminded him. If she could, she would have already been going. She'd always wanted to be a veterinarian.

"I'm paying for it, and no, you're not paying me back and it isn't coming out of your pay. Consider it a wedding gift."

Her mouth dropped open. "That's a hell of a gift."

He shrugged. "You stopped a slayer from going on a killing spree among my people, and Christian's given up Heaven to hang with us bastards. This is the least I can do for both of you."

Christian squeezed her hand and gazed into her eyes. "It was worth it."

"Oh, gag. Take your googly-eyes out into the bar and wait for me before I puke. I'll be out in a minute to take you to Jadyn's apartment."

The dog barked and Rider shushed it. "Go lay down, Kutya. In your bed, now."

Jadyn grinned as the dog stuck its nose in the air and trotted over to the expensive-looking plush bed Rider had placed for him in his office.

"Shoo!" Rider gestured toward the door. "Get out."

Jadyn and Christian laughed as they stood and left the office, unable to stop the googly eyes. Jadyn couldn't stop smiling as they moved down the hall and entered the bar.

"That's a happy face."

"I'm in love," she explained playfully, "and Rider named his dog. I knew he'd love him."

Christian laughed. "Kutya is Hungarian for dog. He literally named the dog, Dog."

"Oh." She shrugged as they moved over to a booth to wait for Rider. "It's a start... and speaking of starts... when can we get married? I don't need a big ceremony."

"Good," Christian answered, looking at her with a devilish gleam in his eye, "because I'd like to stay pure until our wedding night, but I've been pure for centuries. If we can find a minister today, we can be honeymooning by tonight." He waggled his eyebrows.

"Christian!" She gasped and playfully smacked his arm.

"Hey..." He winked at her. "I'm no angel."

The Blood Revelation series continues with *Immortal Rage*.

If you enjoyed meeting Danni, Rider, and the rest of the crew at The Midnight Rider, you can find more of them in the *Twice Bitten* series, available now.

Did you love *Vampire's Halo*? Then you should read *Seta's Fall*[1] by Crystal-Rain Love!

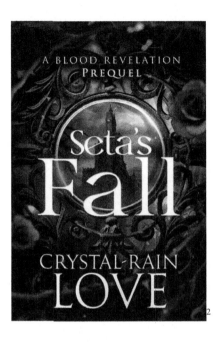[2]

The Blood Revelation Prophecy: Vampires, witches, and shifters will band together to stop the darkness from winning, until one warrior is born to save the world from Satan's wrath. Before she was the baddest vampire-witch to ever walk the dark streets of America, she was a young Spanish servant in Rome, unaware of her own power.

Seduced by Count Roberto Garibaldi and having been promised to wed, Seta gives birth to his son only to find out too late that she had been used to produce the heir his barren wife could not. The count steals the child out of her arms, beats her, and throws her off the cliff just beyond his castle, but Seta's fall does not lead to death.

A guardian has been sent to save her by giving her a second life, a life hidden in shadow where she can not be with her only child.

1. https://books2read.com/u/b5ZvJA

2. https://books2read.com/u/b5ZvJA

Seta must suffer the estrangement from her son until he is old enough to be reunited with her and revenge can be taken upon those who stole him, and she must wrestle with the attraction she has to her sire, a vampire who gave her a new life, but could just as easily take it away.

Read more at https://crystalrainlove.com.

About the Author

Crystal-Rain Love is a romance author specializing in paranormal, suspense, and contemporary subgenres. Her author career began by winning a contest to be one of Sapphire Blue Publishing's debut authors in 2008. She snagged a multi-book contract with Imajinn Books that same year, going on to be published by The Wild Rose Press and eventually venturing out into indie publishing. She resides in the South with her three children and when she's not writing she can usually be found creating unique 3D cakes, hiking, reading, or spending way too much time on FaceBook.

Read more at www.crystalrainlove.com.

Printed in Great Britain
by Amazon

43723754R00169